ADDITIONAL PRAISE FOR

TINY IMPERFECTIONS

"Offers a delightful view inside the cutthroat world of private school admissions that is hilarious, cringe-worthy and all too relevant in today's ultra-competitive educational landscape. I ate this book up like a box of candy; you will too."

—Tara Conklin, author of *The Last Romantics*

"Over-eager parents are just one of the many things heroine Josie Bordelon has to deal with as head of admissions for a tawny private school in San Francisco. These two authors are brave enough to expose the insanity and hilarity that happen during application season. . . . A really funny read."

—Laurie Gelman, author of *Class Mom*

"Youmans and Frank manage to tackle a woman's journey through work, race, and motherhood beautifully in their debut. *Tiny Imperfections* is laugh-out-loud funny and full of heart. I can't wait to see what they bring us next!"

—Alexa Martin, author of *Fumbled*

"Youmans and Frank's deep-dive into private school culture sets the stage for a dishy, charming story of West Coast elitism and parenting at its pushiest. But it's the characters, especially the marvelous Bordelon women, who give this delightful novel its heart and humor—and who make you long to be part of the family even after the last page."

—Amy Poeppel, author of *Small Admissions* and *Limelight*

"Perfectly captures the absurdist bubble of San Francisco's tech upper class. A rollicking good read that reminds us that money, power and influence will never be enough to make someone truly happy."

—Jo Piazza, author of *Charlotte Walsh Likes to Win*

"*Tiny Imperfections* is a funny, heart-warming take on finding love in a most unexpected place."

—Anissa Gray, author of *The Care and Feeding of Ravenously Hungry Girls*

"With a heroine to cheer for and laugh-out-loud delicacies on every page, *Tiny Imperfections* is perfect entertainment! You're in for such a fun ride. I loved it!"

—Lisa Patton, author of *Rush*

"A smart and savvy take on the competitive world of elite kindergarten admissions, *Tiny Imperfections* offers a delightfully refreshing narrative on ambition, family, and love."

—Robinne Lee, author of *The Idea of You*

TINY IMPERFECTIONS

TINY
IMPERFECTIONS

Alli Frank AND Asha Youmans

G. P. PUTNAM'S SONS
NEW YORK

PUTNAM
— EST. 1838 —

G. P. PUTNAM'S SONS
Publishers Since 1838
An imprint of Penguin Random House LLC
penguinrandomhouse.com

Library of Congress Cataloging-in-Publication Data

Names: Frank, Alli, author. | Youmans, Asha, author.
Title: Tiny imperfections / Alli Frank and Asha Youmans.
Description: New York: G. P. Putnam's Sons, [2020] |
Summary: *"The Wedding Date* meets *Class Mom* in this delicious novel of love,
money, and misbehaving parents. 'Delightful . . . Hilarious, cringe-worthy, and
all too relevant. I ate this book up like a box of candy; you will too.' —Tara
Conklin, author of *The Last Romantics"* —Provided by publisher.
Identifiers: LCCN 2019050896 (print) | LCCN 2019050897 (ebook) |
ISBN 9780593085028 (paperback) | ISBN 9780593085035 (ebook)
Classification: LCC PS3606.R3758 T56 2020 (print) |
LCC PS3606.R3758 (ebook) | DDC 813/.6—dc23
LC record available at https://lccn.loc.gov/2019050896
LC ebook record available at https://lccn.loc.gov/2019050897

Printed in the United States of America
1   3   5   7   9   10   8   6   4   2

BOOK DESIGN BY KRISTIN DEL ROSARIO

For my Dad, who was a champion of women long before it was in vogue.

EAF

For my Father who inspired my learning.
For my Husband who inspires my love.
For my Sons who inspire my life.

APY

TINY IMPERFECTIONS

OPEN SEASON

ONE

ᕕᕗᕕᕗᕕᕗᕕᕗ

FROM: Meredith Lawton

DATE: September 24, 2018

SUBJECT: Introduction to our son, Harrison Rutherford Lawton

TO: Josephine Bordelon

Dear Josephine,

I'm Meredith Lawton, close friend of Beatrice Pembrook, who I'm sure you know is a past board chair of Fairchild Country Day School and fourth generation Fairchild alum. It was so good of Beatrice to honor her parents, Ginger and Alfred, after their untimely death by building the school a state-of-the-art black box theatre and a rooftop Olympic swimming pool. Beatrice is such a gem and she should be reaching out to you shortly on behalf of our son, Harrison.

I know admissions season just opened, but last spring we worked on our essays with a Stanford writing coach and have spent the summer perfecting them with our editor from Golden Gate Books so we may be the first to submit our application on the WeeScholars website. I would particularly like to draw your attention to paragraph #4 of essay question #5. I believe it to be a wonderful representation of how worldly and culturally competent Harrison already is at four years, ten months:

"At almost five years of age Harrison has glamped in huts in the Indian Himalayas, cruised down the Mekong in Laos, ridden on a Sherpa's shoulders to Paro Taktsang (the Tiger's Nest Monastery) in Bhutan, been recognized as a reincarnated lama in Nepal, and fed exotic fish all over the world from Mexico to the Great Barrier Reef (thank goodness Harrison got to experience THE REEF before it died completely from environmental hazard—terrible tragedy)."

We will be seeing a lot of each other this year and I look forward to meeting you on our school tour in the beginning of October. If there is anything you would like to learn about Harrison and our family beforehand please do not hesitate to e-mail or call (just not before 10:30 a.m. as I am most likely in yoga, Barry's Boot Camp, or at my weekly cryotherapy appointment).

With much gratitude,
Meredith Lawton

P.S. I couldn't resist sending this adorable picture of Harrison celebrating Chinese New Year in Shanghai. Christopher had to be there for work so OF COURSE we brought Harrison along; one is never too young to be exposed to Mandarin!

I finish reading globe-trotting-mom's e-mail, shift my weight onto one leg at my standing desk—an ergonomic no-no—and look up to a God I'm not 100 percent sure exists because if She did, She certainly wouldn't let people like Meredith Lawton procreate. Or do yoga. Nothing worse than a karmic salutation that screams, *I've found mind body bliss and I'm now superior to you in this life and in the next.*

"Tiger moms are so 2011," I say to a silent, still-empty school campus, except for my own seventeen-year-old daughter, Etta, stretching her enviably smooth mocha, *I-can-eat-Slim-Jims-and-Flamin'-Hot-Cheetos-for-lunch*, ballerina body on the other side of my office. She doesn't bother to acknowledge my deeply profound thought, her sound-canceling headphones to blame.

PRIVATE SCHOOL ADMISSIONS ARE NOW OPEN. Subtext: Let the freaking out, sucking up, buying in, overstating, underlistening, overselling, calling in of favors, pushing boundaries, and, in general, appalling parental antics begin. There should be a torch I light every Monday after Labor Day that stays lit until March 15—since urban private school admissions really are the Olympics of parenting. Instead, I've created a tasteful banner at the top of the Fairchild Country Day School website announcing: NOW AC-CEPTING APPLICATIONS. With a single click on the link, parents are invited to learn more about Fairchild admissions and embrace the truth that their upcoming year will be lost to an abyss of essays, interviews, veiled dinner party conversation, stressful pillow talk, and heavy self-medication, all in the name of kindergarten.

Let's call private school admissions what it is, an obsession for all those families who desperately want a spot on the private school crazy train. In San Francisco, it's a bit different than the famed stories of cutthroat manipulation and desperation that define the Upper East Side of New York City. Don't get me wrong, San Francisco has its overabundance of the rich and anxious, too, but here they're well concealed behind a dirty SUV with a surfboard on top, HOKA running shoes, retro T-shirts, ripped jeans, flip-flops, and a shitload of stock options. The more Bay Area parents feign "It's all good, everything will work out," my stats show what a higher pain-in-the-ass quotient they are.

I actually welcome the occasional New York transplant family who comes into parent interviews owning their perceived superiority in head-to-toe Prada and gray banker suits attempting to establish their dominance through the traditional where they went to school, what they do, and where they work (usually someplace with three last names) introduction. With upfront elitism you immediately know with whom you're dealing and where you stand. When elitism hides behind a white ribbed tank top, aviator sunglasses, and a messy bun it's much more difficult to figure out from where an ambush may come. That's why you can't be fooled by the San Francisco mom in her 24/7 painted-on yoga pants who looks like your best friend or the 100 percent organic lady right out of Goop's weekly online newsletter. Sometimes she's as sweet and detoxed as she looks, but just as often behind that barre-class bod is a momster so determined to get her child into the best school she would toss you off the Golden Gate Bridge while sipping her green juice if she thought your kid was in direct kindergarten competition with hers.

Over the years I've learned the cultural subtlety of West Coast admissions. The first lesson came early in my career when my baby, Etta, was in first grade at Fairchild and I was in my second year as an admissions assistant. I made my first and only mistake of slipping from business English into what Aunt Viv calls "home speak" and getting a little too chummy with an applicant mom who was sweatin' it because her son was channeling mini-Mussolini meets Donald Trump during his kindergarten visit.

"I know how you feel, Charlotte, I'm a mama, too, and sometimes our babies can bring us to our knees." I gave her a big smile in motherly solidarity, but thinking back on it I probably showed too much tooth as this hundred-pound Barbie popped back, "Why you shore is, honey!" and patted my forearm to seal our new "sistahood." Since that moment, I've had to endure Charlotte's ridiculous banter as her son has moved through the grades at Fairchild and her warped sense of our friendship has grown. Luckily, I'm a quick study and I've never slipped into anything resembling black speak again without being related to my audience. Well, except for Lola. I also never told my aunt Viv about my early career slip. She would have skinned me alive.

"Can we go yet? I'll freak if I'm late," Etta yells, to hear herself above her headphones as she rolls her upper torso up from the hideous, stained maroon industrial carpet, her legs split east to west. My office is budgeted for a remodel next year.

I glance at Etta over the top of my computer. After seventeen years it still shocks me that I birthed a child who goes apoplectic if she's not ten minutes early to everything. I didn't even notice when my period was six weeks late eighteen years ago. Time and I have a very loose relationship. "Two Josie minutes," I yell back, holding up a peace sign. Etta's trained to know that means "ten real-time minutes."

FROM: Josephine Bordelon—
    jbordelon@fairchildcountrydayschool.org
DATE: September 24, 2018
CC:
BCC:
SUBJECT: RE: Introduction to our son, Harrison Rutherford Lawton
TO: Meredith Lawton
- -

CONGRATULATIONS, Meredith! You indeed were the first family to submit your application for this coming fall with a post time of twenty-eight seconds after the WeeScholars common application website opened. Our 110-year-old bylaws state that ruthless competitiveness, punctuality, and lama reincarnation are three of the four criteria to qualify Harrison for the golden ticket (YAY! Envision 24K gold confetti raining down, the confetti being compostable, of course), which means he's automatically accepted into the Fairchild Country Day School class of 20-and-who-fucking-cares. No need to tour, attend an open house, or show up for the admissions visit date and parent interview. In fact, you don't even have to wait until March 15 to find out Harrison's elementary school fate like all the other die-hard parents out there.

Fairchild has been waiting years for a family as touched by perfection as yours to attend our school. Please let me know how I can best serve what I can only imagine will be endless, relentless needs and wants every step of Harrison's educational path.

With complete ambivalence that you know Beatrice,
Josie Bordelon

DIRECTOR OF ADMISSIONS
FAIRCHILD COUNTRY DAY SCHOOL

"I've never worked in a school, but I'm pretty sure you'll get fired if you swear in a work e-mail." I didn't even notice Etta hop off the carpet to come snoop over my shoulder. "And you should have a comma after . . ."

DE-LEEEEEEEEEEEEEEEEEEEEEEEEEEEEEEEEEEEEEEE-TE.
Grammar show-off.

Etta certainly did not get her punctuality from me, but her sarcasm—100 percent Bordelon.

As director of admissions this has become my free therapy to keep all the over-the-top parents from chipping away at my sanity. I say my piece and I erase. Then I move on.

"I'm having a hard time rallying for the ridiculousness of the entitled this year. I just want to find some old-school families who parent like it's 1986: roof, food, clothes, water, manners, and if you don't get good grades your ass will get whooped 'cause you gotta earn your keep. I'm looking for black-to-basics parenting." That's my knee-jerk reaction. When I grow weary of the rich, I fall back on my Nawlins Ninth Ward background. Or really Aunt Viv's, since I can only kinda claim my Southern black Baptist roots.

"You're not helping the cause with that e-mail." Etta points to my now-empty screen.

"Yeah, I know, but sometimes it feels good to type the conversation that's going on in my head instead of official director of admissions missives. If only once I could push send on my real thoughts, maybe I could save a privileged child from a life of indulgence and complete cluelessness about the other 99.9 percent of the world. It could be my own act of social justice—to help a rich kid lead a normal life. It's got potential, don't you think?"

"Nope, not at all."

"I'd give my firstborn for the chance to point out to one parent, any parent, when they're in the early stages of ruining their child."

"I'm your firstborn."

"Right, and if I give you away before next August someone else can pay your college tuition." I blow Etta a kiss with a wink. She knows I'd never abandon her; we'd be lost without each other.

"Tell me again why you work in a school? Seems to me at forty you should like what you do. Especially since I'll be gone next year and the only reason you'll have to come to Fairchild is to work hard and watch Headmistress Gooding take all the credit." Etta raises her eyebrows at me.

"Clearly I work here for the fame, money, close relationship with my boss, and, of course, the lice. And because I'll still have to feed you in college—it's called a meal plan. And I do like what I do, sort of, mostly, kind of." Etta turns and pretends to barf in my wastebasket. "And I'm not forty."

"Yet."

Daughters are the worst.

With one Josie minute to spare to get Etta to ballet, I chop out the e-mail that will allow me to pay the bills and keep my kid in leotards.

FROM: Josephine Bordelon—
    jbordelon@fairchildcountrydayschool.org
DATE: September 24, 2018
CC:
BCC:
SUBJECT: RE: Introduction to our son, Harrison Rutherford Lawton
TO: Meredith Lawton

Dear Meredith,

Thank you so much for applying your son, Harrison, to Fairchild Country Day School. We look forward to seeing your family at the first tour.

Warm regards,
Josie Bordelon

DIRECTOR OF ADMISSIONS
FAIRCHILD COUNTRY DAY SCHOOL

Send.

"Good job playing nice, Mama. Now, come oooooon, we gotta go. I'm begging you, don't make me late," Etta stresses, stuffing her headphones in her dance bag, her booty in my face. I know that booty and those endless legs. That was my body eighteen years and twenty pounds ago, strutting down the runway in Tokyo in nothing but a thong, pasties, and an open Jean Paul Gaultier kimono with Japanese characters hand painted on the back. If I had known then what I would know a few short weeks later when I couldn't button my jeans, the characters on that kimono should have read *baby on board*.

"Mama, just send me to ballet in a Lyft. You know how you are the minute admissions opens up—it's like a car crash, you can't stop rubbernecking, or, for you, reading e-mail." Etta huffs at me, a side effect of being artsy and a teenager. I toss her the car keys only because she's not entirely wrong; I do completely lose myself during admissions season.

"I don't have my license yet." Etta says as she deftly snatches my keys out of the air.

"What are all those classes I've been paying for the last three months?"

"Driver's Ed. And it doesn't end until next month. Then I take my driving test."

"Well, I'm not paying for a Lyft when I have a perfectly good car, and I still have the handicap placard from when I sprained my ankle, so drive carefully and park for free. Just don't get caught and text me when you get there." I'm not sweating Etta driving, but I still want to know she's arrived in one piece.

"You're a terrible parent," Etta reprimands, turning to head out of my office. For an on-time ride she's willing to turn a blind eye to the law and drive, but I know she won't use the parking placard; that's playing outside her moral boundaries.

"Nope, I'm just black-to-basics."

I START WORKING ON KINDERGARTEN TOUR AND VISIT DATES for the school year, even as I repeatedly check for a text from Etta.

My phone finally *pings*, stopping me from wondering if I should call the San Francisco County missing persons hotline.

Of course she made it.

I turn back to my computer. Even after thirteen years of kindergarten tours and visits I still find myself eager to show off Fairchild to potential families. The ohhhs and ahhhs from moms, dads, and grandparents remind me of how lucky I felt when I was a student at Fairchild.

It's quite possible I peaked before the turn of the century. At least according to the Fairchild Country Day yearbook and my head of school, Dr. Pearson. During my years as a student he had loved to trot me out to big donors to show that Fairchild was doing its part to not only accept but also to successfully educate a diverse student body. We both wanted to prove that I was not just a product of affirmative action, as many in the Fairchild community in the eighties and nineties wanted to believe. I had, in fact, earned and retained an honest seat in the school, sealed with a spot on the honor roll every semester. Making honor roll should have been all the proof I needed to show I belonged, but while diversity efforts of private schools were all the rage in the nineties, every day I still had to go above and beyond any other student to prove being a member of the graduating class was no fluke.

With an audience seated in a living room with floor-to-ceiling views of the Golden Gate Bridge and the Bay, Dr. Pearson would loudly rattle the phlegm in his throat. It would take three or four additional wet coughs to get the attention of the moneyed alumni sipping Napa Valley Chardonnay and chatting about whether Danielle Steel's new book was based on a fellow Pacific Heights neighbor.

"Allow me to introduce you to Josephine Bordelon." Light applause would follow, and I would join Dr. Pearson at the front of the room. "In our committed diversity efforts, Fairchild gets triple points for Miss Bordelon: She is African American (obviously); is being raised by her aunt Viv, our beloved school cook [lots of knowing nods and ohhhs and ahhhs at the mention of Aunt Viv]; and has been on scholarship since kindergarten. And I have to say [insert stiff chuckle by Dr. Pearson], Josie does more than her fair share to earn her keep and represent Fairchild well. She's an honor's scholar, a track and field phenom, and a breathtaking beauty. If only all our diversity efforts could be this successful, right?"

More than one audience member would dab a tear from the corner of their eye. Poor people of color who triumph among the privileged always make white folks cry. It's fund-raising 101—a recipe, I learned quickly, guaranteed to work:

Take one youth
Add at least half black or Latino or Native American or Asian
    (minus Chinese or Japanese)
Stir in a tale of struggle and perseverance
Bake the sob story for at least ten minutes
Et voilà! Tears and money flow.

If a donor went to four leadership functions in one year, they would see me twice. It was either Diego Rolando, swarthy Bolivian and future professional soccer stud, or me. The two other graduating students of color were either busted, shy, or on academic probation. By the nineties, working alongside or befriending a gay person may have become the norm in San Francisco thanks to Harvey Milk, but diversity efforts in private schools were still being hotly debated behind closed doors (We don't want to water down the rigor and reputation of our school, do we? How many of these people are we talking about? Can they really keep up with the academics? I guess it's okay as long as they don't take my Jameson's spot). What the board of trustees didn't realize was that this was a fair trade. The school got a killer face to rest their diversity laurels on, and I got a first-class education and entrée into the world Aunt Viv wanted for me. And maybe, in my sadder moments, I imagined this was why my mother handed me off to a sister she barely knew.

While today the occasional bitch session with girlfriends about being used as part of a dog and pony show to raise money rears its ugly head, at the time I simply loved to be loved by the Fairchild community. My aunt Viv always told me, "Do what you gotta do, to get where you wanna get." She was strident in her determination that I use the strength of my mind to get ahead; never choosing to dishonor my body or my soul. And I wanted to get myself to New York City. Granted, at seventeen, I had no idea why. I guess I felt like I had never quite belonged anywhere, and New York seemed like the perfect place for people who felt like they were from nowhere but wanted to find somewhere to call their own.

So the story goes, my people are Creole, the result of a lonely French dude gettin' it on with a spicy young house girl. Unknown to the horny Frenchman, in Louisiana sleeping with black women was a bit of a social faux pas, so he hopped the next ship back to the homeland, but not without planting his Brie cheese in my great-great-grandmother.

"I had already helped raise my siblings, no reason to stay in New Orleans, where I would probably end up raising somebody else's children for a living," Aunt Viv would say when I asked why she left Louisiana for California the day after she graduated from high school. "Really the only thing in Louisiana is swamp, sweat, and sadness, and that's God's truth. But I didn't want it to be my truth. I was the oldest of six kids, I wanted my own life." When Hurricane Katrina hit, Aunt Viv muttered this same mantra for months, "See, I told you—just swamp, sweat, and sadness down there. You bettah be happy your mama dropped you off on my doorstep when she did."

I was a baby in a basket, a modern-day female Moses floating down the Mississippi River. Only I was four and my riverboat was a Greyhound bus from New Orleans to San Francisco. My mama told me we were going on a trip to visit her oldest sister, Vivian, whom I'd never met, but by the time I was four the stories of Aunt Viv had reached epic proportions in my people's part of New Orleans. She was nearing thirty and had escaped booze, boys, and babies. In the promised land of California, she slept alone in her own bed, lived alone in her own apartment, and worked in a castle. She also never returned home to the Ninth Ward, not even for Christmas or Mardi Gras.

When Dr. Pearson used to say I was a breathtaking beauty, he had never met my mother, or at least what a four-year-old mind wants to remember of her mother. Her body could stop a Fat Tuesday celebration and her hair made Diana Ross's wigs look limp, but what I remember most was how she could lose herself in music. That woman was twenty years ahead of the twerking curve and her body defied what most thought was anatomically possible. She would sashay down a street, holding my hand; her booty swaying to a constant beat that drummed in her head. I gathered, even at the young age of four, that it was her booty that paid our bills. So at twenty-two, when my mother had saved up her dancing tips for a full year ("stripping" was not yet in my young vocabulary), we headed west to pay Aunt Viv a visit.

I remember thinking that for such a huge adventure we were traveling light with only one bag between us, and my mama let me fill most of it up with my favorite things. But it didn't matter; I had Mama to myself, and a rare pack of multi-fruit flavored Life Savers that had to last me to the famous Golden Gate Bridge. Only who was on the other side of the Golden Gate Bridge didn't know we were coming or that I was about to completely upend her life forever.

TWO

WE HAVEN'T EVEN MADE IT THROUGH THE FIRST FULL WEEK
of school and Lola's already letting me know the struggle is real in
first grade. Her text reads:

LOLA

> **Jesus, one of my kids pooped his pants today.
> Holla back. Lo**

3:26 P.M.

"Shit, Lola," I say when my best friend picks up on the first ring.
"Literally."

Lola teaches at Fairchild's rival school, San Francisco Children's
Academy. She has three boys under eight at home, a husband who is
pretty much her fourth child but with a paycheck, two dogs, a misplaced chinchilla, and a couple of fish I refer to as "water roaches"
because they were supposed to live three weeks when Lola got them
at a white elephant party and three years later they refuse to die. Her

house smells like a YMCA locker room, and she's slowly working her way through an eight-year EdD program at night. With all that she still manages to text me every day to exchange the daily highs and lows within five minutes of kicking her last student out the classroom door.

"How's the new dad pool looking over there?" Lola asks, eager for some crosstown gossip. We're only a few days into the school year and I have yet to look past the overconfident moms of last year's admissions cycle who are now walking their kids into school unsure if they actually want to let their babies go.

"Haven't even had time to notice. Too busy getting ready for admissions tours. The season officially opened yesterday."

"Seriously? Did your vagina die this summer?"

Lola only has two topics she likes to talk about: her beloved students and my relationship status. Lola and I met at a Zumba class twelve years ago, back when she had time to exercise and Aunt Viv claimed I needed to find a hobby. We met just before class started. We were not so subtly looking each other up and down, sniffing out who was the better dressed, the better dancer, the better looking. It's what black people do when they walk into a room. They find the other brothers and sisters and do a quick assessment to see if the competition is going to raise their net worth or take them down. I was wearing a shabby cotton Forty-Niners T-shirt two sizes too big to Lola's Nike scuba-tight lime-green tank top. I'm sure she thought I was the albatross and she had this one on lockdown, but I knew I had her on the dance moves so we more or less broke even as the two women in the room representing black sistas (although most folks barely count Lola as black; she looks like cream with just a drop of coffee).

Ten minutes in we were huffing and puffing, rolling our eyes at each other because misery loves company. Twenty minutes in we were across the street at the neighborhood Mexican cantina holding margaritas and waiting for our chips and guac to arrive.

The first margarita was spent on the general information of Lola's life. Lola was from Toronto, loved her family, but hated hockey and the cold. She moved to the Bay Area right after college, and her first job was as the assistant to a twenty-seven-year-old founder of the next "big" tech start-up during dot-com boom 1.0. She worked seventy hours a week, snorted cocaine on Wednesday nights to get through the rest of the week (which she sometimes still wishes she could do with three kids at home and eighteen in her classroom), and went to Stinson Beach on weekends with girlfriends. But then the founder spent too much time ogling Lola's DDs and not enough on the company's bottom line and it went belly up after two years and junior CEO skipped town. With worthless stock options and a distaste for entrepreneurs, Lola decided on a career where her lady bits were the least of her qualifications. She went back to San Francisco State to get her master's in teaching. A year later she was a first-grade teacher at San Francisco Children's Academy, had traded in cocaine for kombucha, and was head over heels in love with a Puerto Rican professional kite surfer.

I remember Lola looking at me when she finished her light and airy tale assuming she was about to hear something fairly similar. In my first few years back in San Francisco, I hadn't yet found a good man to roll around with at night or a perfect girlfriend to kick it with during the day. Lola seemed like lifelong friend potential, but I didn't want to waste my time on someone who couldn't handle the baggage I was carrying. I decided to let the freak flag fly and share my whole story, starting with being dumped on Aunt Viv's doorstep at four and ending with my return back to Aunt Viv's with my own four-year-old daughter in tow.

After being a lifer at Fairchild Country Day School, single-handedly responsible for bringing in one million plus in donor giving and earning the school multiple 800-meter records in track and field, New York University decided to take a chance on me. My dream to live in New York City came true. I earned an academic scholarship, but the only spending money I had was from Aunt Viv to buy a one-way plane ticket and snacks for the flight. Knowing he owed me big-time for helping him build a new gym, Dr. Pearson found me a job nannying the children of an über-successful Fairchild alumnus on New York's Upper East Side.

Being the first woman in our family not to work as a domestic in the posh Garden Point neighborhood of New Orleans, Aunt Viv didn't want me helping raise other people's children. From the time I was fourteen, Aunt Viv warned me that if some nice-looking lady approaches me askin', "Do you want a job?" I was to pop my hip out and let her know, in no uncertain terms, that "these hips weren't for totin' around nobody's children but my own." Aunt Viv wanted me to get a job in a campus library or in a coffee shop or anywhere that I was not reading bedtime stories to other people's offspring. Thing is, I like kids, always have. In a cynical, cruel world their humor, unpredictability, and pure joy is contagious. And nannying on the UES of Manhattan paid way better than working in Bobst Library at NYU. Freshman year in college kicked off my career working with privileged kiddos as well as not telling Aunt Viv the truth.

One gorgeously warm afternoon the fall of my junior year, I decided to walk from Washington Square Park to 85th and Park Ave to gawk at the swag in the storefronts along the way. Passing through Midtown, even in a crowded sea of people, I felt like someone was following me. By the time I got to the edge of Central Park by the Plaza Hotel a voice was yelling after me, "Hey, tall black girl! Hey, tall black girl!" I put on my best resting bitch face, cocked my hip and channeled Aunt Viv's "I ain't workin' for you" body language, and turned around.

"Whew, I've been following you since Fortieth," panted a middle-aged white lady in impossibly high-heeled boots and a black wrap, pushing her enormous sunglasses to the top of her head.

Resting bitch face did not change.

"Well, then . . ." she started, clearly discomforted by my body language.

"I'll get right to it, I can see you are on your way somewhere important. I work for Ford Models, perhaps you've heard of us?"

"I have," I answered, wondering if I truly looked as naïve as she seemed to think I did.

"Yes, well, my name's Maisie Maxwell and I hate running in heels and I really hate sweating, but I did it for you because I think you're stunning. Seriously, incredible. Have you modeled before?"

I shook my head no.

"I didn't think so, you slouch when you walk. Anyhoo, you have to be almost six feet, legs for days, and your skin is magnificent. Here's my card. Please, please call me. I would love for you to come in for a test shoot. I've been desperately looking for someone new. I'm so bored with the Christie Brinkleys and Brooke Shieldses. All-American is on its way out. I want a model with some piss and vinegar. Some homegrown attitude." Maisie grabbed my hand and shoved her card into my palm.

"Thanks, I think." I didn't look at the card. Was *piss and vinegar* white talk for *ghetto*?

"Please do call me! I have two kids in private school and God do I need to find the next Naomi Campbell. Not that you have to be Naomi Campbell. Actually, please don't be Naomi Campbell; rumor has it she's a bitch of a diva on set. Be whoever you want to be, just please call and cross fingers, maybe you can be my rainmaker. With a mortgage, tuition, my husband's dental school loans, and a witch of a mother-in-law, I need it." Maisie tipped her sunglasses down, gave me a thumbs-up, and limped away in serious pain. I allowed myself to feel flattered that some white lady would run blocks in stiletto boots just to talk to me. But I was done making it rain for other people. If I was going to be Maisie's rainmaker, I was damn well going to make sure it poured on me, too.

Four weeks later I was no longer a nanny; I was on a plane to L.A. for a swimsuit catalog shoot after begging my NYU comparative lit professor to give me an extension on my paper. I told Maisie she didn't need to come with me, I was pretty self-sufficient, but she insisted. As it turned out, during those forty-eight hours in L.A. I only saw her for about twenty minutes. She spent the rest of the time lounging by the hotel pool flipping through a back stack of *Vogue*s. Apparently white women don't actually swim, either. On the way home, she confessed she really needed a vacation from her kids. I remember thinking, I love kids, but I'm never gonna have them. They ruin your life. Look at my mama, look at Aunt Viv having to raise me, and now this lady.

I made more money from that L.A. shoot than I had my entire first year at NYU working twenty hours a week as a nanny. To most people it wasn't much, but to me it was a welcome mat into a whole other lifestyle. I adjusted my NYU class schedule to take the minimum course load to keep my academic scholarship, and also be able to keep up my newfound modeling commitments. I didn't have the heart to tell Aunt Viv I switched my major to psychology so I could model and still graduate without having to take hard classes; she was too busy bragging to all her friends in the Glide Memorial Church gospel choir that I was studying chemistry so I could apply to med school. The money was just too easy and that trumped a tough course load as well as truth telling.

By what should have been my senior year at NYU I was a full semester behind in credits, but my bank account was growing, and I was booked for my first runway show in Milan. Milan was code for *I have arrived* in the world of runway modeling. For months, I had been lusting after a fine-assed David Beckham/Taye Diggs combo. He was a newbie model just like me. Between the green eyes, shaved head, disdain for wearing a shirt to cover up his sculpted torso, and the chip on his left front tooth, he took sexy to a whole new level. Somewhere over the Atlantic he finally noticed me. I had spent so many years being good—studying hard, getting good grades, helping Aunt Viv, training mercilessly for track, getting a scholarship, earning spending money—that I had a moment, one solitary moment of wanting to be bad. David Diggs (or was it Taye Beckham?) and I joined the mile-high club, twice, in the first-class bathroom before the plane touched down in Milan. Cordially, he took me to a nice dinner that night, held my hand near some famous fountain, and kissed me at midnight so I felt no shame.

It turned out I was a massive hit in Milan. As hard as I tried to mimic the dour faces of all the top models as they strutted down the runway, I couldn't do it. The next morning, I was on the front page of the Milan newspaper style section being complimented on my gleaming smile, warmth, and positivity in an ocean of women who look ticked off and hungry. Next thing I knew I was booked for a month of work in Tokyo and heralded as an up-and-coming fashion muse. My mile-high fling and I parted ways in Milan promising to meet again on a future flight, his six-pack abs burned into my memory.

I promptly returned to NYU, quit school, and wrote Aunt Viv a long letter explaining the whole thing, begging her not to worry, telling her that I would make more money in the next ten years without a degree than I ever would after paying off med school loans and thirty years of private practice. Yes, it was fuzzy math, but at twenty-one I was convinced this was a solid life choice. Luckily, this was before cell phones were commonplace, so I never had to hear the depth of disappointment in Aunt Viv's voice.

A month later I sold off what little I had in my dorm room, packed a bag, and flew to Tokyo to live in a postage stamp–sized hotel room in the Shibuya ward. And that is exactly where I found myself at twenty-one: in a thong, pasties, and a kimono, owning the catwalk and blissfully unaware that I was carrying a baby conceived in a bathroom built for one. As far as I knew it was my life that was just beginning, not the lima bean's inside me.

But then my pants didn't fit. Maisie made me pee on four sticks in the Charles de Gaulle Airport to be sure. I spent the next three weeks zigzagging across Europe trying to hunt down my baby daddy. As the hormones raged, so did my anger at my stupidity and his carelessness. I finally tracked him down hunched over a hand-rolled joint outside a swanky hotel in Amsterdam. After I unexpectedly had to remind him who I was, sheer exhaustion and nausea overcame all sensibility and I announced right then and there on the hotel's red-carpeted steps that I was pregnant. He looked at me with a blank stare. "New York to Milan flight?" I hinted to jog his memory. Blank stare. "Gettin' busy in the bathroom?" Blank stare. Clearly, I was not the first woman he had seduced with her booty pressed up against the Purell dispenser.

With all the empathy he could muster, Mr. Mile-High said, "Hey, it could be anyone's baby." But after I explained to him that I had only had sex with two men in my life and the first one was eighteen months before him, his copper skin turned putrid yellow. And after much yelling back and forth in front of that five-star hotel about responsibility and owning your actions, I'm sure it won't shock you to find out that Mr. Mile-High wanted nothing to do with something that would ground him for life. And the hotel wanted nothing further to do with the two of us. Pure pride made me walk away that afternoon, stomaching how unfair it was that my life was on a downward spiral and his was only going to continue to get better—care- and responsibility-free. I guess I could have tried to figure out a way to hold him accountable for his baby, but I was twenty-one, in Europe with no friends and no family, and zero clue how I would even go about getting him to acknowledge the baby was his, let alone to help pay for it. And I was not going to humiliate myself and beg him to take responsibility for me and for his baby. I came from a long line of women who had raised babies on their own or, in my mother's case, had given their baby to their single older sister to raise. In my mind there was no reason I couldn't do the same.

Maisie assured me that if I wanted to get rid of it she could make it happen, and if I wanted to keep it, well, she believed with my body and my youth I would be back on the runway making bank two months after giving birth.

Maisie was right. I was back on the runway nine months later handing off baby girl Etta to whoever would take her while I was in hair, makeup, fitting, and walking. But I was no Heidi Klum. The weight did not just melt off no matter how much Etta nursed. Some body parts (read: boobs and belly) had shifted never to return to their original state. As hard as Maisie tried, the heavy-hitting designers were passing me up. The up-and-coming designers were willing to take a chance on me, but they couldn't pay. I promised Maisie I didn't care, just get me out there, so she did. And as Etta grew on the road, my bank account dwindled and so did my confidence.

After a few years, at the ripe age of twenty-four, I was a geriatric model, and having a toddler hanging off my hip wasn't helping my manufactured image as a desirable, unattainable woman. Fifteen- and sixteen-year-olds were becoming the norm for agencies now. The more infantile the body, the more bookings a model got. The thick Bordelon backside was no longer in vogue. Though I had it in me to work hard to make a lot of things happen, heroin chic was not in the cards.

Then Etta turned four. I knew in a year I would have to put her in kindergarten and we could no longer live on the road. I suppose Etta was a convenient excuse to get out of the modeling business, but the reality was I hadn't really been in it for the past two years and my meager savings proved it. Also, I was tired. Tired of constantly moving around and tired of doing it all on my own. I was never in one place long enough to get past a third date with anyone. In truth, most of the men I had dated were not even worth the second date, I was just desperate for adult companionship.

We landed at the international terminal at the San Francisco Airport, one big bag between us. I hailed a cab with the efficiency of a global traveler, and forty minutes later we were wrapped in a blanket of damp fog on Aunt Viv's doorstep in San Francisco's Outer Richmond neighborhood. Etta held my hand, waiting anxiously to meet the only real mother and true companion I ever had.

By the time I finished my story, Lola was on her third margarita. "Let me get this straight: You were a professional model and THAT is what you wear to Zumba class?" Lola asked before breaking out in hysterics.

What can I say? Milan, Tokyo, Paris . . . that was a lifetime ago.

A dozen years as friends and Lola is still my toughest style critic and most fierce wing-woman, watching my back and always looking out for my front. I pull myself from the memory of our first meeting and get back to my friend on the phone. "No, Lola, my vagina did not die this summer. She's woke and worried about climate change. Now, will you listen?" I say, sucking my teeth like a surly tween.

"Okay, okay, whatchoo got?"

"Big start to the year, Lo, I might be snagging myself a billionaire." I know this little nugget of intel will make my best friend's day.

"Did you swipe right on a billionaire?!?!?!? I didn't think they say that sort of stuff in their profiles. Was he standing in front of a big yacht? Maybe he just cleans it, or maybe he does own it. Probably big bucks, small Johnson." I should have known Lola would fly right by my juicy admissions gossip and dive directly into my personal, or lack thereof, life.

"'Johnson'? Really? That's so old school. And, ewwwww, you know I don't use dating apps."

"We need to change that. You should be using something."

"I do—abstinence."

"Two years of no sex since Michael is not abstinence, it's called celibacy, girlfriend. Michael was fine, I'm not saying he wasn't, but no man is worth livin' a nun's existence. I'm willing to bet my middle child you are the only single woman in America not on at least one dating app. You're virtually nonexistent in the modern dating world. I'll come over tonight and set up your profile. Let's bring you into the 2000s; it'll be fun." Lola rarely takes no for an answer.

"First, Tommy's your least favorite child, so that's a pretty low wager. And second, the billionaire I'm talking about is Christopher Lawton of Lawton, Springfield, and Smith Venture Capital on Sand Hill Road, best friends with Sergey Brin. He and his *wife* tore down three houses to build their mega-mansion in Presidio Heights. It was on the front page of *San Francisco* magazine a few months ago: The house has a helipad on the roof so the Mister can fly to Palo Alto for work and avoid 101 traffic. Anyway, they were the first ones to apply to Fairchild this year. I got a lovely note from the Missus. Apparently, her son is a reincarnated lama."

"A trust-fund lama—that should be a box to check under 'Race' on the common app."

"The category should probably be a bit broader: Caucasian, Hispanic, Black, Pacific Islander, Latino, Religious Icon."

Lola lets loose a throaty cackle before taking a turn for the serious. "Do you know for sure the Lawtons are still married? Have you googled them yet?" For Lola, all roads lead back to my relationship status.

"Yes. They're still married. You know my sensitivity to that since . . ."

"Go-Home-Jerome." Lola answers for me. "I almost forgot about him. It's bad enough to cheat, but then to cheat badly, such a loser."

Pathetically, I was the one who felt like the loser in my first so-called adult relationship. Jerome and I dated for three months about four years after Etta and I settled in San Francisco. He was the first guy to have even an inkling of real potential. Our dates were always a fabulous adventure: wine tasting in Sonoma, dinner in the tiny beach town of Bolinas, a mid-afternoon work hooky date to the movies complete with making out in the dark. And then he went on an island vacation with some "buddies" for ten days. I did a boss job hiding the fact I was counting down the hours until he returned. Aunt Viv took eight-year-old Etta to a church picnic the day Jerome returned so I invited him over for brunch and for proximity to my bed. We passed right by the orange juice and pecan waffles. Jerome was unbuttoning my blouse when I noticed a distinct tan line on his ring finger and my heart dropped. I shoved him hard with both hands shouting, "GO HOME, JEROME!!!!" I spent the next week crying and plotting a revenge I knew I was too soft to act on. For some extra salt in my humiliation wound, I also had to ignore the twenty-plus phone messages he left begging me not to tell his wife. Go-Home-Jerome, Michael, and a handful of dates sprinkled over the years make up the extent of my romantic history. After all that it was easier to sideline my romantic life and focus my energies on Etta.

"Earthquake drill—gotta run." That's our safe word when we want out of a conversation. Well, it's my safe word. Lola will talk about anything; no subject is off limits.

"Liar. Hit me up later."

"Bye, lady."

Meredith Christopher Lawton San Francisco images

I love Google. Researching applicants is a major part of my job. Well 3 percent, but procrastination can make it more like 50 percent. It was officially 10 percent of my job when I was an admissions assistant (so technically now it's Roan's job), but I haven't quite been able to kick the stalking habit. I figure it can't hurt to know what the Lawtons look like before they walk into the conference room this week for the first school tour of the year.

Hundreds of images load of Meredith purring across my screen, a full-on couture kitten. I wonder how Karl Lagerfeld, Yves Saint Laurent, and Tom Ford feel about battling it out for prime real estate on the same five-foot-nothing body. Scrolling down I finally find a picture of Meredith with a man I assume is her husband standing slightly behind her, caught in her shadow. Meredith hovers just above him in five-inch Jimmy Choos, perfectly frayed jeans, and a wrinkled but ready-to-wear button-down shirt tied at the waist with a Gucci belt peeking out. Flawless Californian dress up dress down. Even squinting, I can't quite make out Christopher's features behind his wife's presence.

Twenty more minutes of searching and I now know Christopher Lawton's net worth, his two failed tech start-ups before hitting the mother lode six years ago, and where he earned his collection of PhDs. I develop a soft spot for him because it turns out the couture kitten is actually his first wife, not round two or three. A mythical loyal, wealthy male breed. But what he actually looks like remains a mystery.

THREE

✦✦✦✦✦✦

I WEAR MY HEAD-TO-TOE BLACK OUTFIT FOR EVERY SCHOOL tour. Roan calls it my "death of childhood" uniform. Fitted cashmere crewneck sweater, cigarette pants, and towering heels. Very Vera Wang. I read in a four-year-old *Harper's Bazaar* at the dermatologist's office that a work uniform that never changes is a display of power (and creates an illusion that makes you appear ageless, wait no, I think it was timeless). Anyway, maybe for Carolina Herrera it is, but for me, I just can't compete on the fashionista playing field of the potential Fairchild mom even though the ex-model in me still wants to try. However, in heels I have a good three inches on even the tallest of baby mamas around the conference table—and that's just enough to let each of them know who, exactly, is in charge of their offspring's future.

"You have lipstick on your teeth," Roan says, pulling on his upper lip and pointing to his perfectly bleached white teeth. Roan assures me that in the haughtiest of gay circles he aspires to belong to, flawless teeth are a must. It was a bonding moment between boss and peon because in the mating rituals of my African ancestors the whites of the eyes and teeth are the first sign of good health, thus making the subject in question acceptable dating material. Somehow that nugget of historic folklore has transferred itself into modern sex ed in black families. In the Aunt Viv puberty talk when I was twelve, the first lesson she imparted to me was to check out the whites of the teeth and eyes. From there, decide whether to look down and check out the rest of the package. Roan says white teeth glow better when clubbing.

"That's blood. I ate a small child for lunch."

"I hope you plucked a fat, juicy one off the playground. Not some kid who's all knees and elbows," Roan lobs back, completely non-plussed by the inappropriate banter of a prestigious school adminis-trator such as myself. I love Roan. Best. Hire. Ever.

"You know this is probably the year when the majority of mothers applying their little darlings to school will most likely be closer to my age than yours?"

"How do you figure that?"

"Well, you're thirty-nine, let's say they're on average probably thirty-two or thirty-three and I'm a baby at twenty-nine. So, you know what that means, right?"

"What?" I ask, directing my question more to the marketing ma-terials I'm arranging on the conference table than to Roan.

"You're old."

"You're fired," I say, not looking up from the admission view books.

"No, I'm not."

"How do you know?" I ask, fake annoyed that he's questioning my authority.

"Because you can't stand sending out the rejection e-mails to 90 percent of the applicant pool every year in March. You don't have the stomach to break young hearts and crush young futures all over the Bay Area, so you make me do it. And then, after I push send, you pretend to have a doctor's appointment and go to the Fairmont for a gin-soaked spa afternoon with Lola. You'll keep me around forever just to do that one task. Behind that witchy black wardrobe you wear is a bleeding heart. Mine's Teflon."

"Lola and I meet at the Huntington Hotel for our annual sweat and swill, not the Fairmont," I shoot back at Roan as he heads to his dime-sized closet office across the hall.

Roan's right. For all our verbal sparring over the young and the shallow, Roan is wicked smart and gets private school culture. Though he was raised deep in the almond groves of Modesto, he enjoys the lifestyle of the absurdly rich. He has flourished in this madcap milieu using his gift of gab to develop an astonishing level of cultural competency of the 1 percent. Over the years he has morphed into my work "boo-friend" and I trust him. Like I said, best hire ever.

FROM: Meredith Lawton
DATE: October 2, 2018
SUBJECT: My +1
TO: Josephine Bordelon

Dear Josephine,

Christopher will not be able to attend the tour this afternoon. While he cares deeply about Harrison's educational journey and path to success, the international markets can't wait, and he had to jet to Hong Kong last minute. In his absence our family bodyguard, Randy, will be in attendance.

I assume having personal bodyguards on campus is not an uncommon occurrence given the children who attend Fairchild Country Day. We like to treat our support staff like family (excellent modeling to teach Harrison the importance of being inclusive of all people), so it's critical to us that our bodyguard enjoys the school he may be attending alongside Harrison. I ask that you treat Randy with the same respect and courtesy you give all applicant parents and students. Hopefully there will be another bodyguard or two attending the school, so Randy may make a friend and have someone to eat lunch with once Harrison is comfortably settled.

Looking forward to finally meeting you in person at 1:00. I will be rushing over after having lunch with Beatrice Pembrook at Pizzeria Delfina. Have I mentioned we are the best of friends? Depending on traffic down California, if I'm a tad late please excuse my tardiness, I appreciate you waiting and not starting without me.

Bless you (I just got out of the BEST Vinyasa yoga class. Feeling so centered:-)),

Meredith Lawton

Life being what it is, I expect the occasional last-minute e-mail from a frantic parent that they can't make their coveted tour spot due to a bedridden illness, car trouble, or being pulled into a meeting that, if missed, would cost them their job. I get it, I do. But holding up my tour because of slow restaurant service, no way.

FROM: Josephine Bordelon—
    jbordelon@fairchildcountrydayschool.org
DATE: October 2, 2018
SUBJECT: RE: My +1
CC:
BCC:
TO: Meredith Lawton
- -

A Fairchild school tour waits for no mother. The show must go on. If you can manage to be the first to send in your application and sign up for a school tour, color me crazy, but I suspect you can manage to make it to the tour on time. I'm sure your BFF Beatrice Pembrook will understand if you have to run out without finishing that last sip of prosecco. Consider it excellent training for the next thirteen years of your life driving Harrison and the bodyguard to school for 8:15 a.m. drop-off.

Fondly,
Josie Bordelon

DIRECTOR OF ADMISSIONS
FAIRCHILD COUNTRY DAY SCHOOL

I hear the first footsteps coming up the stairs and into Colson Hall for the tour.

DE-LEEEEEEEEEEEEEEEEEEEEEEEEEEEEEEEEEEEE-TE.

There go my most sincere thoughts along with any time I had to spare to send off an appropriate, if not honest, response.

I pick up the phone to call Roan. "Wife's five-two, French, kitten heels, jeans, white-and-blue-striped boatneck shirt, and a fitted blazer. Oh and Anna Wintour wannabe hair. Casual French chic. Husband works in biotech sumpin' and sumpin', collared shirt, blazer, no tie; fit, but angular face that looks pinched, like he's sucking lemons."

"No, the footsteps are too staccato. I call gay men who know alternative families are all the rage in private schools. One is carrying some extra dad weight. He's the mom. My guess is the dad might be fairly good-looking and they're going to seem like an odd match; so in our post-tour pillow talk we can deconstruct that relationship for a good couple of hours. And I say thank God, this school needs a little more of my flavor."

"Trust me, the school can't handle any more Roan."

"Three, two, one, go."

We both step out of our offices and into the conference room and Roan does a little happy dance behind the backs of the two dads. He nailed it. I do my best to conceal my disappointment. Roan and I play *guess the first family* at every school tour. Whoever wins (or comes closest) based on the sound of the footsteps coming up the stairs has to buy the other lunch before the next school tour. Year after year, Roan is the equivalent of a Vegas card counter at our game and by the end of the twelve-week tour season my bank account is running low and Roan's ego is on a high. I know it's juvenile, but when you've been doing admissions as long as I have you must do what you can to keep things interesting otherwise every year is Groundhog Day— same faces, same stories, same cycle. That said, I really thought I had come out of the gate strong this season with a Frenchie couple. Gay dads threw me for a loop.

"Welcome to Fairchild Country Day School. I'm Josie Bordelon, director of admissions. I'm so happy to have you on our first tour," I say, recovering from my devastating season-opener loss.

Good to note, my lady parts are not dead. Gay or not, one of the dads has given new definition to "dad bod." I almost wish the tour were over so I could call Lola. The other 75 percent of me hopes there are a lot of questions at the end of the tour, so I can stare longingly at Dad #1. Or is he Dad #2? I decide to label the hot one Dad #1.

"I'm Daniel," says Dad #2.

Being the first tour of the year, I remind myself that when trying to build as diverse a class as possible two dads always trumps two lesbians or mixed-race families; it's an accepted industry fact.

"Nice to meet you." I extend my hand and give my well-practiced smile that says *you might be the most important parent I have ever met.* I've given that smile approximately 18,142 times. Approximately.

"We're so happy to be here, we can't even tell you. I mean we've been waiting for this for years and it's better than I ever expected. I can't believe the Palace Legion of Honor is practically in your backyard and the kids can go for hikes on the Land's End trail all while learning in the peaceful environment of the Sea Cliff neighborhood." Daniel blurts out the Fairchild topography with overt enthusiasm, a drop of spittle landing on my right boob. Daniel turns red, I pretend not to notice. I'm going to give him a break since he was smart enough to marry up.

"I'm Ty," says Dad #1 with a radio-smooth voice. He towers over his stumpy husband. Oh what I could do with this blond-haired, blue-eyed gabe (that's what Roan calls a gay babe and I've culturally appropriated it). I immediately rename him Wonder Boy. Like, I wonder if he ever had an awkward stage. I wonder how Daniel snagged him. I wonder if he would let me feel his broad shoulders. I wonder, yet again, why the best-looking men in San Francisco are gay. If this guy were straight we'd make a fabulous salt-and-pepper set. God, I can't wait for the admissions visit dates, when I get to take Polaroids of the families for their files. I want to pin Ty up on the "Admission's Hall of Fame" bulletin board that hangs inside my office storage closet. I'll just cut out Dad #2 and their offspring.

"It's *really* quite nice to meet you." I put my hand out to shake with Wonder Boy. His grip is firm and oozes confidence and safety. I internally shudder at my overemphasis on *really*. Luckily I'm black, because beneath this ebony I'm blushing red velvet. His name already lost to my memory, I turn and smile again at Dad #2 as some sort of consolation prize. I'm sure he's used to playing backup in this duo.

"What's your rising kindergartener's name?" I eke out, thrown off by Wonder Boy and his superhero bod. Roan shakes his head in disgust and leaves the conference room to greet other parents walking up the stairs. I need to steady my footing and reclaim my game.

"We have a daughter, Gracie," Dad #2 says awkwardly, patting Ty on the shoulder and then quickly recoiling. Boom! There it is. The chink in the perfect family chain. Thirteen years in admissions and I can pick up on it with the first physical touch I spy between parents. It's the weak smile, the lack of eye contact, the crossed arms. The dead giveaway: awkward affection.

Daniel, that's Dad #2's name, I remember now. I'm back from my momentary swoon. I know this story like the Aesop's fables Aunt Viv recited to me every night as a child. Daniel desperately wants Gracie to go to private school; Wonder Boy does not. Wonder Boy went to public school and it did him just fine (which I can't argue with, look at him); so if public school was good enough for him it will be good enough for his daughter. Daniel, however, wants this for Gracie. He wants more than what he had. The fine AND industrial arts; the four-year coding AND robotics program; the choice to take Mandarin, Arabic, Latin, or Spanish; the Pembrook Aquatics Center; AND the seventh-grade service trip to Nicaragua. Daniel wants to be a Fairchild family. Ty does not.

"Well, find your name tags, pick up any of the materials on the table that look interesting to you, and help yourself to tea or coffee. We'll get started as soon as all the other parents arrive." I can't dwell too long on one family or the other families who are waiting in line to meet me will stage an uprising. San Francisco private school admissions is an ugly sport, and playground legend states that the first rule of the game is a personal meet and greet with the admissions director, who holds the outcome of every child's future. It's all so pretentious and overly dramatic, but I suspect many of the parents like the pomp and circumstance of it all. I myself have enjoyed a power trip or two.

"Thank you, Josie. We're looking forward to seeing more of this stunning school in person. Years of looking at the pictures online, and now we're finally here!" Daniel nervously giggles, throwing a final Hail Mary pass to impress me. He needs to shut up before I start to like them less.

My phone dings. Saved by text. "Excuse me," I say and turn to peek at my phone screen.

MEREDITH

> **Almost there. Don't start without me. Thx. ☺ Meredith**

Today 12:56 P.M.

Holy hell, how'd she get my cell phone number?

"OKAY, I KNOW YOU'RE DYIN' TO SPILL THE TEA. WHAT WAS the most ridiculous question you got on the tour today?" By pure luck Lola's oldest son has karate on Tuesdays two blocks down from San Francisco Ballet School, where Etta pretty much spends her life.

Every Tuesday afternoon Lola and I walk to Absinthe on Hayes Street. When I was growing up Aunt Viv wouldn't let me hop a bus, get off a bus, or walk a block to find a bus in Hayes Valley. Back then, after the Tenderloin, Hayes was the least desirable neighborhood to walk through unless you had an urge to get mugged. Today, like so many other neighborhoods in San Francisco, Hayes Valley has been revived (or destroyed, depending on your point of view) into a precious haven of artisanal cheesemongers, handwoven rug peddlers from war-torn Middle Eastern countries, fair-trade coffeehouses, and snooty French patisseries. You could choke on the hipness of it all as fit lumber-sexual men cruise the sidewalks hand in hand with equally fit tattooed artistic types, male or female. Usually one of them is licking a goji berry cardamom ice cream cone.

Not that I wouldn't mind a muscled-up Daniel Boone of my own, but Lola and I stick to Absinthe, the oldest establishment in Hayes, because their happy hour champagne is the cheapest in the neighborhood and they will split a burger at no extra cost. We could give two shits if the lettuce and tomato on our burger has been locally sourced and the cow was read Dostoyevsky out in the pasture before being led to slaughter. We talk about everything at school that is supposed to be confidential. It's the best ninety minutes of my week.

"I had one family claim their newly minted five-year-old is doing algebra, and they want to know how Fairchild will be supporting his math genius. Because, of course, they assume their midget brainiac will get in. Oh, and when he tests out of all the math levels at Fairchild will the school pay for him to be bused to UC Berkeley for his math courses. About three other families nodded in agreement. Apparently they also have Nobel Prize–winning popsicle-eating mathematicians. Watch out, Isaac Newton."

"Here's to the Pythagorean theorem." Lola cheers and downs her champagne.

"Is the Pythagorean theorem algebra?"

"No clue. Frankly, I'm impressed I pulled 'Pythagorean theorem' out of my ass." Lola waves down the bartender for another glass. Occasionally it's a two-champagne day, if *occasionally* means three out of four Tuesdays. "And who won the bet?"

"Roan. Now he's even more impressed with himself that his gaydar is so finely tuned that he can detect homo steps. His words, not mine."

"Ohhh, two dads out of the admissions gate. That is some fine work, Ms. Bordelon. I daresay playing the diversity card becomes you. San Francisco Academy needs to hire a disabled Native American lesbian as the admissions director to beat Fairchild at its own game." Lola flutters her eyelashes and puts on her best Southern accent, which, coming from a Canadian, sounds more like Fargo, North Dakota. Lola loves to tease that I'm the reason all the interesting and beautiful people end up attending Fairchild. Interesting and beautiful is code for not unattractive, not white, not straight, not Christian, not 100 percent gender specific, and not poor. And she's not 100 percent wrong.

Thirteen years ago, when Etta and I landed on Aunt Viv's doorstep I had about five hundred dollars to my name and big hopes of getting Etta into Fairchild. I had spent eighteen hundred dollars to fly us from Berlin, the last stop on my mediocre modeling career. Then there were the endless snacks, crayons, and coloring books so Etta could be entertained on the long flight home while I tried to figure out what exactly I was going to say to Aunt Viv. *Déjà vu, Aunt Viv. I know we haven't talked much since I sprang it on you that I was quitting NYU for a modeling career, but here I am with my four-year-old daughter I couldn't find the time to tell you about while I was busy parading my half-naked body in front of ogling audiences all over the world. Her name is Etta and I'm praying you haven't written me out of your life because she needs to go to school and I need help raising her; so far I'm doing a subpar job of it on my own. And then there's the issue of needing to make some money. I'll give you three guesses to figure out who I remind you of.*

Thankfully, Aunt Viv welcomed me and Etta across the threshold of her apartment and the next day escorted me into Dr. Pearson's office. I was looking to beg my way into the open admissions assistant job. Dr. Pearson practically fell over himself with his good fortune. Without a single lick of experience other than walking a straight line down a catwalk surrounded by well-dressed emaciated people, and an unbroken Fairchild track and field record, Dr. Pearson hired me on the spot. I fought back tears in his office. I'd returned home to the place where I had always shined, was the star of the show, and would be remembered for those accomplishments rather than the mess I had made of my life during the past five years.

For Dr. Pearson, I had all the qualifications he needed for an admissions assistant, and he had zero interest in what had transpired since I graduated high school. Here was Josie Bordelon, Fairchild alum, intimately familiar with the ins and outs of tuition assistance, a good-looking first face to represent the school, related to the most loyal employee Dr. Pearson had ever had, oh and the winning lottery ticket, black.

I've since learned that in the private school world, hiring a black or brown person who is smart, loves kids, and sort of likes the parents is the educational equivalent of a Super Bowl ring. Parents of color like to see an ally in the school. If you want some flavor in your classrooms, then families of color better see a few administrators who look like them, or at least they better not all look like Reese Witherspoon.

I desperately needed a job, even if it didn't pay much. After dropping out of NYU to model wasn't the get-rich-quick adventure my twenty-year-old mind had believed it would be, I realized there was a reason my peers had taken the more traditional path of summer internships, graduating college in four years, and landing a job in finance or tech. It was called a 401(k), vision benefits, and paid vacation. While I was living leveled up in Dolce & Gabbana, my Fairchild classmates had been securing a future. Four years later, when the loudest noise in my life was the sound of a wailing toddler, I knew I would never let Etta make the same mistakes I had made. If I worked at Fairchild I could even influence hundreds of next-generation me's to forgo the path less traveled and focus on creating a stable and secure pipeline to a solid future.

"Ohhh, I got something for you." In addition to the champagne I'm about to make Lola's day.

"Gurl! You had sex, didn't you? Please tell me you had sex," Lola says moving her barstool closer to mine, not wanting to miss a single detail.

"Uh, no, sorry for the letdown."

"No worries, I knew I was overreaching."

"And on that pathetic note, the gay dads who Roan called for the win, one of them just may be the hottest dad to pass through Fairchild this decade—I've named him 'Wonder Boy' in honor of the question on the tip of every single woman's tongue in San Francisco—I wonder why, yet again, this truly foxy man isn't straight? I've reserved a spot for him in my closet Hall of Fame." I grab a napkin from the bar and feign a heat flash creeping up my neck. "Every inch of Wonder Boy's six-foot-fourish frame is pure bliss. His handshake was so firm I would let that man grab my dreads and take it from there. And you know how I feel about people touchin' my hair."

"You do not call him Wonder Boy," Lola deadpans. "That is so white!"

"The man is white. White and gay."

"Then I'm pretty sure his interest in grabbing your dreads and taking you anywhere is nada. But I'll give you credit for actually recognizing a hot dad when you see one, that's progress."

"Oh I recognize plenty of hot men, I just haven't been bringing them home. With Etta leaving soon, guess it's time to start imagining future possibilities. Lucky me, I have a great imagination."

"HAAAAAAA!!!" Lola busts out like she won the lotto. "It's about time you kicked Michael's memory to the curb. "

Michael and I met six years ago when he was the city councilman for our district. Aunt Viv always went to the neighborhood meetings when the city councilman was attending. I thought she went to be politically active and have her voice recognized and her concerns heard, but then one night she bribed me to go with her with the promise of wings and potato salad afterward. In the first minute I knew Aunt Viv attending those meetings had nothing to do with politics.

It was love at first glance, but I didn't make it easy for Michael. I refused to give him my number. Told him a city councilman should know how to connect with all his constituents. The next day, an eleven-year-old Etta handed me a business card and told me a guy who was kind of cute stopped by and that I should call. I took the opportunity to teach Etta the first lesson in dating that all women should know: You don't go calling boys; they call you.

Two days later he showed up at a school tour. He took the whole tour, even asked a question during the Q and A. At the end of the tour I worked the room, talking to all the attendees except him. He waited me out. By the time the last overly engaged parent had left it was lunchtime and I was starving. I let him take me to lunch. Then I skipped the rest of the day at work and let him take me to bed.

For four years and three months Michael was the upstanding man three generations of Bordelon women had never experienced. For the first time in our lives Aunt Viv, Etta, and I did not have to do it all on our own. Something broke, Michael fixed it. Aunt Viv couldn't reach a pot on a top shelf, Michael got it for her. Fairchild had a father/daughter dance, Etta got to go. And I got to properly fall in love for the first time at thirty-three.

Then, just a bit over two years ago Michael got an incredible job offer in Sacramento. When we were all together we encouraged him to take this once-in-a-lifetime opportunity. When Michael wasn't around, Aunt Viv assured me she would be just fine if Etta and I moved to Sacramento to be with Michael, not to mess with true love. I invited her to come along, but she told me her life was in San Francisco. Her life had been in San Francisco before I showed up as a babe and it would continue in San Francisco long after I left.

But the invitation to move to Sacramento with Michael never came. There was talk of long distance, there was talk of visiting each other on weekends, but there was never talk of becoming a real family.

Ultimately, I had to let him go for Etta. I didn't want her watching her mother accept anything but true love and commitment from a man. She didn't need the promise of a weekend father that I knew would eventually fade for reasons she was too young to understand. And I didn't need a part-time lover. Alone was better than half-assed. So I took the lead and the three of us let Michael go. What was most heartbreaking was that he didn't seem to mind going. That we, in fact, had been a layover for him on his trip to bigger and better things.

"Josie, as good as those four years were they were not worth closing up shop. Everybody needs some good lovin'." Lola reminds me, more like a big sister than a girlfriend.

"How can you have three kids and have the brain capacity, let alone energy, to think about sex all the time? Nic is one lucky guy."

"Oh I don't spend my time fantasizing about having sex with my husband! You fantasize about your husband folding laundry or emptying the dishwasher or making dinner other than pizza. I think about having sex with anyone but Nic. Let's just say I have a rich imagination, and as much as I would like to imagine you getting it on with Wonder Boy, it's not even worth my very limited brain capacity, you know, since he's GAY." Lola licks the rim of her empty second glass of champagne and hops off her barstool. "Gotta go. My mini—Bruce Lee will be starving for his cheese stick. And, Josie, we are two years and a handful of months past Michael. As much as I applaud your recognition of a good-looking dad—even if he's not straight—it doesn't count as dating progress. Bring me a man who wants to sleep with women. That's something I can work with."

Every woman needs a girlfriend who speaks the truth. At almost forty it's as necessary as a pair of Spanx.

FOUR

"MAMA, WE NEED TO TALK ABOUT NEXT YEAR." ETTA IS SET-
ting the dinner table. I spy Aunt Viv fake minding her own business.
She's been washing the same bunch of collard greens for about five
minutes.

"Not right now, I'm exhausted. I had my first tour today and Lola
made me have two glasses of champagne." I can feel it coming—
three, two, one.

"Now, baby, I don't want to let her go, either, but Etta's time, it's
comin' and Lola don't make you do nothin' you don't want to do.
When you two women gonna stop acting like a couple of girls?
Drinkin' on a Tuesday afternoon waitin' on your kids. I should call
child protective services on you two." How is it Aunt Viv can simul-
taneously make me feel old because Etta will soon be leaving me for
her own life and infantile for loving my Tuesday afternoon drinking
dates with Lola? "Etta, don't you mind your mama, you go right
ahead, I can tell you have things to say. And she's gonna listen, trust
me." Aunt Viv points her chef's knife at me. In almost fourteen years

of collective decision-making the score is currently 823 Aunt Viv and Etta to my 62, and at least 50 of those times Aunt Viv was either out of town or at least out of the house.

Etta strategically moves over to the sink to lock arms with Aunt Viv. They are now a united front looking to take me down.

It's not that I don't want Etta to go to college and become her own person, of course I do. Since she was small, I have planned all the ways I would make sure Etta did early adulthood differently than me. I'm thinking Cornell or Dartmouth, a rural Ivy nowhere near the distracting trappings of big-city life. Etta can study engineering, computer science, or math; she has consistently shown promise in all three areas since second grade. A gorgeous, brainy, black female with that kind of academic background will play well in the job market. Then, if she wants to go to graduate school in New York or D.C. or London on her own dime I'll be fine with it because she will be a fully cooked human being. No pasties and full-body waxes for Etta.

Etta is a smart and focused girl. I'm not saying that as her mother, I'm saying that as a professional who spends her waking days assessing the full range of human aptitude and ability, or lack thereof. The smarts I attribute to her great Fairchild education and genetics (I was a fabulous student, just a lousy decision-maker), the focus to her long-standing dance career with the San Francisco Ballet School. Etta brilliantly uses her body to create beauty and art, something neither her absent grandmother nor I could make happen. Ballet has also kept her out of trouble, healthy, and sheltered from the trappings of the world. Fairchild and ballet are all Etta knows, and I will make sure her next step in life will be as promising (and as safe) as the last fourteen years. What I want for my child is no different than any other parent: I want Etta to be happy, to have options in life, and I want to make sure she doesn't return to my couch. I came back to San Francisco to try to end an unfortunate two-generation cycle of Bordelon women using their bodies rather than their brains to make a living. It will be different for Etta. She will rewrite our family story to be one of brains over beauty, NOT the other way around.

Admittedly, what I don't know is how I'm going to pay for this expensive turn of family events. Even though I'm a Fairchild alum and unquestionably an extraordinary employee (minus the crank calls I make to Roan pretending to be from his favorite Japanese restaurant informing him there is actually pork in his beloved *gyozas*—take that, you vegan freak), this whole applying to college business is far more complicated than I remember and it's leaving me with one feeling—overwhelmed. Historically, when I'm feeling over-whelmed, my MO is to work hard to ignore the situation that is creating the anxiety. This is a learned survival skill I refined early in my childhood. Whenever I would wonder why my mama left me, why she never came back, why she thought Aunt Viv would do a better job raising me than she could, I would compartmentalize my ques-tions because when I tried to ask Aunt Viv she refused to give me answers. I was met with a dismissive, "Oh you don't really want to know anything about that, you've got a good life with me haven't you, child?" To this day I still don't know if all that time Aunt Viv actually knew where my mother was but wouldn't say or if Aunt Viv was as clueless as I was. Either way, growing up, my mother was not a topic up for discussion.

"Okay, you want to talk about next year. Do you have anywhere that you are planning on applying early admit? Perhaps prioritizing Cornell or Dartmouth would be a good idea. Living in upstate New York or rural New Hampshire will be a wholly different experience for you, one I think you would really enjoy." (An opinion I have based on absolutely nothing.) "Tomorrow after school let's talk to Krista in college counseling. She'll help us get this whole early admit thing figured out." Take that, Aunt Viv, I engaged in the post-graduation conversation and I nailed it. Clearly day drinking does not inhibit my above-par parenting skills.

I pull out the cushioned chair at my usual spot, excited that the dining table is crowded with a menu of catfish, greens, and cornbread tonight. Digging into my fried fish I notice Etta shoot Aunt Viv a look of panic. I put down my fork and turn a hard gaze on Aunt Viv.

Aunt Viv takes her time dabbing the corners of her mouth with her napkin and looks to Etta. It occurs to me that Aunt Viv is conveniently wearing her power wig—straightened chin-length bob with a front-bang sweep. She named this one her Queen V one day after she mistakenly heard me call it her "Queen Bey" look. All business—no bullshit.

"You go on, baby girl," Queen V says, smoothing her manufactured hair.

"Okay," Etta starts, barely above a whisper. "Mama, what if I was thinking of maybe, uh, ah, well . . . a less traditional type of college, but still one of the best, I promise?"

"Huh? Take that fork out of your mouth, I can't understand you."

"What if I was thinking of, you know, a less traditional college than the ones you're talking about?"

"I'd say stop thinking." I knew I was not up for this conversation after a two-champagne Tuesday. Aunt Viv needs to learn to mind her own business. I could rip that wig right off her head. Where is this coming from? Etta has never been a kid to stray from the norm, from the expected. I did too good a job making sure of it. The number of times I've tried to get her to skip ballet and come to the movies with me are too many to count. She refuses to miss a day of dance, not wanting to disappoint her master teacher, Jean Georges. Five days a week for the past ten years, Etta has always done exactly what she was supposed to do and that has included not ditching dance class for the movies with her mama.

"Now, Josie, don't be so quick to judge. Your path was not so much of a straight line."

"Exactly, Aunt Viv, and I'm going to save Etta from the sheer idiocy she may be genetically predisposed to when it comes to making big life decisions. Learn from your mother's mistakes, Etta. The less traditional path—I'm here to say, not so glamorous. Unless you define glamorous as standing butt-ass naked in a crowded changing room as two assistants pull the skin around your kneecaps up to your mid-thighs with duct tape so your knees look unnaturally bony like a nine-year-old boy's."

"Hear her out, Josie. This is Etta's life, not yours."

"Oh, Etta's life is my life as long as I'm payin' for it."

"You shush, Josie Bordelon, and listen to this child. Imagine if you had had half an inkling to call me and tell me what your twenty-one-year-old brain was thinkin' before you marched into that college office and dropped out of NYU tryin' to cash in on a modeling career."

"If I had called and told you my plan you would have ripped me in two like an old rag."

"You got that right, but I woulda listened to you first before I'd gone and done it. Etta baby, go ahead, you say your piece. Tell your mama what you're thinkin'. And then let's get back to dinner. God help you two if my fish goes cold." There's no greater offense in Aunt Viv's world than when people around her dinner table allow her food to go cold.

Etta takes a deep breath and sets a steely stare on me. "MOM."

"Before you go down this road, remember: I gave you life. And save that white girl *Mom* talk for your friends. I'm your mama and don't you forget it."

"Seriously, Mama?!?!?!" Etta whines, too easily thrown off her game in my humble opinion. The kid needs to toughen up before she flies the nest. She wouldn't survive a day in New York.

"Alright, alright. Tell me what you're thinking, I promise to have an open mind." Under the table I cross my fingers.

"I want to apply to Juilliard."

"Juilliard? Juilliard, Juilliard? Like in New York City, Juilliard? Like where students dance or sing or strum a guitar and hope they can audition for an understudy role in an off-off-Broadway production that pays literally nothin'?"

"Yes, that's the one," Etta confirms, twisting her napkin around her index finger, not meeting my eyes.

"Etta, my fondest memories of you as a child will always be you on stage, your grace, your beauty, and yes, your talent. But, OVER MY DEAD BODY will you be going to a four-year university, if Juilliard is even considered a university, to focus on dance when I have been paying thirteen years of tuition for you to get a first-class education. That is not part of the Bordelon family plan." I'm feeling ambushed by my family. How long has Aunt Viv known and whose idea was it? And how far down this road have they gone?

"Discounted tuition," Etta shoots back. Oh no she did not! I grip the edge of the table to hold myself back from yanking Etta out of her chair and tossing her into her room.

"Your dead body," Aunt Viv considers, passing the collard greens. "That can be arranged. Now eat, you two. Y'all are acting a fool at my dinner table and this conversation ain't goin' nowhere good tonight."

"This conversation ain't going nowhere ever," I mumble under my breath.

"I heard you," Etta says, not looking up from putting vinegar on her greens.

Good, I think to myself.

FIVE

✦✦✦✦✦✦✦

FROM: Randy Chavez
DATE: October 3, 2018
SUBJECT: School Tour
TO: Josephine Bordelon

Dear Ms. Josephine,

Mrs. Lawton told me I had to write you a thank-you e-mail
after the tour, but I'm not sure what I'm supposed to say.
Mrs. Lawton hired me last year because she was worried
about her husband's safety and said all the big men in
Silicon Valley have bodyguards so her husband needed
one, too. I thought I would be driving Mr. Lawton around,
making sure no one gets close to him, getting him a
sandwich from Subway, and maybe keeping my mouth
shut, you know, if he had a girlfriend or boyfriend or
something. In my line of work you don't judge. I really
didn't know that by bodyguard Mrs. Lawton meant a
dressed-up babysitter for her kid.

So anyway, the school tour was pretty good, not as boring as I thought it would be. I'm thinking of quitting my job, though. I'm not going back to school; I hated it the first time around. Either way, maybe sometime you would like to go out and grab a beer?

Randy

Did I just get asked out on a date by an applicant's disgruntled staff member? Lola's going to love this one. I always send her my best e-mails knowing these little gems make her day. If she actually suggests I go on a date with Randy, though, I'll have to punch her face. Next e-mail.

FROM: Meredith Lawton
DATE: October 3, 2018
SUBJECT: Fairchild School Tour
TO: Josephine Bordelon

- -

Josephine,

I always thought Fairchild would be the perfect school for Harrison, but once I saw the Ingenuity Lab I knew we had made the right choice! Harrison is going to die when he gets his hands on those tools. You do make the children wear hazmat suits when working with power tools right? We don't want anything to happen to Harrison's fingers, his piano teacher would be devastated.

Beatrice Pembrook agrees that Fairchild is the absolute best place for Harrison. Has she talked with you yet? I know it's on her to do list, but she's hosting a dinner for 500 this weekend to raise money for the India Basin/

Hunter's Point redevelopment project so her life is insane. It was a wonder she was able to carve out time for lunch with me yesterday. I guess that's what the closest of friends do for one another though, am I right?

Randy, our bodyguard, should be writing you a thank-you e-mail as well. He shared with me that he could really see himself attending Fairchild alongside Harrison which makes me rest easy when I think about Harrison going off to big-boy school. There are so many crazy people in the world these days, the idea of someone coming after a high-profile child like Harrison is downright terrifying. I'm sure you can understand how having Randy there to protect him will really put Christopher and me at ease. And I know Randy is keen to stay with our family until Harrison is through middle school and has earned his black belt. Randy is beyond committed to our family, I feel so blessed. And don't worry; Christopher will be at the parent interview, he's devastated he couldn't make the tour, truly. Harrison's education is of utmost importance to him.

Off to see my meditation guru. I have upped my sessions with her to three times a week to get me through admissions season. I want to make sure in the midst of this crazy time I maintain being a centered mother and wife. It's so important to prioritize self-care particularly during trying times, don't you think?

Namaste,
Meredith Lawton

Oh, where to begin. How about the fact that Meredith Lawton thinks her child is already in Fairchild? And though I suspect he is not going to last through the month, are the Lawtons willing to pay double tuition for Randy? I need to let this one sink in before I decide whether it deserves a response.

Time to read one last quick e-mail before meeting with Roan.

FROM: Ty Golden
DATE: October 3, 2018
SUBJECT: Kindergarten Tour
TO: Josephine Bordelon

Dear Josie,

Thank you for the school tour yesterday. While Daniel was ecstatic to be there from the get-go, I will admit I came in with some serious reservations. But between your warm smile, your thoughtful answers during the Q and A, and the phenomenal facilities, I have to say I, too, am impressed. Gracie would be a lucky little girl if someone as wonderful as you were to be in her life. Daniel and I look forward to seeing you again for the parent interview. Until then, keep sharing that beautiful smile with the world.

Best,
Ty Golden

Wait a minute, Wonder Boy's last name is *Golden*? Well of course it is, 'cause the universe just kind of works like that. You don't get to be a six-foot-four Adonis with a name like McClumsky. So now Wonder Boy will forever and always be known as Golden Boy. And Golden Boy is either more knowledgeable about how to play the private school game than I gave him credit for or he's working me over with his man charm. If I didn't already know Ty is gay, I might even read between the lines and figure this dad wants more than an acceptance letter. For sure it wouldn't be the first time a dad has hit on me, but it has been a few years. More than likely he's harmlessly flirting with me because he thinks it's upping the family's game.

Overall though, not a bad morning. A date proposal and a compliment from a foxy baby daddy, so I think I'll let Meredith's e-mail sit and not ruin my current good mood. I know she means well and she's not used to having to play by the rules of the real world. She wants the best for her son, and she's settled on Fairchild. While her sense of entitlement chafes me in all the wrong places, I can't totally fault her; I feel the same about Etta, but with more subtlety and finesse, of course. To think that Meredith Lawton and I may have a minuscule something in common gives me pause.

I GRAB THE EXTRA CHAIR IN ROAN'S OFFICE AND POST UP next to his desktop, where he's busy checking the WeeScholars website to see how many applications are in so far. There are 261 applicants, including siblings, for the 36 spots available. About what I expect to have come October. And if we stay on target it will be upward of 625 by December 14.

"Two hundred sixty-one, you know what that means?" I ask Roan, tapping my pencil on his desk. He slaps his hand over the pencil to make it stop.

"Please, I beg of you, don't make me start today. You can have my gift certificate for a mani/pedi on Fillmore if you let me start next week. Trust me, that's a great deal, have you seen your nail beds?" Roan doesn't lie, and I'm tempted, I really do need to stop picking my cuticles.

"We agreed that when applications passed the 250 mark we would start setting up parent interviews. And by *we*, I mean you. Here, I brought you Altoids to get you started." I shake the can at Roan like he's a kitty ready to pounce on a shiny object.

"They can't smell my breath over the phone."

"No, but in two hours when I come back to check on you and your mouth is all dry and cottony from talking to 261 fascinating parents, trust me—rank. You know I always work from a state of self-preservation."

Roan takes a huge swig of coffee and exhales in my general direction.

"Well, I was going to let you wait until next week, but after that act of insubordination, it's game on, Roan."

"You were not. Alright, pop an Altoid yourself and let the cold calling begin." Roan has surrendered to the chief.

"Okay, I want to hear you do your first conversation since it's been a year; put the call on speaker. Remember to be accommodating, enthusiastic, and kind. Don't be pushy, but don't let them manipulate you. Avoid unnecessary conversation, but try to connect over something you may have in common so they feel known and they feel important. Oh, and heard, people love to be heard; psychology 101. Oh, and remember DO NOT get off the phone until you have nailed down an actual date and time, no matter how annoyed you may get. In other words, pretend to be someone you're not."

"Any other advice for a grown man who has successfully been making phone calls long before you came along?"

"Yes, withhold sarcasm, as painful as it may be for you. And if you play nice, I'll buy lunch today AND let you choose where we eat."

"Today's lunch is above and beyond all my school tour wins, right?" Roan questions, raising his eyebrows at me. I notice a few new forehead lines but decide it's in my best interest not to point those out to him now.

"Let the Academy Award–winning performance begin." Roan dials a 917 number for an Alice Allsworth. Must be a New York transplant.

ROAN: Hello, is this Alice Allsworth?

ALICE: Speaking (says Alice with the disdain of a woman being solicited for money by her kid's sleepaway camp).

ROAN (ALREADY ANNOYED BUT MAINTAINING COMPOSURE): This is Roan Dawson from the admissions office at Fairchild Country Day School.

ALICE (WITH A COMPLETE CHANGE IN TONE AND LEVEL OF EXCITEMENT): Oh, well, HELLO, Roan, so lovely of you to call. You just caught me between my Pilates session and running to open my store for the day.

Roan and I quickly skim through the application online to find that Alice owns a high-end denim and chocolate bar on Sacramento Street in Presidio Heights. Seems like either a complete oxymoron or marketing genius. Buy jeans and chocolate. Eat too much chocolate. Need new pair of three-hundred-dollar jeans. I make a mental note to google the shop.

ROAN: Well, I'm calling to set up a day for you and your husband to come in for a parent interview on behalf of your child, Smith.

ALICE: Absolutely, we are wide open. I'm so thrilled to hear from you, this is news we've been waiting for since we sent in our application. Do you have a date and time to suggest? Meeting with Fairchild is our number one priority.

ROAN: How about next Tuesday at three-forty-five?

ALICE: Does Smith attend the interview? Because if he does, Tuesday afternoons are out for us. On Tuesdays he has private CrossFit sessions to work on his core strength and agility for soccer season.

ROAN: No, the interview is just for you and your husband. It takes about twenty to thirty minutes. So then, will Tuesday at three-forty-five work?

ALICE: That should work. No, never mind, Steven has his weekly call with his leadership coach on Tuesdays at four o'clock. They have been together since his first job post–business school. He's more faithful to her than he is to me.

Roan writes down *TMI!* in huge block letters on a notepad.

ROAN: Okay, how about anytime the week of October twenty-second?

ALICE: Well, that would be perfect, but I will be in Tokyo all week at a denim show and it can't be missed. The Japanese are the Chanel of denim, you know.

I see Roan clench his jaw. I meet his TMI comment and raise him a *chillax*.

ROAN: Well, since you are the first family I have called, perhaps you would like to suggest a date and time that will work for you and Steven.

ALICE: That's a brilliant idea. Give me just a minute to scroll through my calendar. Steven and I can come in for a coffee at 7:00 a.m. the first and third Tuesday of every month and, of course, we are always available for drinks after 8:00 p.m. at Spruce. It would be fun to get to know each other over a cocktail, don't you think? The ambiance at Spruce is so intimate; it's a wonderful place to chat. Oh, and we have a nanny on Saturdays and Sundays, too, so weekends are a possibility.

ROAN (POINTING A FINGER GUN TO HIS TEMPLE): While I can think of nothing more I would like to do with my free mornings and evenings, the admissions office has a strict policy of meeting with parents on campus between the business hours of 8:00 a.m.

and 5:00 p.m. I hope that will not be inconvenient for you and Steven.

ALICE (A HINT OF IRRITATION IN HER TONE): Not inconvenient, just not easy. As I said before, this is a priority for us, I assumed there would be more wiggle room and scheduling options for working parents. Oh, I know. I close the store for three weeks over the winter holidays and work slows a bit for Steven just before we head to West Palm Beach to be with our families for Christmas. We are such East Coasters at heart; we miss our weekends down there terribly. There is no substitute for the Atlantic. Am I right? (not waiting for an answer) How about December twelfth at noon?

Roan mouths to me: *She hates the Pacific.* I point to the computer screen for him to focus and check the school calendar. It's the date of the annual holiday sit-down lunch—complete with white linens, candles, and rented china—that the parent council puts on for the faculty and staff every year, but I tell him to book the Allsworths. If he doesn't start moving at a faster clip he'll still be calling to book interviews well into the New Year. Not acceptable.

ROAN: Well, I'm happy that in October you're able to find a date to prioritize us in December.

I slap Roan across the shoulder. I knew telling him to "withhold sarcasm" was going to trip him up, I just didn't expect it on the first call of the season.

ROAN: When you come to the main office on December twelfth, be sure to sign in at the front desk and get visitor passes. You will then be directed to Colson Hall, where the admissions offices are located.

ALICE: That sounds lovely. And you will be sending me a reminder e-mail closer to the date, correct?

ROAN (IGNORING THE REQUEST FOR AN EVITE REMINDER OF THE INTERVIEW): We look forward to seeing you on December twelfth, Alice. I hope you and your family have a lovely fall. Enjoy your trip to Tokyo; I hear the changing leaves are incredible this time of year.

I practically choke on the saccharine dripping from the walls of Roan's office.

ALICE: Yes, they are, thank . . .

ROAN: *Click.*

"Well, I think that went well," I say to Roan, attempting a supportive smile though I know it comes across as slightly pained.

"Yes, beyond delightful. Only 260 more to go, lucky me." Roan pops another Altoid and turns to answer his ringing phone.

ROAN: Hello again, Alice. Oh, it turns out December twelfth isn't going to work for you and Steven after all? Are we available in January? Well, let me take a look.

I sprint out of Roan's office, closing his door behind me. This is his least favorite part of the job and, from prior years' experience, I know right now I am his least favorite person.

SIX

"WHEN I SAID I WOULD TAKE YOU TO LUNCH ANYWHERE you want, I thought it was implied that meant somewhere I would like," I whine to Roan, the two of us joining the line at the *WHAT THE HEMP?* vegan food truck in the Presidio. I'm starving from watching Roan sweat over all those parent phone calls.

"Listen, Ms. Chick-fil-A, you can't pickle yourself in preservatives your whole life. Rumor has it after forty it's a slippery slope to tubby town. Consider this intervention an early birthday present. Plus, can you think of a more stunning place to have lunch on a sunny day? Just look at the view."

I'm looking out at the Bay and the Golden Gate Bridge, but I suspect Roan's looking at the Rasta millennial sporting a frohawk and a Harvard crew T-shirt tidying up the compost station. As we slowly move up the queue I stare at the menu hoping for an option that looks edible and has not been foraged in the wilderness. "Do you think the tempura is a mix of veggies or more like onion rings?" I ask Roan, happy I've found something that actually sounds quite good.

"That's not tempura, Josie," Roan shakes his head, exasperated with my lunching habits, "that's tempeh. It's a fermented soy patty. Delish in a burger."

"Oh. I just thought vegans couldn't spell."

"Just pick something, please. We're almost up to order." I can tell Roan is worried I'm going to accost the urban farmer who will be taking our order with my organic sarcasm.

"Okay, well a burger sounds good, I'll get that."

"You realize it's not a meat burger, right?"

"You just said tempeh is good in a burger."

"The tempeh is the burger."

"Then it's not a burger. A burger has meat."

"Jesus, just order the sweet potato fries and free me from this lunch hell."

"Don't they have real fries?" Roan is speechless. "I'm just messin' with you. That sounds good. Here's some cash. Get me an order of sweet potato fries and a drink from a fruit I've heard of, no hibiscus or elderberry. I'll go find us a picnic table."

I have bought myself five quiet minutes to scroll my IG account on this warm fall day. I have to know what Tracee Ellis Ross is up to. Her fashion sense is off the hook and I can't help but live vicariously through her posts. Lola knows if Tracee ever wants to be my BFF I will drop her like a bad habit. It's a mutual understanding.

I feel a shadow fall over me. I put my phone down to see if fog is rolling in to ruin our lunch. At first glance all I see is a very small pair of running shorts atop some tanned and toned legs. Moving up is a sweaty, powder-blue thin T-shirt sticking to a well-defined six pack. I shield my eyes to look all the way up and smiling down at me is a glistening Golden Boy. Literally. He's blocking my sun so there's a halo of light around his body. It's both magical and disturbing. His package is a mere few inches from my face. Close enough to tell something *good* is definitely wrapped up in that polyester/nylon blend.

"It's Josie, right? I remember your face, but I'm having a hard time placing where we've met." A smile that perfect must have bankrupted Golden Boy's family in orthodontic bills. Beyond his wide pecs, heaving while he catches his breath from his run, Golden Boy has a vibe about him that takes my thoughts places they haven't strayed in a while. He may not completely remember me, but there's no way any man or woman with a pulse could forget him.

"You met us at the Fairchild Country Day School tour with your husband," Roan says, magically appearing at Golden Boy's side and giving him an obvious once-over. "Why don't you sit your sweet self down and join us for lunch?"

"Sure, uh, let me just run over and grab my order. I mean, put my order in and, uh . . . I'll be back in a minute." Golden Boy seems flustered by Roan's presence.

We both watch in silence as Golden Boy jogs away. Even at a slow pace his buns bounce on a beat. I dig into my fries, no use pining after something I can't have.

"I'm not convinced he's throwing down 100 percent on my side," Roan ventures.

"There you go with your twenty-first-century gaydar again. Millennials think everyone is on an elastic sexual spectrum. Can't someone just be plain ol' gay or plain ol' straight anymore?"

"BORING," Roan says, pretending to yawn.

"What are you two talking about?" My hand automatically covers Roan's mouth. Appropriate conversation outside the halls of Fairchild is not his strong suit.

"Have a seat." I shift down the bench hoping Golden Boy's sweat doesn't stink. Or drip. Roan shoots me a look that says, *Move to the other bench so I can sit by this hunk of man.* I hop to.

"Does your husband know you're out here on this gorgeous fall day parading around the Presidio in those microshorts?" Roan asks, propping his chin in his hands and looking straight into Golden Boy's eyes. I should have kept my hand over his mouth.

"Do you run, Josie?" Ty asks me, eager to escape Roan's wistful gaze and tactless question. His question sends Roan into a fit of laughter. The subject of me and running is one of Roan's favorites.

"A few years back I trained for a 10K in Golden Gate Park for breast cancer awareness," I share, which is 100 percent the truth.

"Oh, yeah, how'd it go?" Ty mumbles through a mammoth bite of his falafel gyro.

"Well, I raised twelve hundred dollars for the cause which was great, but then the day before the race I went to pick up my number at registration and they gave me a hideous bubble gum pink shirt. They said all the runners had to wear them in the race."

"What happened after that, Josie?" Roan giggles, giving Ty a flirty slap on his bicep. "This is my favorite part of the story." I kick Roan under the table. He doesn't flinch.

"I took the shirt home and tried to make lemonade out of lemons. I cut off the sleeves, shortened it to above my hips, turned it into a V neck, and then I tried to cut it into a racer tank in the back. The shirt chose to unravel rather than submit to more surgery."

Ty laughs. "So did you go ahead and race in what little was left?" A hint of naughty, naughty in his tone.

"Nah, I sent in the money I raised and went out to brunch with girlfriends the next morning instead."

"Which was probably best because Josie's idea of training was walking on a treadmill in the Fairchild gym gabbing to her best friend, Lola, on the phone," Roan shares, trying to catch Ty's eye. If Roan even attempts to bond with Ty on the athletic front I'm going to call foul. I've never even seen Roan in sneakers.

"Hey, I'll have you know I was a track star when I was at Fairchild. Two of my records still stand. It's just, without a coach barking down my back I seem to lack the motivation to run on my own. It takes some effort in the morning to look this good, I don't want to go messing it up during the day." I toss a lock, to show Roan he isn't the only one with mad man skills.

"I could tell looking at you during the school tour you were a runner. You definitely have the build with all that leg. You should give it a go again. Maybe race with a master's club. I've tried, but I have a tough time doing anything with consistency given my work schedule." This is so typical of an applying parent. Mentioning "work" in general terms so I will take the bait and ask what they do. Then the humble brag of their extensive résumé goes on and on far longer than it should. I'm not falling for it today, not in the mood to feign being impressed.

"Yes, Josie, you would probably slay in the women-over-forty category," Roan offers up. He's enjoying this whole conversation at my expense a little too much.

"I'm not forty," I insist to Ty, though I don't really know why it matters if he knows my age. I guess I can't help but care what a handsome man thinks.

"K, neither am I." Ty shrugs and smiles. "How are the sweet potato fries? I've been meaning to try them, but I always end up getting the same thing. Creature of habit, I guess."

"They're okay if you like food that will help you live to a hundred, unless the lack of taste and satisfaction kills you first."

"HA! No kidding, I'd much rather be saddled up at the Big Easy Beignet food truck over there. My vice is Southern cooking. I'll do anything for a Po'Boy. I run so I can eat. New Orleans has got to have the best food in the country."

"I was born there," I say, smiling at our connection. I wouldn't have thought this West Coast white boy had an ounce of humidity or hot sauce in him.

"Really? You're from New Orleans? I don't hear an accent," Ty says.

"I don't hear one in your voice, either," I volley back, uncomfortable with the spotlight on me, and suddenly aware I'm on the verge of breaking my rule about no personal chitchat with applicants.

"I'm not from New Orleans, but I did a fellowship for a year at Tulane. Practically every older woman I met wanted to feed me, and then they wanted to adopt me when they failed to marry me off to their neighbor's daughter or their own niece. I showed up there with two biological aunts but came back with three new ones. I still write them all. Well, actually two, the third learned to FaceTime at eighty. Now I can't get her off the damn iPad." Roan and I give each other a quick *Who knew?* glance. There's more brain to Golden Boy than what pleasingly meets the eye.

"I have an aunt from NOLA, too," I offer, surprising myself by sharing another personal fact.

"Does she still live there?"

"No, she lives here now. With me, actually."

"Did you ever visit her? That place is something special."

"I knew it once, when I was a little girl, but I don't remember anything really and I haven't been back since."

"That's a shame. Ugh, gotta go, only time for a quick lunch today. Thank you guys for sharing your picnic table and for the good company." Ty lays his hand over mine. I feel my heart rate slow a beat and my body heat rise. This has been one of the more enjoyable lunches I've had in a while. "Guess I'll be seeing you at the parent interview that's coming up in the next month or two, right? I'm not completely sure when it is. Daniel lays out the schedule, and I do what I'm told."

"Yeah, I prefer to be told what to do, too." Roan stands to shake Ty's hand, shattering my moment of bliss. Good thing our business manager never leaves campus to witness things like Roan's half professional, half flirtatious, 100 percent unscrupulous moves. This is an HR disaster in the making.

"Bye, Josie. Good to see you, Roan." Ty grabs his sandwich basket and looks around the grounds for a garbage can. This handsome man even picks up after himself. I give him a quick wave and then I watch Roan watch Ty walk away. He looks like a pointer dog on the brink of chasing his hunt.

"Stand down, soldier." I pull Roan back onto the bench and hold him there. I pop another fake fry into my mouth which, admittedly, tastes pretty good and I, too, watch Golden Boy walk away, unable to avert my gaze.

SEVEN

ETTA

> I'm catching a ride with Poppy. Don't 4get 2 bring leg warmers 4 after dance, don't want to pull hammy. Tell Lola hey. Don't be late. Again.

3:18 P.M.

LOLA

> Bruce Lee not feeling it today. Please don't drink alone. Not a good look. Lo

3:20 P.M.

Damn. Etta's got a ride to dance and Lola's ditching our Tuesday date. Now I have no excuse to avoid building the applicant database, a director of admission's Mount Everest.

I clean out my junk mail, junk drawer, and junk food cabinet. I fluff the pillows on my meet-and-greet chairs, I check the paper in the printer, and I settle into a half-full bag of chocolate pretzels. I stare at the water stain on my ceiling that I think is growing, but I'm not sure. I admire my black patent strappy flats I got for a steal off Gilt. Not terribly comfortable, but damn do they look good. I check WeeScholars—ten more applications this afternoon. I give Facebook a quiet peruse, pretending to read posted *New York Times* articles, but really hunting for upcoming flash sales.

I have an e-mail from Nan Gooding, Fairchild's invisible head of school. Well, invisible if you are a student or one of her administrative staff. If you are a parent or alumnus with wads of cash and, even better, a penis, you have her undivided attention. Nan has yet to find any sense of professional responsibility to mentor the next generation of female school leaders. She would rather be the scarce silk scarf in an ocean of bow ties and blue blazers than share the waters with her own kind. Dealing with her is best done first thing in the morning, when her fresh eight ounces of coffee has kicked in. I give the first of the two e-mails a quick once-over and make a mental note to return to it tomorrow morning, if action or contact is truly necessary.

FROM: Nan Gooding
DATE: October 9, 2018
SUBJECT: Next year's potential donor list
TO: Josephine Bordelon

- -

Josie,

I would like the list of the 20 top potential donors that you have come across so far in this year's applicant pool. As you are aware, this is important information for the head of school to have, so I would appreciate you prioritizing it. Please send it to Elsa, my assistant, when it's ready.

Nan Gooding

HEAD OF SCHOOL
FAIRCHILD COUNTRY DAY SCHOOL

Nan never just says Elsa, but "Elsa, my assistant." It's become one word, or one name, Elsamyassistant, and a constant reminder to everyone in school that she's the only one with a personal assistant. Nan is like that kid in every neighborhood who runs over to your front steps to let you know you just missed the ice cream man while devouring a Big Stick inches from your face. You hate that kid, but there is also a weird reverence for the things she has that you don't.

Once I know all the students are off campus, I open my window for the cool air and consider playing something with an old-school bass line to get myself pumped to start building. The rain is coming down hard outside, so it feels more like a Macklemore kind of day than early Jackson Five—back before Michael started playing plastic-surgery roulette and Tito fancied himself a politician. I crank a little *Gemini*, still unsure if I'm okay with Macklemore flying solo without Ryan Lewis, and decide to check my e-mail one more time before truly diving into learning the new CRM system Fairchild installed over the summer. E-mail is the low-hanging fruit of professional accomplishment.

FROM: Jean Georges Martin
DATE: October 9, 2018
SUBJECT: Your commitment to Etta's dance career
TO: Josephine Bordelon
- -

Dear Ms. Bordelon,

The finance office has again brought it to my attention that you have not yet paid for the fall quarter of the San

Francisco Ballet School. I hate to be the one to tell you that this is the third time in four years you are late with payment. While I know Etta is a fiercely committed ballerina, over the years I have questioned your commitment to your daughter and her promising career. Please visit the finance office at your earliest convenience, meaning this afternoon, to sort this business out. It would be a shame to have to refuse Etta a prominent role in the spring production of *Don Quixote* because her mother did not prioritize her daughter's talent.

I write with only the best intentions on behalf of your daughter, Etta Bordelon.

Merci beaucoup,
Jean Georges Martin

ARTISTIC DIRECTOR
SAN FRANCISCO BALLET SCHOOL

Fucker. To say that Jean Georges and I have a chilly relationship would be like saying hell was slightly hot. Ever since I refused to straighten Etta's hair when she was eight, so it would fit in a perfectly shellacked bun like all the other young partygoers' in *The Nutcracker*, Jean Georges has considered me an unfortunate hurdle he has had to leap over (or knock down) in order to grow Etta's gift. If it hadn't been so obvious by the time Etta turned eight that she would be the pinnacle of his teaching career, he would never have tolerated what he considers my intolerable disregard for rules and, by proxy, him. The missing bobby pins, the passion plum lipstick rather than the ballet school's sanctioned soft orchid rose (no brown-skinned female would be caught dead in pink lipstick), the refusal to buy Etta more than one pair of ballet shoes at a time (less a refusal and more a lack of funds). If it weren't for her unmatchable talent, Jean Georges would have bid Etta and my crazy ass adieu and moved on to a family who reveled in their child being under the tutelage of such a highly regarded—his words, not mine—ballet school director.

"He loves to hate me," I say to no one in particular, throwing my head back over the top of my desk chair, tossing a rubber band ball up into the air. I have held off on paying ballet tuition hoping to use that money for Etta's college application fees. Then, as soon as all Etta's college applications were in, I would pay for fall and winter quarters in one lump sum in January. Yes, a lot late for the fall tuition, but only thirty days late for winter. As expensive as college is going to be, and as sad as I will be to see Etta go, I'm looking forward to the day I no longer have to pay ballet school tuition and receive snooty e-mails from a poorly aging primo ballerino or whatever you call an over-the-hill ex-principal dancer holding too tightly to a youth that is looooong gone.

Never, in all my years as a director of admissions, have I made any family feel as lowly as Jean Georges does to me on a biyearly basis. Maybe he's condescending to all the parents, I'm not sure, but shouldn't he be kissing up to me for birthing the best dancer who will probably ever come through his school? After a few more songs about justice, fighting for what's right, and being fed up with the Man, my Macklemore-fueled sense of empowerment rationalizes postponing direction reading for the CRM (it's a job better suited for Roan anyway), and I lock up my office to drive down to the ballet school to surprise Director Martin with a visit a half hour before pickup.

PLEASE TURN OFF ALL CELL PHONES;
THIS IS AN ENVIRONMENT OF ARTISTIC
PEACE AND BEAUTY.

Usually a sign like that would make me want to turn my ringtone up, but not wanting to piss off Director Martin more than I already have, I slip my hand into my purse and switch off the ringer. A dab of lipstick wouldn't hurt the situation, either, so I feel around in the cavern I call a purse for some long-forgotten stick of something or other. I can only hope it isn't passion plum. Don't want to relive that nightmare with Jean Georges.

My eyesight adjusts as I walk into the dark theatre. All the students are in the stretching studios, so I know I will spare Etta the embarrassment of begging her master teacher for forgiveness. Then, while I'm in this compromised state, I'll ask him for an extension for Etta's fall and winter quarter payments (my take-no-prisoners angry [white man] energy died somewhere around Vallejo Street and Van Ness). While my will is steeled to grovel, my mind betrays me and I start to giggle when I see Jean Georges stride across the stage in a regal purple unitard and black riding boots. The winning touch is the cocked fedora perched on his head and the riding crop he's whipping through the air. I don't care how many professional ballets you've performed in, a unitard after retirement is never a good idea.

"Excuse me, Director Martin." I will my facial muscles not to defy me and break into laughter. Objective achieved.

"Well, hello, Ms. Bordelon. I assume you received my e-mail, thus the inappropriate visit during rehearsal time?" I take a giant step to the left over the shade Jean Georges has laid down. "I'm also going to assume you visited the business office first like I asked you to do in the e-mail?"

Damn. I knew I should have reread the whole thing through one more time before charging into Director Martin's kingdom.

"Well, here's the thing . . ." I start.

"'The thing'? The THING? There shouldn't be a *thing* if you've done as I instructed you to do and paid your bill before paying me a visit." Jean Georges crosses his arms over his chest and looks at me with zero amusement. This is going to be harder than I imagined, and I'm going to have to eat some serious humble pie.

"Actually, there is a thing. The thing is called college. And Etta will be going next year, and I have had to reserve her dance tuition this quarter for application fees. But the good news is, I'm planning on having her apply early so that means she will find out where she's going in December and by January I will be able to pay off the fall and winter tuition. Please don't punish Etta in her last year of dance because I've had to make some difficult financial choices for a couple of months."

"Why would this be her last year of dance?" Jean Georges asks, looking genuinely confused. Did he not just hear me say that Etta's heading to college next year? Though I think I made myself clear, I don't allow myself to get annoyed before launching back into my reasoning a second time.

"Jean Georges, Etta is a senior this year. I'm focusing on her applying early admissions to a few Ivies and maybe Pomona and Claremont McKenna. I need to get Etta into college as soon as possible so I can really start to plan our tuition payment strategy. You see, thirteen years of adjusted tuition at Fairchild, crazy rent, and then ten years in the San Francisco Ballet School, without any financial aid, has made planning for college a little more difficult than I anticipated, but I'm trying as best I can."

I couldn't help myself; I had to throw in a dig that for ten years the ballet school had refused to help me pay for Etta's twenty hours of dance a week even though she has been the most promising dancer to come through the school in well over two decades. Consistently, the ballet school has pointed out to me that I hold an important role in the administration at Fairchild Country Day. And continually I point out that I am a single parent in San Francisco and while everyone around me is getting filthy rich off start-ups and mergers and investments, I am working in education where, even at Fairchild, the salaries are paltry compared to the rest of the professional world and the astronomical cost of living here.

At my lowest, I had to ask Aunt Viv to dip into her retirement to help me make dance payments once Etta went from dancing ten hours a week to twenty. To my continued shame, that transition coincided with my leasing the first new car of my life, a backlog of parking tickets to be paid off to avoid collections, and an irresponsible anxiety-induced shopping bender. While I no longer live a glamorous life, my appreciation for expensive clothes never made the shift from my modeling career to a job in education. I blame Maisie Maxwell for that one.

Aunt Viv lent me the money, no questions asked, but my promises to pay her back so she could retire by seventy have not come to fruition and have left me with three a.m. pangs of guilt. The fact that Aunt Viv arrives an hour early to every one of Etta's performances so she may have the best seat in the house at least assures me she believes in her investment and the choice I've made to let Etta pursue ballet through high school. Dance and Fairchild have kept Etta on a steady, trouble-free path, and for that both Aunt Viv and I are forever grateful.

"Ms. Bordelon, I've spent more time with your daughter than you have the past ten years." I open my mouth to refute this pretentious Frenchman, but he closes his eyes, shakes his head no, and puts his index finger to my lips to silence me. "I know every muscle in her body from fingertip to calloused big toe. I know she works harder than any ballerina I have ever had in this school, and I know she comes alive when she is on stage bringing art to life. I know she does well in school, so you will allow her to dance, and I also know she waits all day in school to come here at three-fifteen and do the one thing she loves most in the world. What I don't know is if she wants to go to college—an Ivy, Pomona, Claremont, or otherwise. Is that a conversation you two have had?"

"We will be having that conversation soon." I say with false authority. In fact, the only conversation we will be having is about which colleges from my list Etta wants to attend.

"What I so very clearly now know is that going to college is what you want her to do whether she wants that for her future or not. Perhaps then, may I suggest that it is you who goes back to college and leave Etta alone to pursue becoming the professional dancer she was born to be."

I'm stunned speechless, a state I'm not sure has happened since Donatella Versace told me though beautifully plump, my nursing tits hung too close to my belly button for her to consider me for her runway collection.

"That unitard makes your balls look lopsided," is all I can think to say as I turn to walk out of the theatre, tears of rage burning my eyes. How can Jean Georges even begin to claim that I don't support Etta's interest? I came back to San Francisco to make sure she had a stable home with a loving, albeit small, family. I got a job as an admissions assistant so I could make sure she got to go to Fairchild and we would qualify for the faculty/staff tuition assistance. I borrowed money from Aunt Viv to make sure Etta could continue ballet through high school. And I will do what it takes to make sure she has a career where she never worries about money like Aunt Viv and I do. I have had thirteen years of making sure Etta has choices I never had because of lack of guidance (though I know Aunt Viv did her best). There was too much emphasis on my looks and not my brain—a bad combo for a young woman let loose in New York City with little understanding of the world. With all I've done, Etta will not end up back on my doorstep in five years.

And I really hate purple.

Alone in the lobby, gathering my composure, I have twenty minutes before Etta is done so I reach in my purse for my phone. Lola loves my Jean Georges impressions, particularly when I mimic him pissed off. I flip on the ringer to give her a call and see that I have had three voice mails and five texts in the twenty minutes I've been playing verbal badminton with ballet Barney. I go right to text.

SANDY

It's Sandy in the main office your aunt Viv
collapsed in the kitchen at school. We have
called paramedics. Call the school.

5:12 P.M.

SANDY

Sandy again paramedics have arrived.

5:18 P.M.

SANDY

There is a woman named Lola also listed as an
emergency contact for your aunt I'm calling her
now since I can't get you.

5:24 P.M.

LOLA

Jo get yourself to UCSF hospital ASAP! Meet
you there. Aunt Viv is on her way in ambulance
where the hell are you? Better not be drinking
without me . . . Lo

5:36 P.M.

ELSA

Josie its Elsa, Nan's Assistant. Sorry to bother
you but Nan told me to text you since you didn't
answer her e-mail. Nan wants you to know she
expects the list of the 20 wealthiest applicants
for the coming school year in her in-box first
thing tomorrow morning. Please include their
individual names and net worth.

5:37 P.M.

This isn't possible! The one time I have my ringer off, Aunt Viv, a woman who has never been sick a day in her life, decides to collapse? How, in one day, one hour, am I failing both Etta and Aunt Viv? And then there's Nan and her need for me to facilitate playdates for her to rub elbows with San Francisco's elite. My hashtag should be #sonotwinningatlife.

"Lola, where are you? Are you at the hospital yet? What happened to Aunt Viv?" I yell into the phone as I run to grab Etta out of class and head across town.

"I'm at the information desk right now trying to find out what room she's in. I'll be with her until you get here. Don't worry, when the apocalypse comes that woman will still be standin', trust." I burst into tears knowing Lola is already at the ER, since it will take me a good forty minutes to get to UCSF hospital at rush hour. "You better turn off those waterworks before you see Aunt Viv, you know she has no patience for soft souls."

"You're right. I'll lose it in the car but pull it together by the time I see Aunt Viv. Promise." Jesus, I better be fine. I'm pretty sure I can't do life *without* Aunt Viv, but I'm 100 percent sure I can't do life *with* Aunt Viv if she thinks I fell to pieces at the first sign of a health issue in her sixty-nine years. I'll never hear the end of it around the house. *Josie, can I trouble you to get me two aspirin without you fallin' all over my casket?*

"Good. Here we go, just found out she's been transferred from the ER to room 502, cardiac floor. By the way, where are you, why weren't you picking up your phone?"

"I was battling with Jean Georges."

"Oh snap, you had to do battle with him sober? Who won?" I can feel Lola sympathy cringe over the phone.

"He did."

"Double snap. Crap day for you. See you soon; room 502."

"See you there."

EIGHT

✳✳✳✳✳✳✳✳

WE DRIVE IN SILENCE THE WHOLE WAY TO THE HOSPITAL,
Etta nervously pulling a loose string hanging from her black wool leg
warmers. Teen stoicism is keeping Etta's face calm, but I'm her
mama. She grew inside me, developed a heart right underneath mine
and sometimes I know what she's feeling before she does.

"Don't worry about Aunt Viv," I say, as much to Etta as to myself,
while parking the car in the underground garage. "She is absolutely
sticking around to see you graduate from college. You're going to
make her proud in every way I failed her, and there's no way she's
going to miss that victory, I promise you that. You're the reason she
gets up in the morning, I'm simply another mouth she has to feed." I
squeeze Etta's hand tight. She squeezes back but can't look at me.
The Bordelon *shed no tears* policy is a tough one for her to follow, her
heart not yet battle-scarred from life like mine. We continue to hold
hands up to the fifth floor, our steps tentative as we get closer to
room 502. I don't do well with uncertainty and not knowing if the
situation that lies behind the door may change our lives forever is
creating a peach pit sized choke in my throat.

I crack open the hospital room door and hear Lola giggling like she's at a sleepover, which seems completely inappropriate in the middle of a crisis. And Aunt Viv is doing the same? I let out the huge breath I've been holding since talking to Lola. I didn't even know Aunt Viv knew how to giggle. Staying light and positive is the name of the game, I know, but I'm eager to hear what the doctor has to say about Aunt Viv's health.

Etta steps in front of me, heartened by the laughter, and pushes the door wide open before I'm mentally ready. Aunt Viv is sitting up in bed, worrying a ball of tissue with her right hand, IV hanging.

"Etta baby." Aunt Viv's face lights up. "Come on over and meet the doctor who's been taking good care of your aunt Viv. He even brought me a cup of those ice chips I like so much." Aunt Viv weakly waves Etta over. Her skin looks ashen to me, but you don't tell that to a proud black woman; ashy elbows and knees being the sign of poor grooming and all. "Josie, you come over here, too, even though the one time you don't answer that damn phone is when my life is teetering on the edge. Remind me to change my emergency contact." Aunt Viv's collapse has not affected her wit. That has to be a good sign.

Lola gently taps the doctor who is lost in Aunt Viv's chart, so he'll turn to greet me. Again with the weird giggle. I'm embarrassed for Lola and this flirty, awkward Catholic schoolgirl thing she's got goin' on. You think you know your best friend . . .

"Josie, this is Dr. Golden, the incredible cardiologist on call who has been helping Aunt Viv since she was checked in. He was able to get her out of the ER and onto the cardiology floor quickly. Dr. Golden, Josie Bordelon is Aunt Viv's niece. They live together and Josie is Viv's primary caretaker. I'm just the loving and dedicated best friend available for all birthday parties, child-rearing advice, and family crises."

"I don't need a caretaker, you watch your language," Aunt Viv scolds Lola.

Shocked to see that Golden Boy is Aunt Viv's doctor, I say the first thing that pops into my brain, "The last time I saw you, you weren't wearing any pants." The room drops dead silent.

Golden Boy, as it turns out, is a golden cardiologist. If I had actually taken the career conversation carrot he had dangled in front of me at the vegan food truck I would have known that. Lola is standing right behind him subtly thrusting her hips and licking her lips. No joke. Here we are on the UCSF cardiology floor with Aunt Viv confined to a hospital bed and Lola is thinking about grindin' up on the doctor.

"The ex–track star turned director of admissions. Do I have it right?" Dr. Golden inquires with a grin.

"Well, there are a few other details before, during, and after those two life events, but more or less, yes, that's me."

"It's nice to see you again, Josie." Dr. Golden bypasses my hand and goes in for a hug. Over his shoulder I see Lola's eyebrows shoot sky high. *Later,* I mouth.

"Not sure it's that nice to see you again under these circumstances," I say, cutting to the chase, but instead, come off sounding like a complete biatch.

"Of course. Let's talk about today." Dr. Golden's smile disappears and he returns to the information on Aunt Viv's chart.

"Good Lawd, Josephine, that's no way to talk to the man who saved my life. You will have to excuse my niece, Dr. Golden, she left her manners I don't know where. Josie, do you need to go look for those manners I taught you that you've clearly misplaced somewhere between the parking garage and comin' on up in my room?" Lola and Aunt Viv have forgotten that we have gathered in this aseptic hospital room to diagnose why Aunt Viv collapsed at school, not to marry me off. Nor do they yet know that their efforts are futile.

"Dr. Golden and I know each other because he and his HUSBAND are applying their daughter to Fairchild," I explain, scanning the room to make sure eye contact and complete understanding of the situation has been achieved with every female in the room. Lola drops her head in defeat. I know she had high hopes for this one.

"Uhhh yes, that's right, we're trying to get Gracie into kindergarten at Fairchild." Dr. Golden seems to be growing increasingly uneasy in the company of four women stuffed into this tiny hospital room. I don't know if it's estrogen overload or if he has some really bad news to give us.

"I know more about medicine than I do about kindergarten, so I think I should stick to my area of expertise. Since Daniel's running the kindergarten admissions show, I'm going to focus on your aunt Viv."

"Excellent idea," I say as I brace myself, desperate to hear that Aunt Viv is going to be okay.

"Your aunt Viv had a mild heart attack. Nothing that a couple weeks of rest and some lifestyle adjustments won't help. Limiting stress, a healthy diet, an aspirin a day, and regular exercise will do wonders to decrease the chance of another, potentially more serious, heart attack."

"You mean so that it will never happen again, right, Dr. Golden?" Etta asks, cautiously speaking up. She is tucked in tightly next to Aunt Viv. I know she's praying that if she hugs her long enough nothing bad can happen. Etta has been doing that with her stuffed elephant since she was little. I choke up again; my whole life is clutching on to each other in a twin-sized hospital bed. None of us is ready to break up the Bordelon girl band on this particular Tuesday afternoon.

"I can't say never. When there has been one heart attack the chances are increased of having another. What I can promise are lower chances of it happening again if you follow my instructions and take good care of yourself, Vivian. No going to work for the rest of this week or the next two. And when I see you for a follow-up appointment I want to hear all about how you are going to incorporate exercise and more fruits and vegetables into your daily routine." Golden Boy affectionately squeezes her left foot. Clearly the good doctor does not know that Southern women of an older generation are allergic to exercise.

"Well, that's not gonna work for me. Tomorrow is tacos and corn torte at school, all the kids love it. I even have fresh kiwis for dessert." In fifty years at Fairchild, Aunt Viv has made every single lunch, except for two, for the 820 children. And those were my fault, temperamental appendix when I was ten. "Oh and then next Friday I'm caterin' the heads' monthly lunch meeting in Grierson Hall. The prosciutto and Gruyère quiche is not gonna make itself, and our head of school insists on it." What doesn't Nan insist on when it comes to her need to be the lead show dog? Does she really think the other Heads of School care what quiche is served? Or does she think that by serving Gruyère instead of common man's cheddar she will establish some perverse private school dominance that is profoundly important to her but inexplicable to anyone else? At least there's comfort in knowing Aunt Viv must be feeling okay because her constant state of ornery is pushing back hard over kiwis and quiche.

"Nor are you going to be making it, Vivian," Dr. Golden insists, his eyes trying to bore a hole through Aunt Viv's thick skull. Medical tough love trumping the scrappiest lady in town. Swoon.

"Are you going to come make it for me then? Those hands of yours don't look like they've seen much time in a kitchen cookin' food and scrubbin' dishes." Aunt Viv is not going down on our couch for the next three weeks without a fight.

"I will if I have to, young lady. And I'm sure Josie would be willing to help me cook if that means we can get you to stay home and rest. Josie, how are you in the torte and quiche department?" Golden Boy comes and stands next to me, looking for us to join forces in this argument that he has mistakenly picked with Aunt Viv.

"Josie will make whatever you want," Lola offers in an unnaturally deep voice. I roll my eyes, pained by Lola's attempt to sound sultry. Good thing Dr. Golden is gay because right now Lola is proving herself a subpar wing-woman.

"Don't let her near my kitchen, she'll burn the whole place down!" Aunt Viv scolds Dr. Golden with a wink. When thirty of my almost forty years of living have been spent in the same house as Aunt Viv, one would think I'd have picked up a skill or two in the kitchen, but all I've picked up is a great appreciation for having someone else do the cooking. In the Bordelon household no one is allowed to go hungry. Call it a knee-jerk reaction to Aunt Viv's childhood of too many mouths to feed and not enough food, but for whatever reason she overcooks and overstuffs us. I don't complain, though my skirts don't exactly fit, either.

Etta buries her head in Aunt Viv's pillow thoroughly mortified by this display of two grown women falling all over themselves to win the favor of the good gay doctor.

"You women are the best thing to happen to me this week. The view is not usually this lovely in the hospital." Golden Boy chuckles. "You let me know when it's time to whip up some of those quiches. I'm actually pretty good with a knife. Prosciutto is a meat, right?" This guy clearly spends way too much time eating hospital grub and food truck fare if he lives in the foodiest city in America and he's questioning if prosciutto is a meat.

Opening the door, Dr. Golden leans over and whispers in my ear, "And, Josie, you're hands down my favorite director of admissions so far. Trust me, Daniel's made me meet them all." His lips are so close to my earlobe he could easily take a nibble. The idea of it makes me shudder and then stifle a snicker knowing Roan will get a real laugh when I tell him we're both turned on by the same eye candy.

"We ARE the best things to happen to you!" Lola shouts after him, clumsily punching the air and kicking her foot to close the door behind him. Yet again, she's momentarily lost control of her limbs and her self-respect.

"What was that?" I ask Lola, horrified by her display of uninhibited dorkiness. "And where did it come from?"

"God, I have no idea," Lola groans, mortified, burying her head in her hands.

"You may be able to handle your liquor, Lola, but you sure can't handle yourself in front of men," Aunt Viv chimes in before laying her head back and closing her eyes to rest.

"Good thing I have a rich fantasy life, because I've completely lost my mojo in the real world. But maybe he has a straight doctor friend for you? Gay or straight, you know good-looking guys always hang together," Lola whispers to me, hoping if we stay quiet enough Aunt Viv will sleep a little. She digs her elbow into my ribs, making sure she's been heard.

"Welcome to my no mojo world, Lo," I say, reaching for Lola's hand. "Now you know why there are dust bunnies rolling through my lady parts."

"Awww, Mama, that's disgusting!" Etta scrunches her face up as if the idea of her mother having sex is akin to taking a big whiff of foul milk. "Just get a man already so I don't have to hear you and Lola talkin' about your dried-up lady parts."

"Etta baby, when your mama was your age she could stop traffic when she crossed the street, she was that beautiful. Problem is, she ain't been out walkin' much since Michael left," Aunt Viv mutters, turning on her left side to get more comfortable. Lola nods her head in complete agreement. Though she has never once said it out loud, I know Aunt Viv still pines for the days of having Michael around the house. I don't know if it's Michael I pine for or if it's for some sign from a man—an employed, attentive, intelligent man—that I'm still in the game, that I'm worthy of love. I know the early morning, twenty-year-old barista at my local café would Mrs. Robinson all over me, but I'm not looking for man-filler. I'm holding out for a winner. Only thing is, I don't know if a winner will be able to find me behind the emotional fortress I've built around myself, brick by brick, over the past eighteen years.

"I think it's time you hit the streets again, Josie. What's the worst thing that could happen to you?" Aunt Viv's words fade as she falls into much-needed sleep.

"I could get hit by a car."

NINE

"PICK YOUR POISON. ON THE TABLE I HAVE A SELECTION OF vegan donut holes, Skittles, blueberries, dark chocolate–covered espresso beans, corn chips, and sparkling water." I have worked hard to create a stress-eating buffet that expresses to Roan that I choose to stand in solidarity with him when it comes to his finicky vegan eating habits.

"I'm off gluten, corn, and sugar," Roan smugly announces, reaching for the blueberries as if there's an audience of health zealots in the conference room ready to give him a standing O. I peg him dead center in the forehead with a powdered donut hole. Take that, you clean-eating buzzkill. "You should try an elimination diet sometime, Josie—it would do wonders for your mood swings."

I remind myself to fire Roan after we get through reading five hundred applications comprised of four essays each, over the next few months. That's two thousand answers attempting to convey how ultimately perfect each family is for the Fairchild community. I would never make it through them all without Roan reading every couple essays or so with an accent to match the applicant—Irish,

Indian, Texan, and Southern Californian are his strong suits. Something has to make the time pass, and nothing does the trick quite like espresso beans and tasteless humor.

"Uh-oh here we go, Roan. Oh, yes, one of our favorite genres has risen to the top: the *perfection is my child's greatest weakness* category. An oldie, but oh so good and overplayed. Remember the parents last year, or was it the year before, who claimed their child's weakness was struggling to make friends because her perfectionistical tendencies intimidate other children. Perfectionistical isn't even a real word. THAT was one of my favorites."

"Really? I liked the year of the parents who said their child was genetically predisposed to genius, since he had dominant traits from both sides of the family. Remember they wanted to know if we are a West Coast testing center for Mensa and complete assurance that their child wouldn't be penalized by the school or by his peers for the intellectually superior gifts he had inherited. Then they spent the next two pages sharing the details of Albert Einstein's miserable, or was it misunderstood, childhood. A failed analogy complete with endless typos. That one belongs in some *What Not to Do When You're Applying to Kindergarten* guidebook."

"I don't remember that one."

"Yes you do, I'm pretty sure it was from my first year. Before I learned to pace myself on the snacks? I almost threw up from a Sour Patch Kids and kettle chip overdose."

"Oh yeah, that's right, you were an admissions virgin."

"And you were the older director who popped an innocent assistant's cherry. Now I daresay the mystery is gone in our relationship." Roan sighs and reaches for another stack of applications.

I open the next family folder.

"Let's hear what Vanessa Grimaldi has to say about her daughter, Antonia. Oh, oh, wait here's a picture of sweet Antonia actually demonstrating her perfection." I hold up the picture of Antonia in painter overalls with a bandana securing her hair hunched over what looks to be a forged van Gogh, *The Starry Night*.

"That's totally photoshopped, you know," Roan huffs, barely giving the photo a second look.

"I don't know, maybe not, she could be a prodigy, it's possible." As director of admissions I have to keep up appearances of neutrality and positivity toward each applicant. Roan doesn't buy it.

"Or it could be paint by numbers. Which basically tells us that, at five, Antonia knows her numbers and primary colors. Hardly a prodigy." Good point, I have to concede. I move on to read the first essay question:

1. What are your child's greatest challenges?

While a typical little girl in many ways (she loves frozen yogurt and having her nanny French braid her hair), since Antonia was born while summering with our families on the Amalfi Coast, Tommaso and I have struggled to find peers for our sweet daughter to play with who are able to keep up with her ability to focus; produce quality drawings, sculptures, and three-dimensional structures; as well as her European tendencies toward more refined food and outings. We encourage Antonia to go outside and play American games with the neighborhood kids so she may be one of them, but she insists on intently working on her own masterpieces in her loft art room overlooking the Bay (views can be so inspirational; perhaps we should move her studio to the basement to encourage her to be a normal child!). Our hope is that by going to a school like Fairchild Antonia will be encouraged to spread her focus and perfectionist tendencies toward other endeavors. We know she has multiple talents and potential capabilities to discover and to share with the world, but right now she is limiting herself to art. Though a true raw talent due to a lineage of famous Italian alfresco painters, she needs to expand her work and her learning, and we believe Fairchild is the best school for her to spread her wings.

Roan grabs the application folder from me and starts thumbing through the whole thing. "Well, one perfect child won't ruin the school. Unless the Grimalidis show up at their parent interview with a six pack of spitting camels we should definitely put them in the *to be considered* pile."

"What? Camels spit? Wait, who's in charge here? We never like nascent divas, you're breaking with tradition."

"That may be true, but we LOVE a nascent diva whose father is heir to an international spa empire. The name Grimaldi doesn't ring a bell? They own Casa di Bella in the Presidio near Lucas Arts. It is three stories of pure five-star Pacific pampering. I've heard their espresso enema followed by a Colombian roast body scrub is to die for. You lose five pounds in ninety minutes, have energy for days, and feel smooth like a peach. We take the kid, I can stay twenty-nine forever or for as long as Antonia is at Fairchild."

"Roan, seriously, you understand we can't do that, right?"

"No, Josie, you don't understand. You're black. Your people don't age. Look at Aunt Viv. She's sixty-nine going on forty-two. She IS the poster child for 'black don't crack.' I'm Irish, we look at a lager and we get all ruddy and age ten years. But that doesn't seem to stop us from drinking. If I keep up my night-clubbing routine, soon I'm going to be thirty going on fifty-four. I need a spa heir in my back pocket. Please, please. Do it for my future children."

"You don't even have a boyfriend."

"Exactly, and I certainly won't ever have a boyfriend and then husband and then said children if I look like a weathered Irish mailman from County Cork. I need the spa to ensure my husband is as hot as Golden Boy." Roan has raised some very fine admission points to consider.

"Well, like I've always said, we do need to prioritize what's best for the children, real or imaginary." I wink at Roan and toss Antonia's file to the top of the *to be considered* pile and open a new folder. Each of us is due our favorites, regardless of rhyme or reason.

DING.

Saturday morning, I wake up feeling fuzzy, sluggish, and regretful from eating a bowl full of Skittles followed by multiple Jack Daniel's shots and a subsequent turn on the karaoke stage. Lola is hands down my sista from another mister, but I do have a few friends from my days as a student at Fairchild who I see from time to time. This year we are all turning forty and these girls don't mess around with their celebratin'. These fortieth birthday parties are going to ensure me an early death. I don't have to look in a mirror to know I look as tired as the entire seventh-grade class on a post–bar mitzvah Monday morning. Only, my headache and puffy eyes are much worse. And who the hell is texting me so early in the morning? I pick up my phone to check. Whoops, it's actually 10:45. Hopefully Etta found a ride to ballet. She's probably texting me to let me know who picked her up; damn, I raised a responsible girl. Even from bed I'm an exceptional mother.

TY

> Hi, Josie. It's Ty Golden. Just want to check in and see how your aunt Viv's doing. I hope you've been able to keep her off her feet and out of the kitchen. Her medication shouldn't be causing any trouble, but for some people it can be upsetting to the stomach. If it's bothering her let me know and I can stop by and check in. Hope it's okay to text on a Saturday morning. I've been at the hospital doing rounds since six and wanted to make sure all is good in the Bordelon house.

10:45 A.M.

I bet Golden Boy has saved multiple lives in the amount of time it's taken me to semi sleep off a hangover. And he texts with perfect grammar. Who does that? Well, better he text this morning than call. I'm not sure I can formulate an intelligent sentence through the cotton field that has sprouted in my mouth. Luckily, even on death's door I can still type.

JOSIE

> Dr. Golden, thanks for check in. Aunt Viv has come to embrace Netflix, Amazon Prime, Hulu, and bossing me around more than usual. My hope is that she continues to get her energy back so she can return to school and boss other people around for a change. I'm an admissions director not a nurse, though you may have been understandably confused given my stellar bedside manner in the hospital. Medication A.O.K.

10:46 A.M.

Ugh, I gotta brush my teeth. I officially can't stand myself.

TY

You don't strike me as the type of woman to take someone bossing you around. You probably got that from your aunt Viv?

10:46 A.M.

Ohhh text banter, I'm really good at that. Fuzzy teeth can wait.

JOSIE

You got that right so don't think you can bribe me with free bedpans and Band-Aids to get Gracie into Fairchild.

10:47 A.M.

TY

Gracie can get herself into Fairchild, that kid rocks. I'm the unacceptable one.

10:47 A.M.

JOSIE

What's unacceptable is saying someone rocks. What is this, 1999?

10:48 A.M.

TY

Might be, I don't get out of the hospital much.

10:48 A.M.

JOSIE

> Speaking of getting out much, I need to get my day started. Seems there must be a life that needs saving, too. Don't lose a patient on account of my witty banter. Have a good weekend.

10:49 A.M.

Ty

> **You, too.**

10:50 A.M.

I brush my teeth and wash my face to dislodge the mascara crumbles, but I decide to forgo the shower at this particular moment. I'm a bit too consumed with worrying whether I overstepped my professional boundaries by sharing that the director of admissions of the school where the good doctor wants to send his kid is a hot mess with a hangover. I gotta start rereading my texts before I hit send. Damn trigger finger.

Though not a requirement for acceptance, I shoot myself an e-mail from my phone to remind myself to write "smart" and "funny" in the Golden file so "hot dad" is not the leading pro for the Golden family. I assume Gracie goes by Golden. I'd rather be obviously related to hot dad than frumpy dude if I were Gracie. Not that Gracie, at four and a half, even knows one of her dads is hot. Yuck, hope not. I need to pull my head out of the gutter; maybe I do need a full shower to wash away the sins of the mind and of my evening.

Tonight, Fairchild is having a reception for families of graduating seniors. The evening's entertainment is the college counselors reviewing the college application process. This is not my idea of a fun-filled Saturday night, spending it back at work with parents who have been in and out of each other's intimate business for the past thirteen years. An administrative decision was made to move the event to a Saturday night after parents complained of out-of-town work commitments during the week and that the least Fairchild could do after a decade plus of tuition is combine a parent cocktail hour with college information night. Steep college costs on top of the nearly-broke-me bills from the past thirteen years of education is enough to make any teetotaling parent drink.

When my breakfast burrito fails to soak up last night's liquor and my headache kicks in, I decide to quit drinking. Or at least I'll quit until tonight, when I'm forced to accept the truth of college tuition and the competing data on whether the outcomes are even worth the price tag. I'll save the option to drink if I need it. I have to see where the night takes me.

After the subpar college conversation at dinner a few days back, I decided I needed to come to the higher-learning discussion 2.0 with Etta a bit more prepared. Some preparation will also help me get the most out of Fairchild's college night. Krista and Sam in college counseling spend their days transitioning the oldest Fairchild students out of the school. I spend my workdays doing the complete opposite, counseling Fairchild's youngest potential students into the school. Though Krista and Sam are friends of mine, it's a rare day that our two departments cross paths, thus we are fairly clueless about the details of one another's jobs.

I open my laptop at the kitchen table to finish off the college Excel spreadsheet I barely started last Sunday night. Mustering my cunning mama smarts yesterday, I suggested to Etta that we go to dinner together before the college night. This will be when I present my succinct spreadsheet that will foretell her future.

Aunt Viv is in the living room consumed with the second season of *Queen Sugar*, a show that strikes a little too close to the train wreck that was her childhood in New Orleans. The characters in the show even share our last name, so I suppose Aunt Viv feels like they're kin. Either way, with Aunt Viv sucked into the Deep South drama, I know I have some time when she won't be prying into what I'm doing or why I look like ten miles of bad road at 11:35 in the morning.

COLLEGE/ UNIVERSITY	EARLY ACTION DUE DATE	EARLY DECISION DUE DATE	REGULAR DECISION DUE DATE	APPLICATION COMPLETED
** CORNELL	10-Nov	N/A	1-Jan	
** DARTMOUTH	10-Nov	N/A	1-Jan	
WILLIAMS	10-Nov	N/A	1-Jan	
DUKE	10-Nov	N/A	3-Jan	
POMONA	10-Nov	N/A	15-Jan	
CLAREMONT	10-Nov	N/A	15-Jan	
UMICHIGAN	10-Nov	N/A	30-Nov	
UCBERKELEY	10-Nov	N/A	30-Nov	
UCDAVIS	10-Nov	N/A	30-Nov	
UCSANTA CRUZ	10-Nov	N/A	30-Nov	

After toggling back and forth between a couple of websites, I realize we can't apply Early Decision anywhere because Etta would have to choose to attend said university before we hear about any kind of tuition assistance package. That's good information to know because in our house it's financial aid first, acceptance second, pack your bags third. That narrows our options down to applying Early Action and Regular Decision. Ugh, Early Action applications are due in two weeks. How has Etta not been on top of this? I'm annoyed that my conscientious seventeen-year-old has chosen now, of all times, to fall down on the teenage job. That said, Etta and I have pulled off more difficult feats in our past, like when Etta was one and I had to lose six pounds in five days for an Alexander McQueen show in London. We made it happen by both of us subsisting on baby food alone for 120 hours. As a grown woman, if I can eat applesauce and strained peas for a week straight, I can get Etta to pull it together to apply to Cornell and Dartmouth Early Action. And then I can march down to the San Francisco Ballet School and shove two quarters' worth of tuition down Jean Georges's leotard.

Getting this college thing tied up before life goes dark with admissions work in January would be a huge relief. Otherwise, I'm not sure how I can pull off yet another intense three-month stretch of the Fairchild admissions season and the stress of getting Etta into a top college regular admissions. The last time life felt this out of my control was when I peed on the pregnancy sticks in Paris, but at least then I got the answer I needed immediately. This waiting to know Etta's future is forcing me to live waaaaay outside my control freak comfort zone.

I decide this is no time to be subtle; immediate action is required no matter how small. I bold and increase the font size for Cornell and Dartmouth and add a few more asterisks for emphasis. When I sit down to show Etta this chart before we head to tonight's odd mix of events—drunk college counseling—I want her to be clear on what the Bordelon game plan is and what our prioritized college picks are for next year.

TEN

"AUNT VIV, ETTA AND I ARE HEADIN' OUT FOR SUSHI ON Geary before we go to Fairchild for college night. Can we bring you back anything?"

"Why you pay good money to eat at a restaurant that don't even cook your food for you is beyond me. I can make you plain rice with a bite-size chunk of raw fish right here, won't cost you nothin'. Sushi, *phf*, what a waste of money. Every time you girls go out for sushi you come home pokin' around my kitchen looking for somethin' real to eat 'cause you still hungry."

I knew that would be her answer, hence why we're going to sushi. Bringing Aunt Viv any kind of takeout is a testament to patience and, knowing elder abuse, will land you in jail. Doesn't matter where the food comes from, according to Aunt Viv it's always cold, limp, and tastes like plastic by the time it reaches her plate. "All right, I've cut up a ton of veggies for you in the fridge and there is some good lentil soup to heat up. Dr. Golden's gonna ask you about your diet at your follow-up. So stay away from the chicken pot pie and the thin mint chocolate chip ice cream Etta bought this afternoon. Both are off limits."

Aunt Viv is about to launch into a snappy comeback when Etta walks in the room. We are both confused by her choice of outfits for the evening. I do a quick scan of potential parental comebacks that are filed in my brain that may (or may not) be suitable for this occasion and decide to enter into the inappropriate clothing conversation from the angle of motherly love and support. Here's hoping . . .

"Etta baby, the lavender leotard looks divine on you." (Her nipples are showing.) "And I do love it with the flowy skirt." (I can see her crotch.) "But, well, tonight at the college event there will be university booths for us to visit as well as all the other senior Fairchild families," otherwise known as smarmy divorced dads three times her age who will have no problem lusting after a young woman built like a Roman goddess with the innocence, or so I will continue to believe, of the Virgin Mary.

Etta looks down at her outfit, as if noticing for the first time this evening what she's wearing. "But this is who I am, and this is what I do. I'm a dancer; I dance. These clothes don't bother you when I wear them Monday through Saturday."

Aunt Viv is enjoying viewing this interaction in silence. I know what the smirk on her face says. That one eyebrow creeping toward her wig line is a reminder of my 1994 fashion phase of only wanting to wear black lacy bras under see-through white T-shirts. Not a look Aunt Viv appreciated for church on Sundays no matter how liberal Glide Memorial Church was or still is. After a few weeks of Aunt Viv tolerating my rebellious look, rather than talking about it she took action. I came home on a Saturday afternoon after a track meet to find a pile of my black lace bras cut into tiny pieces with Aunt Viv's shearing scissors. Next to the pile was a brand-new crisp, white button-down shirt and an unadorned neutral padded bra with a note: *The Lord would prefer you wore this.*

Big parental pause. I take several inconspicuous breaths and remind myself to play the long game. The goal is an acceptance to an

Ivy League school. Parenting is a marathon, not a sprint. Out loud, sweet as molasses, I say, "Yes, you are a dancer, it is one of the most incredible things about you. But maybe for tonight, you can emphasize something else that is phenomenal about yourself, the fact that you have near-perfect grades, have been on the Dean's List every semester, and that you rocked the SATs." Oh my God I can't believe I said *rocked*. I'll have to tell Dr. Golden.

"So you, who always tells me to be exactly who I am and whatevs to anyone who wants me to be something or someone different, is telling me that tonight I should be someone I'm not?"

I'm startled by Etta's aggressiveness. Disrespectful children may rule the roost in white folks' homes, but in black households, the mama rules supreme when it comes to attitude. It's been like that for generations and history is not about to go changin' tonight in the Outer Richmond. "But that IS who you are! You are a well-rounded, top student in a competitive school in a competitive city, and I want you to be well prepared to compete with the other students who will be applying to top colleges, too. We can't afford to make even the tiniest of mistakes in the home stretch of senior year."

"But I don't need to compete with those kids because I don't want to go to those schools; I want to go to Juilliard. And Director Martin thinks I have a really good chance of getting in." The edge is off her tone because she is smart enough to know what's good for her and back down, but she also knows the mere mention of Director Martin can send me into a tailspin. And, indeed, it does. Mission accomplished.

"Have mercy on your sweet soul, you talked to Jean Georges about college before you talked to me?" I start to sweat at the mere mention of Jean Georges. How is it that he's become the man of the household, directing life decisions for the daughter that I have spent the last eighteen years raising?

"I haven't talked to him about college. I've talked to him about

Juilliard. Director Martin and Aunt Viv listen to me because you don't. You're literally incapable of listening to me about what I want to do next year. It's like you want me to make up for all the mistakes you made when you were my age."

I never thought Etta would go there, but she did—pointing out how my past mistakes have affected our lives, and have the potential to ruin her future, too. I knew Etta and I might be exchanging words at some point this evening, but I thought we would at least get past the edamame and miso soup. At this point our reservation has come and gone.

I slowly turn to Aunt Viv. She pulls her afghan over her head. How dare she talk with Etta about her future behind my back. We've always been on the same page when it came to prioritizing Etta's education so she can go on to live a life unshackled by financial insecurity and professional regrets. I'm not stupid, I know Juilliard is one of the best possible stepping-stones for a career in the arts. But when you look at the short list of famous Juilliard graduates they are overwhelmingly actors and musicians. One Google search and a person is hard pressed to find a famous Juilliard dancer, let alone one who actually made a decent living spinning around on stage. Plus, assuming limitless talent and no injuries, how long is a dance career going to last? Eight, ten, fifteen years max? And then what? She becomes the next Jean Georges holding on a little too tightly to a long-lost past of curtain calls and starvation? No thank you, not for my daughter.

Through the afghan holes Aunt Viv speaks up, "I got you the job at Fairchild. I'm one of the reasons Etta has attended that world-class school. I have paid some of her ballet tuition over the years and I'm always the first one seated at her opening nights. I'm allowed to listen, and I'm allowed to have a say in the future of my baby girl." So that's how they are going to play it, yet again, two against one—with me forever the bad guy.

"May I remind you, Aunt Viv," I respond through clenched teeth, "that Etta is MY baby. And, Etta, you would do well to remember that, too. Aunt Viv don't make the decisions about what's next for you. And Jean Georges shore don't make the decisions about what's next for you. You know who does that? I do. Your mother." My temper is hotter than fish grease. I don't even want my drawers touchin' me right now. Have these two lost their minds? It was me who missed the window for an epidural and pushed and puffed in excruciating pain all alone in that hospital room to bring this big-headed girl into the world. It was me who cried alone in that same hospital room when the nurse's assistant, averting her eyes, handed me Etta's birth certificate with the declaration of paternity to fill out. And it was ME who decided that since I left the space labeled "FATHER" empty, I would do both jobs of mother and father myself. I might be leasing the boat by living with Aunt Viv, but I AM captain of this ship.

"Do you hear me, Etta? 'Cause I'm definitely hearin' me. And right now I've decided that you will go change your clothes. And I will go to the car. And when you get in that passenger seat I want to see Etta the intellectual. Etta the academic. Etta the Fairchild student, who is interested in imagining a future wider and brighter than ballet."

"I hear you, Mom, but I wish you would try to hear me," Etta whines and turns on her toes to go to her room. I turn on my heel and head to the car to cool off. Aunt Viv decides to keep her head under the blanket until we are long gone.

EVEN THOUGH WE'RE GOING TO FAIRCHILD AS PARENT AND daughter, I still have to put on my professional game face the moment I walk through the front doors, whether I want to or not. Occupational requirement: When you're a parent and an administrator at a school, leave your baggage in the parking garage.

Since we missed dinner I bring Etta a plate of cheese, crackers, and grapes to make up for the sushi. I grab a glass of Chardonnay that I recognize from the locked storage closet in the director of development's office. Not my favorite, but holding it gives my hands something to do other than want to cover up the backless black leotard Etta swapped for the lavender one. I didn't see it until she walked into the gym ahead of me and shed her coat. I have underestimated Etta's cunning ways, but she quite possibly has also underestimated mine.

"Sam has done a fabulous job pulling this evening together. I think it represents the high standards of execution I have set for Fairchild." Like a slick cat Nan has slid in next to me, watching over the sea of mothers and fathers, taking in the view of soon-to-be-potential-alumni-parent donors. I can almost see dollar signs in her irises.

"I believe it was Krista who brought this event together. Sam has only been here a year, so I think he's still learning quite a bit." While Krista and Sam work closely together, I want credit to go where credit's due.

"Yes, well, in his short time here, I can tell Sam has true leadership qualities. He is going to make something of that college counseling department. Excuse me, Josie, I see the Jacksons and I have my eye on them funding the completion of our glass-blowing studio." Nan is off to hang on the arm of a father who will undoubtedly believe the compliments she showers upon him as she pickpockets his financial portfolio. Tonight, I am a parent and not an administrator, so I salute her fund-raising efforts and watch her go.

I take a big breath, refocus on the college acceptance goal at hand, and remind myself that, as the adult, I should smooth things over with Etta. I cross the room over to her gaggle of friends and tap her on the shoulder. "Come on, let's sit down, I think the counselors are about to start," I say softly to Etta in an attempt to repair some of the damage done tonight. I head to two chairs at the front of the gym, and as I take a seat I see Etta hang back and sit down with two of her best friends. Okay, Etta, message received loud and clear. You hate me right at this moment. But, please, have a little faith. When you have everything in life you could ever want, you will thank me. You'll be part of a professional power girl posse. You'll find a man who wouldn't dream of walkin' out on you, and one day you will have a child and you'll realize every move I made, every thought I had, was in your best interest.

To my surprise, Nan steps out from behind the curtains onto the stage. She has managed a new coat of lipstick to soften the biannual lip filler she had done on Friday afternoon, when she had Elsamy-assistant e-mail the faculty and staff to say she was "out of the office" having quality "face time" with other San Francisco school heads.

"Thank you for gathering tonight for our college cocktail hour. For years I have been begging Krista to come up with a better way to fully share with parents about the college application experience because this is where Fairchild Country Day really shines. Last year we had nineteen students go to Ivy League colleges and three to Stanford. Go Fairchild Flyers!" Nan gives an uncomfortable woo-hoo and fist pump, her team spirit falling flat in front of this anxious audience. I shrink in my seat. Witnessing Nan out of her element is painful.

When no one cheers back in response to her callout, Nan clears her throat and continues, "Lucky for this graduating class, Sam and I fell upon the fabulous idea of combining two of Fairchild's favorite activities: counting Ivy League applications and socializing." Nan pauses hoping this will elicit a rousing round of applause, but again she is met with lukewarm claps. "I look out at this room and see a landscape of parents who have raised the next poet laureates, neurosurgeons, and tech billionaires." I turn in my chair and look around me. Statistically speaking, there are parents of at least three Uber drivers and one kid here tonight is headed for the clink.

"Before I bring Krista out here for the less inspirational information on the nuts and bolts of the college process, let me say that I have dedicated my life to ensuring that your children not only succeed, but achieve their greatest aspirations. I want you to know that whatever the final outcome of your child's college acceptances, it is not for my lack of effort to provide your child with a quality education. I want you to know no one in this school cares more for your child than I do. Best of luck to you all!"

Krista walks onto the stage, a strained smile plastered across her face. Nan exits quickly without even a glance in Krista's direction. A sense of relief overcomes me. Even though Nan has alpha dogged me publicly at least two dozen times by now, I always wind up in analysis paralysis, deconstructing each slight to figure out what I could have done differently to make her like me more, support me more, maybe even go so far as to praise my work to the Fairchild Board of Trustees. But apparently, I'm not the only woman regularly snubbed by our head of school. Krista, I feel you, sister.

As Krista adjusts the mic at the podium, the sense of being alone in this parenting game flares. I know this feeling well; it has been a constant companion for eighteen years. It's the feeling I had the first time I rushed baby Etta to the ER with a 104 temperature in the middle of the night while working in London. The feeling I had flying with Etta over the Atlantic to start a new life for her in San Francisco and reengage in an old life for me. It's the feeling I have time and time again walking around the city with Etta knowing I'm being judged by strangers for being yet another single black woman parenting a child I probably had no business birthing at barely twenty-two. And it's the feeling that became my truth when Michael left us—not even for another woman, but because he chose to be alone rather than being with me. I know alone, and I've learned to do it well. That said, there's definitely a difference between being alone and feeling lonely in the uncharted waters of parenting a teenager. Tonight, both plague me.

"Welcome to Fairchild Country Day School, a school that has been an intimate part of your day-to-day family life for upward of thirteen years for those who started with us in kindergarten. Together we have eighty-eight incredible human beings, have we not?" Applause erupts and woo-hoos break out. I do love Krista. She always knows how to reach right in and pull on the heartstrings. I give her a thumbs-up and she winks, which I know is for me, but I suspect the balding dad in flannel at the end of my row thinks it's for him as he smirks and winks back. Ah, men. They can be flaccid, stanky, and wearing a spaghetti-stained T-shirt and they will still believe every woman looking their way has been touched by their testosterone magic.

"There are two rules of the college application process that I want each and every parent in this room to take to heart. Students, I want you to hear this, too. RULE NUMBER ONE: Deciding where to APPLY to college is a partnership between parents and child. This is a family conversation to happen over multiple dinners together, on college trips, during lazy Sunday afternoons, after receiving SAT and ACT scores. As a family you will talk about school size and location: east, west, south, north, urban, rural. You will discuss program specialties, housing, transportation, social environment, and, of course, cost, scholarships, and tuition assistance. THIS stage of the process is a team effort." See, Etta, I knew I was right. So glad to know Krista is on my side and she just shared it with the world, or at least with this unique microcosm. Despite their general thinking, teenagers do not know everything,

"RULE NUMBER TWO: And, parents, you really want to listen up on this one. Deciding where to GO to college is ultimately your child's decision, because remember, you have agreed to everywhere your child has applied if you have properly followed rule number one. At this point in the process it is NO longer a team sport, it is for the individual to decide. Your child may or may not ask for your consultation in these final moments. This fact may be painfully difficult for some of you"—Krista looks pointedly in what I hope is flannel dad's direction—"but please wait to be asked for your consult at this final stage of the process. Additionally, after acceptances have been received and your child is leaning one way or another, you must remember this exact moment, when, a few minutes ago, we were all clapping and cheering and congratulating ourselves for raising incredible human beings. They are capable of making the important decision of where to go to college. We have been preparing them for this exact moment for years. After all, you have been to college and you have created your life path. The time has come to let your child follow their chosen path, the successes and the stumbles. Best to stomach this difficult fact now and not when the acceptances come because—trust us in the college counseling department—in that moment, your child will know exactly where he wants to go, and your job will be enthusiasm and excitement for their journey. Yes, I said THEIR journey. Not your journey, theirs."

I can feel Etta's eyes drilling a hole into the back of my head from four rows behind. *Krista, you are dead to me*, I decide on the spot. I will have to text her and let her know I'm canceling our walk on Thursday. Oh wait . . . On the walk she's telling me all the juicy info she knows about the athletic director at Three Winds Academy being fired effective immediately, vital gossip given the competitiveness of admissions among San Francisco private schools. Okay we'll go for our walk, but after that she's officially dead to me.

MID-SEASON

ELEVEN

FROM: Nan Gooding
DATE: November 6, 2018
SUBJECT: Admissions Check-in
TO: Josephine Bordelon

- -

Dear Josie,

I can't believe it's that time of year again to dig our heels in and get to work on admissions. Let's meet on Thursday from 1:00–1:30 p.m. so you can tell me how things are looking for this year and I can tell you what I need you to do to ensure that we have our best admissions season yet. Check in with Elsa, my assistant, first and don't be late, I'm booked solid with meetings in my office so there will be a line at my door of people waiting to meet with me.

I will see you at our scheduled time, 1:00 p.m. sharp.

Your Head of School,
Nan Gooding

HEAD OF SCHOOL
FAIRCHILD COUNTRY DAY SCHOOL

About mid-admissions season Nan sticks her head out of her oak-paneled office decorated with portraits of past school heads to meet with me for an admissions status update. The moment always reminds me of a gopher sticking its head out of a ground hole checking for predators to make sure it's safe to come out and scurry about. I wish I could say after a few years her directive e-mails wash right off my back, but I'd be lying. Every single e-mail that comes my way I want to clap back with:

> Nan, I know you ain't talkin' to me like that, did you mean to send this to someone else?

But I do like my job, and after checking my bank account balance last night I know I need this job. So I reply politely that I look forward to meeting with her.

And then show up at 1:04 p.m.

Our brief biyearly admissions updates have, without fail, gone something like this the past six years:

NAN (CLEANING HER GLASSES): How are the numbers looking this year, Josie?

ME (STICKING TO SCRIPT): As strong as last year.

NAN (NEEDING MORE): Stronger than when Dr. Pearson was here?

ME (RECOGNIZING WHEN AN EGO NEEDS TO BE STROKED): Absolutely, Nan, I never saw numbers like this under Dr. Pearson.

NAN (PLAYING WITH HER SILK NECK SCARF): Good, good. Admissions has always been one of my strong suits as head of school.

ME (NOTHING)

NAN (A BIT LOST IN SELF-CONGRATULATIONS): Not that I care, but the board of trustees will want to know the admissions numbers.

ME (IN MOCK AGREEMENT): Yes, yes, for the board of trustees.

NAN (RETURNING TO HER ALL-BUSINESS TONE): Here is my list of three "must accept" families. They will need to go through the full admissions process like all families, of course, but will be accepted to Fairchild no matter what. And I may have a fourth.

For thirteen years as a student and for my first six years as an employee in admissions, I had never known any head of school other than Dr. Pearson. For generations of students and their families, there hadn't been a Fairchild without Dr. Pearson. For thirty-eight years the school was his life aside from his wife, Della, who was as loved as Dr. Pearson by the student body, with her warm, reassuring presence and the sacks of tulip bulbs she planted with each incoming kindergarten class in the fall.

As far as anyone knew, Dr. Pearson had no children, no friends, no hobbies, and no interest in travel. He had Della and he had Fairchild. That is probably why, under Dr. Pearson's leadership, the school endowment grew to sixty million dollars. Even through two dot-com busts, the campus gained four new state-of-the-art buildings, a couple of playing fields, and a parking garage. And, along the way, Fairchild became the most competitive private school in the Bay Area. From tech billionaires living in Presidio Heights to moody, persnickety chefs planted firmly in Mission Dolores, the one thing they had in common, aside from their Range Rovers, was the desire to have their kids attend Fairchild.

In the fall of my fifth year working as an admissions assistant, Della passed away suddenly. The whole community was sure Dr. Pearson, who was healthy as a horse, would follow shortly thereafter from a broken heart. A secret head of school search committee was formed to make sure the school was fully prepared to find an exceptional new head for when that fateful and devastating day came.

Dr. Pearson took off the month of November. The board offered him more paid leave through the winter holidays even though he probably could have taken off two full paid years given the amount of unused sick time the man had accumulated during his tenure. But Dr. Pearson kindly declined the offer and returned to school the Monday after Thanksgiving vacation looking tanned and fit. Still, the community stayed braced for him to drop dead any minute.

But then the one-year anniversary of Della's passing came and went and Dr. Pearson showed no signs of slowing down. The school thrived and, oddly, Dr. Pearson began to show up at school looking younger and appearing more vital than ever, mentioning dinners at San Francisco's trendiest restaurants. It seemed Dr. Pearson was going to go on forever as head of Fairchild Country Day and that was just fine by me because in that time of personal renaissance he promoted me to director of admissions. For the first time, I felt like I had some financial wiggle room. By no means rolling in cash, I could at least start to pay down my NYU loans and not have to choose between rent, groceries, and new ballet shoes for Etta. I had finally been given a break in life, and I was ready to coast a little bit.

The spring of my second year as director of admissions, Dr. Pearson was discovered by Fairchild's upper school's dean of students, pants down around his ankles in the art supply closet with Señorita Flores, the Spanish teacher. This in and of itself may not have been that big of a deal. In fact, most of us would probably have been rooting for him, knowing he was getting a second chance at love. That was until Bea Cornwall, Dr. Pearson's long, long, longtime executive assistant went batshit crazy and destroyed his office with the new nine iron he had her pick up for him since his late-in-life interest in golfing developed. She put that nine iron right through his head of school portrait. It turned out all these years Dr. Pearson *had* had a hobby: Bea Cornwall. It also turned out that Bea Cornwall had simply been biding the appropriate amount of time (whatever that is) after the Della era for Dr. Pearson to pick up the pieces and ask for her hand in marriage. By the end of the Week of Love all three were gone from Fairchild and the middle school art supply closet had been emptied, disinfected, and restocked. What remained of Dr. Pearson's thirty-eight-year legacy was a Greek tragedy that would haunt the next head of school, Nan Gooding, and Fairchild's reputation for the first couple of years of her headship.

I went from being an admissions assistant in May to director of admissions in July to acting head of school eighteen months later while the board scrambled to find a new head late in the private school hiring cycle. Why me? you may wonder. Why not the CFO or the assistant head of school like all the other private schools in the country would do when they are in need of an immediate interim head of school? I have a two-word answer for you—white males. Dr. Pearson was not the only administrator in our school who enjoyed a good striped bow tie from Brooks Brothers or Thomas Pink. The board of trustees thought, given the nature of Dr. Pearson's sudden departure from Fairchild, that a woman in the head's role would be a nice change of scenery. I was a twofer, being black and all. The hope was that any memory of the old guard—khakis, cuff links, wandering penises—would be erased from short- and long-term memory when I was in charge. I represented a new era for Fairchild.

Only I had no idea what I was doing. Luckily, it was April and admissions were complete. New parents had signed their enrollment contracts and put down their deposits mere days before the private school gossip wires were set aflame.

I still remember watching Dr. Pearson pack up his office. Ms. Cornwall was already checked-in to a "retreat" in Napa, her nerves unable to survive the public embarrassment of losing her marbles and losing her lifetime-coveted love. Her desk sat as she had left it before being tranquilized and hauled away by paramedics post face-off with Señorita Flores. The front office went from a bar brawl to a ghost town in a matter of hours. The board of trustees wanted me present as Dr. Pearson packed up almost four decades in his office to ensure there was no extraneous funny business.

While I understood why Dr. Pearson had to go, my heart was conflicted. Here was a man who had always believed in me and held me to high standards of academics and conduct. He was the first to brag about me to anyone who would listen and then he welcomed me home to Fairchild, no questions asked. Dr. Pearson was the closest thing to a father I had ever had and letting him go, even given the circumstances, proved difficult.

In quiet moments throughout my life, I wondered if having a father would have improved my luck with men. I fantasized about my dad being something like Dr. Pearson, graying temples and a tweed jacket even on warm days. When I was nine I made the mistake of telling Aunt Viv. Her boisterous voice shook the apartment walls as she repeated, "Tweed? What black man have you ever seen wearing tweed?" and then she would break out in hysterics all over again slapping her velour-covered knee at my ignorance. "Girl, you'd do better imagining an Afro and some shoes that need resoling as fast as he skipped town!" At my disappointed expression, Aunt Viv softened a bit and reached for my hands, "Don't worry about it, baby girl. Tweed or no tweed, that daddy of yours is gonna be mighty sad he ever walked anywhere away from you. No man will ever do that to you again." But here was Dr. Pearson in his best tweed jacket preparing to do just that. And a handful of years later, Michael walked out on me, too. This was officially a pattern I had no interest in repeating.

I was only acting head for five draining months before Nan Gooding arrived at Fairchild to save what some speculated might soon be a sinking ship without Dr. Pearson. And thank God she arrived when she did because I knew within a few short hours of my first day as interim head, I had no desire to ever hold the position permanently. Turned out, I loved being director of admissions! Being around families on their Sunday church behavior as the director of admissions, having them shower you with compliments and delightful conversation—all good cheer and gratitude—is where I shine. Easy, I know. Give these same people five minutes in the front door of a new school year and some of the best and the brightest parents of a generation turn into cold, complaining, sniveling shells of their formerly optimistic selves. After only two phone calls and six e-mails as head, I couldn't deal with the entitled and disgruntled customers coming at me from all grade levels. Who knew serving corn on the cob with hamburgers on a gorgeous spring day in May was too many carbs in one meal, thus why Charlie Taylor in third grade was unable to make it through his select soccer tryouts? Apparently Fairchild was to blame for his spiked insulin followed by a carbohydrate crash. Little Charlie's father did a three-way call between him, Charlie's pediatrician, and me to make sure I understood the severity of the mishap. What I understood was that Charlie had a dad out to single-handedly dismantle the tradition of the great American picnic. To say I was beyond ecstatic when Nan was hired, and a start date was confirmed, would be an understatement. I looked forward to the moment I could return to my office in Colson Hall, where the loudest complainer was Roan after a spray tan gone awry.

From the get-go, I think my relationship with Nan could best be described as frosty. I'm not sure how it spiraled downhill so fast. My two-cent speculation is that Nan didn't grow up with many girlfriends. Any girlfriends. I think she grew up seeing other capable, competent girls as enemies who had to be edged-out for her to earn the accolades and get the boys. Trying to be head of a private school only fertilized these nasty characteristics. In an industry that is at least 80 percent male and still discriminates against hiring women into head of school positions, female candidates can quickly become, as Aunt Viv loves to say, *women with sharp elbows.*

Funny thing is, of the three finalists, Nan was my favorite candidate. She had done her homework on the history and current state of Fairchild and had reputable research to back up her personal philosophy on education and leadership style. The two male candidates tried to skate by on charm, cronyism, and white male privilege.

Nan, unfortunately, viewed my enthusiasm for her appointment and imminent start date with a healthy dose of skepticism. I shared with her my gratefulness to turn the reins of the Fairchild wagon over to her and even pointed out the big piles of horse crap to watch out for as she took the old wagon on her first spin. Somehow Nan took my offer to share some advice as a vote of no confidence and she's been working hard to prove her exceptionalism and superiority ever since. I just wish Nan could get off the power trip she's been on for six years. One would imagine she's tired from all that travel.

With each passing year she seems to leave the security of her oak-paneled office less and less and rely on commanding e-mails and sporadic public displays of self-congratulations more and more.

IT'S 1:27 P.M. ON THURSDAY AND OUR ADMISSIONS CHECK-IN is coming to a close. True to Nan form, she throws me a curveball.

NAN (SWEETENING HER TONE AS I'M ABOUT TO EXIT OUR AD-MISSIONS CONVERSATION): Oh, one more thing, Josie, I'm thinking of throwing a fiftieth anniversary party for your aunt Viv in late February or early March-ish. She is the longest standing employee Fairchild School has ever had since founding Head of

School Balthazar Fairchild, so I think we should celebrate her tenure. I want it to be a party like Fairchild never experienced under Dr. Pearson. Of course, I will need Viv to do the food, but everything else Elsamyassistant can take care of.

ME (BEING THE AUNT VIV EXPERT IN THE ROOM AND KNOWING SHE WILL HATE THIS IDEA): Well, Nan, that's a very kind offer, but Aunt Viv is not one for a big fuss. I'm not sure a massive party is how she'll want to celebrate being at Fairchild for fifty years. What about dedicating the cafeteria to her with a lovely plaque and maybe a gift certificate to her favorite Cajun restaurant?

NAN (WANTING TO PROVE ONCE AGAIN SHE KNOWS BETTER THAN ME, EVEN ON THE SUBJECT OF AUNT VIV): Nonsense. Of course Viv will love a party. I will deliver a speech that honors her well.

ME (TESTING THE LIMITS OF MY PATIENCE): I know you would, but given her recent heart attack and need to take it easy, I'm not sure making food for hundreds of people for her own party is a great idea. I want her to have a good couple of months to recover without added stress.

NAN (DISMISSING MY RESPONSE WITH A WAVE): It will just be heavy apps, which we both know Viv can whip up with her eyes closed.

ME (GRASPING AT STRAWS): That's true, but you always talk about how important it is for faculty and staff to take care of their health so they can perform to the best of their ability at school.

NAN (IGNORING ME): We will invite alumni families, faculty, and staff from the past fifty years as well as the current community. And perhaps my four top choice families for the incoming year. I'm thinking black tie—you know, do it up right, make it extravagant—there hasn't been a formal party in the grand entry of the school since Dr. Pearson left. Yes, yes, the more I think about it the more the community will love a good excuse to get dressed up. I think you will be surprised by how much Viv will enjoy herself and appreciate the gesture. Trust me, Josie, I'm certain I know best on this one.

ME (KNOWING AUNT VIV WILL SHOOT THE MESSENGER WHEN SHE FINDS OUT ABOUT THE PARTY. I PUT THE TARGET ON NAN'S BACK): Well, it's such a generous offer, and since it's your great idea, I think you should be the one to tell Aunt Viv. She'll love to hear the news directly from you, and don't leave out a single exciting detail. Particularly the part about it being black tie.

NAN (QUITE PROUD OF HERSELF): You're right, she should hear it from me, her head of school. It will mean so much more coming from me. I'll send her an e-mail.

ME (NOW ENJOYING THE ONCOMING DISASTER A LITTLE TOO MUCH): Nan, I think Aunt Viv will want to hear news this exciting in person.

NAN (SHAKING HER HEAD IN CONTEMPLATION, A BIT TENTATIVE NOW): Okay, I'll head over to the cafeteria right now. Ummm, Josie . . .

ME (OFFICIALLY DONE WITH THE CONVERSATION AND IT'S 1:30 ON THE DOT): Yes.

NAN (SLIGHTLY SHEEPISH, BUT TRYING NOT TO SHOW IT SO HER DOMINANCE ISN'T DIMINISHED): Where's the kitchen office?

TWELVE

⸙⸙⸙⸙⸙⸙⸙

THE PICTURE WINDOWS OF MY OFFICE ARE BORDERED WITH colored Victorian lead glass. Intricate cutouts frame the thick swirling fog outside, which blocks any distractions that might normally keep me from focusing on my work. Oh goody a text.

TY

> Aunt Viv promised me her special apple crumble coffee cake at our parent interview with you next week. BTW I know you call me Golden Boy.

9:52 A.M.

I knew I shouldn't have let Aunt Viv go to her post–heart attack checkup on her own. I thought she was going to see her primary care doctor, but apparently the rendezvous was with Dr. Golden. She came home flushed like a teen in lust and began scurrying around the kitchen singing the praises of her Golden doctor and explaining that a man that charming could only be from the South. I didn't have the heart to tell her the application says he's from Omaha.

JOSIE

I didn't realize she was your aunt, too. And the coffee cake, I'm thinking that's a recruiting tactic and in this admissions office we play by the rules. I can't speak to Aunt Viv's unethical behavior.

10:02 A.M.

TY

I saved her life, thus the moniker of affection for Aunt Viv. What have you done other than share a bit of DNA?

10:05 A.M.

JOSIE

I ruined her prime adult years by showing up on her doorstep at age 4 needing a mother. Then I showed up again on her doorstep during her golden years needing help raising my daughter. You get to call someone your aunt when you single-handedly ruin her life not once, but twice.

10:11 A.M.

TY

Touché. So that was your daughter in the hospital room?

10:18 A.M.

JOSIE

Yep, Etta. She's seventeen & a senior at Fairchild. Total smarty-pants.

10:19 A.M.

TY

What's she doing next year?

10:22 A.M.

JOSIE

Going to Cornell or Dartmouth, hopefully.

10: 25 A.M.

TY

I went to Cornell for undergrad and medical school! And I volunteer for the Cornell Bay Area Alumni Association. My kid needs help with admissions, your kid needs help with admissions—maybe we can help each other out. I'm just saying . . .

10:26 A.M.

Ugh I should be saying NO, but instead I leave the text banter at that and hope this conversation doesn't get picked back up next week at the Golden parent interview. Face-to-face I'm not sure I can turn down an offer to help Etta get into Cornell.

• • •

JOSIE

Lo—Aunt Viv told the hot dr. I call him Golden Boy. DYING. Since the heart attack didn't get her I may have to kill her.

11:42 A.M.

LOLA

Aunt Viv didn't tell him I did.

11:44 A.M.

JOSIE

WHAT?!?!? When did you see him?

11:45 A.M.

LOLA

I picked Aunt Viv up from her Dr.'s appt, you know, because you suck as her niece. It just kind of slipped out. He's so good-looking I lost all sensibility again. I gotta say though, worth the trek across town to get a glimpse.

11:46 A.M.

JOSIE

Why didn't you tell him YOU call him Golden Boy? Clearly this is my punishment for not taking Aunt Viv to the Dr.

11:48 A.M.

LOLA

Duh I wouldn't want to embarrass MYSELF would I? Gotta go teach now. Ava has pencils sticking out of every orifice on her head. Holla. Lo

11:49 A.M.

Aside from the carpeting, I have a beautiful office because parents come to see me more than anyone else in the school, though Nan would argue otherwise. It doesn't have the stately appearance of Nan's oak-and-Tiffany glass–fortress, but from where I sit during parent interviews I can gaze right over Baker Beach and out to the Bay. When I'm conducting an interview and the most painful of parents talk incessantly about their budding thigh-high Steve Jobs, their recent vacation, or their most current venture fund investment, I can appear engaged while staring at a view I never tire of.

I have two Herman Miller knockoff chairs, a coffee table (covered in Fairchild materials), and a killer couch that is perfect for a mid-afternoon catch-up snooze (of course, never when I'm interviewing although every year there are always a few that I have to fight to keep my eyes open). Sometimes Aunt Viv sneaks in for a few winks if she has to cater a reception in the evening after cooking all day for the kids. I like that she has a place she can come and rest. Her work is not easy for a woman in her late sixties. The school (Nan) treats her like she's still in her early thirties, and I often feel like they (Nan) are taking advantage of her, but then she always says yes to whatever is asked of her. I know Aunt Viv comes from a time and a place when a job, any job that is not as a domestic, is worth putting up with the Nans of the world. But I don't come from that time and this is California, not Louisiana. I think she's too accommodating, she says she likes to feel needed. A difference of opinion I guess, which Aunt Viv reminds me to keep to myself. Only problem is, the work does exhaust her, and now I have her heart to worry about, too. Also, when she comes to my office for a quick nap Aunt Viv snores something awful. If she's snoozing on my couch and starts her guttural roar I can fairly accurately peg her with a chocolate pretzel or a paper clip from my desk. She usually rolls over and quiets down before anyone outside my office hears her and blows our napping cover, but I do worry one day she will come into my office when I'm not there, get all comfortable, start sawing logs, and the jig will be up.

"Save me!" Roan demands, blowing into my office and slamming the door.

"It's too late for you, Roan, you best end it now. It's been a good twenty-nine-year run, but time's up for you." I'm feeling feisty after my text exchange with Golden Boy.

"Aren't you so not funny this morning, Wanda Sykes. Your twelve-thirty is here for their interview."

"Not following your drama."

"Meredith Lawton is here for her parent interview. I invited her to wait for you in my office, but she says she can't, she needs to start immediately. She has a hydrotherapy appointment at one-fifteen that she *must* make."

"Seriously, she told you she has a hydrotherapy appointment?"

"Yeah, is that a big deal? I'm an easy guy to talk to. You know: open, approachable, and . . ."

"Judgmental. Hydrotherapy is code for a colonic."

"I wonder if she shits diamonds?"

"Okay too far, even for me. What does Christopher look like?"

"There's no Christopher. She said he's in the Middle East for work and her friend Beatrice Pembrook will be joining her for the interview."

"But no Beatrice yet?"

"Nope, the aristocracy of alumni has not shown up yet."

"Hmm . . . Seems Beatrice doesn't care much about Meredith's colonic appointment, either. Give me three minutes then show her in."

"Yes, my queen." Roan gives me a sarcastic curtsy and backs out of my office sure not to make eye contact. Clearly, he's been watching too much PBS.

I heat the water in my teapot to offer Meredith a warm drink before we jump into our conversation. I grab Harrison's file off my desk and quickly review his teacher recommendation. Despite his over-the-top five-year-old lifestyle, he sounds like a pretty down-to-earth child according to his preschool teacher. Shares easily with fellow classmates and is a well-liked community member. He engages in creative imaginary play, willingly cleans up, enjoys doing his classroom jobs, and he is steady with his emotions. The cherry on any entering kindergarten application, he can go to the bathroom without adult supervision. I suspect his aim is off from time to time being a rising kindergarten boy and all, but at least he can wipe. Go, Harrison! The last question of the teacher recommendation form is about parent participation in the school. Harrison's teacher has switched from black font to red for the answer. Interesting to note.

We have never met Mr. Lawton, but we have to assume Harrison's kind and giving personality comes from his father's side of the family. While Mrs. Lawton means as well as any other mother in the school community, her version of parental involvement and support differs greatly from the definition provided in the People of the Pacific Primary School *parent handbook. When we asked for families to collect used and found objects to contribute to our art studio (buttons, egg cartons, yarn, cardboard, etc.), Meredith hired her interior decorator to come work with the students for a week to teach them about color matching, textiles, and textures. Apparently, she spends so much time at the Lawton house that Mrs. Lawton considers her family or at least on the family payroll and offered her up to fulfill Mrs. Lawton's required parent volunteer hours for the month of March. When we asked families to sign up to bring various items to the school potluck and art show, the Lawtons flew in one hundred lobsters from Maine and hired a chef to dish them up for the community. Once a week we have Ready Set Read time where parents read to groups of three or four kids for about twenty minutes. This fall Mrs. Lawton signed up her new bodyguard, Randy, to come every week. Initially he terrified the kids in his black suit and dark sunglasses, but I do have to say a few weeks into the school year, the kids have gotten to*

*know him and love his undercover spy uniform. Mrs. Lawton
also volunteered to fly in Dav Pilkey, author of the* Captain
Underpants *series, but we politely declined. This is all to say
that the Lawtons are a very generous, supportive, and involved
family, it's just that their involvement is based on their own
unique interpretation of what the school says it needs and how
the school would like its parent volunteers to help.*

A diplomatic recommendation, but I get the preschool teacher's
drift. Mrs. Lawton outlandishly outsources her school commitments,
but she views it as being highly involved in her child's school and
education. Noted. A dab of lip gloss, and I'm ready for you, Meredith.
I open the door to my office to see Roan shifting uncomfortably in
the hallway and Meredith texting away on her phone. He wasn't joking when he said she refused to wait in his office.

"Hello, Meredith, it's lovely to see you again," I say, shaking her
hand firmly, a conscious power move I always employ in parent interviews.

"Oh, Josie, I think by this point we know each other well enough
to kiss hello, don't you? You're kinda like a sista to me by now." Meredith goes in for the customary French double cheek kiss. Nowhere in
the Lawton application did I note French lineage or anything else that
would lead me to believe we could be sisterly in any way. Meredith has
added herself to the long list of white folks who knowingly or unknowingly put on an air of ghetto thinking we will then be able to better
relate. They throw out a *sista* here or *brotha* there, a claim to love fried
chicken or Jay-Z's jacked teeth and then, presto, we're practically bosom buddies. Whether it is conscious or subconscious, there's an assumption that the change in tone and language will somehow bridge
a racial divide between the two of us. All it does is put a person's ignorance on display and deflate the conversation before it has even started.
I am no more ghetto than Meredith is poor and from the hood.

While Meredith is working overtime trying to up her street cred, I notice her Miu Miu fur slides. Only two hundred pairs of them were made this season. The model in me has not totally died. I still covet the most unique and gorgeous of clothing and shoe design and indulge myself now and again with a couture eBay "YAY ME!" present. The hunt, the find, and the low-bid for the win are my Triple Crown. I can't deny that I would love to slip my foot into one of those soft leather slides and let the world be jealous.

"Would you like a cup of tea before we get started?" I grab my tea box to show her my selection.

"Oh, yes, I would indeed, but I always travel with my favorite tea, which Christopher brings me whenever he goes to China. They have yet to import this tea to the States and it's absolutely divine and detoxifying. Would you like to try some? I have several bags with me."

I can't help but wonder how much one needs to detoxify prior to a colonic. Doesn't that completely clean you out? But I know it will serve me well to accept her offer and not ask too many questions.

"Yes, I would love to try your tea, thank you." I fill our cups with water and carry them over to the coffee table, so we can sit down and get started. Before Meredith drops the two tea bags, which smell like rancid garden fertilizer, into our cups she chants something vaguely Hindi under her breath.

"Do you mind if I leave the door open a crack, so Beatrice will feel comfortable walking right in when she gets here?" Meredith asks once her tea ceremony is over. Not waiting for an answer, she opens the door. "Christopher so wishes he could be here, but his company is opening an office in Abu Dhabi, and he has to be there for a few weeks to get everything up and running. He invited me to join him, but I told him I absolutely cannot leave the States during admissions season, impossible." Meredith is excitable as she talks, playing with her rings and wristwatch while checking the door every ten seconds. I notice she seems to lack the confidence that she will be enough to carry the Lawton family interview. "I just don't know what could be holding Beatrice up. She promised she would join me today in lieu of Christopher."

"Well, since this meeting is about *your* family, why don't you start by telling me what activities you, Christopher, and Harrison enjoy doing together?"

Meredith is momentarily put off by my disregard for Beatrice joining the interview, but then reconsiders and launches into the story about the first Lawton family vacation to Bali when Harrison was six months old. As the urban legend of the rich and well-traveled goes, he was swimming on his own in the resort pool and in that moment Christopher and Meredith considered contacting Michael Phelps's head coach to find out the proper age to start training Harrison for the Olympics. He has continued to show swimming prowess, and they are currently lifting up the four-story mansion they just built and putting an indoor swimming pool underground, so Harrison has a place to train. I stare out the window and wonder why she can't just take his butt down the hill to the YMCA for guppy swim team like a normal kid. I nod my head to encourage her to keep going . . . The Bay sparkling in the sun is one of the most beautiful sights on earth, a view I can lose myself in again and again. Or perhaps that's not actually Mother Nature doing her best work; it's just Meredith's enormous diamond stud earrings reflecting off my windows.

ETTA AND I ARE HEADING TO THE SCHOOL PARKING LOT when I hear Nan calling after me. I keep walking, not feeling up to engaging with her at the moment, but Etta, always kind, stops and waves.

Ignoring Etta, "Josie, was that Meredith Lawton I saw leaving the campus around lunchtime?" Nan huffs, a bit out of breath. I would have thought those five-mile early morning runs she takes along the waterfront would be doing a little more for her cardiovascular system.

"Yes, it was. I had the Lawton parent interview today."

"Remember, Josie, they're on my list of for-sure acceptances. You cannot, under any circumstances, blow this for me. For Fairchild. The Fairchild community needs the Lawtons. They will be integral to the capital campaign I'm launching next year to build the new STEAMS building."

"What's the S at the end for?" I ask, genuinely curious. Schools all over the country are building STEM and STEAM facilities, but STEAMS is new to me.

"Science, Technology, Engineering, Art, Math, and Social Responsibility. Being a school in the Bay Area, the technological epicenter of the world, it is never too early to grow a new type of generation: a Larry Ellison meets Al Gore type. I want to make sure we are the first STEAMS school in the country because this is my brain baby and I want to be recognized for, I mean, I want Fairchild to be recognized for it. The project must start next year, and I need the Lawtons to lead the campaign effort."

I have to give it to Nan; sometimes her insecurity and need to win at all costs does lead to great thinking and fast action. I decide to throw her a bone and make her afternoon.

"Nan, that's truly brilliant. You'll make my admissions job so easy with a STEAMS facility; everyone will be begging to come to Fairchild. Well done." I wear a look of mock amazement knowing she will thrive on the facial as well as verbal adulation.

"Well, everyone already wants to come to Fairchild, but this will place us so far in front of the competition that I'm sure the National Association of Independent Schools will want me to be the keynote speaker at an annual conference in the next year or two. It is a brilliant idea, isn't it? This is why they pay me the big bucks, Josie." Nan beams and points to her brain. I stand motionless. When I don't agree with her she turns to head back into the building.

I might have actually meant the compliment I dished out if she could have just said, "Thank you" and left it at that.

THIRTEEN

FROM: Krista McCann
DATE: November 12, 2018
SUBJECT: Etta's college essays
TO: Josephine Bordelon

- -

Hey, Josie,

Well, no easy way to say this, but I know you like things told to you straight so here it is . . . Etta's essays suck. There's no way she can send these to Dartmouth and Cornell early decision (or any school for that matter, that's how bad they are). And there's no time to fix them since they are due in two days. Actually, there's nothing to fix; she needs to scrap them and start over for regular decision. I think you and Etta need to meet with me today after school. Can you guys swing by before ballet?

Please try not to kill Etta between now and 3:00 p.m. I'm sure she has a good explanation.

See you later,
Krista

DIRECTOR OF COLLEGE COUNSELING
FAIRCHILD COUNTRY DAY SCHOOL

Deep breath. Even I need some of that namaste, crystals, and higher-power voodoo right now to keep me from marching into Etta's first block Calculus II class and dragging her bony booty out by her ballet bun. What has gotten into that child? Krista was so nice to offer to read Etta's admissions essays last minute. The school rule is that college counselors need a minimum two-week lead with each essay before it's due or it's a no-go on feedback. Krista made an exception for Etta, and I made sure Etta knew that Krista had gone above and beyond by reviewing her essays this late in the game. Etta insisted that though she was late with her essays, everything was under control. And I believed her because she has had everything under control for her whole life.

When Etta was working on her essays I tried everything I could think of to let her know I was available to help. I folded laundry in her room while she was on her computer. I made her bed while she was on the common application website. I was even so brave as to ask her straight up if she would like my help with her applications. That was a terrible idea. I was met with stone-cold silence and then a surprising teenage tantrum that started with, "You don't think I can do anything right! You've never believed in me!" and ended with a heartwarming declaration of, "YOU ARE THE WORST MOTHER EVER!!" If Etta had ever talked to me like that in the past I would have grabbed a duffel bag, stuffed her clothes in it, thrown it on the front stoop, and told her not to let the doorknob hit her in the ass on the way out. But against all instincts I bit my lip, gave her a dark stare that said, *One more word out of you and your life will be over in thirty seconds or less*, and walked out of her room. Or really my room, she is simply a boarder on a fourteen-year lease—payment due immediately if she does not change her attitude and get these applications in on time.

I decided to believe Etta would do this college application thing right. I chose to be the best mother of an almost college-aged kid and back off. And guess what? IT WAS A TERRIBLE FUCKING DECISION! Because here we are. No early options due to crap essays and that means, thanks to my prima ballerina, more flack to be taken from Jean Georges and the bill collectors from the San Francisco Ballet School. I promise this: Today is going to go down in history as one of Etta's least favorite days of her life.

"Mama, what are you doing here?" Etta asks, surprised to see me cut into her circle of friends as they pack up their backpacks at the end of physics. "Is Mrs. Chen not driving me to ballet? Poppy said she's driving us today."

"Hello, ladies." I nod to Etta's posse. "I texted Mrs. Chen. She's picking up Poppy, but you're coming with me." I grab Etta by the wrist and pull her through the circle. I usually do my best not to embarrass my daughter in front of her friends, but today humiliating her a little feels a lot good. "We have a date with Krista. Wasn't that nice of her to invite us both to meet with her in her office? We are going to have some tea, maybe a cookie or two, and hear all about how your essays stink. That sounds lovely, don't you think?"

"Oh."

"I hope by the time we get to Krista's office you have a little more to say to the two of us than just 'oh.'"

"Oh, no?"

"That's more like it."

Entering the college counseling center is like entering the television set of *This Could Be Your Life*. Pennants of dozens of colleges line the walls. A reader board announces the dates of all upcoming on-campus college visits. A beautiful bleached oak conference table is stacked with college viewbooks and laptops line the conference room walls, a quiet place for kids to take practice SAT tests or work on their applications. Any future seems possible in this center. How I wish I could go back in time and start over knowing what I know now.

Etta is biting her cuticles, the true sign that her nerves are rustling and that she's related to me. My heart softens a bit. Yes, I wish I could go back and do things differently, but then I wouldn't have Etta and I wouldn't have had the chance to share the majority of my life with Aunt Viv. I have become a better woman given what I have learned from being a mother and a pseudo daughter. Aunt Viv has made me tough, self-reliant, willful, and able to find humor in the worst of times. Etta has made me softer, kinder, and more empathetic to others. I have matured into a pretty good combination of Aunt Viv and Etta, if I say so myself. Maybe I don't really want another life. I think what I really want is to get to choose this life over others, not just have this life chosen for me based on a series of thoughtless events.

I knock three times. "Hi, Krista, we're here."

"Hi, Josie. Etta, nice to see your mother brought you here in one piece." Krista smiles at me. Etta laughs uncomfortably. Krista and I both know it will only take one meeting declaring our disappointment that Etta has not risen to her true potential to get her back on the right path. I also know Krista is going to take the lead playing good cop and once more I'll be left to reprise my role as bad cop.

"So, Etta," Krista starts in from behind her desk, "I have known you your whole life at Fairchild. The good of that is I know all your talents and your exquisite personality intimately and I can share that with colleges on your behalf. The bad of knowing you so well is that I know what you sent me for your college essays is, well, garbage. And I'm not just talking about your writing ability. The topics and stories you have chosen to focus on, they make you sound like every other college-going kid in America and you, Etta Bordelon, are not every other kid. You have incredible grit, unmatched by any other student in your graduating class. You have used that grit to become an upstanding scholar, Fairchild community member, and exceptional dancer at the San Francisco Ballet School. With all that, why would you choose to write about your hamster dying when you were nine?"

Shocked, I burst out laughing. The laughter continues, a strong cover-up for the angry cop about to go ballistic. Wow, when Etta blows it she blows it big-time. As president of the mile-high club I can say this is one of the less positive Bordelon traits for sure. "Seriously, you wrote about Husky our fat hamster?!?! Why in the world would you do that?"

Etta turns her whole body to face me, completely ignoring the fact that Krista is in the room, or the fact that this is Krista's office for that matter. Her voice is calm, and her body is poised.

"If you won't take me wanting to apply to Juilliard seriously then I'm not going to take applying to the schools you want me to go to seriously. Why would you spend all that money for the past ten years of my life on ballet if you never wanted me to be any good at it? Besides, Juilliard is a great college and you won't even consider it for a second."

Etta's adult composure is rattling me. I need to stay on top of my parental game despite the fury collecting inside.

"Of course I wanted you to be good at ballet. I want you to work hard and be good at whatever you try. That's why we came back to San Francisco, so you could get a first-rate education and have all options open to you. I know Juilliard is a good school. Great, in fact. Great for kids who choose to put their art first and their academic studies second. That is not what is going to happen here, Etta. You will be putting your academics first. And let go of the idea that I don't care about your dancing—that's not true. All the universities I have on our college list have dance classes available to non-dance majors and have many dance troupes for extracurricular activity. Juilliard, on the other hand, offers only three majors—drama, music, and dance. A school like Dartmouth or UC Berkeley has, I don't know, hundreds if not thousands of majors for you to explore and choose from. Back me up here, Krista, why should Etta limit herself to just dance? Baby, trust me on this one, you want access to as many choices as possible, to figure out what you really want."

"You raised me, Mama, so why don't you trust me? All I want is the option to apply to Juilliard. I'm not saying you have to let me go. All I'm asking for now is that you let me apply. That you help me apply. And that maybe you spend more time on you and less time tryin' to fix me. I think Aunt Viv's right: Being single makes you cranky."

I can see by the way Krista is looking at me that she's trying hard not to bust a gut laughing. The tables have now turned and she's sliding toward Etta's side, even after my eloquent explanation of how it's going to be. Yet again, the bad cop stands alone.

I hesitate, but knowing I'll win in the long run I concede. "Okay, I'll make you a deal. If you put your very best effort into your college essays, and I mean write like your continued invitation to be a part of our family depends on it, then I will give you the money to apply to Juilliard."

"Mama, I thi—"

"Not finished. Cornell and Dartmouth are the FIRST essays you will finish, followed by the other schools that I have on the college spreadsheet. And when I say, 'put your very best effort into your college essays,' I mean that Krista and I both get to see them by December 1 and you best impress us beyond our wildest imaginations or else there is no applying to Juilliard."

"Okay. It's a—"

"Still not finished. The only way you get to go to dance on the weekends is if you show me you've been working on your essays during the week AND over winter break, if that's what it comes to. Because those college applications WILL be sent by December 31."

"And if you want good essays and applications done by December 31, then in exchange you are going to have to help me get my Juilliard portfolio ready, which is due at the same time. I get a fair shot at every school—your favorites and mine." I'm not sure where Etta has picked up her strong negotiating skills, but I have to say I kind of like that she's throwing down and making me work for it. Maybe she could hold her own in a big city, after all.

"Before I agree, because let it be understood that your future is based on my generous spirit and good mood, I want your absolute promise that there will be no essays about Husky. Those are the kind of essays I get for kindergarten applications. 'Taylor is an animal lover and expresses sincere interest in being a small-animal veterinarian.'"

"Yes, I promise."

"And you will keep your opinions and, apparently, Aunt Viv's opinions on my dating life to yourself."

"That's going to be tough one. Aunt Viv and I talk about it all the time."

"Why you two caught up in my business? Whatever, not negotiable."

"Okay fine. Deal."

"Krista, you heard her, right? So, if she falls down on the job again, I cannot be held responsible for my actions. Bordelon women are known for dropping their ungrateful children off on the side of the road as deadweight on the family's upward mobility." I can tell from Krista's expression she doesn't know if I'm kidding or not. I look at Etta. She's biting her cuticles again. She doesn't know whether I'm kidding, either.

FOURTEEN

"I THINK MATEO IS GOING TO GET KICKED OUT OF SF CHILdren's Academy." It's not like Lola to allow her concern for her boys to get in the way of our Tuesday afternoon drinking. "The ultimate humiliation, right, a teacher's kid kicked out of school? That's gonna mean sufferin' at least a week's worth of gossip on the school playground. Complete with side-glances and awkward smiles when I walk from my classroom to the faculty lounge."

Mateo is what teachers in elementary school refer to as "excessively energetic" or "spirited," often having to be excused from the classroom to run a few laps around the grassy fields to burn off some wiggles, but he's far from a bad kid.

"Yesterday the fourth graders were lined up to go to music. Apparently, Mateo leaned over and bit the class sweetheart right on her lower neck, pretty much where your trapezoid muscle is." Lola reaches over and pinches me at the base of my neck in case I skipped anatomy in college.

"Ouch! Why'd he bite her there? Or really, why did he bite her at all? Seems a strange thing to do in fourth grade."

"Oh he had a very logical explanation, or at least logical to him. My opinion leans more toward the diabolical. When I basically asked him the motherly version of 'WTF?!?!?' he told me he wanted to find out if the fourth-grade cutie tastes like vanilla or tastes like chicken."

Any sense of self-control defies me. "HA! That's the funniest thing I've ever heard! What was his conclusion?"

"Yeah, I'm sure that's what Hannibal Lecter's mother's best friend said to her when Hannibal was in fourth grade. And he said she tastes like a stale snickerdoodle. My kid is so weird."

"Mateo will grow up to be better looking than Hannibal Lecter. He has that swarthy Latino thing going on from his dad."

"Oh, well that's comforting. I'm no longer worried."

"Want to hear something that will make you feel better?"

"I want to hear it and I want to drink it. Can you get me another glass of champagne while I check to see if the school has called yet to let me know Hannibal's fate?"

I decide to have one more with Lola so she doesn't have to feel like a failing parent and a lush at the same time.

"Dr. Golden and Dad #2, Daniel, are coming in for their parent interview tomorrow. Apparently Aunt Viv promised to have her famous apple crumble coffee cake waiting for them when they show up to sell themselves to Fairchild."

"Don't think there needs to be much of a sales job there. I can't think of any affliction their kid could have that would trump getting to see Golden Boy on campus for the next thirteen years. As witnessed at SF Academy, private schools accept all kinds of families, even ones with a budding cannibal." I always know Lola is coming out of a funk when she starts making crude jokes about her children.

"Well, there is one sticky situation when it comes to Gracie and her eye-candy daddy." Lola leans in, now that she's really interested in this conversation. I know she thinks it's something sexual, but she got to spend the first twenty minutes of our Tuesday date talking about her kid, so now it's my turn. "Dr. Golden alluded over text that he would or, I guess, really he said he could"—I scroll back through my texts to double-check—"'*help*' Etta get into Cornell if I did my part to get Gracie into Fairchild."

"You text with Golden Boy?" Lola asks with a hint of excitement.

"I'm talking about Etta's future here and how far I'm willing to bend the rules of general ethics when it comes to taking favors for admissions. It's always been so cut and dry for me, but now we're talkin' about Etta and the rules are getting a little fuzzier. I wanna play fair, I think, but I also know the backroom deals white folks have been doing forever to get their kids into college. I don't want my kid gettin' screwed because her mama had a brief moment of morality." I successfully avoid Lola's question and make her feel guilty for steering the conversation off the torturous topic of my child's future.

"Right, Etta's future. Girl, you know I love you, right?" Lola asks me, pulling her barstool closer to mine. "And us bein' sista-friends, we choose to be honest with each other so neither of us looks like a fool or makes foolish mistakes." I know Lola is talking about the time I stopped her from shaving her head to prove the point to her husband that she feels invisible in a house full of men who eat, burp, fight, and fart all day. I literally had to grab the clippers out of her hand and point out to her that her ears are not her best feature.

"Well then, here it is, Josie. You need to get off Etta's back and let that girl apply to Juilliard with your blessing. Straight up. If you don't, she's going to go off to college and drop you like a bad habit because you don't see your daughter for who she really is. She's an artist, a dancer, who also happens to be good in school. Not a top student who also happens to be good at dance. You have to let her live her life, whether you agree with her choices or not, or you're going to lose her forever. And then you are going to end up like me, no daughter to take care of you when you're old."

"You'll take care of me when I'm old."

"Not if you don't let Etta seriously consider Juilliard."

"How do you know about Juilliard anyway?" I never brought it up with Lola before.

"Etta talked to me since she hasn't been able to talk to her mother about it."

"So Etta talked to you, Aunt Viv, and Jean Georges all about Juilliard. Any other secrets you know about my daughter that I should probably be aware of since she's my kid?" I'm getting upset. What happened to keeping Bordelon family issues private? Unless I'm the one blabbing to Lola, of course.

"I mean this from the bottom of my heart, Jo, you can be a one-track-thinkin', don't-get-in-my-way-'cause-I-know-what-I-want, the-world-best-hop-on-MY-train, stubborn you-know-what type of person. I've never known a woman who can dig her heels in harder than you can. And I say that with love. And awe." Lola downs the last of her drink signaling that this conversation is done and it's time to pick up her ninja warrior.

"I really should have let you shave your head."

"But you never would have, because at the end of the day once you climb up and out of your own way you always know the right thing to do." Lola stands to put on her coat and scarf to steel herself against the San Francisco fog and wind.

"You think it's so cute that Mateo can play 'When the Saints Go Marching In' on his guitar. Just wait another seven years, when he tells you he wants to run off and join some alt rock band rather than go to college. Or worse, try out for a reality television show. Then let's talk. I'll remind you to let him find his own way at seventeen, for you to get out of the way of his dream that is heading nowhere good."

"Hey, as long as that little cannibal doesn't turn into Ozzy Osbourne and bite the heads off birds on stage I'm all good." I can't wait to remind her of this conversation when Mateo goes Goth at fifteen. If creamy Latino black kids can go Goth. Never really thought about that one. Regardless, we'll see who is the hyper-controlling, know-it-all momster then.

Lola pushes her chair in place and leans over to give me a kiss on the cheek. "You just count yourself lucky I don't rat you out to Aunt Viv that you failed to walk me to my car. Leave a good tip, Hugo's my favorite bartender."

It's my week to pick up the tab and I still have a sip or two of champagne left. I disregard Aunt Viv's golden rule of friendship: "You go together, you leave together." No one's going to mug Lola on the way to her mini-van one block up Franklin. I stay at the bar a few moments more to think about my deal with Etta. I told Etta she could apply to Juilliard and that I would even help make her portfolio video, but I have no intention of actually allowing her to go. But is Juilliard worth losing my daughter over? Is there a middle road we could agree on, like, maybe a reputable college with a strong dance program where she could double major? Seems like Duke is that kind of school, worth double-checking my research at least. Or, if I just stick to my plan and wait it out will she come to see I'm right and thank me later? Deep down I know there is no one right path for Etta to take, but I also know that New York City is littered with many tempting wrong paths. I leave the philosophical for the mundane and signal Hugo for the check. Teenagers have no tolerance for late pickup.

"CHECK YOU OUT!" ROAN GROWLS AS I SMOOTH DOWN THE back of my skirt and give a little shimmy. "Someone's got it bad for the gays."

When I wanna look good, I can look so damn good even Nan will stop and take notice. This morning, she used up her once-a-year compliment admiring my mint-colored blouse that casually ties at the neck with a little peek-a-boo hole that shows some well-moisturized chocolate skin. I've paired my top with a knee-length Kelly-green pencil skirt. And, if that weren't enough, I took the ensemble over the Fairchild fashion edge with my metallic silver ankle booties. BAM! I'm lookin' fly today and I know it. Take that, middle age! I ain't ready for you yet.

Knock. Knock.

The smell at the door gives it away. "Come in, Aunt Viv." As promised, she has arrived fifteen minutes before the Golden parent interview to deliver her apple crumb coffee cake.

"Now remember, Josephine, unless you want me to die earlier than I plan to, you let that good doctor's daughter in this school. I have never once asked for any favors where your job is concerned, but I'm askin' now." Aunt Viv is tearing at the Kleenex she has permanently stuffed up her sleeve. She's visibly anxious, not her usual calm, authoritative self.

"Aunt Viv, you know I can only admit her if she's a right fit for Fairchild. And if her parents are a decent fit, too."

"Puh-lease, child, I've seen you and three directors of admissions before you accept plenty of children who had no business bein' here other than their parents could buy somethin' for the school that it couldn't buy for itself. I've been here a long time. I've seen a lot of things, and I know how it goes. If your parents have more money than Mississippi, Georgia, and Louisiana combined you get in. If you look like you shop at the Ferry Building's farmers market on the weekends, you get in. It's all the families in the middle who have to play by the rules. Private schools color outside the lines. Don't try to tell me otherwise. I need that doctor to be happy that his daughter gets to go to a good school, this school. I'm not up for dyin', Josie, so the least you can do for me is accept that nice family, so I can get on with livin'."

Since her heart attack this is the first time Aunt Viv has actually talked about dying. I know I've thought about it, I know Etta's thought about it, but up until this moment it was unclear to me if the idea of dying was anything Aunt Viv spent much time thinking about. She's not one to delve into emotions and "all that therapy nonsense you younger generations spend too much time talkin' about." This turn of events, me doing what needs to be done to take care of Aunt Viv, is uncharted territory. Aunt Viv is the caretaker. Aunt Viv is the lawmaker. And in full disclosure, Aunt Viv is the steady hand that runs our house and reigns over our land, and I'm in no hurry to step into that family role quite yet.

"Well, Aunt Viv, if I were a betting woman, which I swear to God I'm not"—Aunt Viv detests gambling—"I would bet on the Goldens. I can't think of a time since I've been at Fairchild that we didn't take two dads."

"Now, that's not true. Remember those large fellows with the thick Russian accents you could barely understand? For a whole year every time I came by your office I had to listen to Roan talk in a Russian accent and ask if I knew how to make *piroshkies*. Those men had a son and you didn't take him."

"Aunt Viv, they weren't gay, they were brothers. They just wore too much jewelry. Anyway, we didn't take their kid because SFPD came to Fairchild looking for information we had on them. Turns out they were part of an underground Russian mob out of Moscow that had been steadily growing in the Bay Area for over a decade."

"Okay, so they were brothers, but still you didn't take them is all I'm sayin'. So, unless you plan on startin' to do more of the cookin' and cleanin' around the house I strongly suggest you find love in your heart for the Golden family." Ohhh I hate it when Aunt Viv threatens me with going on a cooking strike. Laundry and vacuuming I can handle, dinner not so much. "And don't touch the coffee cake, it's not for you." Aunt Viv throws the shredded Kleenex in my garbage, kisses my forehead, and gives me a good look up and down. "You look nice today, Josephine. Your hair's all laid and lookin' pretty." A compliment from Nan and Aunt Viv in one day, now I know pigs fly and hell could possibly freeze over. If Golden Boy isn't a foodie, hopefully he's a designer diva and I can get another fashion compliment for the trifecta win. As I begin to preen just a little, Aunt Viv follows up her compliment with, "Cuz yesterday ya had cookabugs hangin' from them dreads. Now stand up straight like I bothered to teach you anything." As orderly as she arrived, Aunt Viv walks out my office door, with perfect posture, I note.

I check my e-mail in the five minutes I have before the Goldens show up.

FROM: Yu Yan (Helen) Wu
DATE: November 14, 2018
SUBJECT: Liu family of Shanghai
TO: Josephine Bordelon

Hello, Josephine,

Lovely to make your acquaintance. I am Helen Wu, senior partner at Admit International, Hong Kong office, and I am the educational consultant for the Liu family of Shanghai. The Liu family will be moving to San Francisco in two months' time, though the head of the household, Wang Wei Liu, will be spending most of his time at his multinational company based in China. The Liu family purchased the Greek consulate two blocks from Fairchild and they have spent three years refurbishing the building to create an acceptable home for a family of such international renown.

Now that the house is complete, the Lius need to find a reputable school for their children. One boy. One girl. Twins. The children will be entering the American equivalent of grade nine.

A colleague of mine in Singapore shared with the Liu family that Fairchild Country Day School is an academically rigorous and highly regarded school with students eventually matriculating into Ivy League universities. This pleases Mr. Liu greatly and he would like me to share with you that his children have been raised with impeccable manners, can sit and focus for extended periods of time, are fluent in the Queen's English, and will be studying hard to ensure acceptance into Harvard University.

Since Harvard is the number one university choice for his children, Mr. Liu would like you to send to me, and I will forward to him, your statistics on Fairchild graduates attending Ivy League universities for the past twenty years. Mr. Liu is well informed that Stanford is an internationally recognized university, but he prefers a school with a longer-standing history of excellence and tradition.

Please inform me, within the next forty-eight hours, as to the correct immediate application steps for the Liu family.

Thank you for your attention to this important matter.

Yu Yan (Helen) Wu

EDUCATION CONSULTANT
ADMIT INTERNATIONAL, HONG KONG

Every year during tours parents ask me what are the biggest trends I am seeing in private school admissions. I don't tell them the truth. It would be too deflating and, frankly, possibly make me sound a bit racist. But here it is. Mad-rich Asians who are gunning for an Ivy League college education so they can return home to Shanghai, Beijing, or Shenzhen and build multibillion-dollar companies in the wild, wild East that is currently the economic climate in China. The

Chinese are moving to the West Coast in droves, gobbling up the best real estate with cash, and flooding private schools with the equivalent of professional students. The wealth of the parents and the drive of the children are astounding. I get at least one or two e-mails from a Chinese education consultant a week. A few years ago, I thought these e-mails were a scam, but after a three-year trend of more than twenty families applying to Fairchild a year from China, this is no scam, this trend is the real deal. I search my sent box for a similar reply I wrote a few weeks ago to another consultant from Shenzhen—copy, paste, and send. I know in less than twelve hours I will receive a perfectly manicured application from Helen Wu on behalf of the Liu family.

Roan blows into my office in a flurry.

"They're here! How do I look? Would you cheat on your husband with me if you were Golden Boy? Or maybe Golden Boy has a gay Golden brother?" Roan has temporarily gone insane thinking he's at the club with his friends and not talking to his boss. I love it.

"Slow down there, Grinder Greg. You're at work. Pull yourself together. And more important, pretend you have some sense in that head and don't embarrass me." I stand up to straighten my blouse and adjust a few locks so you can see a hint of my glittering chandelier earrings. There's little better than being showered with clothing compliments from a couple of queens. "Bring Mama some gold!" I strut over to pose by the couch, feeling my stock rise.

"Terrible play on words." Roan smirks and exits my office. My stock plummets. I thought it was pretty good.

"Josie, nice to see you again." Daniel walks in first, clearly excited to get the interview started. "Please pardon Ty, he rushed here from the hospital and didn't have time to change out of his scrubs. He told me about the coincidence of being your aunt's doctor. I hope she's doing well, or at least getting better."

"Thank you for asking. She is back at school and close to being

100 percent her old self. And no need to apologize for your husband, there are no admission points given for best dressed." Daniel and Ty smile at me. I allow for a pause after the easy opening that I lobbed them for a compliment on my outfit. Not a peep. Really? Nothing? No comment on how utterly fabulous I look? How can they be gay and have nothing to say, not even on the shoes? I've been spoiled by Roan, who notices everything about me. The good and the bad.

"I see Aunt Viv delivered on her promise. I haven't eaten since five a.m. Hope it's okay if I dive right in." Not waiting for an invitation to help himself, Golden Boy grabs a napkin and the two biggest pieces of coffee cake. He devours the first piece in two bites, a trickle of cinnamon crumbs decorating my carpet. How does he eat like that and look like this? I glance away for a moment to give him privacy to wipe his mouth.

"Please have a seat. I'd love to hear how you two met and a little about your family and what the three of you like to do together." I launch into my standard opening interview question, but with the added twist of wanting to know how these two guys who seem so very, very different got together.

"We meft throu my sistar," Ty shares, spreading powdered sugar shrapnel everywhere as piece number two disappears. I could have waited to hear that boring version of their love story until after he finished chewing. I notice Daniel is dying a slow death in the chair next to him.

"You'll have to excuse my sleep-deprived husband. He's been on call for the past two days. What he means to say is that his sister, Caroline, introduced us. Caroline works for Salesforce, and they were at an early Dreamforce event together. I think it was 2010. Stevie Wonder and Will.i.am played. They were amazing. Do you know who Will.i.am is?"

I let the question hang in the air, allowing Daniel time to realize how ridiculous it is. I want so badly to say, "Why, no, I don't," but instead I choose to behave. Crimson rises from his shirt collar and discolors his face.

"Please continue with the story . . ." I say when I think I have tortured him long enough with silence.

"Ty had spent the past ten years in medical school and in fellowships and hadn't had much time socializing in the real world. Caroline brought him along to try to sharpen his dulled social skills. I saw them across the room staring at me just as I was staring at them; both Caroline and Ty are strikingly good-looking. When Caroline finally caught me glancing their way she marched right over and asked me outright if I was single. And then she burst out in a laugh so loud you would have thought it impossible coming from such a petite human being. Ty dared her to come over and meet me out of the blue. I think he owed her twenty dollars after that. Can you believe meeting me was worth only twenty dollars?"

"To be fair, in 2010 twenty dollars was a lot of money for a poor doctor a few years out of medical school drowning in student debt," Ty defends himself, reaching for one more chunk of coffee cake. Daniel slaps his forearm before he can fondle a third piece.

"Since Dream Force 2010 the three of us have been pretty inseparable." Daniel pats Ty's leg a little too aggressively.

"Three meaning you, Ty, and Gracie?" I ask quizzically. The math doesn't add up for me, Gracie is only four and a half.

"No me, Ty, and Caroline."

"And why is it you would like Gracie to attend Fairchild Country Day?" I decide the relationship topic has been exhausted and it's time to return to the script and learn more about Gracie and their hopes for her as a potential Fairchild student.

"Caroline's the one who wants it," they both say at the same time.

A-ha. A real twist in the Golden family history has presented itself. "Wow, so your sister has quite a big influence when it comes to Gracie's education?" I ask, fishing for the real story. My guess is that the sister is the biological mom who donated her eggs. Or maybe she didn't donate her eggs maybe she cooked Gracie for nine months herself. So then she must be Daniel's daughter for sure. It certainly wouldn't be Ty's kid, right? Would that be incest or just really, really messed up?

"She has a strong influence over everything when it comes to Gracie," Ty blurts out but gives me no more information. "You have no idea." Daniel sneaks Ty a sly evil eye, not happy with the direction the interview is going. It's clear they have no interest in taking this part of the conversation further.

"Oh, I know about strong-willed aunts, remember I have Aunt Viv."

"Yeah, well, Aunt Viv and my sister, Caroline, could go toe to toe, trust me. They are well matched." Ty leans in to high-five me. A first in a parent interview. Daniel can't help but nod in agreement reaching for Ty's hand, embarrassed by his husband's high-five attempt.

I like the dads. While I find their honesty refreshing, I can tell by the beads of sweat at Daniel's hairline he is sure Ty has blown it for them. I fake check my watch and tell the Goldens that I have a lunch I have to get to but that I have enjoyed our time spent together enormously. Daniel looks relieved when I put my arm around his shoulders and walk with him to the door. I leave Golden Boy to follow behind us. I want to assuage any doubt Daniel may have about their parental performance by giving him a little extra physical assurance, which is a big deal for me because, as an overall rule, I don't touch people I don't really know. Call it a germ thing, call it an energy suck thing, all I know is: If I touched every parent who came into my office on edge, or left my office having completely nosedived off a ledge during an interview, I would be a walking petri dish.

"I really appreciate your time today, Josie. We hope to see you again soon," Daniel says, the color having returned to his cheeks.

"Yep, what he said," Ty mumbles, breezing by me having snagged

two more pieces of Aunt Viv's coffee cake when Daniel wasn't looking. I can't help but think if that guy made it into Cornell not once,
but twice for undergrad and medical school, Etta for sure has a solid
chance. Overall, that was thirty minutes well spent. By the end I
think Daniel turned a corner and again feels good about Gracie's
kindergarten prospects. Similarly, I am feeling better and better about
Etta's chances of nailing the college game given my time with Ty.

"NAN. WHAT ARE YOU DOING HERE?" I ASK, IN SHOCK THAT
Nan has actually left her oak-paneled fortress and shown up for an
admissions committee meeting. Every year I invite her to join Roan,
myself, and the seven teachers (two kindergarten, two third, two
sixth, and one ninth) who meet five times during the admission season to run the children's visit dates and to work through the selection
process after Roan and I have taken an initial pass through the five-
hundred-plus applications. Extending the olive branch is more a
gesture than a true invitation; plus, she never shows up. It's a little
director of admissions, head of school game of cat and mouse we
play. Until today.

"It has come to my attention that you may not be taking my requests for the incoming class seriously. You know, as head of school,
I do have the ultimate say as to who attends this institution I have
built." I bite down hard on my lip to avoid pointing out to Nan that
she has only been at Fairchild for six of its 150-year tradition. "I'm
not convinced you have shared with the committee the families I
want to see at Fairchild. In talking with the committee before you
arrived six minutes late for YOUR meeting, they do not seem aware
of the list of families that I gave you to make sure are accepted for
the incoming kindergarten class. I have grave concerns with your job
performance as it pertains to information gathering and dissemina-
tion." Roan is behind Nan silently yelling, NOT ME! NOT ME!

"As well, I had Elsamyassistant check into your admissions database and I have to say the system you have set up to rank, track, and comment on each applying child is, to be frank, novice at best, and I daresay, tragically simple. I've seen more sophisticated systems at the Tiny Trees preschool down the street."

"I think our system works pretty well. Look at all the great families we have enrolled right now," Elizabeth one of the third-grade teachers chimes in, trying to interrupt my public humiliation that Nan is enjoying a little too much.

"Well, yes, Josie has probably convinced you that her system works well, but I am here to tell you I have seen more erudite systems at our rival schools. I believe Josie is really holding back progress at Fairchild and I have to say I'm terribly concerned, thus why I'm here." For a second time Roan is silently screaming at me, *WHAT DOES ERUDITE MEAN?!?!?!* I give him a subtle shrug. I have a bigger problem on my hands than a limited vocabulary.

I remind myself I have made it further into this school year than in years past before I start to hate Nan all over again. Once a year, somewhere between early November and mid-December, Nan does something to remind me how my professional enjoyment and satisfaction is directly linked to how threatened she is feeling by me at any given moment. Usually the abuse takes place in private, but this year she has ratcheted it up a notch by taking her superior stance against me public.

"In fact, Nan, we use the same admissions evaluation and measurement standards as every other private school in the Bay Area. The directors of admissions across all the schools spent two years developing the standards together, beta testing it together, and it has now been in use in all the schools for four years; a decision we agreed upon—together. You would know this if you had ever bothered to attend an admissions committee meeting prior to today." I'm swinging just shy of the fences by putting Nan on Front Street like this. I can't afford to get fired, but I certainly am not going to take Nan's humiliation in front of my committee lying down.

"Well, this system of yours had better produce enough money, I mean, quality families, to build my STEAMS program. Good to see you all. Don't let me stop your work from continuing. I'm sure you eight educational powerhouses can more than make up for Josie's shortcomings. For your commitment and service to keeping Fairchild a highly regarded school, I have Jane's on Fillmore delivering a selection of healthy, organic, locally sourced salads, a vast assortment of baked goods, and an array of juices for your lunch. And, Josie, I haven't had time to tell Aunt Viv about the fabulous party I'm throwing for her. Since it's almost the holiday break I've decided I'm indeed going to leave it to you to give her the good news. Oh, and, Roan, don't worry, I remembered that the beet, carrot, apple, and ginger juice is your favorite." Nan gives Roan a smile and heads out the conference room door.

"OH GOODY!!!!!" Roan squeals, clapping his hands together like a toddler moving up the line to see Santa.

"Touch that juice when it's delivered and you're dead," is the only thing I can think to say to control my temper and also reestablish some sense of governance in the room. Yeah, that's right, I'm making Roan pick between Nan and me over a juice that makes you shit red.

STRESS SEASON

FIFTEEN

✦✦✦✦✦✦✦✦

THANKSGIVING HAS COME AND GONE, AND I STILL HAVEN'T mentioned anything about the anniversary party to Aunt Viv. This is my silent protest against The Man or, really, Nan.

If I'm truly laying it all out there, I was hopeful Nan's recent rant against me had forced her to reconsider if she wanted to celebrate any Bordelon at all. Or at least not spend Fairchild money on an event Aunt Viv would detest: two hundred people stuffed in gowns and tuxes crowded in Fairchild's grand black-and-white foyer to celebrate her famous third Friday of the month macaroni and cheese. For weeks after Nan suggested the party I had night terrors that she would insist there be a receiving line for people to offer Aunt Viv their congratulations and for Nan to receive accolades for dreaming up such a glorious celebration. Nan loves any formality that reeks of royalty and power. If I can make it to the New Year without Nan asking if I shared the news of the party with Aunt Viv, perhaps we will all be off the hook.

"Come on, Aunt Viv. If you take much longer you won't officially be the first person seated for this year's *Nutcracker*. Do you really want to ruin your ten-year early bird record?" I yell down the hall. Etta's final year attending the San Francisco Ballet School and she's been selected to dance the part of the Sugar Plum Fairy. She burst into tears when she found out in early November and it gave me a tinge of warm fuzzy that Jean Georges could put aside our differences and grant Etta this iconic solo for her final season. I send myself a reminder e-mail from my phone to put Jean Georges on the list of people in Etta's life to receive a senior picture and a graduation announcement. Though he's one of my least favorite people, Etta would not be the person she is without him. E-mail sent, but still no Aunt Viv. I scroll through my Fairchild account pretty sure I won't have any new e-mail on a Sunday afternoon, but thinking I can use these few minutes of quiet to clean out my in-box while Aunt Viv finishes getting ready.

FROM: Jean Georges Martin
DATE: December 9, 2018
SUBJECT: Sugar Plum Fairy
TO: Josephine Bordelon

Josie,

It has come to my attention that Etta has twice left *Nutcracker* rehearsal early and she has requested her understudy for not one, but two performances so she may work on her college applications. I'm sure this brings you great joy to know Etta is neglecting her role in one of the top *Nutcracker* performances in the country. Instead she is using her time to apply to colleges she has no desire to attend, but apparently you do. I hope the parents' weekend lives up to your expectations.

While I have never been a parent I have had the best interest of over 800 students in my heart and in my mind for the 18 years I have been Artistic Director of the San Francisco Ballet School. It seems to me that you, as a mother, could take a mere moment to do the same with your one child.

I expect Etta will not need to miss any rehearsals or performances after you have read this e-mail.

May the holidays bring good tidings to Etta and Aunt Viv.

Merci beacoup,
Jean Georges Martin

ARTISTIC DIRECTOR
SAN FRANCISCO BALLET SCHOOL

And with one click my *Nutcracker* has been ruined. That wrinkled rat king really knows how to piss me off. I didn't ask Etta to miss rehearsals or performances to work on her essays; she concluded that she needs that time to honor our arrangement all on her own. If she can get the essays and applications done without missing any ballet that's fine by me. My only request was to get it done by December 31 and like you said, Herr Drosseldick, she is my daughter and my word is the law.

Aunt Viv walks down the long, narrow hallway from our bedrooms toward the light streaming through the bay window at the front of the apartment. She is wearing her best suit, the one that's reserved for homegoings, important church meetings, and the occasional wedding. Until Aunt Viv is clearly in the light it's difficult to distinguish between the dark roast of her skin and the midnight-blue of her suit. Her red lipstick outlines the greatest smile and the wickedest tongue I've ever known. Her matching purse and white gloves pick at a memory so deep in my mind I'm not sure if it's real. I vaguely remember my grandmother extending her white-gloved hand to hold mine as we walked to church when I was still living in New Orleans. Or was it my mother? Or was that Aunt Viv when I first arrived in San Francisco?

"You look beautiful, Aunt Viv." I get up and walk across the room to give her a kiss on the cheek.

"Don't be wastin' that nonsense on an old woman like me," Aunt Viv scolds, but I know she loves the compliment. "You have that special phone of yours that takes pictures and videotapes?" Aunt Viv is still working on the ins and outs of her flip-phone, circa 2004.

"It's called an iPhone, Aunt Viv, no one videotapes anymore, but yes, my phone does take video."

"Good. Give it to me. I've been reading on the computer how to take good video when people are moving around a lot. I do believe I know what I'm doin'. I just want to do a little practicin' in the car." Aunt Viv sees my phone on the coffee table and swiftly picks it up and drops it in her purse. She gives it a pat to make sure it's landed where it's supposed to. "Okay, I'm ready to go."

"And what do you think you'll be doing with my phone?" I ask, elbowing her in the side knowing she and technology will never be friends.

"I will be gettin' Etta into Juilliard, that's what I'll be doin'. Now what you don't want to be doin' is makin' me late for Etta's performance."

"JOSIE. JOSIE! JOSIE, DEAR!"

Aunt Viv is busy talking with Krista from college counseling and her three-year-old daughter, who just saw her first *Nutcracker*. I turn to try to locate who in the crowd is calling my name.

"Josie, it's Meredith Lawton and Vanessa Grimaldi. What a surprise to see you here." Meredith yells over the crowd then begins to push her way toward me dragging behind her someone who could only be Harrison. Vanessa follows suit with Antonia drowning in layers of pink tulle.

"Darling, wasn't that performance absolutely grand?" Vanessa purrs in her Italian accent. As much as I dislike running into potential parents outside of school I could listen to that accent all day, the perfect mix of culture and sex. "That Sugar Plum Fairy was simply magnificent. Maybe one day that could be you, darling?" Vanessa coos, brushing Antonia's flushed cheek with the back of her hand.

"That was my daughter."

"Who's your daughter?" Meredith asks, looking behind both shoulders.

"The Sugar Plum Fairy."

"No! Really? Beatrice never told me you have a daughter who is a talented ballerina."

"Well, I don't talk to Beatrice all that often since her children graduated Fairchild, so I can't imagine an occasion where I would have shared that piece of information with her." Can Meredith not stand on her own two feet without the mention of Beatrice?

"You mean you haven't spoken to her on Harrison's behalf yet?"

"Not yet."

Meredith is visibly flustered. Or maybe she's shaking from lack of nutrients, her leather pants hanging loose over a nonexistent backside. All I can think is that someone needs to get this woman a cheeseburger and some self-love.

"It's five-thirty, we need to be heading backstage to grab Etta," I say to Aunt Viv, loud enough for Meredith and Vanessa to hear. "It was lovely to see you both." I put my hand on Meredith's upper arm to give her a reassuring squeeze; all I get is a handful of bone. I thank

God borderline anorexic has never been a black beauty standard as my stomach rumbles for the fried chicken Aunt Viv promised Etta post performance. I bend down to Harrison's and Antonia's eye level before I go. "My name's Josie, and I think in a couple of weeks you're going to come to my school to play and meet other kids and have loads of fun. I can't wait for you to visit so I can show you all the interesting things we have to play with at Fairchild Country Day School."

"Do you have a drone?" Harrison asks with eager eyes.

"No drone."

"Do you have robots?" Antonia asks, twirling in her tulle.

"No robots."

"Then what kind of toys do you have?" Harrison questions, genuinely perplexed.

"Everyday toys like basketballs and blocks. See ya in a few weeks." I stand up and leave the mini MIT graduates-in-training wondering what's "everyday" about playing with drones and robots before age five.

EVEN DURING VACATION LOLA AND I STICK TO OUR TUES-day afternoon Absinthe date. *The Nutcracker* is over, and the fall karate session is done, but there are still inappropriate topics to discuss, champagne to be drunk, and children to be avoided. Most people teach for the great vacation schedule and summers off. Lola may be the only teacher I know who lives for when school is IN session. For her, vacation is akin to being taken hostage in a zoo full of foul smells, two-hour feeding schedules, and the messy habits of four males. Lola always returns to school looking more haggard than when she left after a week or two or ten spent with her boys. This is why we generally start drinking earlier than four o'clock during holidays. We make our annual winter break meet-up a champagne brunch—shake it up a little. The time, not the cocktail.

I roll into Absinthe with an infinity scarf wrapped around my dreads, the San Francisco staple puffy coat to fight off the winter wind and fog whipping through the city, and a pair of red patent leather Chelsea boots I snuck from the set of a Jimmy Choo shoot back when Tamara Mellon was just launching the company and no one knew how loco Jimmy or Tamara really were. The boot never made it to market because it's a flat.

First thing I notice when I walk in Absinthe are the two women, who are not me and Lola, sitting on our stools. I'm thrown. Lola comes in right after me and stops dead in her tracks when she sees the imposters.

"Oh no they didn't," Lola snaps a little too loudly.

"Oh yes they did."

"How dare they?"

"I know, right?" I say back to Lola, unable to take my eyes off the interlopers. They're probably having a bit of a rest after shopping for precious pastel macarons, organic persimmons, and chemical-free makeup at the boutique marketplace that used to be a corner liquor store and hooker hangout when I was a kid.

"Well, we actually need table space this morning anyway. Two, please," Lola tells the hostess. I don't say a thing; I'm too busy wondering if it will feel weird to drink champagne at a table.

Once we're seated, Lola reaches into her hobo bag, pulls out her laptop, and scoots her bistro chair closer to mine. I pluck a feather out of a seam of her down jacket.

"I have a Christmas present for you," she says tentatively.

"You givin' me your laptop?"

"Girl, please. No. Your present is on my laptop." Lola hugs the laptop to her chest as if she's adding another protective layer between her and the cold.

"Oooh! You're going to show me something online, so I can tell you if I want it or not?" I ask, slightly giddy with anticipation. It's been a long time since someone has bought me a present.

"Something like that," Lola says, putting down the laptop and opening Safari. "I signed you up for Bumble and I made you a profile page."

"That definitely is not on my Christmas list."

"I know, I know, but hear me out. One month is all I ask. Try it for one month, and if you don't like it we close down the account. Thirty days is not going to kill you, and I'm paying for the first month anyway so, you know, Merry Christmas." I can't stand listening to Lola whine and beg at the same time. "I don't suppose you got me anything?" Lola asks, already knowing the answer.

"Yeah, another year of friendship unless this online dating thing goes sideways. How does this even work? I'm not up for men judging me by a couple of pictures, which, by the way, I have yet to approve."

Lola takes this as a *yes* and claps her hands with the enthusiasm of a little kid.

"This is Bumble and the best part is the women have all the power. Men can't choose you, you choose them. How great is that! Let's take your profile for a little spin."

"Right now?!?!?"

"Yeah, right now, what else you gotta do? I know you can drink and type, I've seen you do it a thousand times."

"Jeez, okay, but let me see my pictures first." I have to give it to Lola: She has chosen four quality photos of me. One is a little misleading, I don't usually parade around in head-to-toe motorcycle chic. That photo was from a fund-raiser at the Ritz-Carlton, Leather for School Lunches. I know these pictures are going to attract bees to this honey, but I just want to be sure I don't get stung again. Other than that Lola did okay. Even her write-up is spot on, with a touch of exaggeration. I'm ready. "Okay, now what do we do?"

Lola looks at me funny. I think she was expecting more of a fight, not complete participation.

"Well, we actually search on your phone." Lola grabs my phone and in a matter of thirty seconds the Bumble app is downloaded. "Next we start looking through the men. We swipe left to look at their pictures and read the profiles and right if we want to tell them we're interested in a match. I mean, if *you're* interested in a match."

"No, you were right the first time, this is definitely a WE project."

"Are you ready to give it a try?"

"I'm a thirty-nine-year-old swiping virgin. Alright, let's do this."

Tavis
Restaurateur, 39
San Diego State, 2000

Swipe left.

Andre
BMX Racer, 36
Sonoma Community College

Swipe left.

TJ
Architect, 55
University of Wisconsin, Madison, 1984

"TJ's not bad looking and he might be kinda interesting. And trustworthy since he's a Midwestern boy." Lola's squinting at him two inches from the screen like she's examining his pores. "Swipe right?" she asks tentatively, unsure of TJ's qualifications to date her best friend.

"Swipe left, he's fifty-five. I'm looking for a boyfriend, not a father. Can you change my age range to just below when a person qualifies for AARP?" A girl has to have standards.

Lola and I get a feel for the swiping thing pretty quickly and also for the hidden language of online dating. "Self-employed" means "Unemployed." "Entrepreneur" means "three failed start-ups and no one wants to hire me," and "looking for a casual relationship" means "booty call." A picture that looks like it has been torn in half means the wife is on the discarded side. Sunglasses in all the pictures means serial killer. And then we land on one that takes my breath away.

"Oh shit, Jo." Lola grabs my hand. I'm busy reading and not blinking.

Michael, 45

Environmental Lobbyist

Howard University, 1994

He's as beautiful as I remember. Close-shaved head and beard, sleepy eyes, teeth so bright his smile is blinding. And in one of the pictures he's wearing the Battistoni Roma tie I bought him on our trip to L.A. I had to come home and quit my gym membership for the year to pay it down, but seeing him wear it always made me smile and then rip it off him.

Looking at Michael makes my heart hitch. The only man I allowed to become part of Etta's life, breaking my *no men around my baby* rule. I had been so certain he was "the one." With a career on the upswing, money in the bank to put a down payment on a house, flawless manners with all the women in my life, and only eyes for me in the bedroom, he could do no wrong. I was ready to have eighteen more babies with that man, I was so sure he was going nowhere anytime soon.

I can't stop staring at his picture and Lola knows better than to say a word. She simply grabs my phone, deletes the app, and holds my hand.

"Two whiskeys, neat," Lola tells the waitress as she walks by. "Champagne's not going to cut it today."

SIXTEEN

I KNOW PEOPLE JUDGE ME AND THINK I'M A BAD NIECE BE-
cause I don't drive Aunt Viv to school. Truth is, she's never wanted
me to. Morning is her time. Don't ask her what she's doing, who she's
with, or where she's going, just leave her be. Aunt Viv rises long before Etta and I even know the sun's thinking about coming up. Our
alarm clock is Aunt Viv slamming the front door. For the thirteen
years Etta and I have lived with Aunt Viv, her routine has never
changed.

Monday–Friday out the door at 6:15 a.m.
Saturday cards start at noon, rotating location
Sunday out the door at 8:00 a.m. to be at Glide Memorial
    Church early (Etta and I slide in the pew next to Aunt Viv
    on average five minutes late)

One morning a few years ago, curiosity got the best of me and I
followed Aunt Viv out the front door at 6:15 a.m. into the dark of

Outer Richmond. Aunt Viv walked a brisk six blocks past our favorite burrito shop, an Irish pub that closes at 2:00 a.m. but reopens at 6:00 a.m. for those who need a pint before work, and the You Like Beauty hair-care store. I don't know how the Kwon family that owns the store does it, but they carry the best black girl hair-smoothing products in the city. I've been buying all the products I need for my crown from Mr. and Mrs. Kwon for as long as I can remember. Years of following me around the store as a teen and then a dozen credit card approvals as an adult finally convinced the Kwons I was no shea butter thief. Now, before any opening night performance Etta stops by You Like Beauty to show Mrs. Kwon her perfectly smoothed and shellacked bun.

Aunt Viv took a left at Starbucks, the first in Richmond back when I was in high school, walked three more blocks, and then a right at Clement Street. On Clement, about eight blocks after the rush of traffic on Park Presidio, Aunt Viv, chef extraordinaire, marched right into Allstar Donuts. All of Allstar Donuts greeted her with a "Morning, V! Got your seat right here." Still hidden by the winter morning darkness I spied from the sidewalk and witnessed a whole community I never knew Aunt Viv had. Clearly she didn't want me to know since she'd never mentioned word one about her Allstar Donuts posse.

A group of about ten men and women—Asian, black, and white, as far as I could tell—gathered around two pushed-together Formica tables welcoming the day with warm embraces and conversation. I saw one man in a trucker baseball hat with gray curls escaping the sides put an arm around Aunt Viv's chair. He seemed to have an easy laugh at anything said at the table, and I could have sworn I saw Aunt Viv put a hand on his knee. Did Aunt Viv have a secret lover? A friend? A closet husband? It was hard to tell because at that point I had fogged up my small peeping corner of the window.

At exactly 7:30 Aunt Viv said her good-byes to the coffee klatch and headed out as economically as she had arrived. I hid in the bushes of the bodega next door and watched her hop a 7:45 bus to Fairchild, which was no more than a mile away. The next several days I had to fight my instinct to probe Aunt Viv about Gentleman Trucker Hat, but I never did. Aunt Viv had escaped New Orleans for San Francisco to start fresh and lead her own quiet life. That all came to an abrupt halt when I showed up roughly a decade later and altered Aunt Viv's life plans, whatever they may have been. If Aunt Viv needed something to be all hers, well, I gotta let her have it. She's never once complained about raising children she didn't birth, never once mentioned a life she wished she could have led. If she needed to have her own private world from 6:15–7:45 a.m. Monday through Friday, who am I to take away that hour and a half of life that belongs only to her.

SCHOOL'S BACK IN SESSION AFTER THE HOLIDAYS AND ETTA and I both held up our end of the bargain, though I wouldn't say this was the jolliest of holiday seasons. Etta wrote an amazing essay on how the difference between a good dancer and a great one is caring about the tiny imperfections that no one else may notice, but as a dancer you do. What sets her apart from her peers is, though all humans are flawed, she enjoys the journey of working on her imperfections to try to become a better version of herself. She doesn't do it for her teachers, for her family, or for her friends; she does it for herself because it is on stage that she comes alive as the best version of herself. Etta definitely stepped it up from the Husky the fat hamster essay. I tried to compliment her on her recent efforts when she stopped to give me the time of day, which was never long enough for me to finish my sentence. Merry Christmas to me.

I held up my end of the bargain, too, by helping Etta get her application and prescreening content done and submitted to Juilliard by December 20. I was happy to learn that as a junior and senior Etta could take liberal arts credits at Columbia and Barnard. In fact, she could potentially become well-educated in addition to becoming an accomplished dancer. But, no matter how many classes she may take at Columbia that degree will still say Juilliard, not Columbia. I'm willing to bet not many tech start-ups or investment banking training programs are hiring Juilliard graduates.

I also learned that if Etta passes the prescreening process, I will have to send her to New York for a live audition and interview. Add a plane ticket to New York City and a hotel room to the loss column of the ongoing Bordelon profit and loss, loss, and more loss statement. Note to self: Don't even think about hitting the post-Christmas sales at Neiman's or Bloomingdale's. I text Lola and tell her it's her job to not let me travel south of Pine Street to Union Square for the next several months.

FROM: Nan Gooding
DATE: January 25, 2019
SUBJECT: Viv's party
TO: Josephine Bordelon
- -

Josie,

Please come down to my office to talk about your aunt Viv's party. It's less than six weeks away. Elsa, my assistant, will let me know when you arrive.

Please be on time. 10:15 sharp.

Nan Gooding

HEAD OF SCHOOL
FAIRCHILD COUNTRY DAY SCHOOL

Holy hell. I had prayed that the idea for Aunt Viv's party died with the Christmas chrysanthemums and Nan's holiday cheer. I put a little lipstick on and head to Nan's office.

"Hi, Nan." I walk past Elsa and knock directly on Nan's door, opening it a smidge. Her irritation at me has yet to subside since the admissions committee incident. My insubordination in bypassing Elsa and coming straight into her office only adds insult to recent injury.

"Is Elsamyassistant not at her desk?" Nan leans over her laptop to look out to the foyer.

"What would you like to talk about, Nan? I thought the party wasn't happening since you haven't mentioned it to me since mid-November. And I know you must be so busy working on your STEAMS project that I can't imagine you have time to organize a party."

"Well, yes, I am very busy with my STEAMS project. It's not even up and running yet and I can't keep up with the requests from around the country to come and speak at different schools on behalf of the project. The head of school at Hotchkiss has been pestering me non-stop to come speak to his faculty and board of trustees, but I finally had to put my foot down and tell him that Fairchild requires me here. I can't spend all my time on planes and at speaking engagements up and down the East Coast. So, yes, STEAMS does seem to keep me locked up in my office most of the day, but I'm a woman who can wear many hats and I'm still planning on hosting Viv's party."

I struggle not to show my disappointment at this decision.

"You've told Viv about the party like I asked you to, haven't you, Josie?"

"I was waiting to make sure the party was a go for sure. You know, I didn't want to raise Aunt Viv's hopes only to have them dashed." If only there were a trapdoor I could drop through and disappear from this conversation.

"When have I ever changed my mind on a decision that I have made public in front of faculty and staff? Again, Josie. I ask you to do something, and again you disappoint." Nan shakes her head. My fists are in balls at my side, nails digging into my flesh. It's either self-inflicted pain or Nan is going to get a beat down.

"When *do* you plan on telling your aunt Viv about the party? I know she'll want plenty of time to prepare," Nan asks, her eyebrows raised so that they are hiding under her bangs. The only time and preparation Aunt Viv needs is to bitch and moan to me about the party, bitch and moan about my inability to cancel the party to her card group, and bitch and moan to Etta that I'm a terrible niece and when she dies, all her worldly possessions will skip me and go directly to Etta.

"Trust me, Nan, I'm the last person in the world Aunt Viv wants to hear from about this party. Like I said before the break, I think it will mean so much more coming from you." I don't want to be the messenger who gets shot.

"Well, I'm just so busy here, Josie, I don't know when I'll find the time to find, er, I mean, go to the kitchen and tell Viv about the party. I would send her an e-mail, but you were the one who told me that the invitation should be delivered in person." I have a pile of admissions files back in Colson Hall to go through and, frankly, I don't have the time right now for a verbal badminton match that I'm eventually going to lose since Nan's my boss. I throw the match but with a caveat.

"Okay, Nan. I'll do it tonight, but I want to see the invite list so I can show Aunt Viv who's been invited so she'll get excited for the party."

"Yes, fine, fine, fine. Elsamyassistant will e-mail the Viva la Viv list to you. I think we are done here, don't you?" Nan has surpassed her standard two minutes of human interaction. "Elsamyassistant will see you out now."

SEVENTEEN

I STARE AT THE APP STORE BUTTON ON MY PHONE. I'VE BEEN doing this about six times a day ever since Lola and I came across Michael's profile on Bumble. There are so many unanswered questions I have, and I want Bumble to be able to answer them for me. What happened to the job in Sacramento? When did Michael move back to San Francisco? Where does he live? Does he have a girlfriend? A wife? Is her booty bigger than mine? And since he's been back in San Francisco has he ever been compelled to get ahold of me? To find out how Etta's doing? I haven't had the guts to download the app again, but it doesn't mean every time I look at my phone I don't want to. Sheer willpower and pride have kept me from going down the ex-boyfriend rabbit hole.

TY

> S.O.S. Daniel's NOT going to be happy with me.
> I can't make the date of our Fairchild visit date
> for Gracie. I haven't told him yet. Can you help
> an absentminded doctor out of an ugly domestic
> situation and schedule us for another date?
> Please, I'm begging you. If you don't my
> sister will kill me and then who will take care
> of Aunt Viv?

10:22 A.M.

Excellent, a distraction. I swipe over to text.

JOSIE

> I will.

10:22 A.M.

TY

> I know for a fact she would prefer the care of a
> golden doctor.

10:23 A.M.

JOSIE

> That's fair. Then what's the favor worth to you?

10:24 A.M.

TY

> I will insist on doing Etta's Cornell alumni
> interview and I'll bring you a HUGE bag of
> chocolate pretzels.

10:32 A.M.

JOSIE

How do you know I like chocolate pretzels? Another nugget of information Lola should have kept to herself?

10:33 A.M.

TY

No, I saw one crushed into your carpet when we had our parent interview.

10:34 A.M.

So Golden Boy couldn't manage to notice my fabulous outfit, but he noticed food ground into my carpet. He's a unique breed of gay, I have to say.

JOSIE

The way you wolfed down Aunt Viv's coffee cake it's a wonder you didn't dive after that chocolate pretzel.

10:36 A.M.

TY

No kidding. You would think for tuition of 40K a year you could at least have a cheese plate at the interviews.

10:37 A.M.

JOSIE

No cheese plate and no go on changing the visit date. JK. Let me see what I can do.

10:38 A.M.

TY

Your good deed will not go unnoticed. I have some things to drop off for your aunt Viv. She around this evening?

10:40 A.M.

JOSIE

She's going to the movies with her friend Louise. She has a crush on Morgan Freeman and he's in some new medical thriller. But don't tell her I told you, she wouldn't want you to know she's cheating on you with another doctor.

10:41 A.M.

TY

Lips sealed. Heart broken. You home then?

10:43 A.M.

JOSIE

Should be after 5:30.

10:44 A.M.

TY

Great. I'll swing by for a house call.

10:44 A.M.

"Oh my G.O.D. Josie, the Liu twins are in the front office with their Chinese *ayi* for their school visit. They ARE NOT what I, you, we would expect from the ed consultant's e-mails and from reading the twins' applications."

"What's an *ayi*?"

"That's Chinese for nanny. I had to look it up when the consultant e-mailed to tell me the twins would be arriving with their *ayi* and she wanted to know where their two drivers could park." It's not even worth my mental energy to ask why two drivers. "I'm pretty sure their parents are back in Shanghai and didn't see how the twins walked out of the penthouse this morning. You have to take a look at these two before I take them on the tour you pawned off on me. Plus, I have to run and grab Cindi, the new Mandarin teacher, so she can tag along and interpret for me in case I talk too fast like I tend to when I'm, um . . ."

"Nervous?"

"Yeah that."

"Why would you be nervous, you're the MC who moves the crowd."

"You're right. I got this." In front of my eyes Roan grows an inch.

"Now, brush your shoulders off and do this thing."

Before I leave, I turn to Roan to clarify: "Wait, so I understand correctly, the Lius are not here to see the school? They just sent their children?"

"And the nanny—sorry, *ayi*—and the two drivers. And I'm going to go out on a limb and guess the *ayi* has very little power and sway over the twins."

"Okay, meet you in the front office in two. I gotta check these kids out and then I'm passing the baton to you."

I walk through the back door of the front office and spy two lumps slouched in the oversized leather wingback chairs, their phones two inches from their faces. The chairs sit directly beneath a sign that reads: NO CELL PHONE USE IN THE FRONT OFFICE, THANK YOU. Interesting, I remember on their international applications that it was marked "proficient in English." With the intensity they are texting, I can understand the consultant's claim that they are "focused." I think what they are truly proficient in is surly teen.

"Hello, my name's Josie Bordelon and I'm the director of admissions at Fairchild Country Day School," I say to the *ayi* with what I believe is a warm and inviting *Welcome to America* face. Her eyes grow big and she bows her head and mumbles in soft Mandarin. Is this an act of servitude, reverence, lack of English, or has she never been this close to a black person before?

I move to stand in front of the tech twins, but still they don't look up. The pearl-encrusted Hello Kitty phone case belonging to Mei is blinding me, so I take a step to the right. Mei's legs are crossed and she's cluelessly swinging her stiletto-clad foot at me. I can see too much leg, but it's almost okay because it's impossible to note the short skirt when your eyes are drawn to the diamond chain belt circling her hips. From the waist down, she looks like a Bergdorf window gone bad.

Bai has on Chanel sunglasses—indoors on the cloudiest of San Francisco days. Several thick gold chains hang from his pencil neck. I'm a bit perplexed how this pimply, skinny teen can hold his Lil Wayne jewelry up. His sneakers are a brand I've never seen and perfectly unblemished. I have to believe he put them on in the car and then had his driver carry him into the school and plop him in the leather chair. He looks up to say *hello*, or so I think, but instead looks right through me and then bows his head again to the God of all things tech.

Mei finally looks up with a smile and a bit of life in her eyes; this feels promising. "When will we be done here? I want to go to the Apple Store and get iPads for my friends." She doesn't wait for my answer before reengaging with her phone. Her English is perfect.

I decide I'm no longer needed here, turn quickly on my kitten heels, and head out. Roan has handled tougher audiences than the Liu twins in my absence and I'm fully confident they won't break him. I have more pressing concerns like cleaning the living room before Dr. Golden comes over. If Aunt Viv finds out he stepped one foot in our apartment in its current condition, I'll be the next Bordelon to end up in the hospital.

I'm actually looking forward to Golden Boy stopping by. I don't particularly like a quiet house when my mind has free rein to contemplate all sorts of topics buried deep in my brain. Is gravity really going to take over after forty? Am I prepared to date now that Etta's leaving for college? How many more years can I tolerate working for Nan? Are there new trends in body hairstyling? Is the Brazilian still popular?

The doorbell buzzes and I take a last quick look around the apartment. It may not be Aunt Viv's military-standard clean, but I give myself a solid B.

"Wow. You really went out of your way to dress up for me," Dr. Golden says, giving me a quick bottom-up once-over. I look down at my sweats. Really? He didn't notice my fabulous outfit at his parent interview, but now he's become RuPaul on *Drag Race*?

"I didn't realize tonight was a formal affair," I clap back, nodding at Ty's wool charcoal pinstripe suit, crisp white shirt, and magenta-and-navy striped tie. Looking at this man, dressed up in a suit so beautiful there is no way he found it on a sale rack, I can't decide which Golden Boy is hotter: the athlete, the doctor, or the gentleman.

"Oh this old thing?" Ty gives me a mock look of surprise. "I had two hundred fifty cardiologists to impress at a conference today. I was one of the keynote speakers."

"I imagine that's a real fashionista crowd."

"Not a lot of fashion, but a whole lot of heart."

"I should shut the door on you for that corny-ass joke. Good thing I'm in a generous mood this evening and wouldn't mind a little company. Come on in."

Golden Boy fills out his suit as well from the backside as from the front. DANG! That Daniel is one lucky husband. I decide then and there I'll stretch waaaaaaaay out of my comfort zone this evening and casually ask Dr. Golden if he has any single, straight friends to set me up with. This is a limb I'm not sure I'm ready to step out onto, but it's not lost on me that I need to put an end to my celibacy streak and I would prefer to do it with someone as handsome as Dr. Golden.

"I brought a few things to help Aunt Viv start building some more muscle mass and flexibility. You know, start small, ten minutes a day, but even that can do wonders for her physical fitness over time. Then, once she's more fit, we can bump her up to thirty minutes a day, ideally with it happening in the school gym with real exercise equipment. End goal, we get her to an hour of exercise four to five times a week. Low impact, of course, but an hour is what we're going for." Ty pulls out a blue TheraBand and two purple five-pound hand weights from his oversized murse. "A wellness company was giving these away at the conference today and I thought maybe Aunt Viv would love them. Gives her a solid place to start building an honest exercise routine."

"There are a lot of things Aunt Viv would love," I barely squeak out, I'm laughing so hard, "but exercise equipment is nowhere on, near, or next to that list." I pick up the TheraBand and pretend I'm about to slingshot it across the room. Dr. Golden lunges to grab it from me and ends up chest bumping my chin. That man smells good even after a long day of talking to medical nerds.

"Come on, you don't know that, Josie. When Aunt Viv and I talked about diet and exercise at her follow-up appointment she was nodding *yes* the whole time. She told me she absolutely would change her habits, that she understands why it's necessary moving forward. She promised."

I wipe the tears of laughter pooled in the outside corners of my eyes. "She may have been shaking her head yes, but trust me, she was thinking no way, no how. How many seventy-year-old Southern black women do you see lifting weights, doing crunches, and munching fennel? I'll tell you how many, none. And I'll tell you why, 'cause it's hot as hell under a perfectly set wig. Aunt Viv's not buying into your white doctor voodoo woo-woo medicine. Not today, not ever. In her world there's nothing gumbo can't fix. But please, feel free to leave the goodies on the coffee table and I'll let you know how it all goes down, Boy Scout." I'm glad Dr. Golden came over tonight, I haven't had a big belly laugh in a good while. I might have to video Aunt Viv's reaction to her hand-delivered home gym equipment and send it to Dr. Golden for proof of non-compliance. Oh, I'm gonna have so much fun with this . . .

"I think you're underestimating your aunt Viv. She seems committed to me."

"Oh, she's definitely committed to you. That woman's got a mad teenage love crush on you, Golden Boy, that's for sure."

"The woman's got good taste in men, what can I say. And don't underestimate the power of love. She may be running with me on Chrissy Field before you know it."

"She don't love you that much," I assure Ty. I'm definitely sending his cocky self a video of Aunt Viv passing by her gifted home gym, paying it no mind.

"Speaking of love, what about you? I'm assuming no husband if you and Etta live with Aunt Viv. Do you have a fiancé or boyfriend or something?" Dr. Golden is looking around the room like I might be hiding a lover in the drapes.

"You assume right." Ohhhhh, here goes nothing. I'm stepping into the deep end. "I do a lot of things well, but my history shows dating is not one of them. And, um, you remember my friend, Lola? From the hospital?"

"Yeah." Ty is looking confused. I'm not sure I'm wading into this conversation quite right so screw it, I'm diving right in.

"Lola thought maybe you might know of a single doctor, or, I guess, really any colleague or friend you could set me up with." Now it's out there. And the world didn't end. I cringe in mock pain waiting for the answer.

"Why do you look like you're smelling expired milk?" I relax my face and open my eyes as my body temperature rises in embarrass-ment. I don't care how brave this is, it's beyond humiliating.

"I'm cringing that at my age my love life is so pathetic that I'm asking my aunt's cardiologist if he knows anyone he can set me up with. Since Michael, that's my ex, it's been me, Etta, and Aunt Viv—and our tight threesome has been enough. But Etta will be off to college in six months and Aunt Viv is getting older and her recent heart attack and . . ." What were tears of laughter two minutes ago morph into rolling tears of fear out of nowhere. Or really from some-where buried deep where I haven't been willing to go since I first saw Aunt Viv in the hospital bed. I'm pretty sure Dr. Golden is getting ready to run for the door.

"I think these tears call for alcohol. Can I check your fridge?"

"I don't really feel like a drink, thanks though." I push the heels of my hands against my eyes and breathe deep as I plop down on the couch.

"Okay, but is it alright if I grab one? Two hundred fifty cardiolo-gists and one hot mess of a woman is a lot for a guy to take on in one day. Give me two gulps and then we're going to get down to business talking about your future."

"Help yourself." While Dr. Golden's getting a beer I try to wipe my raccoon eyes off on my sweater. Turns out my mascara is water-proof. Score one for Revlon.

"Who's Michael?" is the first question Ty asks after downing half a beer in one gulp.

"I'm in tears because my aunt Viv could drop dead any moment, leaving me alone in this world—or at least alone in California—and you want the dirt on my ex-boyfriend? Good thing you didn't become a shrink, your priorities are whack."

"Josie." Golden Boy sets his beer down on the side table, unbut-tons his suit jacket, and sits down next to me on the couch. He picks up my hands and examines them for a moment before speaking.

"Aunt Viv is not dropping dead. If I have anything to say about it the only thing she'll be dropping is about twenty to twenty-five pounds."

"She'll definitely be dead before she does that. Tough to lose weight when you fry everything in lard and soak your Cheerios in buttermilk."

"As Viv's cardiologist, I really wish I didn't just hear you say that." Ty puts his hands over his ears and shakes his head. "Seriously though, Josie, why are you so worried that your aunt Viv is going to die? You see her every day. She's back at work, back to doing things with her friends." The genuine concern on Dr. Golden's face is reassuring. It seems he actually wants to help me sort through my tangled emotions.

"It's just, well, I already lost one mother when I was four. You would think twenty-six years later I would be strong enough to lose another, but I don't think I am. I'm not ready."

"Wait, I thought you were almost forty?"

"Okay fine, I'm not ready to lose another mother thirty-six years later, but who's counting, genius."

"Apparently you are, backward by ten." Ty chuckles and picks up his beer for another swig. "So your mom died when you were four and Aunt Viv raised you?"

"Kind of. My mom left me at Aunt Viv's front door and I haven't seen her since. She could be dead or she could be very much alive."

"Must have been something big for a mother to leave a beautiful child like you and trust someone else to raise her. I can't imagine." Golden Boy actually looks pained as he pictures a little girl left behind by her mother. He's probably thinking about Gracie and finding it unimaginable that he or Daniel would or could ever do that to her. There's something about how open he is to my history that I launch into details only three people in my world know.

"Well, since you're going all therapist on me, I actually don't know why my mother left me." I don't want to look Ty in the eye, so I start scratching at some gunk on his suit pant leg with my index finger.

"Your aunt Viv never told you?" Ty lifts my chin up with his thumb, so I have to look at him when I answer.

"Aunt Viv has never been willing to talk about it with me and over time I've gotten too scared to ask. It must have been something awful if Aunt Viv won't talk about it 'cause that woman will talk about anything. After all these years it's become the taboo topic in our family. Even Etta knows not to bring it up. Now it's a three-generation Bordelon secret." My body feels tired and heavy and I wish I could crawl over and curl up in Ty's lap. I have enough self-awareness to know that that's taking the doctor/patient's closest relative relationship too far, even for the Golden cardiologist.

"Secrets are exhausting to keep. Particularly family secrets," Ty says, looking like he's all too familiar with this topic. I wonder if it took him years to come out to his family. If maybe, even though he's a handsome, successful, kind doctor, his parents still struggle with his sexuality.

Ty's phone beeps in his pocket as if it knows I am ready for the attention to shift off me.

"Ugh, that's Daniel. I'm sorry to do this to you. I'd love to stay for a second beer, but I have to get going. It's my turn to pick up Gracie at gymnastics, or what I like to call the world's most expensive cartwheel." Ty stands and puts out his hand to pull me up. Just like at lunch in the Presidio, his hands feel warm and strong, like if he wraps them around you everything will be alright. I understand why Aunt Viv has put her faith in him as her doctor. "Oh, I almost forgot." In three large steps with his long legs he reaches into his bag and grabs the dumbbells and lines them up perfectly on the coffee table, laying the TheraBand over the top.

"Do you want to date a doctor?" Ty stops halfway to the door to ask. "I mean, they're kind of an egotistical, pain-in-the-butt, know-it-all bunch. And you're right, they got no swag."

"Sure, I guess I would. Hadn't really thought that deeply about it, but why not? Free medical advice." I can tell Ty is trying to brighten the mood before he leaves me alone in my apartment, so I follow his lead.

"Okay then, I'll see what I can do. I might know someone. He won't be as great as I am, but I promise he won't be sloppy seconds, either. Tell Aunt Viv I said hello and to get to work pumping iron." I can't help but wish my future blind doctor date will be just like Golden Boy.

"Yeah, I'll be sure to tell her. And I can assure you she will ignore me. But, so you know, your professional effort is filed away and appreciated. By both of us."

"I'll start with appreciation and in a few months you two will be fully idol worshiping me, you'll see."

"Noted. Now get out of here before Gracie is the last Simone Biles wannabe to be picked up at the gym." I shove Dr. Golden out the door, knowing how stressed Etta gets when she is the last girl standing at ballet.

I hear knocking at the door and quickly scan the room to see if Ty has forgotten anything before I open it. "Yes?"

"Next time, I want to hear about Michael. Don't think you glossed right over that topic without me noticing." Gays love gossip.

EIGHTEEN

MY DAY HAS PASSED IN RELATIVE EASE: NO STRESSING PAR-
ents or demanding Nan. But it's all about to go downhill fast because
the sand has run through the hourglass: I have to tell Aunt Viv about
the party. I decide to tell her the faux good news at the apartment. If
I tell her at school, she may get home before me and change the
locks. If I do it at home at least I'm assured a roof over my head for
another night.

I take the long route and walk from school through Golden Gate
Park to work out how I'm going to open a conversation that I know
Aunt Viv is going to immediately shut down. When I gave Etta the
keys to the car so she could drive herself and Poppy to dance, she
hugged me in the upper school hallway. IN FRONT OF HER
FRIENDS. I know this moment of fleeting parental kindness is going to include a stop at Starbucks for Venti Frappuccinos, a quick
shopping trip on Union Street, and texting at all the wrong times; it
was worth it to get some public affection from Etta after weeks of the
cold shoulder and one-word answers as we worked through college
applications. I remind Etta not to take her purse into Lululemon and

keep her hands out of her pockets. Etta knows what my reminder means without my having to explain it in front of her friends. The art of *public propriety* is a lesson all black boys and girls are taught at the feet of their parents if their mamas and daddies are worth a grain of salt. Don't give any shop owner reason to call the police. We may reside in progressive San Francisco, but we live in America and no one is going to go accusing my daughter of shoplifting. I don't want to have to hurt anybody for their sheer stupidity.

On my walk home, I stop in front of the De Young Museum. With my back to the copper wire tower, the De Young's signature statement, I stare across the park to the California Academy of Sciences. Aunt Viv and I used to love to take Etta to CAS on the day when admission was free. We would be in line first thing in the morning before the crazy crowds showed up, so we would feel like paying customers who come to the museum and don't have to jockey for a view. Every time, Etta made a beeline to the aquarium, the animal dioramas, and the planetarium. Aunt Viv and I would stand behind her and speculate what kind of scientist she would one day become: anthropologist, veterinarian, or epidemiologist. In those moments, I knew Aunt Viv used to do this exact same thing with me when I was young. I didn't fulfill her doctor dreams, but I felt confident Etta would with two strong women behind her, guiding her. When Etta was six it seemed her possibilities were endless. Though we haven't been to the Academy in years, I still hold on to wanting Etta's options to stay open. I want to know the scientist housed in that grown dancer's body still has a fighting chance.

I stop to see if the snack bar is open at Stowe Lake House. For some reason I'm craving a Drumstick ice cream cone, but no such luck—it closes at 5:00. I take this as a sign to get myself home to face Aunt Viv. Maybe she will surprise me and be excited about the party, but I doubt it.

My favorite things about San Francisco are the brightly painted

Victorian homes, which are a staple of the city's neighborhoods street after street. If a house were painted hot pink with lime green and white trim in Seattle or Chicago the neighbors would talk in hushed tones about the tackiness. In San Francisco, passing a turquoise and cranberry two-unit building makes you feel right at home.

With no ice cream to boost me up for going a few rounds with Aunt Viv, I need late-afternoon caffeine. I hop into one of the zillion coffee shops between the park and my apartment hoping they serve Blue Bottle coffee. That stuff is like rocket fuel to propel you through the worst of what might be comin' your way. The shop is packed, clumps of twos and threes huddled over laptops, talking at rapid speed, eager to think up, develop, expand, and then take public the newest, latest, and greatest tech company—in three years or less. And they can say it all started in a little coffee shop in the Richmond when they are interviewed by *Fast Company* magazine. I applaud the optimism that is a hallmark of the San Francisco professional's mentality, however, the millennial arrogance of thinking that at twenty-eight, post business school, you can take your idea from talk to tech in twenty-four hours or less grates on me. The Bay Area landscape is now littered with teens thinking they're failures because the business plans they developed in their after-school entrepreneurial clubs couldn't raise a seed round.

As I climb the front stairs to our second-floor unit I smile at the yellow door, our own contribution to the colorfulness that is San Francisco. It was Etta's choice. We promised her when she was seven that as soon as she could say "yellow" instead of "lellow" we would paint the door. In second grade when her front teeth corrected, and the pronunciation did, too, the three of us went to Ace Hardware on California Street, got ourselves a can of bumblebee-yellow paint, and went to town on the front door. I still love it.

"Aunt Viv, you home?" I yell, hearing shuffling coming from the back bedroom.

"Folding laundry in my room," Aunt Viv singsongs back. I can hear Zydeco faintly playing. Fifty years in San Francisco and she still holds fast to the iconic Bayou music of her childhood.

I drop my purse in the kitchen, take off my shoes, and spread my toes. A few deep breaths and I wonder if this is how sheep feel when they realize they are being led to slaughter. I grab a handful of pistachios from a bowl on the counter and head down the hall.

"Hey, baby, can you fold a few towels for me?" Aunt Viv leans in for a kiss. I grab a basket of towels. This lady doesn't know what's coming for her. "You have a good day? I picked up a meaty ham hock on my way home, gonna make us some soup with those navy beans I been soakin' since this morning. My bones need some warmin' from a chill I haven't been able to shake all day."

"Soup sounds great." I fold two towels perfectly and Aunt Viv gives me a nod for a job done to her satisfaction. "Aunt Viv, have you given any thought to how you want to celebrate your fifty years at Fairchild?" I ask as casually as possible while holding up a sheet between us to hide my terrified face.

"Good Lord willin' and the creek don't rise, I will celebrate with a fifty-first year at Fairchild. That's what I'll do." I knew at some point in this conversation a creek might be rising, I just didn't know it would happen so soon.

"Yeah, but I mean, don't you want to do something special to celebrate this year? Let's be honest, that school would have sunk into the Bay long ago if you hadn't been there for the last five decades holdin' it up." I'm working the flattery angle.

"Josie, you tryin' to make me sound old?" Aunt Viv purses her lips at me and places a hand on her hip. "I suppose it would be nice to go to the Mission and try out Alba Ray's with you and Etta and maybe Louise" (Aunt Viv's best friend slash nemesis from her card game). "Alba Ray's is s'posed to be good, though I'm not sure how 'cause I read somewhere that none of those boys who started the restaurant

are from Louisiana, so what can they really know about cookin' Cajun? You gotta be born with it in your soul. But, I've been craving me
some crawfish étouffée. You know I don't like cookin' crawfish at
home. Can't get rid of that stank for days."

"Well, that sounds nice, Aunt Viv. Etta and I can definitely take
you and Louise to Alba Ray's, but I was thinking a little bigger,
maybe something more along the lines of a party." I keep my voice
upbeat and cheerful, hopeful she will follow suit.

"A what?"

"You know, Aunt Viv, a party, a celebration, a reason to get dressed
up. Maybe something special at Fairchild. Invite families and alumni
from throughout your career who would love to honor you." As it
comes out of my mouth I know it sounds as bad as I think it does.

"Now why would I want to go prancin' around some Fairchild
party pretending to be fancy? Have you lost your mind? Ain't no one
wants to go celebratin' some old woman. I've just been making people
their lunch all these years; I wasn't savin' their lives."

"Ask any tired, hangry teenage boy at Fairchild and they'd probably say feeding them is saving their life."

"Don't go back-talking me, Josephine Bordelon. You live in my
house, you do as I say. There will be no party, you hear me straight?
You act like you don't know nothin' about me. I raised you, and as an
adult I can't get rid of ya'. You act like you don't know me at all.
Where has your common sense gone, child?"

This is going exactly as horribly as I was expecting it to. Time to
throw down the raw truth.

"Truth is, Aunt Viv, I was just being nice asking if you want a
party. There is going to be a party and there is nothing we can do
about it. Nan's been planning it since before winter break. She's calling it Viva la Viv. She's thinking a Miami nightclub kind of theme.
I'm afraid she thinks New Orleans and Miami are more or less the
same thing. I tried to talk her out of it, I really did, but she insists

and she's not backing down." There, it's out. I take two steps back just in case Aunt Viv comes out swinging.

"You tryin' to tell me that twig of a thing beat you? Please. I know when you tryin', Josephine, and I know when you're not tryin' hard enough. Whether there's a party or there's not I AIN'T GOIN'. And that's God's honest truth. A party—ridiculous. Now get out of my way. I gotta put this laundry away and talk myself out of wantin' to wring your neck." Aunt Viv snatches up the laundry basket and heads down the hall. I follow after her, a little miffed now that she didn't even give the party one split second of thought.

"Aunt Viv, did it ever occur to you that I did try to get Nan to back down from the party? That I tried to tell her you aren't exactly the celebrating type, that maybe she could try to think of a less public way to honor you? But she wants this party. She wants a reason to show off the school and her generosity and herself to decades of alumni. You are a convenient reason!" I realize this sounds harsh, and I take a moment to shift gears back to the rational. "At the end of the day, Aunt Viv, Nan's our boss and we've got to do what our boss tells us to do, and she's telling ME to make sure I get YOU to this party. I have college tuition to pay the next four years and it would be nice if you could retire someday soon and I could take care of the both of us. So you see, I CAN'T get fired because my stubborn old mule of an aunt refuses to show up at her own party!" I should have left the mule out of the conversation.

"I'm not gonna go, Josie, so you best figure out another way to keep your job. A party, what a waste of money. That school could use the money for the party I never asked for in the first place to help some child and his mama pay for a Fairchild education. That's what I would want to mark my fifty years at Fairchild, to help some mama get her child a good education. If anyone had even had an ounce of common courtesy to ask me what I want, that's what I would've told them."

Ouch. Yet again, Aunt Viv is right, on too many fronts. Why didn't Nan or I ask Aunt Viv what she wanted to commemorate her anniversary at the school back in September? Why was the only possible public recognition a party? The least I could have done is force Nan to ask Aunt Viv how she would like to commemorate fifty years. At her fingertips, Aunt Viv was able to come up with an idea that would contribute to the school community and not waste its financial resources on Grey Goose vodka and mediocre merlot.

"Damn, Aunt Viv, that's a great idea, that really is." Aunt Viv is looking right at me like *No shit, Sherlock.* "I'm sorry I didn't ask you directly how you would want to celebrate this milestone. I'm even more sorry I didn't work harder to get Nan to ask you directly. Your scholarship idea is so good that I promise to work on it. I want to make this happen for you. I will do everything I can to make this happen for you." I pause for a moment and reach out for Aunt Viv's hand to seal the promise. She reluctantly takes it and smooths the top of my hand with her other palm, forever the reassuring adult of our household. "But in the meantime there's still going to be a party and you're still going to have to g—"

"Aunt Viv, Aunt Viv, I got an audition at Juilliard!!!! You home? Did you hear me? I got an audition at Juilliard!!!!" Etta comes bounding up the front steps screaming at the top of her lungs. "Aunt Viv, they want me, they really want me! Can you believe it??!!" The front door slams and moments later Etta bursts into our conversation and flings her whole body over Aunt Viv. She doesn't even notice I'm there. Aunt Viv drops my hand to embrace Etta.

"How do you know, baby girl?" Aunt Viv asks Etta, the two of them jumping up and down in pure joy.

"There was an e-mail from the director of admissions, Ms. Sanchez or Santos or something like that, inviting me to come for a live audition on Monday, March 4. Can you believe it, Aunt Viv? Is this the best news ever or what?" As Etta and Aunt Viv embrace again, I catch tears streaming down Aunt Viv's face. She quickly wipes them away before Etta lets go a second time.

Etta finally notices I'm standing right there, the woman who gave her life. "Oh, hi, Mama. The car's parked right out front, can't believe I scored a prime parking spot. A live audition at Juilliard and I didn't have to circle the block five times to find parking, this is like a miracle day."

"I'm proud of you, Etta. You deserve that audition and they would have been idiots not to give it to you."

"Yeah, but you probably won't even let me go to the audition since Juilliard's not Ivy League," Etta says, throwing a knowing glance at Aunt Viv. That stings.

"Oh, trust me, she's gonna let you go," Aunt Viv pipes in.

"She is?" Etta doesn't even try to hide her surprise.

"Yes. You see, your mama and I were havin' a discussion before you came in that she needs me to attend a party I really don't want to go to, but she's gonna force me to go. That's okay, though, 'cause in exchange for me going to this party of hers your mama agreed that if you got an audition at Juilliard not only would you get to go, but the three of us would go to New York to make sure you have the best possible audition the good Lord grants you. Isn't that right, Josephine? Isn't that what we were just discussin' before Etta blew in like a hurricane rippin' through a cane field?"

"Well, that's not exactly how I remember the conversation, but there are a few small truths to what you're sayin'."

"I believe that's EXACTLY how the conversation was goin' if you want me to attend this party of yours, Josephine."

"Aunt Viv, it's not MY party, it's YOUR party that Nan is insisting on throwing for you."

"Oh and one more thing, Josephine, if there's going to be a party in my honor I want Dr. Golden there. If it weren't for him there would be no me to celebrate. Although if I die before this ridiculous party then I suppose I wouldn't have to go now, would I? But, since I don't really plan on dyin' I guess we're goin'. To the party AND to New York. You can bring Lola as your date."

"I thought Etta would be my date."

Grabbing Etta's hand, "No, Dr. Golden AND baby girl are my dates."

"Mama, we're sittin' here talking about a party where the three of us are going to be all dressed up and lookin' FIIIIIINE as all get-out and you thought you'd take me as your date? That's just . . . sad, Mama. Sad, sad, sad. Take a risk, Mama, find a date."

"Not Roan!" My clan yells at me in surround sound.

What's sad is that, once again, I'm the odd woman out in this threesome. And I'm the one stuck with the bill for our trip to New York. "Aunt Viv, how do you think we're going to pay for this Bordelon family vacation?" I ask pointedly, annoyed that my own aunt and daughter are expertly manhandling me.

"Oh, I imagine you'll figure that one out, Josephine. I trust you'll get that all laid out nice and neat if you know what's good for you," Aunt Viv says, caressing Etta's hand but looking directly at me with a steely stare. "Whew, all this party and trip takin' talk has got me kinda hungry. Etta, you want to walk with your aunt Viv to Allstar Donuts?"

"Mama, are we really all going to go to New York together?" Etta's excitement is on overload. This news has forced her to allow me to join in on their two-way family celebration.

"Sounds like we are," I say, not taking my eyes off Aunt Viv.

"Yes! Aunt Viv, let's go get apple fritters to celebrate! Can I tell you what I'm thinking about doing for my different dance pieces at the audition? I haven't been able to stop thinking about it since I opened the e-mail! I'm dying to tell someone, and you've seen everything I've done, so you can help me!" Etta is talking only in exclamation points. This is the happiest I've seen her since the stress of her Fairchild senior year began to ramp up in October. Admittedly, Etta's sheer joy is contagious, and I start to think a trip to New York with all three of us might be fun. That is, until I remember Aunt Viv's varsity, A-level, never-knew-she-had-it-in-her, devious negotiation skills.

"Hey, Aunt Viv," I call after her as she's putting on her jacket.

"Yes, Josephine."

"I'm telling Dr. Golden you're eating donuts and he's not going to be happy with you. This IS NOT part of your post–heart attack health plan." Jesus, what am I six?!?!

"Tattletale! You just concentrate on telling him to come to my party. And remember, if he can't come, deal's off. Can we bring you back a donut so you have something to nibble on while you find our flights? I ain't never been to New York and I can't wait to go. You think we'll have time to see a Broadway show or maybe those Rock-ettes?" Aunt Viv chitchats with Etta like schoolgirl besties as they head toward the door.

"Stop spending money we don't have!" I yell after them. How, in a matter of ten minutes, did this party I never wanted to happen, and Aunt Viv surely never wanted to attend, end up costing me a trip to New York? Is there any way I can expense our plane tickets to the party?

"While we're gone you need to stir the soup. And put some cream on those hands and elbows of yours, Josephine. Bordelon women don't do ashy. We don't want you embarrassin' us in New York, isn't that right, Etta?" I swear I detect Aunt Viv humming Frank Sinatra's "New York, New York" on the way out the door.

NINETEEN

THE HOUSE IS UP EARLY GETTING READY FOR OUR SATUR-
day. Aunt Viv has cards at Louise's house and I have my fifth Saturday of kindergarten visit dates at Fairchild. I reach past Aunt Viv for
my 32 oz. to-go cup and lid. She's singing Alicia Keys's "Empire State
of Mind" for what feels like the seventy-fifth time. Her anticipation
is endearing, but the tune is getting old. I grab a pear, give Aunt Viv
a little pat on the booty, and remind her to wake up Etta in time to
shower and study up for her Duke interview at noon. I dash out the
door into the San Francisco Indian summer that comes every mid- to
late-February—72 degrees and sunny. The whole city is in a good
mood.

I always settle into the chaos of visit-date-Saturdays with a half
hour to quietly read through e-mails in my office for anything last
minute or urgent (which usually means a panicked parent because
Junior woke up with a fever, and is it possible to reschedule otherwise Junior will end up in juvie, unemployable, then destitute and
living on the streets, and it will all be my fault). I send Etta a quick
text to make sure she's up.

JOSIE

What are you wearing for your interview?

8:32 A.M.

Nope. Can't send that. It's just begging for a snotty response from a teenage daughter.

DE-LEEEEEEEEEEEEEEEEEEEEEEEEEEEEEEEEEEEEE-TE.

Hope you slept well can't wait to hear about interview when I get home. Where is it again?

ETTA

Guy just texted moved it to 3 @ peets coffee in laurel village I could have slept in.

8:33 A.M.

JOSIE

K. I'll check in later. Love you. Go back to sleep.

8:33 A.M.

Perfect! I'll be done by three o'clock and I promised to swing by the grocery store for Aunt Viv, so I'll go to Cal-Mart and casually walk by Peet's and see if I can spot Etta. I know she's upheld her end of the college application bargain, but still I find myself worrying about her interview. One minute it's about her grooming, the next it's her test scores. Should she share her SATs since they're so good? A quick spy will calm my nerves. Nothing creepy or overbearing, of course. I won't introduce myself to Mr. Duke or share a few key facts about my intelligent daughter. I'm not that parent.

FROM: Yu Yan (Helen) Wu
DATE: February 16, 2019
SUBJECT: Liu Twins
TO: Josephine Bordelon

Dear Josephine,

I hope this e-mail finds you well. Mr. Liu has been waiting patiently to hear from Fairchild, per the twins' attendance. As you can imagine he is a very busy man and he would like to settle the acceptance and tuition payment for Mei and Bai as soon as possible. In your reply Mr. Liu would like to better understand why the tuition is so high as the school does not make a profit. He also asked me to share with you that he has had his assistant do research on the neighborhood where Fairchild is located, and it has come to his attention that the house next to the school is for sale. Mr. Liu is willing to buy the house for cash and lease it to Fairchild for market price, so the school can have more space for programming. The Liu's *ayi* told him that the school is "compact" and is in need of more buildings.

Additionally, Mr. Liu would like to know exactly how many sports and extra school activities per week Mei and Bai need to do when the family moves to San Francisco, so they will be appropriately groomed for Harvard acceptance. And if you could advise exactly what sports and what activities would be best that would greatly assist Mr. Liu.

A check for $73,000 is in the mail to cover tuition as well as a small gift to Fairchild for expediting the application and acceptance process. Please e-mail me when you receive the check, so I may officially inform Mr. Liu that the children are enrolled in school. Lastly, after you have spoken to the head of school please share with me if you would like Mr. Liu to buy the adjacent property and draw up a lease for Fairchild and the Liu Corporation to sign.

Thank you,
Yu Yan (Helen) Wu

EDUCATION CONSULTANT
ADMIT INTERNATIONAL, HONG KONG

Ugh, this is neither last-minute nor urgent, it's just annoying. Did Helen and the Lius not read the detailed instructions on how to apply to Fairchild as an international applicant? All acceptances, U.S. or foreign, are given on the same day and that day is not today. Plus, she wasn't joking with the small gift comment. Tuition is $36,400. The $200 Liu gift is not going to buy them any influence.

Today is dedicated to buying local—not imports. In ten minutes six of the most well-bribed rising kindergarteners in the Bay Area will be ushered by their parents across the Fairchild threshold for the finals of the private school admissions Olympics—the visit date with strangers. But, before I tear myself away from e-mail I indulge in a little wishful shade and peck out a reply to Helen.

FROM: Josephine Bordelon
DATE: February 16, 2019
SUBJECT: RE: Liu Twins
TO: Yu Yan (Helen) Wu

Dear Helen,

If I had a dollar for every time a parent wanted to buy us a mansion in exchange for admitting their kid to Fairchild I could damn near pay for my three plane tickets to New York City. But wait, I just reread your e-mail and Mr. Liu does not want to buy us a mansion he wants to buy himself yet another mansion and rent it back to us at ridiculous San Francisco market prices because one of his childrens' several nannies didn't like the looks of our campus. Please tell Mr. Liu to save his money; his children will need it to continue their personal passion to build the world's largest teen Louis Vuitton collection.

All my best,
Josie Bordelon

DIRECTOR OF ADMISSIONS
FAIRCHILD COUNTRY DAY SCHOOL

With my finger hovering over the keyboard I consider that this is one rant I really should send. I could send it in the vein of wanting to help the Lius become culturally competent in the ways of the American private school system. Or at least give a boost to Helen's education consulting business—you know, educator-to-educator, woman-to-woman. I've got to tell her this is not the way to go about getting your clients into top American schools and increasing your personal placement batting average.

"Are you a richist?" Roan has snuck up on me and helped himself to an eyeful.

"What's that?" I ask Roan after he finishes reading my e-mail. I want his opinion if I should send it, even though I know the answer.

"You know, it's like a racist, but you hate rich people."

I spray my coffee all over my keyboard. "How can I hate rich people, Roan? My body, mind and, soul revolve around fulfilling their greatest parenting fantasies."

204 · ALLI FRANK and ASHA YOUMANS

"Well, the dads' maybe."

"And a few butch moms." Both of us crumble into exhausted laughter. We have been working six days a week since winter break and it's starting to wear on our base-level humanity.

"Okay, got it. Message received."

DE-LEEEEEEEEEEEEEEEEEEEEEEEEEEEEEEEEEEEEEEE-TE.

Roan offers me his elbow. "Alrighty then, shall we go meet the six little wonders of the world and their momsters and fathers who are eagerly awaiting our arrival?" Moms always get a bad rap.

As we head into Fairchild's grand foyer to greet today's group of nervous parents and their offspring, it's nice that the first faces I see are Daniel's and Ty's. Holding hands between them, Gracie is a budding hipster in her skinny jeans, red Converse high tops, plaid shirt, and mini horn-rimmed glasses. Her helmet of brown curls clearly hasn't been touched in days. "Hi, my name's Gracie and my daddy says if I do everything you say and shake your hand nice he will buy me a pair of Uggs." I look up at Daniel who is rigid in disbelief that he's been outed in the first minute of the audition. I can tell Gracie and I are going to get along just fine. I like an honest woman. I reach out to shake her extended hand.

I brush by Ty and whisper through my classic admissions director grin while making eye contact with the gathered parents in the room, "After the visit date I need you to hang back a minute. I have a big favor to ask you. And before you even ask, no, the weights have not made it off the coffee table."

"I'm intrigued." He leans in to whisper back.

"Don't be," I say with a reassuring pat on his shoulder. It's as sculpted as I remember from our lunch at the vegan food truck.

In my opinion, the visit dates have always had a striking resemblance to horrific reality TV kid beauty pageants. Whoever's child can look the freshest, stay clean the longest, come across the smartest, and not completely melt down and show their true selves, wins.

There's a little boy sitting by himself in khakis and a mini blue blazer with a vintage Superman T-shirt peeking out. It looks as if the gold blazer button may pop at any moment from the pressure of his belly chub. He's glancing through Eric Carle's *The Very Hungry Caterpillar*, one of my personal favorites. From a distance I think I may be in love. As I get closer to introduce myself I know I recognize this little boy. Then his mother turns around.

"Good morning, Josie, and a most glorious New Year to you," Meredith says loudly, giving me an air kiss on each cheek. I know this move; she's trying to intimidate the other parents by acting chummy with me like we're lifelong family friends and she has a secret key to the Fairchild kingdom that no one else has. It's so admissions 2008. I do have to admit that Meredith is looking radiant from the inside out. She must have managed to get herself to an early morning yoga class, showered, juiced, and slipped into the Burberry quilted jacket that I've been coveting for years in the same amount of time it took me to get up, pour a vat of coffee, and make it to work.

"Nice to see you and Harrison. I see you're looking at one of my very favorite books," I say, turning away from Meredith to focus on my new little friend. Harrison beams me a smile and returns to his hungry caterpillar.

"Oh, he's most likely reading it, his tutor has him running phonic drills at home. Isn't it wonderful that you and Harrison already have so much in common, a love of the same literature." Meredith gives a forced laugh and I decide, out of common courtesy in a public space, to not tell her that all kids love *The Very Hungry Caterpillar*; that's why it's considered a classic.

I give Meredith a thumbs-up because I don't have words. I try to walk politely away when Meredith grabs me by the wrist. "Oh, and Christopher sends his regrets for not being here. Poor darling, it's just tearing him up inside that he's missing all the admissions fun. His flight out of Istanbul was canceled, but Harrison's education . . ."

"I know, Meredith, is of utmost importance to him. That's how all the parents here feel. In fact, it's how all the families who apply to Fairchild feel. Everyone wants the best for their son or daughter." Meredith gives me a slight "hmpf," perturbed that I have lumped her in with the rest of the parents. Or it could be that she's not used to someone who looks like me putting a woman who looks like her in her place.

Antonia Grimaldi is on the corner bench picking her nose and wiping it on her bite-sized cashmere sweater. Her father is reading out loud to her from the *Wall Street Journal*. Amani and Dev Shah are sitting on their mother's lap chewing something gummy. I go over and give Priya, the boys' mother, a big hug that includes the kids. The Shahs are a Fairchild family favorite. Their twin girls graduated from ninth grade last year and are now at Thatcher for boarding school. Priya calls her one-in-a-billion second set of twins her "happy mistake." Arjun calls them the party favors from a friend's over-the-top wedding in L.A. It seems silly to make them go through the whole Fairchild admission song and dance with Amani and Dev, but since the first set of twins are no longer at Fairchild the second set are not given sibling preference. True to the Shah family, Priya and Arjun don't mind doing the whole routine all over again. Clearly, it's all for show that the rules and protocols are 100 percent followed. Amani and Dev and Priya and Arjun are shoo-ins given their reputation for being completely normal, down-to-earth parents. Next to being a potential million-dollar donor, being normal, rational parents in an era of parenting through irrationality, will earn you a spot in any number of private schools. If more of the parents applying to Fairchild understood this fun little fact my job would be infinitely easier.

I know there is one more child who is supposed to be here for the 9:00 a.m. group. I look around the room and I spy two eyes peeking out from between her father's knees. Dad is trying to move her around to the front of him, but she's having none of it. I sit down on the floor right in front of Dad's kneecaps. My mystery student closes her eyes and rattles her cornrows back and forth signaling to me that she's not coming out. Dad tilts his head down and tells me her name's Ruby.

"Ruby, do you know that you are named after the most beautiful gemstone in the whole entire world?" The cornrows shake up and down with a rattle. I count a nonverbal "yes" as progress.

"Ruby red is such a beautiful color. It can be the color of a crayon, the color of a heart, the color of lipstick, the color of a big bouncy ball I have for us to play with in the gym."

"My little sister's name is Opal. It's an ugly color," says Dad's knees. I bite my lip to keep from laughing.

"Can you hold my hand and show me something in this room that looks like the color opal? I'm not sure what color that is." I slide my hands between Dad's knees, knowing he thinks I'm either a miracle worker or feeling him up. Ruby takes my hand and pushes her dad's legs apart to come out and greet me.

The emotions that wash over me when this milk chocolate bunny appears are startling. I'm suddenly transported to the day fourteen years ago when Etta and I sat in this exact foyer waiting for our kindergarten visit date to begin. It was her first of many auditions and Etta could sense my hopes and fears for our future. She refused to come out from under my skirt, so I had to walk with her and the other kids to the playroom like Mother Ginger in *The Nutcracker* since Etta was busy trying to crawl back into my womb. When we got to the playroom, I quickly lifted my skirt, flashed my underwear to the crowd of teachers, pushed Etta out, and ran for my life, shutting the door behind me before Etta could make a run for it. After that embarrassing display of parenting I figured at best we would be put on the waitlist and, at worst, the Fairchild director of admissions, who was soon to be my boss, would be calling CPS.

In the midst of all these new parents christening their children's educational journey today, it occurs to me that in a few short weeks Etta and I will be back where we started—trying out for admission to a highly selective school with rigorous standards and hundreds of applicants richer than us and perhaps more talented than Etta. We aren't going to New York for a Bordelon family vacation; we're going to try out for Etta's future. And even though I don't want Etta to go to Juilliard, if they judge my baby based on one performance and a few essays and she doesn't get in my heart will shatter and I will demand answers, if not someone's head served to me on a platter. From professional experience, I know that someone's head will be the director of admissions. As uncomfortable as it makes me to admit, I know I'm like every other overbearing and unbearable parent in this room. I shake my head and blink aggressively one, two, three times and pull myself back to my current reality, twelve little eyes staring eagerly at me.

"Ruby, Amani, Dev, Antonia, Gracie, and Harrison, can you come sit in a circle with me? Your big people will stay standing by the wall not far from you, but I would love it if you could come find a seat on the carpet with me, and I'm going to tell you about the fun we are going to have." Ever so slowly six children tentatively make their way from their parents to the circle. Harrison is the last one to arrive, finding it difficult to part with his book.

"Today you're going to follow me and my friend Roan to a room that has all sorts of toys in it and a few more super fun grown-ups. In that room you are going to get the chance to do lots of interesting things with letters and numbers and drawing and blocks, and there will be some surprise toys, too. Then Roan will read you a story, and finally you will get to go outside and into the gym and run around and be silly. While you are having so much fun I get to spend some time talking with your parents in a big-people room. But I promise you, your parents are not far away, in fact, when you are on the playground if you look up I bet you will be able to see us in the window! How does that sound?"

Five heads nod okay, Gracie looks a bit like a deer in the head-lights.

"So, before we take you all over to the playroom, does anyone have a question they would like to ask? I want to make sure everyone feels comfortable with the plan and the adventure we are all about to have."

Amani raises his hand.

"Yes, Amani?"

"Ummm, when you're playing on the slide and it's cold outside does your pee pee tickle?"

And just like that, in thirteen years of doing this job I can still be asked a question I would have never thought of in a million years.

"Why yes it does, Amani. It really does." It's always best not to argue with a five-year-old and I'm pretty sure none of these parents are looking for me to launch into an anatomy lesson. Amani seems satisfied with my answer.

As I lead the line of kids from the foyer over one building to the playroom I feel a small hand slip into mine. I look down and see Ruby gazing up at me. I smile, and we hold hands in silence the rest of the way to make sure everyone concentrates on walking. I haven't had a broken bone or a lawsuit at an admission visit date yet and I'm not about to start now.

When we get in the room, I tell all the kids to take off their jackets and hang them on the hooks. Roan quietly shuts the door, not wanting to startle the kids into thinking they have been locked in a kid clink. Ruby refuses to let go of my hand. She pulls two times on it and wiggles the index finger of her free hand signaling me to bend down. "I don't have a mommy." I take a moment to process this in-formation. I don't want to say the wrong thing.

"There's another thing we have in common. We both think the

color Ruby is beautiful, and I don't have a mommy, either." Ruby's eyes light up with surprise.

"Is your mommy up in the clouds watching you, too?" Ruby's same index finger points to the ceiling.

"Your mommy gets to watch you every minute of every day? That's a lucky mommy." I'm willing tears not to start trickling.

"That's what my daddy says, too, but I sure wish my mommy could be here to watch me."

"I bet she wishes that, too, baby. Wouldn't she be so proud to see you being a big girl at a school visit date?"

"My mommy and daddy used to make funny noises in their bedroom. Did your mommy and daddy do that?"

"Yes, at some point they certainly did."

"Help, Josie, we got a runner!" Roan yells and dashes through a now-open playroom door. For all his baby chub, Harrison certainly is lightning-fast.

After the visit, I get an almond milk chai latte from the Starbucks at the opposite end of Laurel Village from Peet's Coffee. Groceries are in the car and it's 3:08. I'm just going to do a quick walk by the oversized windows of Peet's Coffee on my way to the Wells Fargo cash machine next door. I legitimately need cash, sort of. Etta better be well dressed, no leotards. I'm hoping Aunt Viv was home to give her a once-over.

I pull a baseball hat from my purse and put on my oversized sunglasses. A believable disguise for a sunny day. I pick up the pace as I near Peet's, ready to move swiftly but staring with laser focus. Turns out I don't have to look too hard. Etta is sitting at the window counter with a white man much older than she, who I assume is doing the interview. I guess, for some reason I can't quite put my finger on, I thought a black alumnus would interview Etta. If for no other reason than to prove that it's not only white folks or black athletes who end up at Duke. I crouch down quickly so I'm below Etta's eyesight level, but I'm intrigued by who this older gentleman is. I back up, cross California Street, walk one block down toward the Jewish Community Center, then cross back over to the same side of the street as Peet's so I can see Etta in her interview from the opposite view. As I approach the front door to the coffee shop I rip off my glasses in disbelief. Etta, is indeed having coffee with an older gentleman—JEAN GEORGES! I don't even take a momentary pause to cool down the mom fire that has been lit. I throw open the door and in six swift steps I'm standing between Etta and Jean Georges, surprisingly unable to say anything I'm so angry.

"Josie," Jean Georges says in a measured, nonplussed tone. Etta ceases to blink.

"I know why you're here, Etta, or at least I thought I did. What I don't know is why you're here with Jean Georges. What I'm hoping is that it's mere coincidence you two ran into each other here, at the exact time you're supposed to be having an interview for Duke. And the second part of that story best be that your interviewer texted and he's running late. Is that what you want to tell me, Etta?" I'm flexing my hands together behind my back to keep my fingers from wringing Etta's neck.

"Mama, why are you here?!?!?" Etta whines through clenched teeth.

"I was at Cal-Mart picking up some groceries for Aunt Viv, as I promised her I would do. And as you know, Bordelon women follow through on their promises to their family members. And then I realized I needed some cash." I'm definitely relieved I had my cover story worked out beforehand. It holds serious weight in the middle of this sting operation. "So tell me, is your interviewer early or late?" Silence.

"EARLY OR LATE, ROSETTA FAYE BORDELON?"

"There's no interview." Etta says, barely audible, not meeting my eyes.

"Come again? 'There's no interview,' why not?"

"I canceled it." I take a big, deep breath at this news I was not expecting from my rule-following, perfection-seeking daughter. Peet's is a small coffee shop with not-so-great acoustics, so if I lose my shit and start screaming it will certainly reverberate off the walls.

"You better pray to God that I think the reason you canceled that interview is a good one. You have ten seconds to convince me. Go."

"I wanted to review my performance choices for my Juilliard audition with Director Martin and this was the only time he could do it this week."

I hold my hand up and take a step back. "I need a moment to process without any more information input." Silence hangs in the air, again. "Just so I'm perfectly clear, there is no Duke interview."

"Umm-hum."

"What was that. I can't hear you."

Etta replies in a small voice, "Yes, that's right Mama, but I still have a chance of getting in. The interviews aren't required, they're optional."

"Oh, yes, I know. BUT any student who WANTS to go to Duke does everything in their power to make sure they have an alumni interview. Only uninterested, unqualified applicants are stupid enough not to have an interview." At this point I need to calm myself down, 'cause I'm getting heated. "It's called 'building your admissions case,' of which you now have none. So now you have not only disqualified yourself from any kind of early college action or decision due to your juvenile first round of essays, but now we can also cross Duke off your college list."

"I never put Duke on the list, you did."

"Excuse me?" My voice is rising, again. I'm no longer accountable for what may happen.

"She said it was you, not her, who put Duke on her college list," Jean Georges offers snidely.

"Director Martin, yet again, you've offered unsolicited counsel to our family. This coffee date is over. Etta, get your backpack, we're heading home to review how you have successfully managed, before even graduating from high school, to narrow your life choices. That's something even I didn't do." I swivel my neck to glare at my next target. "And you, Director Martin, go find another ballet protégé to lead astray 'cause I swear I've never laid hands on a soul in my life . . . don't you be the first."

"*Au revoir*, Etta," Jean Georges says, standing to pick up his fedora and meticulously place it on his head. "Her ballet arrangement for Juilliard is incredible, Josie. Just remember, it's human nature to put effort into the things we really care about, the things we really want. Be the mother who knows what's best for her daughter because she knows who her daughter is down deep in her core and what it is she wants most out of life." Swiftly Jean Georges pivots on his toes and heads out the door, leaving me with my lying teenage prima ballerina.

Etta would have looked so good in Blue Devil blue.

TWENTY

FROM: Josephine Bordelon
DATE: February 18, 2019
SUBJECT: My aunt, Vivian Bordelon
TO: Beatrice Pembrook

Dear Beatrice,

I hope this e-mail finds you happy and healthy and enjoying our beautiful weather. If I remember correctly, Dash finished law school and is now working in Boston. He must be enjoying the city; it's a fun place to be in your twenties.

I'm not sure if you've heard, but my aunt Viv is celebrating her 50th year at Fairchild School. While Nan has been kind enough to plan the Viva la Viv party for her (I hope you and Ethan will be able to make it), there's one specific thing Aunt Viv would like most to commemorate her fifty years at the school.

I looked at Aunt Viv's finances and between the two of us we can put together $1,000 a year to contribute to a Vivian Bordelon tuition assistance scholarship to support a single parent who is applying their rising kindergartener to Fairchild. The school was so generous to Aunt Viv when she was raising me. Then, a generation later, the school stepped up and has been equally kind as Aunt Viv and I have raised Etta. Aunt Viv would like to pay it forward to another parent who is working hard to do it all on their own and wants to provide an education of a lifetime for their child. I am hoping to start the Vivian Bordelon Scholarship.

One thousand dollars a year is not going to make much headway in a tuition payment. I'm writing to ask, with great humility as I know you have already been overly generous with Fairchild, if you would be willing to do any sort of match with us to help me bring Aunt Viv's scholarship closer to life. Again, I know this is an unusual ask and one that under other circumstances would come from the head of school, but given that this is my aunt Viv, I would like to establish the scholarship myself.

This is a surprise to reveal to my aunt Viv at her party so please keep my request between the two of us. I thank you for considering a $1,000 matching donation and if you are unable to make a gift at this time but have some advice on how I may go forward trying to build the Vivian Bordelon Scholarship, I would greatly appreciate it.

Warm regards,
Josie Bordelon

DIRECTOR OF ADMISSIONS
FAIRCHILD COUNTRY DAY SCHOOL

My finger hovers over the send icon knowing when Nan gets wind of me going around her to ask Beatrice Pembrook to fund a scholarship in honor of Aunt Viv, she's going to hit the roof. Nan is the monarch of our small nation, but all the buildings and portraits occupying her land feature men who have instrumentally forwarded the mission of the school. NEVER would Nan allow the first female publicly named anything on the Fairchild campus be for a woman other than herself, particularly not for a cook. Her story will be one of a woman who played with the big boys at Fairchild—and won. If I hit send, Nan will see my e-mail as a complete and total act of insubordination and toying with her legacy. If I don't hit send, Aunt Viv will think I was blowin' smoke at her request. It's an ugly choice either way.

Send.

I mumble a small prayer, asking whoever is up there listening to make sure Nan doesn't learn about the scholarship before the one minute she has allotted for my remarks at Aunt Viv's party. Fifty-nine seconds is long enough to present Aunt Viv with the surprise scholarship as long as I talk quickly and take minimal breaths.

Nan has made it clear since the beginning of her tenure that only she and the director of development can approach the monied families of Fairchild to ask for cash to fund a project. And if it's the director of development who does the bidding, Nan still gets credit. Nan has always held the Fairchild purse strings tight and I imagine Beatrice is on her short personal ask list for her STEAMS program or maybe an unnamed TBD legacy project like a Gooding Art Gallery. I know if the Vivian Bordelon Scholarship takes a dime from any Nan initiative I'm toast at Fairchild. Hell, I may be toast at the school simply for not telling Nan that I'm doing this, but if I don't get the scholarship up and running as I promised Aunt Viv, I'm toast at home. Rock, meet hard place.

I'm momentarily drunk with power from sending one e-mail. I'm sick of Nan man-, well, woman-handling commemorating Aunt Viv's fifty years of dedication to Fairchild when she has only been around a small fraction of that time. Really, I'm just sick of Nan and her disregard for the hard work of everyone at Fairchild. Yes, me included. I want ownership back over the Bordelon destiny. I want . . .

Ding. Shit! Is that Nan already? How does she know?

> TY
>
> I swear I was intrigued by your mystery favor yesterday, but my beeper went off and I had to head to the hospital immediately. What can someone like me do for someone like you?
>
> 2:42 P.M.

Whew, not Nan. I wasn't quite ready to text fight with her so soon. Plus, what am I crazy? She's not Oz. How would she know about my e-mail to Beatrice in twenty seconds or less?

> JOSIE
>
> You know you could make some serious money teaching straight men how to text flirt? Might even be able to give up that lame doctor gig you got going on.
>
> 2:44 P.M.

> TY
>
> But then what would I do with all that extra sleep I'd be getting? My body would be confused if it weren't in a perpetual state of stress and exhaustion.
>
> 2:46 P.M.

JOSIE

Well now I feel guilty asking you my favor since you're so busy making the world a better place . . . but here goes. Fairchild is throwing a big party for my aunt Viv who has worked at the school for fifty years. She hates parties, so you can imagine how thrilled she was when I told her about it. After a rough round of Josie-bashing Aunt Viv agreed to go if you were invited and you agreed to show up.

2:49 P.M.

TY

Are you asking me out on a date?

2:50 P.M.

JOSIE

No, Aunt Viv is.

2:50 P.M.

TY

You're going to be there though, right?

2:51 P.M.

JOSIE

Yes, of course. Aunt Viv will make sure I suffer alongside her or she'll make me the coat check girl; not sure which one.

2:51 P.M.

TY

> **Then I'll be there. Gotta go—someone's heart just fell out of their chest.**

2:52 P.M.

Ty really does give good text, lucky Daniel. Back to e-mail. Ohhh, look at that, Nan's not online, but Beatrice is.

FROM: Beatrice Pembrook
DATE: February 18, 2019
SUBJECT: RE: My aunt, Vivian Bordelon
TO: Josephine Bordelon

- -

Dear Josie,

I feel so privileged that you thought to ask me to join you in supporting the Vivian Bordelon Scholarship. When I was a child my mother was traveling all the time and your aunt Viv acted as the mother I never really had. She made sure I had treats to bring to my class when it was my birthday and she came to all my school band concerts (which, trust me, was an act of love because I was a terrible flute player). She was even the one to take me to the dentist when I knocked my two front teeth out climbing the jungle gym. My own mother was in Morocco, but Viv was right there holding my hand.

Is $30,000 a year enough or would you rather do $35,000? I'm not sure what tuition is these days. Whatever is necessary to make this happen, let's do it and do it right.

With much appreciation for being included,
Beatrice

I run a victory lap around the kitchen table, raisin' the roof. Aunt Viv is going to bust a gut when I present her with the Vivian Bordelon Scholarship at Viva la Viv. Who's the master negotiator now, Aunt Viv? Me, that's who! Well, I really didn't have to negotiate much to make this happen. Okay, I didn't have to negotiate at all. Beatrice Pembrook is, in fact, the gem that Meredith Lawton rambles on and on about, I have to give her that. I push to the back of my brain how I'm going to need to explain this to Nan when her permanent lockjaw drops to the floor at the party. Instead I call Lola. The Nan conundrum can wait for another day.

MONDAY MORNINGS ARE MY DROP-OFF DUTY AT FAIRCHILD. I enjoy standing in front of the school welcoming students to a new week as they tumble out of their Teslas. As I walk through the grand foyer to the front doors this Monday morning, I see Nan slipping into her office. I pop my head in uninvited and unannounced by Elsamyassistant. Early this morning after an extra-large cup of inspirational coffee I decided I'm going to bury Nan in kindness and compliments in the days leading up to the party. If I'm on my best behavior now, perhaps there's a chance she won't go ballistic on me later when she finds out about the scholarship in front of the Fairchild community. That's all I got for a viable Nan-handling strategy, so now is as good a time as any to kick it off.

"Hey, Nan, I'm heading out front for drop-off duty, you want to tag along with me?"

"Wha—!" I startle Nan unintentionally. "Did Elsamyassistant tell you to come in unannounced?" Nan asks flustered as she sets her weekly peonies arrangement down on her desk. "I need to talk with her about protocol. She's been particularly loose on her duties as of late."

"Elsa isn't out front, Nan, I just thought you might like to come say hello to some students with me. Come on, hanging out with the kids is the best way to start a Monday morning." Already the hard work of being fake nice is exhausting me.

"Well, I don't know, there's so much for me to do here . . ."

"If you come with me I'll tell you what I found out about the valuation of the Stuarts' company. Remember, they're on your acceptance list."

"I just knew I picked the right families for next year! I swear I have a sixth sense for who will truly be able to help Fairchild become the best day school in America." Nan bangs her fist on her desk, the exclamation point to her perceived personal triumph.

"Let's go, I'll give you all the juice out front." Not even the strongest of educators can resist a little gossip; Nan concedes.

"Alright, ten minutes, but then I must catch up with Elsamyassistant to review my hectic week."

Nan and I push open the heavy eighteenth-century bronze double doors that serve as the main entry into Fairchild Country Day. Originally a mansion from the Gold Rush, as the school grew, Dr. Pearson did a beautiful job adding modern wings to the historic home. Nan likes to trash talk the multiple renovations Dr. Pearson did, but *Architectural Digest* has twice written articles that beg to differ.

"Good morning, Annie, have a great day at school! Myles, I can't wait to see your presentation on Islamic art. Sean, how'd the lacrosse tournament go this weekend?" Nan watches as I greet each of the children who stumble over growing feet in a rush to embrace best friends, and hustle along the stragglers who are taking their own sweet time getting to their classrooms.

"You seem to know a lot about these children," Nan states—an observation more than a compliment.

"For me, that's the fun of working in a school, being around the kids and learning all about who they are. Kids are pretty hilarious and entertaining." How you become a head of school if you don't enjoy the company of children is beyond me. Nan shifts uncomfortably in her Ferragamos.

"I prefer to focus on the parents. Now, tell me, what is it that you know about the sale of the Stuart company that I don't?"

"Give it a try, Nan, chat up one student for kicks and giggles and then I'll give you all the intel, promise." I can almost see dollar signs in her irises.

"Fine. I think I recognize these two girls coming up the stairs now. Good morning, ladies, I trust that you slept well, had a good breakfast, and are ready to work hard today?" Nan smiles tersely, keeping her distance, so it's understood there will be no physical contact.

"Nan, this is my daughter, Etta, and her best friend, Poppy. They've been here since kindergarten."

"Oh, yes, well, I knew I recognized her," Nan strains out, nodding to the three of us. "Now, back inside, Josie, so we can talk. Can't waste time chitchatting on the front steps of school all day, can we?"

"I'm right behind you, Nan." I shake my head in defeat.

"Mama, when I leave next year I don't wanna hear on *TMZ* about some crazy lady who offed her boss and tossed her in the Bay. If I do, I'll know it's you," Etta warns me, even though she knows she isn't exactly at the top of my favorite people list right now, either.

"Yes, well, I can't make any promises."

TWENTY-ONE

IT'S THE END OF FEBRUARY, THE HOMESTRETCH OF ADMIS-
sions season and I'm exhausted. "I can't take it anymore. The kids are
too cute and the parents too absurd," I confess to Roan, thunking my
head on a pile of admission files. I'm sick of looking at the four walls
of this conference room, and the roof of my mouth is raw from an
excessive amount of cinnamon gummy bears. "What happened to a
family trip being camping in Yosemite where the biggest excitement
is someone getting carsick on the way down?"

"It was swapped for hot-air balloon rides over the Serengeti or
master junior chef pasta classes in Tuscany," Roan lobs back, only
half paying attention to my mouth ailment and to me.

"I can't even spell Serengeti," I huff. Why's Roan not playing
along with my superficial rage at the good fortune of others?

"Okay I've gone through this pile of twenty-five applicants and
here are my seven acceptances." Roan hands them over to me and
then stands to twist and stretch his back. The committee has nar-
rowed it down to one hundred admissible children. Roan and I flip
through the files as I have the final, final jurisdiction.

"Ummm, Roan, we can't have a class solely comprised of budding Mr. and Miss Americas. Is there substance behind the surface of these seven Gap Kids models?"

"Between the seven of them they speak eleven languages, practice four religions, play five instruments, were born in three different countries, know how to share and touch their toes, all can wipe themselves, one is a Taurus—go bulls—and three of them gave me compliments on my shoes during their visit dates. Oh, and only one has a mom we red flagged, but I think she travels a lot for work so it's worth the risk."

"Excellent work, Colonel Mustard. Did you find these applicants in the library with the candlestick?"

"HA, Ms. Scarlet! Don't be a hater 'cause you lost the game."

"Alright, put them in the acceptance pile with Harrison Lawton, Antonia Grimaldi, and the Shah twins. Oh, and Ruby Vassar. She will be a nice calm energy to balance out the Joan Rivers–meets–Amy Schumer–wannabe I noticed you have in the *yes* pile. What about Gracie Golden? She must be in your pile; she's not in mine."

"I don't know. She really didn't interact with any of the other kids, kept to herself, and refused to share the dinosaurs. And she wasn't much interested in working with the teachers at the math and reading stations. Oh, and look in her file at her self-portrait." Before I can grab the file, Roan pulls the drawing out for me.

I snort laugh so hard my Diet Coke stings my nostrils. In front of me are two big pink nipples and an oddly anatomically correct drawing of a vagina. Clearly Gracie has a doctor for a father who has already explained the importance of these unique attributes of the female body. "Well, she certainly knows she's a girl. And, I might say, possesses a passion for biology and anatomy."

"You know she's going to be the one in third grade spreading all the wrong rumors about where babies come from." I look a little more closely at the picture.

"Yeah, I can see that. But I don't think she'll be the downer ruining Christmas for all the kids by sharing Santa's a fraud."

"I always hate that kid."

"Me, too. But every class has a holiday downer, plus, our acceptance pile is a growing list of heteros. As you like to remind me, we need a little more Roan fairy dust sprinkled in this place."

"That we do, Josie. Gracie, welcome to Fairchild Country Day School." Roan slams Gracie's application on top of the *yes* pile and does his version of a touchdown dance which looks more like the closing number of *A Chorus Line*.

• • •

LOLA

What are you wearing to Aunt Viv's ball?

1:02 P.M.

JOSIE

Don't call it a ball. I have no clue. You want to swap champagne for shopping today?

1:03 P.M.

LOLA

Aren't you a Cinderella buzzkill. How about I grab two empty water bottles from the sports store that is my front closet, snag a bottle of champagne at the liquor store on my way to get you and we drink while we shop? Now that, my friend, is how you find a dress.

1:03 P.M.

JOSIE

Your brilliance is inspiring.

1:04 P.M.

LOLA

That's what my first graders say. C U after school.

1:05 P.M.

Lola and I meet at Bloomingdale's in the Westfield San Francisco Centre mall. If it's a bust, then Nordstrom is right around the corner.

"Roan's on call. He doesn't want either of us to buy anything until we have snapped a picture, sent it to him, and he has given his blessing. And we can't take a picture under the horrid fluorescent lights in the dressing room. He wants us to go out onto the sales floor and take it. He says more everyday light. Dressing room light is designed to highlight all tragic flaws as well as some we don't even know we have."

"I prefer to call them battle scars," Lola says, craning her neck to see her backside in a three-way mirror.

"My life is littered with those," I mumble as I attempt to slip on a dress that doesn't even make it past my rack.

"Josie, when is your body going to drop like the rest of us? I should have had my babies in my early twenties, too. When number three is born at thirty-seven nothing is ever the same again," Lola says, speaking more to her naked boobs than to me as she attempts to lift them up to her clavicle.

"Maybe if you stopped wearing your saggy nursing bra that is two years past its expiration date your girls would reclaim their proper place. Or at least they might with a little help from a new friend called underwire."

"You're so right. I'd forgotten bras are actually supposed to hook in the back, not the front. I suppose if my baby is old enough to crack open a can of Coke it's time to buy some new bras. Do you think Roan wants final approval on my boulder holders, too?"

In less than two hours we manage to rebuild Lola's lingerie collection and find her a black sheath dress that skims her thick thighs in all the right places and a pair of black strappy sandals with costume amethyst–encrusted buckles. I swear Roan had a tear in his eye he was so proud of Lola and her ability to purchase something that did not come in denim or was "boyfriend" cut.

Our water bottles of champagne have run dry and so has my patience for finding something for myself. I'm heading home empty-handed. As we walk past Saks Fifth Avenue to meet Nic and the boys for dinner at Sears Fine Foods (the deviled eggs are so delicious even Aunt Viv travels from the comfort of her own kitchen for them), my dress is waving at me from the window. Literally. A saleswoman taking the mannequin down stopped and waved at me as I walked by before she tucked the mannequin under her arm and headed to who knows where. But wherever she was heading she was carrying my dress because you know who looks good in orange? This woman. And I'm not talking the fruit or bad seventies shag carpet orange. I'm talking the orange that is so rich you've only seen it in pictures of Tibetan monks in their prayer robes or on jeweled crowns worn by royal families. Black women are who those orange dresses are made for. And when I say *black women* I mean those like Aunt Viv and me—even with some white blood coursing through our DNA—our black runs so dark it absorbs all the colors of the rainbow and, damn, do we wear it well.

I peel off so quickly Lola's suddenly standing solo on the corner. I knock on the glass from inside the Saks door as Lola startles then follows me in. My dress is heading up the escalator and we hop on to rescue it. I jump off at the top and sprint to catch the saleswoman. Those quick twitch track muscles occasionally still come in handy.

"Excuse me, miss, where are you taking that dress?" I ask, stopping the saleswoman by pulling the mannequin's hand.

"Oh, hi, yes, um it's time to switch out the windows and, frankly, we haven't had the best luck selling this dress. It's a rare woman who can pull it off. The cut is quite low in the front, it takes a certain décolletage."

"Have you met this rare specimen of a woman who I am lucky enough to call my best friend?" Lola chimes in, reaching over my shoulders to cup my breasts. I smile because the best feeling in the world is having someone in your corner, telling the world you are perfect even when you both know you're not. Though I could have done without the public fondling.

"Do you want to try it on?" the saleswoman asks hopefully.

"What size is it?"

"It's a size four, but runs quite long."

"Don't need to try it on, I'll take it."

"Wait. Should we FaceTime Roan before you hand over your credit card?" Lola grabs my arm before I can reach for my wallet.

"No, I got this. I know magic when I see it."

ETTA HANDS ME A SMALL ENVELOPE AT DINNER. I SHOVE IT in my purse to look at later. It's probably from Poppy's mom, who writes me thank-you notes for every minuscule nice thing we do for Poppy. Last month she wrote me four paragraphs on my limitless kindness after I had Poppy spend the weekend with us so her mom could go visit her sister's new baby. I didn't have the heart to tell her the girls watched too much Netflix and ate a whole tube of raw cookie dough between dance rehearsals.

Hopping in bed that night I remember the letter and grab it out of my purse. The off-white envelope has no writing on it, nor is there a picture on the front of the card. The handwriting inside is beautiful and I turn it over to see who it's from before I read the message. Jean Georges. I pause and blow out a huge puff of air. Do I really want to end this successful day on a sour note? I know Etta will ask about the letter in the morning so better to ruin the end of this day than ruin the start of tomorrow.

Dear Josie,

Even though we both work in schools I know we don't see eye-to-eye on what makes for an exceptional education. I can't imagine a life without art. You can't imagine a life without professional success. One thing we can agree on is that Etta is capable of both. Thank you for allowing her to audition for Juilliard and giving a life of art a chance. I'm hoping I've misjudged you all these years.

Jean Georges

I'm speechless. I flip the card over a few times looking to see if there's a passive-aggressive, or plain ol' aggressive, jab hiding somewhere. Nope. 97 percent sincerity, 3 percent shade. I certainly didn't see that coming. Maybe the magic of my dress is already spreading good juju from the hanging bag in the corner.

"I'M COMING, I'M COMING!" I YELL AT THE DOORBELL, AS-suming Aunt Viv's locked herself out and after all these years I can finally catch her in the act of heading to Allstar Donuts before dawn. A thirteen-year truth about to be revealed.

"Meredith, it's Wednesday at six-thirty in the morning. WHAT are you doing at my house? Wait—how do you even know where I live?!?!" I'm standing in front of one of the biggest prospective parents and donors Fairchild has ever known in pajama bottoms with Michelle Obama faces all over them and a skimpy Target tank top. My eyes are crusted over and still half asleep, but at least I have the wherewithal to cross my arms over my chest as my nipples turn hard from the blast of early morning cold air coming through the front door.

Meredith ignores both of my questions. "I need to talk to you, Josie, I'm desperate." She pushes past me to come inside. Her determination and disregard for social protocol shake me awake. I take in not the Meredith Lawton I have come to know but a Meredith Lawton who more resembles how the other 99.99 percent of mothers live. Her hair is disheveled and her breath is stank. Her pristine white T-shirt has coffee dribbled down the front and I see a hint of leftover red lipstick in the creases of her lips. Imperfect as all get out. This is the first time I feel like we are the same gender let alone that I could possibly, one day, maybe, like this very real person who stands before me.

"Do the three of you actually live in a place this small?" Meredith asks from the center of our living room that I have always described as "oversized" for a two-unit Victorian. And just like that, my capacity to embrace Meredith, flaws and all, has died. I choose not to acknowledge her question with an answer.

"Why are you here, Meredith? We could have met at school in daylight. I always make time for potential parents during working hours."

"It's all fallen apart, Josie. Randy gave his two-week notice last night. Harrison's scores from the educational psychologist came yesterday and they are . . ." Meredith looks like she's choking, and I grab the back of a chair ready to Heimlich her if I have to, "his scores are in the average range. Can you believe it? The shock of it nearly sent me into a tailspin, but luckily my meditation guru was willing to talk to me from his retreat center in Goa. He's on a fourteen-day talking cleanse, but for me he was willing to break his vow of silence. He knows an emergency when he hears one. Then, when I finally get off the phone with him once my energy has calmed and my chakras have realigned, Christopher sashays into my sanctuary and flippantly announces he can't make it to Viv's party this weekend. He cancels on the party as casually as he cancels his daily session with his trainer. When I lost it he merely shrugged and said, 'No harm, no foul.' But I informed him with every decibel I could muster that his actions are indeed harmful to Harrison's future!" Meredith flops on the couch, grabbing a pillow to her chest. "And if that wasn't enough to break the strongest of women down to the core, get this, Beatrice hasn't returned any of my calls, e-mails, texts, or Facebook messages. It's like the universe is conspiring against me, Josie. And I don't understand why. I spend countless hours on my yoga mat setting positive intentions and sending healing vibrations out into the world, so that karma will support me when I need it most. But instead, what do I get in return? I get a normal child and a husband who doesn't seem to care about his future, which, to note, just got increasingly difficult to sort out given his test scores. I don't understand; we had a tutor for six months working with Harrison to prepare for the exam. What am I going to do with a normal kid, Josie? WHAT?!?!? His social and professional prospects are now so limited!"

As Meredith is talking my mind wanders to contemplating if I could start a new business that provides private school "admissions therapy." I'm pretty sure I could charge $200 an hour for one-hour phone consults and $350 for in-person consults for the month leading up to March 15, when school decisions go out. If I'm willing to go a month without sleep and be available for twenty-four-hour round-the-clock house calls, I bet I could make enough money to skip working the other eleven months of the year. I think I'm on to something. This would definitely help with the college tuition hurdle.

"Meredith, you know what I think would be most helpful to you?" I'm making up my first official go as an admissions therapist on the

fly, 'cause I need to get Meredith off my couch. In the spirit of generosity and wanting to make Meredith not my problem, I decide to
make Nan's day without her even knowing about it. This is a deliber-
ate last move in my "kill Nan with kindness" strategy before it expires
Saturday night. "A good sit-down chat with Nan Gooding, that's what
you need. I'm sure she would love to hear the details of your current
predicaments. She's a very good listener and she loves to help Fairchild's most cherished potential families. I am texting Nan's assistant, Elsa, right now, even though the sun has yet to come up. She
usually gets in around seven-thirty and she will get back to you and
I know Nan will want to see you immediately, if not sooner." I put
down my iPhone so I can look intently into Meredith's eyes and send
her ESP signals to leave my house pronto. "Nan will help you feel
better about this whole being normal dilemma, I promise."

There's no sign on Meredith's face that she has registered what I
have just said or done, and she is making no gestures to get up and
leave despite my best efforts. "I—I will just die if Harrison is, Harrison is, well, you know, actually normal. Maybe the tests are wrong,
maybe we need to get a second opinion from another educational
psychologist." Meredith scrunches her face up tight, like she was just
dared to suck the pulp off a lime. "So, I'll get a second opinion. Yes,
yes that's what I'll do, I'm definitely scheduling an appointment for
another opinion. And then I'm writing a scathing Yelp review of the
doctor who claims Harrison is normal. *Pfft*—where'd she go to
school? UC San Diego? I need a doctor from a real school."

"I know it must be tough, Meredith, but the good news is billions
of us function successfully every day with diagnosed and undiag-
nosed afflictions of normalcy. It really is remarkable what healthy,
normal people can do and how fulfilling their lives can be in this day
and age." The fact that I'm standing here discussing a nonexistent
problem, when NOBODY in my community comes to a person's
house this early unless someone is dead, is not lost on me. I also

know that if Meredith doesn't get off my couch soon she's gonna be that dead somebody.

Meredith smooths her hair back. She doesn't acknowledge a word I've said and, frankly, she may have forgotten I'm in the room. "It's still several months until Harrison starts school, so I have plenty of time to replace Randy," Meredith says with an increasing air of confidence and can-do spirit. "A meeting with Nan will be good; this is a situation that may be over your head, Josie, no offense. I'm glad we agree something this important needs to go to the top. And Beatrice is probably on holiday, don't you think? I'm sure that's it." A truthful answer from me is not really what Meredith is looking for.

"Way to go, girl, love your problem-solving initiative!" I give a little attagirl punch in the air and point Meredith to the door before her moment of personal power disintegrates. She picks up some momentum to get off the couch but looks at my phone on the side table when a text dings. I let the rudeness of checking out my electronic personal life go in lieu of her leaving swiftly.

"You know, these are the moments in life that really test who you are in the universe and how you overcome the obstacles of your earthbound and celestial journey. I can't wait until my yoga teacher gets back from Esalen, so I can tell her how I was able to asana my way through this trial and envision my way out of the darkness and into the light. I'm a survivor, and Harrison will be, too, despite his diagnosis. You know, I'm going to go straight home and vision board about this. By the way, if indeed Harrison has a diagnosis of normal, does that count as diversity?"

This may possibly be the weirdest morning I've had since Etta was born. Pre-Etta, I believe it was cartwheeling down the beaches of Nice with a gaggle of Cirque du Soleil drag queens after a private Prada show in a French castle owned by a Russian oligarch. But this, I have to say, is a close second.

TWENTY-TWO

.ᶜᵗᵗᵗᵗᵗᵗᵗᵗ

TY

I'll pick up you all up at 6:50. Looking forward to the party tonight.

4:47 P.M.

JOSIE

Why don't we just meet you and Daniel there?

4:48 P.M.

TY

Is chivalry dead? My sister couldn't babysit so he's home with Gracie. Besides, I'm Viv's date tonight, not Daniel's.

4:49 P.M.

JOSIE

Etta's Aunt Viv's date.

4:50 P.M.

TY

She's dumping me before the evening has even started?

5:51 P.M.

JOSIE

Not a chance, she's double-dipping. You were my bargaining chip to get her to come to this par-tay in the first place. That said, she may ask you to check her pulse and her pupils in the car. She's been a little skittish lately. She thinks all these fancy veggies and grains you've been telling her to eat are what's going to kill her. Maybe bring your tongue depressor, too. Thanks for the ride offer. See you around 6:50.

5:52 P.M.

By 3:00 p.m. the day of Viva la Viv I have taken Aunt Viv to the beauty salon to have her hair—her real hair—lined up and cake-cut. A handful of times a year Aunt Viv decides to go au naturel 'cause she can pull it off; apparently tonight is one of those nights. Then we go to the nail salon for a specific cherries jubilee red that, according to Aunt Viv, only exists at one salon on all of Clemente Street. I start to tell Aunt Viv that any of the twenty nail salons within a twelve-block radius of our house can paint her nails cherry red if she buys the polish herself, but she's having such a good time bossing me around from the passenger seat of the car I decide not to ruin her one-day dictatorship. While her nails are drying, and gossip is flowing with the other ladies in the salon, I have to run to the tailor's to pick up her dress. Then I'm off to the shoe repair shop to pick up her beloved beaded purse that is being resurrected from near extinction to match Aunt Viv's emerald-green dress. Our final stop is Walgreens to buy a pack of tissues small enough to fit in her newly fixed purse and some Epsom salts to soak in, so she will feel loose in the joints all night. I asked Aunt Viv why all this fuss for a party she didn't want to attend in the first place. She acknowledges my sincere curiosity by ignoring it and begins humming Billy Joel's "New York State of Mind," her current go-to method to shut me up before our flight tomorrow. How Aunt Viv even knows that song is out of my realm of guessing; Billy Joel is not exactly Zydeco. I run into Starbucks across from Walgreens for a triple espresso and a necessary four minutes of freedom to get me through the rest of this day.

Arriving home, I'm met with, "Mama, you packed? We can't be late to the airport tomorrow. Promise me we won't be late." When Etta goes to school next year, I won't miss her badgering me about time. That kid has never heard of, nor practiced, the art of being fashionably late.

"I'm packed Etta, promise, but we don't leave until mid-afternoon, so we have plenty of time to finish getting ready in the morning," I call from the bathroom. Is it too much to ask to have thirty minutes to clean myself up for tonight?

"Do you plan on parading around New York naked, Mama? If so, then please don't show up for my interview with the Juilliard director of admissions," Etta says, standing in the doorway to the bathroom holding my empty suitcase. It's trying having a seventeen-year-old for a mother.

"I promise that bag will be stuffed to the top with appropriate clothing by the time we leave for the airport tomorrow. Now, how 'bout you go snooping in your aunt Viv's suitcase and leave me alone so I can get dressed? You know, before I had you, I had a whole team dedicated to making me look good, now I gotta do it all by myself and it's a task that takes focus."

"Don't need to check Aunt Viv's bag; it's already packed and by the front door. She doesn't want to miss our flight, either. You know we'll leave you behind if we have to. Aunt Viv and I can have a good time without you." Etta is practically levitating she's so excited to go to New York.

"Oh, I have no doubt." What is it with these type A ladies I'm livin' with? I'm like the chill in the middle of an uptight sandwich.

"While it may only be for a few more months, I'm still runnin' this show and you, baby girl, need to go get dressed. I didn't buy you that jumpsuit you begged for to watch it hang in your closet. And remember, we can't look too amazing, don't want to upstage Aunt Viv on her big night." I give Etta a wink and a swat on her tight booty to usher her along. God bless that child, I hope that backside lifted high to the heavens doesn't get her in all kinds of trouble in college. My fear is real. I see how Lola's boys look at Etta. Even though the oldest is only eleven, those boys know an angel when they see one.

Etta hip checks me and runs out of the bathroom before I swat that backside for real.

· · ·

TY

In Lyft, be there in two. And if I do say so myself I'm looking fine.

6:42 P.M.

JOSIE

Lookin' fine is kind of like rockin' it. No one says it anymore. Come up with something from this decade.

6:43 P.M.

TY

Sharp, hot, dope, handsome, fab, sizzlin', fly?

6:44 P.M.

JOSIE

Okay, Eminem, stick to looking fine.

6:45 P.M.

TY

And it's looking like I'm right outside your door.

6:46 P.M.

JOSIE

Can you wait there for 5? I'm pretty sure Aunt Viv wants to make an entrance. A woman never loses her need to impress a man. Lay it on thick, this is her night and so far she's really eating up being Queen for a day.

6:47 P.M.

"Aunt Viv, Etta, Dr. Golden's here." How is it those two are always complaining about me being the late one and here I am waiting on them to cross the finish line on this evening's primping marathon? I can only imagine the amount of product littered across every inch of the bathroom. A shea butter cemetery surrounded by a MAC mess.

"Now where's that doctor of mine?" Aunt Viv giggles, making her way down the hall holding Etta's hand. We stand shoulder to shoulder in front of the coat closet mirror, a vision of color and style and grace—Aunt Viv regal in her emerald-green chiffon dress, me in rich orange, and Etta killin' it in canary yellow. We are a glorious rainbow of love and femininity.

Dr. Golden knocks on the front door. Aunt Viv smooths the back of her dress like all women do before stepping into view of a handsome man. She stands straight like the matriarch of our family that she is, clears her throat, and opens the door.

"Good evening, Dr. Golden. I appreciate you getting all gussied up in your best church clothes for me," Aunt Viv singsongs. *Those are no church clothes*, I think to myself, slightly slack-jawed and staring at Dr. Golden. He's in a deep midnight–blue European-cut suit that accentuates his God-given ocean-blue eyes, swimmer's shoulders, and slim waist. His suit jacket cuts a perfect V. Ty's lavender shirt collar is conservatively open, showing a hint of baby-smooth chest. He's wearing shoes that look straight out of a Milanese leather factory, nearly causing me a fashion orgasm.

"Good evening, Viv. Do you think after one heart attack and two checkups we can move our relationship to the next level and you call me Ty? After all, I have seen you in a hospital gown, front side and back." Aunt Viv lifts her hand to her mouth to stifle another giggle, but the golden doctor intercepts it on the way to give it a kiss. Etta and I watch in awe; we've never seen Aunt Viv so intimate with a man. "I got you this wrist corsage, Viv. The honoree of this evening's soirée must have flowers so everyone in the room knows exactly who she is. May I put it on you?"

"Of course, Doctor—I mean, Ty. Thank you." Aunt Viv blushes. I wipe a tear from the corner of my eye before Aunt Viv can notice and scold me for making a fuss. Even if the rest of the evening is a bust, witnessing the tenderness and reverence Golden Boy is showering on Aunt Viv makes the last month of complaints about the party and the earlier eight hours of schlepping Aunt Viv around San Francisco worth it. This is Aunt Viv's fifteen minutes of fame and, deservedly, this little corner of the world is revolving around her.

"Well, there you go, Viv, you look absolutely beautiful. I knew you were a sight, but, woman, you take my breath away." Aunt Viv fingers the yellow flowers on her wrist, demurely tips her chin at Ty, and strides out the front door. Etta swallows a snicker and we roll our eyes at one another, a nonverbal agreement that Aunt Viv is going to be unbearable for the next couple days riding high from tonight's attention. I'm unsure if there will be enough room in the Lyft for the two of us, Dr. Golden, Aunt Viv, and her ego.

I send Etta out behind Aunt Viv and then grab my purse and keys to lock the door. Ty is waiting for me on the front stoop. Damn if his mama didn't teach him good manners. I pull the door shut, lock it, and shimmy past Ty.

"And you're looking damn fine, too, Ms. Bordelon," Ty whispers in my ear, flicking the bow of my dress at the back of my neck. My skin erupts in goose bumps. I've really got to start dating. If I get goose bumps from a gay man's touch, imagine what might happen with someone who actually wants to rip my clothes off. Watching him make Aunt Viv swoon reminds me how a man can make a woman feel with the right kind of sweet attention. With Etta leaving soon, Aunt Viv's recent heart attack, and coming across Michael again, I find myself needing, well, truthfully wanting, some of that sweetness for myself.

TY WASN'T LYING; I DO LOOK FINE. THE COMBINATION OF college application stress with Etta, the crunch of mid-admissions season, and a shortage of my favorite chocolate pretzels at Trader Joe's, and I'm within eight pounds of my fighting weight, a number I haven't seen since 2003.

As we roll up to the school, we hear the live Afro-Cuban music coming from Fairchild's grand foyer. Etta's unconsciously swaying in her seat, her body incapable of not moving when it hears a sweet beat. The car parks right in front of the twenty stately stairs covered in red carpet. Etta hops out of the car first and floats up to the main entrance, her hips continuing to keep in time with the Cuban groove. I take in a sharp breath. Etta's confidence as she half dances, half glides her way into the party throws me deep into one of the few memories I have of being with my mother. She moved through the streets of New Orleans, skin glistening from the summer humidity, shoulders swaying to whatever tune was in her head. I don't recall the specifics of my mother's features, I just know she was a mere five years older than Etta in my last memory of her before she dropped me like a milk delivery on Aunt Viv's doorstep. Watching Etta, I know it's true that her body was born to move, and I can't help but wonder, with a bit of fear, if Etta is a next generation Ophelia Bordelon. And if she is, how will those roots and seeds play out in her future, since no one knows what happened to my mother.

I bring myself back to the present when I see Nan, erect and tidy, greeting guests at the summit of the stairs. I have to give it to her, she did indeed go all out with the Miami-meets–New Orleans mash-up theme for Viva la Viv. From the live band to a couple of classic red and baby blue 1940s Fords lining the curb, Nan did what she could to turn this expansive Seacliff estate into a mini-Havana. Complete with strobe lights the whole vibe feels very Buena Vista Social Club with palm trees, forced heat, trayed cigars, and plenty of Cuba Libres at every turn. While I do give Nan a pile of credit for sparing no expense on behalf of Aunt Viv, I can't help but wonder if Nan realizes she has confused Cuban with Creole. Communism with Cajun. Does Nan even know where we're from? Or care? Given her efforts I suspect she knows but doesn't care.

• • •

LOLA

God I wish I was a lesbian, Jo!

7:17 P.M.

JOSIE

Where you at?

7:17 P.M.

LOLA

Staring at you from the bar.

7:18 P.M.

JOSIE

Get me a glass of champagne and then get over here. And thank you. When Nic dies we can be lesbians if you want.

7:18 P.M.

LOLA

Done.

7:19 P.M.

Roan gets to me before Lola does. "Grrrrllll! Give. It. A. Whirl!" He gives me two sharp snaps and puts his hand out to me and I grab hold for a slow *take it all in, baby* three-sixty. The heavy orange satin feels buttery on my skin as it lifts just a hair to let in a slight breeze and show off my cocoa-buttered legs. My locks are swept up in a bun to highlight my long neck that's framed by gold hoop earrings. The highlight of this outfit is my purple suede heels that have only known concrete twice. Once on my first "official" date with Michael and tonight. These are not everyday shoes, these are *I've got something to prove* shoes. And tonight, once I saw Aunt Viv in her emerald green and Etta (who is one of five people in the whole world who can crush a canary yellow strapless jumpsuit) I knew this was the night that the Bordelon women came to slay.

Lola saunters over carrying two flutes of champagne. As she's about to enter our circle she does her own twirl making sure our group gets a full view of every inch of her glory. Ty chokes on an ice cube. The plunging V at the back of Lola's dress, which is a mere couple of inches from playing peek-a-boo with the icing on her cakes, takes him by surprise.

"Ooooooo la la, Lola! Look at you!" Roan gushes all over Lola. Lola has known Roan for all the years he's worked for me and she can speak Roan fluently.

"Look at me? Look at you?!?! Top to toe, toe to top, Tom Ford is weeping with joy right now. Slap you on a billboard, it couldn't be any better if you tried—FAB-U-LUSH!" Lola fans herself like she's over-heating. The love affair between Roan and Lola is strong and it is real. I've been the third wheel since I introduced the two.

"Roan, Lola, you remember Ty Golden?" I ask, shifting the con-versation off our vain selves to avoid seeming vapid in the midst of someone who, you know, massages hearts with his bare hands.

"I do remember you," Roan says, placing a hand on Ty's chest and looking right into his eyes challenging him to a game of who will blink first. We are now officially playing with the admissions gods. If Nan knew Ty was a potential parent, not invited specifically by her, Roan and I would be updating our LinkedIn profiles. For once, I give

244 · ALLI FRANK and ASHA YOUMANS

thanks to Nan's indifference to the admissions process of the middle-class applicant. "You're San Francisco's very own gay Hermès with inexhaustible stamina and an ungodly metabolism." I forgot Roan was a classics major at Santa Clara.

I duck under Roan's arm to step between the two men before this whole scene turns into one big Greek tragedy.

"Nice suit." Roan brushes the lapel and then winks at Ty before taking two steps back. Thankfully he picked up the *down boy* signal I was vibin' his way, but the pause comes with a curious lift of his left eyebrow. Roan is either shooting Ty some shade or he now recognizes him from someplace other than the vegan food truck and admissions. Oh dear God, infidelity is not necessary information for a director of admissions to know about an applying family. I choose to pretend I didn't see their subtle exchange, but my stomach lurches nonetheless.

Lola heads off to chat up a Fairchild parent whose son is on her oldest's soccer team. Roan spies a relatively famous alumnus who is a fairly important human rights attorney at the fresh age of thirty. And since Roan believes human rights in San Francisco means gay rights and gay rights means potential boyfriend material he heads over to fancy himself a flirt. Roan likes to do right in the world through association.

Ty and I are left standing together, Aunt Viv already lost to a crowd of admirers. "So, do you, Daniel, and Gracie have any fun plans coming up? I remember Daniel saying in your parent interview that he loves to head to Washington in April for the tulip festival and then somewhere to taste Washington wines." This seems like very safe conversation given that having Ty here is playing outside the admissions rulebook. Plus, it proves that I listen and pay attention in the parent interviews. Usually.

"Yeah, about that."

"About tulips?"

"No, no not tulips."

"Wine?"

"Well, yes, kind of about wine. Liquid courage and all. I need to . . ."

"You need to get yourself a refill and get me one, too, please. I think I'm going to stick to red tonight, no more champagne. No, white, I'll stick to white wine; don't want to potentially stain my dress. If you don't mind grabbing us two glasses, I'm going to check in on your date."

"Okay, sure, but then I have to talk to you about this whole kindergarten thing, Josie."

"Probably best if Daniel's part of the conversation, don't you think? E-mail me tomorrow and we'll set up a time for you and Daniel to come in when I get back from New York." I'm used to people wanting to talk shop with me when I'm trying to be a regular person and have some fun. It used to annoy me, but now I just tell them to make an appointment and walk away.

"I need to talk to you tonight, Josie. Daniel doesn't know."

And ugh, there it is. Dr. Golden is no different than Meredith Lawton pretending to be my friend; Vanessa Grimaldi offering me free facials; or the myriad of other parents who want to give me Giants tickets, symphony tickets, backstage passes, or a weekend in Sonoma to butter me up so I will admit their child. Often in a couple there is one parent who plays outside the rules, and Dr. Golden willingly being Aunt Viv's date must be his version of transferred airline miles. Pricey tit for costly tat. How did I not see it? Did his good looks and care for Aunt Viv really throw me that far off my game? I needed something from him and he most definitely needs something from me. I'm sure he sees this evening as a fair trade.

I'm not going to ruin tonight for Aunt Viv, so I will have to effortlessly avoid getting locked into a one-on-one conversation with Ty. I see him walking toward me with our wine and I quickly scan the room for Aunt Viv. She's by the grand piano being showered with compliments from a couple of boys, now young men, who I remember hanging out in the kitchen between school and basketball practice begging Aunt Viv for scraps, they were such hungry, growing food receptacles. Actually, they were more like stray dogs—the more Aunt Viv fed them, the more they showed up before practice. And now here they are, filled out and tuxedoed. I don't want to bust up their lovefest, but I need someplace to hide.

"How are you doing, Aunt Viv? Enjoying yourself?" I ask, awkwardly inserting myself into the middle of the conversation.

"I'm having a lovely time chatting with Eric, Ben, and Riley, who I haven't seen in ages. Did you know Eric wrote one of his college essays about workin' with me in the kitchen? Imagine. But you I get to sit next to on a six-hour flight tomorrow, so if you could just let the four of us continue our delightful conversation that would be wonderful." With a pat on my shoulder, Aunt Viv waves me off and turns her back, closing off the circle. Damn, who knew Aunt Viv could be such a mean girl. New plan. Find a corner to practice my fifty-nine-seconds scholarship speech one last time. Crap, Golden Boy is heading right for me doubling down with two wineglasses.

"Ty, I'd love for you to get to know Etta a little better. She can tell you all about being a lifer student at Fairchild. Let's go find her." I grab my glass of wine out of his hand and redirect him through the crowd to look for Etta.

"Sure, sounds good, but we do need to talk at some point, Josie. It's pretty important."

Then it hits me; maybe it's not about admissions for Gracie, maybe something came back on Aunt Viv's last round of tests and that something is not good. Really, really not good. And he wants to tell me, so we can figure out how best, together, to break the news to Aunt Viv after her big night. Oh my God I'm sure that's it. When are we going to tell her? Tomorrow morning before we fly out to New

York? We can't do that. It will destroy Etta's focus for her audition and ruin our first big Bordelon vacation. But if we wait until we get back and Aunt Viv finds out I have known for days without telling her she will disown me. I knew that heart attack was worse than Aunt Viv and Dr. Golden were letting on. My eyes start to heat up and tear. *Don't cry, Josie. Not here, not now, don't cry.* I fan my eyes a few times to dry them out.

"There she is, Josie." Ty guides my elbow over toward the band where Etta, Poppy, and a few girls who graduated last year are talking.

"Ty, this is Etta's good friend Poppy, who she dances with, and these two extraordinary Fairchild graduates are Simone and Freya. Actually, Freya is at Cornell. Go Big Red!" I weakly cheer as I introduce Ty to the group. Or maybe that's it; maybe what he wants to talk about is Etta and her application to Cornell. I told him back in January that she submitted all her materials on time. Perhaps the school has contacted him to do her alumni interview. Does he have second thoughts about interviewing her because now he knows us a little too well between applying his daughter to Fairchild and being Aunt Viv's doctor? If he doesn't interview Etta I'm not sure I want to be seeing his face around campus next year and all the years after that. *You aren't the only who can dance this dance, Dr. Golden.*

"Umm, Mama, I think Headmistress Gooding is trying to get your attention. She's over near the bar." I pull myself out of my thoughts on Ty, Etta, Cornell, and his screwing up her collegiate chances. I look toward the bar and see Nan beckoning me to come over. Elsamyassistant is standing at attention nearby ready to serve, but not close enough that anyone can detect Nan's need for a social crutch.

"Ty, I have to go talk to the head of school. You going to be alright with these ladies? You'll learn a lot to prepare yourself for Gracie's teen years."

"I'm both curious and terrified, but yes, I'm alright. After you talk with Ms. Gooding, please come find me." Ty seems visibly rattled and nervous. I smile and nod, but I don't give him a verbal yes. As I walk away it hits me. How did I miss it when I have seen it dozens of times? The awkward affection at the parent interview, Daniel staying home with Gracie tonight rather than coming with Ty to Aunt Viv's party. The golden gay couple must be getting divorced! Daniel doesn't want to say anything until after decision letters go out, Ty can't hold it in any longer. Sometimes it's so easy to miss the most obvious clues.

TWENTY-THREE

APPROACHING NAN I NOTICE SHE HAS A SLIGHT SLUR TO her speech, no doubt the combination of two Cuba Libres and zero *comida*. Nan never eats in public. She's wearing a black taffeta two-piece suit that looks most appropriate for a funeral. I need to come up with a compliment to thaw the inexplicably icier-than-usual vibe I've been getting this week while bustin' my hump to be extra nice.

"Your drop pearl earrings are beautiful, Nan. Are they a family heirloom?" I ask with a gracious smile and warm eye contact aided by alcohol.

Nan looks away after a glance. "Not everything's about family, Josie. You would be wise to think more critically about the ramifications of always putting family first." Okay, I'm not sure what to do with that random comment coming from Nan, or the Cuba Libres, and I'm not sure who's doing the talking. "I'm going to give my speech now and present Viv with her gift. Yes, I, too, have a surprise gift for Viv. My gift may cause you to want to adjust your brief remarks, so I suggest listening closely. You aren't the only one capable of surprises, Josie. And speaking of surprises, I forgot to thank you for your suggested meeting with Meredith Lawton. It was most informative." Nan's breath could be lit on fire she reeks so strongly of Captain Morgan rum.

"Two can play at your game, Josie. I'm feeling very underappreci- ated for all my effort on behalf of your family." Nan's elbow slips off the bar and she stumbles but catches herself mid-chastise. "You know, I am unbelievably busy and I was still able to find the time to pull together this night on a level Fairchild has never seen before. I have taken care of you, Viv, and that daughter of yours and how do you show your appreciation? By going behind my back, that's how. Now, please go make sure your aunt Viv is ready to take the stage."

I'm starting to feel nervous. This is a step above Nan's usual nasty behavior, one I haven't seen before and there's nothing about it I like. I bite my tongue to avoid clappin' back with something I'll regret. I pray Nan's gift to Aunt Viv is small and can keep the focus of the evening on her celebration instead of turning the spotlight to Nan and her self-serving generosity. Or her distaste for me.

I tell Nan I can't wait to hear what the gift is to keep the conver- sation neutral. I don't want a battle of the bitches since Nan is clearly gearing up for a fight.

"Do you need help up the stairs?" I have to ask as she teeters a step away from the bar toward the stage.

"No, Josie, I'm fine thank you. Where's Elsamyassistant?" Nan hands me her drink, looks around but doesn't register Elsa right next to her and weaves toward the stage parting the crowd on her own. I head the opposite direction to grab Ty and Aunt Viv but am am- bushed by Meredith Lawton.

"You know I took your advice and met with Nan. In our meeting it became clear to me that you have not been doing everything in your power to ensure Harrison a spot in the incoming kindergar- ten class. Nan and I talked at length and she assured me a kinder- garten spot for Harrison; she only needed a small favor from me in return. Though Christopher is unable to attend, I'm here tonight to support Nan in her speech for Aunt Viv. Nan asked me to be here." Great that Meredith took my advice to heart and successfully climbed the admissions ladder from Beatrice Pembrook, to me, to Nan. I'm thankful that any future early morning meltdowns over Harrison's education can happen at Nan's house, not mine.

"I'm so happy you and Nan have gotten a chance to know each other, you two seem like a formidable pair, but I need to find my aunt Viv. Nan's about to thank her for her service."

"Yes, we are becoming fast friends, Nan and me. I'm so looking forward to hearing her words of thanks to your aunt Viv. Oh, and by the way, Josie, I thought you told me you were not in contact with Beatrice Pembrook?" Meredith asks and accuses at the same time. How quick she is to drop me like last year's must-have designer handbag.

"I'm not. As I've said to you before, Meredith, Beatrice's children are long out of Fairchild."

"Interesting. Then why did I see a text on your phone from her about a scholarship the morning I stopped by your house in crisis and you could barely spare me two seconds of your time? And, my oh my, was Nan surprised when I mentioned it to her the next day at our meeting."

I don't think ruining lives is what Steve Jobs envisioned when he developed the iPhone.

"MAMA, MS. GOODING DOESN'T LOOK SO GOOD," ETTA whispers in my ear as the audience watches Nan wrestle the microphone out of its stand. Aunt Viv, Ty, Roan, and Etta have gathered around me. Lola is nowhere to be found. Though she likes to pretend she's a minimalist parent, I'm positive she's in the bathroom talking to Nic making sure no one has veered off the four pages of instructions she left to ensure everyone is still breathing and the house is still standing by the time she gets home. "You don't look so good, either, what's going on?" Etta asks, and I shake my head. This is not the time or the place to let Etta know I have risked her college tuition—hell, our entire family's financial stability—on a catfight I wanted to win with Nan over how to honor Aunt Viv. I feel so childish standing next to my grown daughter.

I have my phone ready to take video as soon as Nan begins to gush about Aunt Viv. It won't be sincere. Nan will put aside her fury at me for secretly contacting Beatrice and put on an Oscar-worthy performance to convince the gathered party how much she cares about Aunt Viv, after she describes how well the school year has been humming along with her at the helm. Meredith has planted herself to my left and offers Nan an enthusiastic golf clap.

"Now for the main event of the evening," Nan continues, after exhausting her list of recent accomplishments. "I would like to invite our guest of honor, Vivian Bordelon, and community-at-large member, Meredith Lawton, to join me on stage." Aunt Viv looks at me like I put one past her, her stare down informs me that once we are out of the public eye she will torture me mercilessly. I feign shock to match hers. I mouth to her *I have no idea what's going on* as she heads over to the stage followed by Meredith. Meredith offers her a hand to help her up the stairs, but Aunt Viv vigorously waves it away. She plasters a smile on her face, lifts the skirt of her dress just an inch and climbs onto the platform with her chin raised. I capture it all on video because I'm terrified and curious at the same time about the surprise that awaits us.

"I spent months considering what would be the best way to commemorate our dear dedicated, hardworking Vivian Bordelon for her fiftieth year at Fairchild. I know for many, your fondest memories of Fairchild are the bell that would ring to signal hot cookies coming out of the oven, the thoughtful snack boxes complete with individual notes Viv made for traveling sports teams, and my personal favorite, the quiches she bakes and sends home with me when she knows I will be working late into the night and won't be able to make myself a proper supper. Dairy free of course." Nan pauses and pats her stomach allowing a moment for the audience to register her svelte figure. "In these hours I've reflected on your career, dear Vivian, I'm in awe of how much you have done for this community while raising your niece, Josie Bordelon, and your grandniece, Etta Bordelon, all on your own. Single parenting can't be easy. That is why I'm thrilled to announce that I, in partnership with the brand-new Lawton Family Foundation, have started, for the upcoming year, the Vivian Bordelon Scholarship for a qualified student of a single parent to attend Fairchild School."

Aunt Viv's jaw drops. Nan takes a bow, tipping too far left but catching herself on Aunt Viv's sleeve. Meredith Lawton continues her golf clap from the stage staring right at me.

"Next in the evening's events Vivian's niece, Josie, was meant to give a few brief words, but she's a bit speechless after hearing of my generous scholarship. I think at this point in the night it's time to raise your glasses and give a big VIVA LA VIV toast! Let the dancing commence."

Aunt Viv gives Nan a strong hug that makes sure to hold her up, so they can exit the stage together before Nan embarrasses herself. Meredith waves to the ongoing applause and follows two steps behind for an extra set of hands. I continue to video, my utter shock keeping me from knowing what to do next.

As Nan brushes by me she stops to spread the last of her drunken cheer, "Don't you ever go behind my back and try to upstage me. Did you think I wouldn't hear about you asking Beatrice Pembrook of all people for money for your piddly scholarship? I hold the purse strings on all the current money and future funding for this school. You can't even buy a bottle of Perrier for your school tours without going

through me first. You think just because you're a black female administrator you can get whatever you want, whenever and however you
want, without working hard for it like I've had to do? That diversity
is on your side? Well, I'm here to tell you that you can't. I won't allow
it. I had to fight hard for decades in a field of stupid, unqualified,
balding, preppy men to be taken seriously as a female leader in this
male-dominated industry. If you think I'm going to let you sashay
through the halls of Fairchild all black power and upstage the years
of fighting and climbing I've had to do to come out on top, you are
seriously mistaken. I'm not your mentor, I'm not your friend, I'm not
here fighting for social justice, and I'm certainly not your cheerleader
happy to pave an easier road for you. I'm your competition, so you
better watch out. If it weren't for Fairchild—and for me—you would
have been nothing, your daughter would be nothing, and most certainly your aunt Viv would have nothing. Remember this, your job
security and your aunt Viv's job security rests on my mood, and right
now, my goodwill has run dry."

TWENTY-FOUR

⚘⚘⚘⚘⚘⚘

IF THIS WERE A BET MADE-FOR-TV MOVIE, I WOULD BE TAK-
ing out my earrings right now readying myself to claw that bitch's
face off. But it's not, so I do the next best thing.

JOSIE

> **LO. WHERE THE F ARE YOU?!** You missed it all
> go down **HARD.** I'm about to send you an e-mail.
> Check it. Then come find me **ASAP!**

9:12 P.M.

My phone was on the entire time Nan was laying down the heat.
I can't believe Lola missed this whole thing. While I didn't get Nan's
face on-screen dishing out drunken threats, I did get her voice loud
and clear going dark and nasty on me. And thank God I did because
Lola would never believe me otherwise. I hurriedly tap an L to pull
up my contacts list and shoot Lola the video file on the down low.
When complaining about Nan, Lola has sometimes said I'm just

used to Dr. Pearson, who was always sweet on me. Lola assumes any woman who goes into education is way, way too compassionate, kind, and hell-bent on improving the world. Present company excluded.

While Aunt Viv is showing her framed letter of recognition to another flock of admirers, Ty startles me by putting his hand firmly on my back to steer me someplace out of the fray. All I can think about is what bothers Nan more: me being black or me being female? Or is it the combo that has sent her over the edge? Where is Lola and why is Nan such a ghastly drunk? AND WHERE IS LOLA?

"I'm so happy to see Aunt Viv enjoying herself tonight, but what's up with your boss?" Ty says, leading me past the dessert table.

"Long story, but short version is she hates women."

"Ouch. I want more on that later. Right now I need to talk to you." Dr. Golden has no idea what just transpired, nor the fact that my interest in hearing anything he has to say is zilch. I want to hunt down Meredith and hopefully come across Lola on my witch-seeking mission, but Ty body blocks my path and steers me deep into a quiet corner. This night has become an utter disaster, what a waste of a good dress and spectacular shoes. Let's get it over with, Golden Boy so Etta, Aunt Viv, and I can go home, wake up tomorrow, and escape to New York for a few days. Right now, San Francisco is not big enough for Nan Gooding and me.

"What is it, Ty? What's so important? Are you and Daniel separating? In the throes of an ugly divorce? If so, I'm very sorry for you two, I really am, but I'm in the middle of a serious professional soap opera." I shake my head, annoyed. Honestly I have no extra emotional energy for another person.

"Josie . . ." Big pause . . .

"What, Ty? Say it. You agreed to be Aunt Viv's date tonight because you're worried a divorce will harm Gracie's chance of getting into Fairchild? Is that right? You want a special favor like every other just-shy-of-certifiable, playground gossiping, manipulative parent in

San Francisco? Is that what you want—a guarantee for Gracie?" Ty shakes his head no. Okay, maybe that was a little harsh, particularly if he's nursing a broken heart. Clearly my anger is unsure where to land.

"No? So, what then—Aunt Viv has a serious heart condition and you picked this inopportune moment to tell me? You could have asked me to make an appointment for Aunt Viv. Jesus, say what you came here to say so we can get on with it and end this disaster of a night. I'm so tired. Nan is pissed at me. I'm probably going to lose my job, and I have to get on a plane tomorrow and pretend to be excited for Etta to visit a college that costs upward of 70K a year for my brilliant daughter to dance around half naked." At this moment my life feels like an endless game of not getting what I want, and I'm done with losing. "Please, out with it so I can find Lola, Aunt Viv, and Etta and bring this night to a close."

"I'm not gay."

TWENTY-FIVE

✦✦✦✦✦✦✦✦

"SAY WHAT?"

"I'm not gay. In fact, I'm the opposite of gay. And I like you. I mean I like, like you."

I stand in silence. My nineteen-year-old resting bitch face is back. "What?!?!"

"I'm saying I like you, Josie. I think you rock." Ty's face lights up in a huge grin, an adolescent twinkle in his eyes.

"I told you never to say that."

"I know you did, but it's true. I'm hoping you heard me say I'm not gay."

I'm in such a state of disbelief, my mind is stuttering. Words fail me momentarily and my jaw drops wide enough to catch flies. My stomach is cartwheeling like a second-grade girl at recess: Is it the fried plantains or maybe the ceviche turned at the buffet? I know it's neither. This is a reaction to Ty's big fat lie, or perhaps an inkling of excitement over his out of the blue admission.

"Is that why you and Daniel are getting a divorce, you've decided you're not gay? Is that possible? Did I make you not gay? I've heard of supposedly straight husbands coming out to their wives, but I've never heard of it happening the other way around."

"No, no, no, Daniel and I aren't getting divorced—"

"And you 'like, like' me?" I interrupt. "Are we in eighth grade and you're about to hand me a note asking me to mark *yes* or *no* if I like you back?"

"Well, we are currently standing in a school. And while the note thing is not a half bad idea, what I want to know is: Did you hear me say I'm not gay? Yes or no?"

"I don't understand. You're *not* gay. But I never once caught you checking me out."

"Oh, trust me, I was checking you out, even in those ratty sweats you were sporting when I came over for the house call. Maybe you just weren't paying attention, you know, since you thought I was gay and all. Do you really think I have time to make house calls to every single one of my patients? I made a house call to get to see you."

"Are you sure you aren't confusing needing a beard with liking me? 'Cause if you need one I'm already spoken for. Roan and I have mad gay man–straight woman love."

Ty shakes his head no. "I look terrible with a beard."

"So, you're talking man-woman um, like? The opposite of what you and Daniel got going on." I need to get myself really clear on what he's sayin'.

"Yes . . . I'm talking man-woman like. Glad to know you've heard of it."

"So then, are you bi? Cis? Pan? Trans? Fluid? What have I forgotten that you can possibly be that might explain the past six months? Wait, does Daniel know I'm the reason your family is breaking up?" I don't know what universe I'm existing in because it sure isn't the one called my reality that I left back at the apartment a few hours ago.

"Nope, none of those. I'm just your average, boring, old-school, straight, heterosexual white guy. Except I can dance. I'm actually a really good dancer by anyone's standards. That's what I've wanted to tell you all night."

"You've wanted to tell me you're a good dancer?"

"No. I want you to know that I'm crazy attracted to you and I'm done lying about it. C'mon, Josie, is this really so hard to believe? I swear I've caught you checking me out." He's got me there, but I'm not admitting it. My brain can't digest the information enough to construct a coherent response to Ty's confession. This is hands down the most bizarre professional encounter I've ever had with a potential parent, actually any parent. This is beyond more than I can handle for one night, and more than I've ever had to deal with in one admissions season. At a loss for words I start to wander off, bombarded by my own thoughts, but Ty pulls me back in.

"Josie, hear me out." Ty waves his hand inches from my face to wake me into reality, well, this altered reality. He does it with the efficiency of a doctor who has performed this exact move a hundred times on patients in shock. Still, my mind is having trouble focusing, flipping from Nan and Meredith, to the scholarship, then the threat, to Aunt Viv and Etta, to Ty. And why can't I find Lola?

"Josie, focus, please. I can explain." Golden Boy picks up my hands hanging limp at my sides. His palms feel familiar. Ty has touched me before and my body remembers: at lunch overlooking the Bay; in Aunt Viv's hospital room; and, of course, my mini breakdown during his house call. All those times I convinced myself it was an act of professional courtesy—his and mine. The truth is settling in and it's starting to feel good. "Caroline is my sister, and Daniel is her husband, my brother-in-law. Well, first he was my best friend in college, then my brother-in-law. Gracie is their kid, my niece, and I would do absolutely anything for her. Are you following me?"

"Uh-huh." I'm listening—after thirteen years in admissions I really thought I had heard it all, but I guess there's always room for something new.

"Caroline desperately wants Gracie to go to Fairchild, more than anything in the world, and she is a force like none other. I mean, she was a force not to be messed with before she had kids, but now that she's a mom there's no obstacle she can't figure out how to go over, around, or under to get what she wants for Gracie. It's impressive and terrifying at the same time. And she helped me pay for medical school, so I kinda owe her." Ty pauses for a breath and makes eye contact with me to make sure I'm tracking. Dang. He's a good doctor and a good brother. I've wanted to find someone like Ty, thoughtful and kind, whose humor is as sharp as mine. Who knew all this time it could be Golden Boy bringing my sexy back.

"Caroline knows that their hurdle to getting Gracie into Fairchild is that they are an average, middle-class, hetero white family—well, they are if you subtract Caroline's world-class cunning and Daniel's exceptional lying. I was surprised by our acting chops, but more surprised to find you."

Thinking back, Ty's texts were flirty for a doctor checking in on his patient. If he wasn't so deliciously good-looking and, at the time, gay, I would probably have considered the texts hugely inappropriate, particularly when he could have called Aunt Viv directly. Or maybe I wouldn't have because that's how desperate I am for a bit of male attention, fake gay or not. I guess it's possible Golden Boy was slyly checking me out while stuffing his face with Aunt Viv's coffee cake. How'd I miss all that?

"Anyway, my sister's a recruiter for Salesforce, Daniel's an accountant, and they live in a town house they rent in Jordan Park. You can write their life script from there. Their chances of getting Gracie into a snooty private school are slim. Sorry, but it's true. I mean, look at this party; a lot of these people, they're not normal. Follow me on rounds at the hospital, I'll show you everyday people." I consider telling Ty he's not wrong, that many of these people, if not all, strive to be anything but normal. "There's nothing exotic, special, diverse, or, frankly, terribly interesting about Caroline and Daniel. They're loving parents who want the best for their kid, just like everyone else. So that's where I came in—as the gay husband." A pained expression flashes across Ty's face, hopeful for some recognition that I'm following the story he's laying down.

"Daniel does look like an accountant. That's the first thing that rings completely true since you started talking."

"I know, right? Such a numbers nerd!"

"Not the point. Keep going."

"Well, since they can't build Fairchild a new gym, Caroline thought if Daniel and I posed as a gay couple the chances of Gracie getting into the school would be higher."

Maybe. But this story better have a good ending. "Go on." My mind still needs convincing, but below the neck I'm hopping on board.

"Daniel is my family. Has been since we met over beer pong sophomore year in college, and Gracie won my heart the minute I held her for the first time in the hospital. But, man, I didn't realize how much time this whole private school application thing takes—it's like a second job. I thought I'd have to sign a few documents, show up a time or two, and be done." The look I throw him says, *You don't know nothin' about raising a kid in the city.*

"I'm sure my colleagues at the hospital think I'm having some kind of illicit affair because I keep leaving for two hours here and there for tours, visit dates, parent interviews—and no one knows what I'm doing or where I'm going. The plan was working pretty well. You believed us. I was a little worried about Roan. We hadn't planned on a gay guy to sniff us out, but, hell, we even fooled him!" Ty's momentary look of triumph is followed swiftly by one of remorse.

"But it turned out Roan wasn't our Achilles' heel; it was that I was attracted to you." Ty runs his index finger from my bare shoulder across my collarbone, stopping at the neckline of my dress. "That I *am* attracted to you. Like in the *I can't stop thinking about you morning, noon, and night sort of way.*" His eyes implore me to forgive him, to give some indication that I feel the same. "I kept wanting to ask you out to coffee or dinner or something, but Caroline begged me to wait until after the acceptance letters come out. I've been counting down the weeks. I thought I could keep my feelings under control for Gracie's sake, I really did, but then you show up in that dress and those heels and what's a straight guy supposed to do?" His touch is winning me over, but I'm not ready to surrender. I want him to work for it a little bit longer.

"Am I going to ignore my chance to be with a stunning woman who consumes my every thought just for a coveted seat in a fancy kindergarten? I mean, I was going to have to keep up this ruse for the long haul. That's why I'm throwing my niece under the bus now, hoping there may be a shot that perhaps you can get over this whole lying thing and let me ask you out on a date. Not an interview. Not a doctor's visit. Not a house call. A real date." Finally, a pause and a moment of quiet. I didn't realize Ty was such a talker.

Now I have questions. "So, when you were 'gay' you didn't notice my fabulous outfit at your parent interview, but now that you're straight you love my dress and shoes?"

"I love how the dress accentuates what's underneath. I couldn't give a shit about the shoes." His eyes leisurely roam my body, taking it all in for the first time as a straight man. Or at least a straight man to me.

"That's such a guy's answer," I deadpan; humor my go-to whenever I feel vulnerable.

"I know. I've had a lifetime of practice." Ty's hands move up my arms to cradle my face in his palms. He uses his strength to pull me in for a kiss. Butterflies trapped since Obama's second inauguration are set free as I roll onto the tips of my toes, reach for his shoulders to steady myself, and fall into the smooth hold of Golden Boy's lips.

If his kiss could talk, it would say, *Now that I've got you, I know I want more.* If my body could talk, it would say, *FIN-A-LLY.*

"Ouch!" Golden Boy pulls back from what had quickly become a deep, delicious kiss and touches his lower lip. "What'd you bite me for?"

"That's for lying to me the last six months," I say. "This is for coming clean." I take hold of Golden Boy by the belt buckle and whisper, "Let's do that again." I allow my heart to admit that kissing Ty had crossed my mind. Damn, I think I like, like him, too.

We come up for air, but Ty doesn't release me. It's as if he's keeping me from averting my eyes from his sincerity and his moment of truth. "So, now what do you think?"

"I think I wanna know what your mama's gonna say about you dating a black girl."

"There's only one way for us to find out."

"Hey, guys, what's up?" The look on Lola's face tells me she knows something I don't. Oh, how wrong she is. Standing shoulder to shoulder, Ty holds my hand, our intertwined fingers hidden in the folds of my dress. I'm caught between wanting to dish with Lola and never wanting this moment to end.

"Where've you been?!" I can't help barking at Lola for abandoning me in the midst of this catastrophic, but revelatory, evening. "I have some big news that's going to blow your mind," I tell Lola, tightening my grip on Ty's hand so he can't skulk away. He gets to explain this one to my best friend because she will definitely think I made this story up.

"Yeah, I got somethin' to tell you, too. You go first," Lola says, acting like her tea is hotter than mine. How wrong she is.

"Well, you'll need a cocktail to hear my headline." It's like our first meeting at Zumba all over again, sniffing the competition, trying to one-up each other. "Ty's not gay. And he likes me. Like, LIKE likes me," I emphasize, in case she's not picking up what I'm putting down.

Lola gives us the one eyebrow raise but doesn't break stride.

"And you accidentally e-mailed that video of Nan out to the whole invite list for Aunt Viv's party. Instead of selecting 'Lola Valencia,' you selected 'Viva la Viv.' So now Nan, your boss, and Fairchild families past, present, and a few future, think you sent out a video of Nan puttin' you on blast." My jaw drops. "Giiiiiiiiiiiirl, hold on tight because it's about to go down."

TWENTY-SIX

NEEDING IMMEDIATE SPACE AFTER HEARING LOLA'S BREAK-
ing news, I leave Ty with a smooch and a whisper in his ear to text
me and step outside for some fresh air. On the one hand, the result
of my trigger finger could end up on the front page of Sunday's
Chronicle as the most recent exposé of the rich and richer—
something I don't want for the Fairchild community. On the other
hand, Nan brought this on herself showing her true colors by behav-
ing so badly. Despite Nan's actions, Fairchild is family and I'd never
do anything to intentionally harm the school. I can't believe I'm going
to have to deal with this fallout during our family's mini-vacation and
Etta's audition. Bottom line, I'm pissed at Nan for comin' for me.

I bundle up my Bordelon bookends and order an Uber XL. As we
pull away from Fairchild, Aunt Viv yawns, showing every molar and
filling in her mouth. The night's excitement is catching up with her,
telling me she's gonna blink out the minute her head hits her Pos-
turepedic. As much as I want to let the night's celebration settle into
Aunt Viv's bones, I know I won't be able to sleep if I don't tell my
squad about Ty. The three of us bust up laughing when I tell them

he has it bad for me. When Aunt Viv asks how I know, I recount the details, including the toe-curling kiss. Etta can't stop howling, but eventually is able to eke out that he seems great, and maybe a white daddy wouldn't be so bad. Then the giggles start all over again. Aunt Viv rests her hand on my leg, leans her head back on the seat, and declares, "Well, ain't that somethin'. A good doctor and good taste in women."

"There's something else, too." Since we're stuck in evening traffic a few blocks from home, I figure now is as good a time as any to show them the video I mistakenly sent out to the entire party invite list. The car is silent listening to Nan spew her drunken venom.

"Mama, we can turn around right now and snap that skinny stick in two." Etta is on fire, her teenage night owl energy kicking in as the rest of the family is winding down.

"Thanks for the offer, love. I know you got my back. But our family has had enough drama for one night." I give Etta a kiss on the cheek and open the car door as our Uber arrives in front of our building. "I think it's best if we all focus on getting a good night's sleep. We have a big day of travel tomorrow."

I follow Aunt Viv to her room to say good night. I know there's no way nothing's going to be said before she turns out the lights.

"You learn the truth about a person when they been drinkin'," Aunt Viv claims, sitting on her bed rubbing her feet after too many hours in heels. "And what I learned tonight is what I was suspectin' all along. Nan Gooding is only out for herself. She don't really care if you black, brown, red, yellow, or white. Don't try to make a mark in her territory."

I move to her side to help as Aunt Viv works to unclasp her necklace. "I feel sorry for her. Only carin' 'bout yourself is a lonely place to live. I've been caring for Fairchild children for fifty years, you for thirty-five, and Etta for fourteen, and I ain't ever been lonely. And you know what? I ain't ever been unhappy, neither. Oooh, child," she whoops. "This was a wonderful night. I'm glad you made me go. I've always been proud of you and proud of Etta, but it never crossed my mind to feel proud of myself. Tonight, I do." With a kiss good night planted firmly on my cheek, Aunt Viv waves me off to bed.

"G'night, Aunt Viv." As I'm about to close my bedroom door, Aunt Viv's voice floats through the apartment with one last comment for the evening. I'm not surprised, that woman likes to have the last word. "Josie, you best be givin' that good doctor a chance. You know, you ain't been shakin' them sheets in a while."

"You might be right, Aunt Viv." I've been leading life with my head these last few years, but maybe it's time I start paying attention to my heart, too.

TWENTY-SEVEN

FROM: Yu Yan (Helen) Wu
DATE: March 3, 2019
SUBJECT: Liu family
TO: Josephine Bordelon

Dear Josie,

Mr. Liu has decided his children will continue enrollment at
Shanghai American School. The school has had over 40
graduates go to Harvard in the last ten years and he
prefers clear numbers to Fairchild's limited evidence. I
hope Fairchild will take the Liu decision as an opportunity
to better gather Ivy League acceptance statistics and
market to prospective parents more aggressively. Mr. Liu
will retain the property next to the school for an
investment, but it is no longer available to rent for
Fairchild. If the school would like to consider a sale,
he is amiable to a cash offer.

Thank you,
Yu Yan (Helen) Wu

EDUCATION CONSULTANT
ADMIT INTERNATIONAL, HONG KONG

Other than Helen Wu, my inbox is mysteriously empty given the video debacle. Thank goodness because Lola and I have been blowin' it up over text all morning breaking down this video thing. I had to keep her from marching down to lodge a complaint at the NAACP at 7:00 a.m. on a Sunday. I'm choosing to view the e-mail silence as a lukewarm sign over the fate of my job, and will do my best to leave the drama in San Francisco to focus on Etta once we hit the airport.

I couldn't sleep last night between Nanageddon and thinking about Ty as a straight man, maybe *my* man and not Daniel's husband. It hasn't even been sixteen hours since the big reveal and already I'm acting like a fifteen-year-old girl staring at my phone wondering when he's going to text. If he's going to text. If indeed last night was legit or if he woke up this morning and realized it was the booze talking. He better not be waiting for me to make the next move.

Etta and Aunt Viv flank me as we wait at SFO to board our plane to JFK. Aunt Viv tells me that if I'm sittin' next to her on the plane I have to put my damn phone away, she ain't no stranger takin' up a seat next to me. This is a family trip and we're gonna spend our time with each other, whether we laughin', cryin', or doin' something someplace in between.

It was a fairly quiet morning at the house, Etta giving me my space after the craziness of the night before and choosing to spend her last hours before our trip stretching so her muscles don't stiffen on the long plane ride. Her audition is tomorrow morning and though her mother's career may have ended last night, Etta is staying focused on the next forty-eight hours and her future. Aunt Viv putters around the apartment preoccupied by something, but I'm not sure what. She checks and double-checks her luggage, her purse, and her wallet. No word about Nan or the video or Ty from Aunt Viv, either. All three of us are quiet, immersed in our own worlds—past, present, and future.

I put my Out of Office; in an emergency, contact admissions assistant, Roan Dawson message on my e-mail and say a prayer that Roan doesn't quit after being left to deal with Nan's misplaced post-party wrath since I'm out of town. While I wish we were on our way to Dartmouth, I'll take anything across the country to get me out of town at this exact moment. I write myself a note in my phone to give Roan a raise when I get back, that is, if I have a job. And maybe beg him mercilessly not to take another job and leave me alone at Fairchild. If I get canned it's going to be unbearable, but if I get to stay, that very well may be unbearable, too.

On the plane Aunt Viv adjusts her neck pillow, puts her magazines in the back of the seat in front of her, shoves a new tissue up her sleeve, and pops in a mint. Settled in, she places her hand over mine and lifts our entwined fingers to give them a kiss, something she hasn't done since I was little and gripped in some sort of childhood nightmare. "We have a big couple of days ahead of us, Josie. Let's close our eyes and rest up, we'll need our energy." Aunt Viv moves my hand to her cheek. "This trip is going to be a great reminder of the lengths we will go to for our family, the ones we love most. Through the good and the bad, you and Etta mean everything to me." Aunt Viv doesn't open her eyes but lays my hand back in my lap. Her face twitches and her body jerks as she drifts off to sleep. It's not like Aunt Viv to get all philosophical and lovey. Something seems to be weighing heavy on her mind, but I have no idea what since the party is over and Nan's unmentionable behavior does not seem to be registering any weight with her. With Aunt Viv asleep, I reach under the seat and pull out her purse. Using the dexterity of a surgeon I riffle through her bag looking for any sort of clue to her unnatural sentimental behavior. Etta watches me and I'm sure she's going to cry thief and startle Aunt Viv awake, but instead she puts out her hand for a piece of gum.

I come up empty-handed. I envy Aunt Viv as she sleeps soundly. I'm not sure she fully understands the damage I've done with the casual touch of the send button, but it seems she's willing to leave the drama of San Francisco behind and set her sights on the adventure ahead. I, on the other hand, have already bitten every cuticle down to its nub.

"Mama, don't be so nervous, I promise I'll be okay tomorrow," Etta assures me as she watches me dig into my thumb bed.

"I know you will, baby." I smile across Aunt Viv at my grown-up little girl. *But will I be okay?* That's the real question.

YESTERDAY'S ARRIVAL IN NEW YORK WENT SMOOTHLY, BUT today is Etta's reckoning day. As our cab pulls up to Lincoln Center we step into a world of endless possibilities. That's how I remember feeling about New York City when I first arrived twenty-one years prior; watching Etta full of awe as she heads to the front doors of Juilliard is the greatest of déjà vus. Only, while I was unsure of what I could or could not ask of this limitless world as a young black woman, Etta is nobody's fool. She walks with poise, her taut muscles flexing through her blush-pink tights. Her bun is near perfection, my refusal to tame her lion's mane at Jean Georges's request, a distant memory. Her shoulders are set with purpose. It takes all my restraint to not point out to the strangers walking by that the essence of power and grace that just glided past them is my daughter comin' to get what she came for. There may be plenty of things I haven't done right, but that . . . that girl right there, I did that right.

LOLA

I have three minutes alone before the enemy line infiltrates my classroom from recess and I'm a goner. How's the audition going? I'm dying here I can't stand it. Holla. Lo

9:42 A.M.

JOSIE

I don't know how it's going in there, they won't let parents in.

9:43 A.M.

LOLA

Imagine that, dance moms not allowed.

9:43 A.M.

JOSIE

You know I'm not a dance mom Lo.

9:44 A.M.

LOLA

Yet. But if they don't take Etta God help that director of admissions. How's Aunt Viv?

9:44 A.M.

JOSIE

A wreck. She went to get coffee and take a walk around Lincoln Center. I don't think she can handle the pressure. And she might be nervous for this afternoon. We're all meeting the director of admissions before Etta's interview. Can you believe the director of admissions at a college wants to meet the family of each applicant? Seems overkill for college, if you ask me. Do you think they're trying to sniff out helicopter parents?

9:46 A.M.

LOLA

For 70K a year nothin's overkill. Call me when you hear about our girl. And don't think you're off the hook about Ty. Must hear more . . .

9:52 A.M.

While I wait alone in the vast, contemporary atrium I scroll through my phone to check e-mail. Before I touch the envelope icon I make myself a promise only to read, not respond. My emotions are still too hot from the weekend and if I answer even one e-mail my out-of-office cover will be blown and Saturday night's fiasco will be relentlessly staring me down.

Roughly sixty e-mails line up like little soldiers waiting for me to run inspection. I knew it was only a matter of time before the floodgates opened. The subject on Meredith's intrigues me enough to chance opening it though I thought Saturday night had put an end to our short-term relationship.

FROM: Meredith Lawton
DATE: March 4, 2019
SUBJECT: I didn't know . . .
TO: Josephine Bordelon

Dear Josie,

I must say, Josie, you looked drop-dead gorgeous on Saturday night. It takes a certain complexion to pull off that color orange and you were simply radiant. I'm so disappointed Christopher couldn't be there to meet you, I know you two will get along famously. I've always known you are the top director of admissions of any private school in town, but in that outfit, there couldn't be a possible doubter in the room.

Speaking of doubt, I want you to know that I have never doubted your professionalism and power to determine if Harrison is a qualified Fairchild Country Day School student. When I told Nan about the scholarship you were putting together with Beatrice Pembrook I simply wanted to support your aunt Viv and her service to the school since you and I have become such good friends through this whole emotional admissions process. I was so distraught at your house the other morning I didn't know which way was up. That's why I read your text from Beatrice. Obviously, I wasn't myself. But again, Nan seemed thrilled with the news about the scholarship when I told her about it and asked that I not share with you, so it could be an even bigger surprise for you and your aunt Viv at the party. I promise I was by no means trying to skirt around you to be in cahoots with Nan to ensure Harrison's entrance into Fairchild. I would never do that—that would be plain silly, right? We both know what a truly remarkable candidate Harrison is.

It would be fun if you, Christopher, and I grabbed dinner sometime. We would love to get to know you better in the next couple of weeks. Are you available this Thursday?

Love and peace in these difficult times,
Meredith

Revisionist history is a remarkable thing. People love to spin a story to make themselves look good, as an innocent bystander or a victim of circumstances, all to ensure they end up with what they originally wanted. I believe that's what plantation owners did until the Civil War came along. And that's what black people have been watching white people do since the founding of this country. Talk about a tale as old as time. I'm sure Aunt Viv has an old-school Aesop's fable about this exact scenario.

Oh, how I wish I could e-mail back to Meredith, if my job wasn't already teetering on the edge. At least I think it is, based on the six e-mails I passed over from Elsamyassistant asking me to call the school immediately, if not sooner, at Nan's insistence. I'd like to tell Meredith that jumping from my ship to Nan's make-believe yacht was a novice parenting move, not to mention a completely transparent one. How Meredith missed the *future is female* memo that you don't step on the necks of other women to climb your way to the top, is beyond me.

TWENTY-EIGHT

ETTA BURSTS THROUGH THE AUDITORIUM DOORS RIGHT
into my arms. The tears flow immediately and while I should be asking her what's wrong, my first thought is one of relief—*my baby still
needs me*. And while it may not feel like it right now, or in a couple
of days, it will be okay that the audition didn't go well. Like I've always known down deep where a mother's intuition lives, it's her brain
that's going to take Etta to the places she needs to go. Meredith
Lawton, this is what real parenting looks like. I squeeze Etta even
harder and remind myself that the money we spent to go on this trip
will be worth it if it opens Etta up to considering other options for
her future. Cornell and Dartmouth, you still have a chance.

"Oh, baby, don't cry. I know you. I know you tried your absolute
hardest. Today just wasn't your day and that's okay, the world is still
waiting for you to do amazing things. Whatever you set your mind to
I know you can do, your determination inspires me every single day."
As we hug, I stroke her back and I can feel the heat radiating off her
body from giving her audition maximal effort. Her body weight falls
heavy in my arms as she releases months of preparation and desire

and now it's all over. I will myself not to think about the snot she's rubbing on the shoulder of my favorite celadon-green cashmere sweater.

"No, Mama, you don't understand," Etta ekes out through sobs or hiccups, I'm not sure what farm sound she's making now. I do understand. The pained expression on her face is a carbon copy of me as I looked back and forth over four pregnancy tests in the Charles de Gaulle Airport. Eighteen years later and I still remember the horror of realizing the course of my life as I had envisioned it had changed forever. The sobs and wrecked face are the first acknowledgment of the end of an era. In this kind of moment there is no imagining there can be any sort of good or positive next step, but time will prove otherwise even if it does not completely heal. "Mama, I was incredible. The best I've ever been. I did it. I really did it!"

I pull back from Etta, so I can clearly see her face. "These are tears of joy?" I ask, thoroughly confused.

"I think they're mostly tears of relief." Etta wipes her cheeks with the back of her hands, pulling herself together. "And yes, happiness, too. But mostly relief. Mama, you should have seen me up there, I was a star. My best ever. I promise if you had seen me you would know this is where I'm meant to go to school. I'm meant to dance, Mama, I know it. I know I'm meant to be a dancer." I take a step back to get a full view of Etta. Her limbs are long and lean, held naturally in first position. The baby pink of her leotard and tights is in sharp contrast to the young woman standing in front of me. Her smile is so broad it might break her face. Her whole body oozes an aura of hopefulness. And in this moment, though I don't want to admit it, I, too, know she's meant to be a dancer. Etta is not meant to study the science of motion, she's meant to be in motion and, after all these years of nurturing this girl into a strong, independent young woman, who am I to stand in the way of her trajectory?

"Where's Aunt Viv? I can't wait to tell her all about it." While Etta pulls on her leg warmers, pants, and wrap sweater I group text Etta's San Francisco fan club: Lola, Roan, Poppy, Krista, Jean Georges, and Ty.

Their responses flood in.

Krista . . .

KRISTA

👍 ☺

1:18 P.M.

Roan . . .

ROAN

LOVE THAT GRRRRL!!! And by the way Nan hasn't left her office once today.

1:19 P.M.

Jean Georges . . .

JEAN GEORGES

I always knew Etta was destined to be a professional dancer. Even when others doubted . . .

1:19 P.M.

Lola . . .

LOLA

> You tell Etta her Aunt Lola is crying in the 1st grade bathroom she's so proud of her. BTW, it is beyond gross in here.

1:19 P.M.

And Ty . . .

TY

> I think great things await Etta and her mom (if she lets them) . . .

1:20 P.M.

"Mama, I know you're proud of me, but that smile of yours is telling me there's more to the story," Etta says, locking arms with me.

I show Etta my phone.

"You gonna give him a chance, right? Just don't be givin' up the boo too early." Etta laughs and hip checks me. A tiny, girly shriek escapes my mouth.

"Oooooh, Etta, you still not old enough to talk to your mama like that!" But deep down I kinda like it. My baby may slowly be becoming my friend.

Aunt Viv is sitting stiff and perfectly upright squeezing the life out of Etta's hand. Since there were two hours between Etta's audition and our interview with the director of admissions, Etta and I wanted to explore around Lincoln Center a bit, but Aunt Viv insisted we eat lunch close by so we could be early to the interview. Then, after commandeering our plan, the woman barely touched her sandwich. I'm so consumed by the increasing reality of Etta being accepted to Juilliard that I don't mark any of Aunt Viv's odd actions with great concern. That is, until she doesn't ask the waitress to wrap up her untouched sandwich. Aunt Viv detests people who allow perfectly good food to go to waste. There can be one cookie left on a tray of three hundred at an admissions open house and Aunt Viv will wrap it in a napkin, bring it home, and have it with her coffee the next day. When you grow up poor with six siblings and only enough food to feed half of them, you are well trained to stretch every last crumb on a plate.

"Aunt Viv, where'd you go during my audition?" Etta asks. I, too, want to know the answer to this question, but I don't want to get my head bitten off given Aunt Viv's peculiar behavior since we left San Francisco.

"I needed to check out a few things around the school. Make sure everything is okay, you know, no hiccups with our visit."

"Check out what things?" I ask, a bit miffed, since that's my job as Etta's mother, though it never occurred to me that there was anything specific that needed double-checking.

"We best be going." Aunt Viv doesn't even register my question. She raises her hand for the check and then digs into her purse to reapply her lipstick. Aunt Viv is going into this interview with a winner's attitude.

We are a whole fifteen minutes early for the interview and I can feel the anxiety creeping back up among the three of us. This is what I wanted to avoid by taking a walk around the West Side to get some fresh air and regain a calm perspective on this whole college admissions process. Instead, the three of us are squished together on an uncomfortably firm modern couch freaking out in our own individual ways.

I reach around Etta's shoulders to rub Aunt Viv's back. I can feel her heart beating fast and firm through her blouse. It doesn't feel normal to me. I lean forward to peek at Aunt Viv and her skin looks dull. We're sitting, which is good, but I'm wondering if I should excuse myself and go call Golden Boy—Dr. Golden—Ty, oh whatever the hell I should call him now that he's no longer a prospective Fairchild dad, but still Aunt Viv's cardiologist and possibly my new bae, too.

"Etta, Vivian, Josephine Bordelon, Mrs. Santos will see you now." Seems in university admissions you get your own Elsamyassistant. Duly noted.

Aunt Viv stands, presses down the front of her skirt, and briskly walks in the office ahead of us like all she wants to do is get this interview over with and get on with her day. For a woman who deeply wants Etta's dream of going to Juilliard to come true, this is a pretty bold move since this is Etta's interview. With the three of us safely inside the office, I'm immediately struck by the unbelievable resemblance between Mrs. Santos and Aunt Viv. Despite the difficulty white folks have, not all black people look alike. I guess there's an exception to every stereotype, and I'm standing in front of her.

"Josie," Aunt Viv is the first to speak up. Etta looks confused by Aunt Viv talking first. Pure rudeness, if you ask me, but Aunt Viv has been off her etiquette game since Sunday morning. So I pause to hear what she has to say since Etta's future is now riding on her big mouth. It better be good. "I would like to introduce you to Mrs. Santos. Ophelia. Bordelon. Santos. Your mother."

TWENTY-NINE

OUR HOTEL ROOM HAS TWO QUEEN BEDS, BUT AUNT VIV
lies right beside me on mine. We've been horizontal for almost an
hour, a word yet to pass. I don't know what to say or ask first and
Aunt Viv has never been one to put words in my mouth. At our urg-
ing Etta continued with the plan to spend the afternoon and evening
with a Juilliard dance program ambassador learning about the school
from a student's perspective. I figure on a Monday night that perspective can't involve too much alcohol or late-night clubbing.

I pick up the remote to turn on the TV because clearly I'm not
ready to talk. Aunt Viv places her hand over the remote and lowers it
back down, keeping her hand on it for a lingering moment. "I think
we've had enough drama for one day, no need to add someone else's."
Tears well in my eyes and slide down my temples. I'm frozen in place.
Aunt Viv pulls a Kleenex out of her sleeve and dabs my face dry. I
can see where the scars from fifty years of working in a kitchen and
the natural wrinkles of time have intersected. These hands have held
together both the Fairchild community and our family for decades. I

don't know where to start without risking hurting Aunt Viv by bringing up questions with answers she keeps buried deep and out of sight.

"Have you always known?" I guess that's as good a place to start as any.

"I've known since September."

"How? And why now?"

"Well, when Etta started talkin' about Juilliard she showed me stuff about the school on their website. There was a picture that caught my eye." Aunt Viv takes a long pause to inhale and to choose her words carefully. I'm not sure if she's going to continue or if that's the end of the story. "You know I hate those laptops. Print's too small for an old lady like me. But after that night with Etta, I asked Ms. Gooding if she could get me a computer with a bigger screen. Said my eyes couldn't read recipes on a laptop. Took me a while to convince her though, she thought after fifty years of cookin' for Fairchild I don't need recipes no more." Aunt Viv gives me a tickled grin. "Which, between you and me and these hotel walls, is the truth, but she don't need to know that."

"Not sure if that was about the recipes or about Nan not wanting to part with money and her fucked-up power trips," I shoot back.

"Watch your language, Josephine Bordelon. You may be hurtin', but you're still a lady. And either way, she ended up givin' me her big screen thing that sits on her desk."

"Her monitor?"

"Yeah, that. And she got a nice new one. And then I went to work trying to find out about the woman in the picture on the Juilliard website."

"So how long did it take you to figure it out?" My real mother has been such a distant mirage in my life. Once I got my own life going in college and modeling and then back in San Francisco, it only occasionally crossed my mind to search for her online. It certainly was never something I mentioned to Aunt Viv since she spent my childhood dismissing such talk as a waste of time.

"Once I got that monitor I started going through every page of the Juilliard website. I've read every single word and I've studied every single picture. Then I got to admissions. There was a letter written by her to all the kids applying to the school. The letter was signed Ophelia Santos. Between the picture, the name Ophelia, and my sneaking suspicion that after your mama dropped you off with me she just might figure her way to New York to try to make it as a dancer I knew it had to be her. And, shore enough, I knew right."

"Why didn't you ask me if I wanted to meet her? It should have been my decision to make."

"Well I did consider that, and maybe it should have been your choice, but once Etta got that audition, there was no decision to make. You were gonna have to meet your mother whether you wanted to or not. And for Etta's sake, I couldn't give you one more reason not to let her follow through on her dream of applying to Juilliard." Fair point.

"She looks like you." I roll on my side to look at Aunt Viv for the first time since the conversation started.

"Maybe. But she's built like you and Etta. Ain't no mistakin' you all got the same blood."

"So, I couldn't make it as a model. And ended up working in school admissions. Ophelia couldn't make it as a dancer and she ended up working in school admissions. Both of us leaving family thinkin' New York City would make our dreams come true and then the city gave us anything but our dreams in return. The similarities are too much. See why I don't want this life for Etta? There's a strong Bordelon pull to New York to get your soul crushed and I don't want that for my daughter. I want anything but that for her. I could handle the disappointment when it was mine, but I don't think my heart has room for Etta's broken dreams and disappointments, too. It would snap me and I feel, like . . . like . . ." I'm stuttering now, trying to express years of anxiety, love, and deep concern all at once. "In the past few years, after being a young baby mama, barely making ends meet on an assistant's salary and then Michael leaving us, I have finally healed the broken pieces and I'm whole again. I want to stay whole."

Aunt Viv chews on my words for a moment and then continues, almost as if what I said washed past her ears. "I called Ophelia around late November, when I knew for sure Etta was going to apply to Juilliard. When Ophelia left you with me all those years ago I made her promise she would never try to get in contact with you or with me, again. That she would go on and live her life and leave us be. But I never said that I wouldn't contact her."

I sit up on the bed and look out over the city from the twenty-second floor. A weariness from the past forty-eight hours' events overcomes me and I feel closer to fifty than forty.

"You know I'm a good bit older than your mama and growin' up I liked to look after her like she was my own. Well, truth tell it, our own mama was so busy raisin' all of us that we had to help raise each other. But your mama was my favorite. As a young girl she was so pretty. My grandfather, Joseph, who you're named after, would heft Ophelia up in his arms and say 'Ooooooweee, yous pretty as a speckled pig.' And Ophelia would squeal back like a baby hog. It was their own little show, those two."

I was fairly certain I couldn't handle hearing any more. This seemed enough for the last two days if not my last almost forty years.

"By the time I was plannin' my own path outta the wards of Nawlins I was worried sick 'bout your mama's future. I could see dem hook-headed boys from aroun' de way lookin' at her sideways. I knew down deep tellin' her to keep her dress down wasn't going to be enough."

I turn to look at Aunt Viv, surprised by how thoroughly she's slipped into home speak. Her mind is no longer focused on me. Aunt Viv's lost in memories long, long past.

"You know the whole family, including me, wanted the best for your mama. But I don't think any of us stopped to check on what your mama wanted. Her being so pretty and all, we thought our only job was to keep them boys at arms distance. No one bothered to find out much else about her. In the end, Josie, I think, just like me, your mama wanted out, she wanted the chance to become who she was meant to become. We didn't know any better back then that life could be bigger and fuller, Josie, and we lost your mama because of it. But you and I, we know better, don't we? We really do. So, we gotta let Etta go to Juilliard because we can't risk losin' Etta like the family lost your mama. And like I lost you for a bit of time, too. Those were the hardest six years of my life and it can't happen to our family again, Josie. It just can't."

I reluctantly nod my head yes. Not because I agree that Etta should go to Juilliard, but because I agree we can't lose her. Witnessing decades of pain surface in Aunt Viv, I know we would not survive Etta abandoning our family in search of her future.

"And there is a happy ending to this story, too. I have to give it to Ophelia; she did make her dreams come true in New York. She didn't come here just to dance, she told me on the phone. Ever since she was a young girl she dreamed of being a dancer and a teacher. She came to New York to do both and that's exactly what she made happen. For twenty-two years she taught dance at Juilliard, first as an assistant teacher and then moving up to master teacher. Time caught up to her, like it does for everyone, and her body needed a break from dance. By that time she was married, a true New Yorker, and a respected member of the Juilliard community. So, she was offered a job in admissions. One she says she loves since she gets to make dreams come true for young, talented artists like Etta."

"You know my next question, don't you?" Water pooled again in my eyes, threatening to rain down.

"I imagine so, but I'm not one to go thinkin' for you, Josie. There are so many questions you must have, baby."

"Does Ophelia have other children?" I can barely give the question voice. I have to reach deep in my diaphragm to push it out.

"That was the second part of our agreement when you came to live with me. If I were to raise you, Ophelia had to promise me she wanted no children. It wasn't that she just didn't want you. And maybe I was being selfish, but I couldn't see peepin' out the window my whole life wonderin' if she was going to bring me more kids to raise." Aunt Viv places her hand over my heart. "For what it's worth, she kept that promise to me and to you."

I nod.

"She has a nice-sounding husband, but you still her only child."

"But Aunt Viv, you let your sister drop me on your doorstep and turn your life upside down. You've never had financial security, you've never had a great love. You gave all that up for Ophelia and for me. Why?"

"I didn't give up nothin', Josie, I got somethin'. I got you. But to answer your question, black women in our family have been raisin' babies on their own for quite some time for all sorts of reasons we don't need to go into tonight. And we've tried hard to do it as best as we could with what we were workin' with. For me, I just couldn't see bringin' a man into our world and risk you feelin' abandoned for a second time. That was my choice, Josie, and I think I made the right one. But right now I want you to hear me loud as church bells. Etta ain't known nothin' but love and security from the day she was born. She has a solid foundation and she's ready to fly right. That means there's plenty of room for new love in your life. For even more love than the full cup you already got."

There it is, the whole story. Or as much of it as I'm able to stomach for one day. I thank Aunt Viv for her honesty but tell her that's enough for now.

"That city out there"—Aunt Viv points to the New York skyline, millions of lights turning on as day turns to dusk—"it may not have done right by you, Josie, but it's done right by your mama. And she wants to help make sure it does right by your baby, her grand-baby."

"Etta's your grandbaby, Aunt Viv." And the sobs come. And come. And come. I don't have the strength to fight them off any longer.

"Yes, she is, Josie, but I'm willing to share her now. And I'm willing to share my daughter, too."

NEXT SEASON

THIRTY

LOLA

Can you talk in 10? September is already killin' me. Holla.

7:40 A.M.

JOSIE

Yep.

7:40 A.M.

"What's happened already, Lo? It's only the first day of school," I answer the phone, worried Hannibal-the-Cannibal Valencia has already scouted out his next victim.

"Nothin's wrong, I just wanted to make sure I got to check on my girl before the day got away. Was it weird going to Fairchild this morning without Etta? Have you cried? Are you standing upright? I'm worried about you. Do you need a drink?"

"It's not even 8:00 a.m."

"But it's 5:00 p.m. somewhere and it's Monday, which I think means it's Tuesday in Australia. Plus, everyone needs a drink after the first day of school. It's a mandated law of parenting."

"Maybe you need the drink?"

"I do. And a trophy for getting three boys in pants this morning. I could not look at their flammable Warriors basketball shorts for one more day. All three are pissed at me. Even the cannibal, who usually doesn't care what he wears. But I actually won a battle fought on the home front before 7:30 a.m. so I'm officially declaring my first day of school a victory. Come on, you can tell me if you miss Etta."

"You know, I think I'm alright for today. No guarantees for tomorrow though."

Lola's been worried about me missing Etta since I came home from dropping her off at Juilliard two weeks ago. What Lola doesn't know is that I littered the United terminal at JFK with tear-soaked tissues. I thought I was keeping my emotions in check until I spied a mom walking to her gate holding hands with her toddler daughter dressed head to toe in full-on ballerina. The memories of leotards, toe shoes, and tights, and even Jean Georges became too much, and the universe got to see my ugly cry. I was unfit for public consumption, but still I had to make it home. Meanwhile, Aunt Viv was in San Francisco manically cooking her sadness away. We now have enough jambalaya and cornbread to open a parish soup kitchen.

"I'll take an alright. That's good for now. Okay, enough about you, on to the important stuff. Expecting any new hot dads this year? Straight ones?"

"Actually, there is one."

"There is? You noticed? Who are you and what have you done with my best friend?"

"Yeah, yeah, yeah. It's Ruby Vassar's dad. Did you know he sold his first software chip platform blah de blah something or other tech company for 128 million when he was thirty-one? I never knew of a brotha who survived the South Bay long enough to make millions and not become a casualty of the great Silicon Valley hope of fast money and faster fame. And to do it by thirty-one. Where was he when I was single?"

"Clearly you were falling down on the job. I thought as director of admissions you had professional online stalker status. I think we both can agree you lost your edge last year when you let Etta's future get in the way of your own. Plus, I've heard softening around the edges is what happens when forty is just around the corner. Like next week." Lola never misses an opportunity to lean on her youth, being a whole ten months younger than me.

"What about you? Did you scope out any hot new dads at the parent orientation on Saturday? And do they know you come with baggage, like a husband and three kids?"

"Everyone comes with baggage at our age. And men love Nic; he's one of my best features. But no. Pretty weak new dad showing at San Francisco Children's Academy this year. But you know who is really bringing their A game?" If Lola says the granddads I'm going to vomit in Nan's ex-office. "The uncles. That Gracie Golden has one fiiiiiiiiiiiiiiiine-looking uncle. Mmmm . . . I could stare at that man all day. Good-looking *and* a doctor. Wait 'til all the single yummy mummies find out, it's going to be a catfight of epic proportions to get their claws in that one at Back to School Night."

"Uh, no it won't, 'cause I'll be there right beside him. I'm not stupid. No way is my man walking into that den of single momsters all alone." With just the mention of Ty my whole body heats up on this sun-soaked San Francisco morning.

Propping my feet up on what used to be Nan's desk, I admire my new back-to-school Choos. Now that I'm interim head of school, again, I gotta dress the part. Looking around this oak-paneled cigar room of an office, I can't help but reflect on how everything went down last spring.

The official story is that the week after my video went out as a surprise Viva la Viv party favor, Nan's mother in Arizona was diagnosed with an unspecified terminal illness with an unspecified amount of time to live. Nan took a six-month leave of absence. Five months in and any attempt by the board of trustees to reach Nan had been met with voicemail and out-of-office e-mail replies.

Turns out, the Bordelon women were the talk of Fairchild after the Viva la Viv party. And the talk of San Francisco Children's Academy and the talk of the forty-six other private schools across the Bay Area, though by some miracle the video of Nan never went viral or made the news.

On the flight home from New York I ordered myself a mini Chardonnay, plugged some early Drake into my ears, opened my laptop, and said a prayer. Out loud, I think, because Aunt Viv elbowed me hard after my amen.

As I opened my first e-mail, I closed my eyes and took several big, deep meditative breaths to calm myself for what may be waiting for me on my screen. Turns out, you live in the Bay Area long enough and no one is immune to all that Eastern philosophy mantra mumbo jumbo.

FROM: Beatrice Pembrook
DATE: March 6, 2019
SUBJECT: Scholarship
TO: Josephine Bordelon

Dear Josie,

I'm feeling badly about what happened with Viv's scholarship. I was so excited when you asked me to participate that it inspired me to reengage with the Fairchild Community. I called Nan to tell her that I would like to serve on the Advancement Committee or maybe even as a board member again. Who knows, soon I may have a grandchild to attend the school. Nan acted like she was familiar with the Vivian Bordelon Scholarship, but now that I reflect on our conversation her questions were quite probing and her exit from our call quite curt.

I'm not sure what the future holds for Nan Gooding and her tenure at Fairchild, but I want to assure you my offer to support the scholarship well into the future still stands.

All my best,
Beatrice

P.S. I have been meaning to tell you that I am an acquaintance of Meredith Lawton. While she can be, shall we say, a bit of an unhinged prima donna (sorry, but more appropriate words are escaping me at the moment), her son and her husband, Christopher, are absolutely delightful. The Lawton men are worth the trouble of taking Meredith on as a package deal.

So, it was both Meredith and Beatrice who blew my cover on the Vivian Bordelon Scholarship. Oh, how happy Meredith would be to know she and Beatrice shared the same social faux pas.

FROM: Elsanansassistant
DATE: March 6, 2019
SUBJECT: Nan would like to talk to you
TO: Josephine Bordelon

Please call Nan at your very earliest convenience. She will
be in her office all day.

Elsa

FROM: James Dyer
DATE: March 7, 2019
SUBJECT: Interim Head Position
TO: Josephine Bordelon

Dear Josie,

I have been informed that you are on a college visit with
your daughter. In light of this weekend's events, Nan, with
the support of the board, will be taking a six-month leave
of absence. In her place the Fairchild Country Day School
Board of Trustees unanimously voted for you to act as
interim head of school given your previous experience in
the job. Please contact me at your first availability.

Warm regards,
James

FROM: Elsanansassistant
DATE: March 8, 2019
SUBJECT: Nan's leave of absence
TO: Josephine Bordelon

Dear Josie,

I believe I will now be your assistant. Please let me know if you need anything. Nan only allowed me two bathroom breaks a day. Would it be possible to have one or two additional ones? I would love to go a whole year without a bladder infection.

Yours,
Elsa

FROM: Roan Dawson
DATE: March 8, 2019
SUBJECT: Interim Head of School
TO: Josephine Bordelon

Does this mean I get to be Director of Admissions?!?!?

Roan Dawson

ADMISSIONS ASSISTANT
FAIRCHILD COUNTRY DAY SCHOOL

It was a two-Chardonnay flight. Or maybe four. I lost count.

"DAMN I LOVE THESE SHOES." I SAY OUT LOUD TO A QUIET office. Who knew ecru could look so good on a pair of size-ten black feet.

I head out of the large bronze doors and down the stairs to the sidewalk to stand front and center for first day of school drop-off. While my summer was full of budgets and facilities issues and the annual audit—all boring head of school stuff I have no desire to

continue once a new head of school is found—I love being in front
of the school on the first day. Day one is particularly magical with
fresh haircuts, summer sun freckles, giant hugs for favorite teachers,
and effortlessly clean backpacks. The first day of school always says,
*Anything is possible. The past does not have to dictate the future.
Everyone gets a fresh start.*

Some of my favorite parents are the ones who, though living in
the middle of a city, figure out a way to bike with their child to
school. Perhaps it's because I never got to (I can't imagine Aunt Viv
riding a bike), or maybe it's because it makes the Bay Area, the epicenter of technology and investment, seem sweet and simple. A small
bicycle brigade comes down the block and as they pull up to the
sidewalk there's a man I don't recognize. He's in scruffy khaki shorts
with a bit of a rip starting on the thigh and an unkempt beard. He's
wearing a faded red *Friends* T-shirt, circa 2000, and Converse shoes
that, I can tell from here, must smell something awful.

I approach the vagrant-looking man—prepared to ask him where
he needs to be, and can I help him be on his way—when I see a boy
on the back of his bike. The boy taps the man on his shoulder and
he turns around to unbuckle the child's helmet. As it comes off, the
boy beams and raises his arms to be lifted up. The man kisses an
exposed chubby cheek and lifts the little boy off the bike. As I walk
closer, I see a flash of tummy roll peeking out from under a well-
worn Superman shirt. Harrison Lawton gives me a shy wave and
then grabs for his dad's hand proud, that his father will deliver him
to his first day of kindergarten.

"Hello, I'm Christopher. Meredith has told me so many great
things about you and about Fairchild. Harrison is raring to go—
aren't you, buddy? Been talking about kindergarten for weeks."

So, this, finally, is the infamous Christopher Lawton. Certainly
not what I expected, but the surprise is a pleasant one. For the first
time since I met her almost a year ago, I give Meredith credit for

having a big heart in the right place. Only a woman who can see past the exterior to love the interior could hop in bed night after night with this affable Linus lookalike.

"It's wonderful to finally meet you, Christopher. And, Harrison, you're going to love Ms. Brooks, she's the best kindergarten teacher in the whole world." I shake Christopher's hand and he picks up Harrison and throws him on his shoulders, a ride into kindergarten fit for a king. A happy tear drops on my nose. There is nowhere else a person can work where there is so much boundless, endless love. Working in schools . . . Best. Job. Ever.

With the children tucked happily in their new classrooms I head to Nan's, I mean, *my* office to check a few things before my 10:00 a.m. meeting in the conference room. It's never too early for chocolate pretzels so I bust open one of the five bags I have tucked away. A new stash for a new year.

I've never been a person to have pictures on my desk, but like I say, new year, new beginnings. To the left of my computer screen is a goofy picture of Etta and Ty from the observation deck of the Empire State Building. They look like they're caught in a wind tunnel, but the expression on their faces is pure joy. I was hesitant to invite Ty to come with me to drop Etta off at Juilliard, afraid it was too much too soon for Etta and for me. Aunt Viv reminded me that nothin' good comes from movin' slow at my age and, more important, I needed someone to put together the IKEA furniture for Etta's dorm room. I couldn't disagree with her, the fantasy of Golden Boy and me riding off into the sunset or at least on a 747, pure bliss. And it helped to have a shoulder to cry on for the plane ride home. That man took every snotty tissue without hesitation.

After the Viva la Viv confession, it took Ty a few weeks to persuade me to go on a public date with him. I held him off until after admissions acceptance letters had gone out (call it a separation of church and state kind of thing) and then I folded. Once we dipped our toes in the waters of dinners out, it only took him a few meals to convince me that we have other things to talk about than Aunt Viv's health and the possibility of her dying. He continues to assure me that time is years and years away. As summer progressed, so did my need to see him, to be near him, and certainly to have my hands all over him. But it was always with the caveat that getting Etta organized for and settled into Juilliard was my priority until the end of August. He happily let me set the dating pace, but maybe now that Etta's launched, I can let my freak flag fly a little bit. Golden Boy might get an eyeful of me in a naughty nurse's uniform. I look juicy as hell in white.

Oh goody, a text. Even heads of school procrastinate.

TY

Hope you're wielding your power wisely over there, Head of School Bordelon. No going full dictator on me.

9:18 A.M.

JOSIE

Are we role-playing over text, Golden Boy?

9:18 A.M.

TY

Is that a thing?

9:20 A.M.

JOSIE

Could be our thing . . .

9:20 A.M.

TY

> **Getting to be with you is my thing. Damn, gotta run, someone was rude enough to have a heart attack in the midst of my sexting. See you tonight.**

9:21 A.M.

I reread our text strand three more times because that's what you do when you're a woman in the honeymoon phase of romance. You text, you reread it a zillion times for hidden meaning, and then you think about it for hours on end. Doesn't matter if you're fourteen, twenty-four, or almost the big four-oh, the behavior is similarly pathetic and yet still causes the internal tickle of excitement we all crave. Lola is eating up every moment, waiting and willing to plan a wedding since she has no daughters. I'm just planning what I'm wearing tonight for my back-to-school dinner date with Ty at the Slanted Door. One thing Lola and I do agree on is that we now have something new to talk about at Absinthe on Tuesday afternoons.

Before I dive into a day of excruciating meetings concerning things I care zero about (seriously a meeting about standard vs. miniature toilets in the lower school?) I hop on my computer to check on a few things. I go to the Fairchild website and beam like the proud mama that I am. Roan remembered. At the top of the home page is a banner in Fairchild's signature cornflower blue.

FAIRCHILD SCHOOL IS NOW ACCEPTING APPLICATIONS

Like I've always said . . . Best. Hire. Ever.

The Bordelon women made it through Etta's senior year and today feels like a fresh start. Etta is settled into her life at Juilliard, Aunt Viv is continuing for her fifty-first year as head cook at Fairchild, and I have another opportunity to enjoy being head of school for the first time. To top it all off, I have been given another chance to discover if I like being one half of a pair.

There is one loose end I've been avoiding dealing with all spring and summer, unsure what I want the outcome to be. To my surprise, Aunt Viv has not inserted her opinion once, but in this particular instance it is her opinion that matters to me most. Regardless, it's time to get this task off my to-do list and move on.

FROM: Josephine Bordelon
DATE: September 20, 2019
SUBJECT: Us
TO: Ophelia Santos

- -

Ophelia,

I'm sorry I couldn't see you when I was in New York getting Etta settled into Juilliard. I could make all sorts of excuses about needing to focus on Etta, getting her settled in her dorm and having it be all about her, but I'd be lying. I was the one who needed the trip to be about Etta and me, not about you and me. I wasn't ready.

Aunt Viv and I will be back for Etta's first performance in early December and perhaps I'll be ready to see you then. It will be frigid cold in New York for this California girl so maybe we can get coffee.

Josie Bordelon

INTERIM HEAD OF SCHOOL
FAIRCHILD COUNTRY DAY SCHOOL

I reread my e-mail several times with my finger hovering over the delete button. I want to make sure this is what I want to say to my mother six months after meeting her for a second time.

And then I hit send.

GOLDEN BOY SCOOTS IN NEXT TO ME ON THE BOOTH SIDE of our table at the Slanted Door. Nothing says new romance to a packed house more than two people who can't even stand to be separated by a two-top. I tuck myself tight up under his arm. Perfect spot 'cause when I turn to talk to him my nose catches the soapy aroma of his neck. Divine. Ty is twirling his index finger in the strap of my dress. Every time his finger brushes my shoulder my lady parts remind me that, at forty, they are in the best shape of their lives.

"I got you something for your first day back." Ty reaches under the table and I hear a rustling of plastic.

"Better not be a mug. News flash, people who work in schools hate mugs, particularly ones with trite sayings. And theme jewelry. We also hate theme jewelry. I hope to God you didn't get me pumpkin earrings or a Flag Day scarf."

"Oh I got you something far better. Something that's a little bit for you and a little bit for me, so maybe I should call it a *we* present." Lord, men are so predictable. I put my hand out ready to see what Ty's fantasy lingerie looks like. Is he a traditional black satin man or more of a modern see-through red silk kind of guy? Is it long and flowy or does it play peek-a-boo with my goodies? Instead, he hands me a shoe box with STELLA MCCARTNEY in big black block letters across the top. Damn, I think I just fell a little bit in love.

"Should I open it now?" I ask, petting the box, hardly able to contain my crazy couture excitement. I pop the top off before Golden Boy is able to answer.

There, in mint condition, are a pair of brand-new, never-been-worn, not-from-eBay pair of Stella McCartney Eclypse turquoise lace-up running sneakers, and a matching tank top and running tights.

"I thought you might be willing to go running with me if you had the right outfit to wear. Do you like it?"

"It's perfect," I gush, caressing the gorgeous workmanship of the shoes. I slip off my purple suede heels, out for their third date ever, and tie up my new kicks. "Just beware, my Fairchild track record still stands for a reason. I'm fast. So fast I might leave you in the dust."

"Don't you worry, Josie Bordelon, I plan on keeping pace."

"I sure hope you do, Golden Boy."

ACKNOWLEDGMENTS

Asha, who knew my hours of sitting on your PreK counter, eating your mac and cheese, laughing our heads off, would lead to this moment. Working side by side with you has been the best part of this journey called writing a book. If we are blessed to get to do this a second time, I promise not to eat all your tortilla chips, but keep the mac and cheese comin'. Though Josie would cringe, I have to say it: You rock.

Some are born with the gift of speed, a natural hand at drawing, a mind for numbers. I was born with the gift of always choosing to surround myself with strong, highly-capable women with sharp senses of humor and boundless positivity. After two decades of working in education, when I told my closest friends I wanted to write not one of these women doubted I could do it. Not one questioned my ability to make this leap, of which there was zero evidence I had any skill or talent. These women have cheered me on relentlessly, they are my Lolas: Nicole Avril, Shelley Bransten, Kristy Clark, Stephanie Griggs, Ally Gwozdz, Elizabeth Herrick, Caren O'Connor, Beth Scheer, Beth Silber, and Deborah Zipser.

Mom and Dad, I won the parent lottery. I really don't know what else to say. Mom, you are such a warm and open person on stage, in public, with all people. I am more reserved, but it turns out these incredible attributes you possess do live in me too, via, the characters of this book. Thank you for wanting this for me as much as I wanted it for myself. Dad, never could I have imagined a more perfect fit for a father. You get me. You always have. Thank you for letting me be me.

Scott, I waited many years for you and you showed up! Your patience, patience, patience as I found my stride as a writer did not go unnoticed. We are so lucky to have us and to have our girls, Lila and Lexi. My greatest hope in life is that you will find, own, and share your voices—the world wants to hear what you have to say. Aunt Viv would tell you to, "Do what you gotta do, to get where you want to get." I'm telling you to be fierce in your own ways. Love you forever.

—ALLI FRANK

Thanks so much to my coauthor, Alli, for the invitation to this party and for all the laughs. Our meeting among a roomful of frolicsome preschoolers and their hopeful, hand-wringing parents is proof magic happens in schools. The years we spent in service to our students and their families are the foundation of our common values, familiar histories, and similar senses of humor. On our writing journey, you put the zing in the yin to my zany yang and I look forward to more adventures among the pages with you.

Premiere praise goes to my family, who are my greatest source of strength and who showed me how to value life, laugh out loud, and believe in love. My late father, TJ Vassar, is my hero who taught me that the secret to connecting with others, and finding myself, could be found within the pages of books. My mother, Lynda Vassar, is my role model in womanhood who instilled in me that being a fabulous wife and mother can include a healthy sense of self and enduring independence; I am the woman I am because of her. My sister, Mikelle Vassar, and my brother, TJ Vassar III, are my cradle-to-crypt crew, who never make me face a fight alone. There are no better road dawgs than these two and I love them fiercely. My in-laws, Fred and Mary Ann Youmans, and my brothers-in-law, Chris Youmans, Matt Youmans, and Greg Youmans, are the extended family of my dreams and true family in my heart, whose support is unfailing. And I can't forget Ma and the Luna family, the members of my village who are always there to show me the way home.

A huge shout-out to the people in my life who added to the spirit of the characters in this book. You are part of a colorful sista-hood and I am grateful for your friendship: Latasia Lanier, Sarah Kietzer, YC Spring Chang, the Moore Hall Corner Crew, and the YoGreenies.

Finally, my greatest gratitude is for my three guys at home. To my sons, Jared and Michael: You boys taught me all the greatest lessons of my life; I am humbled and proud to be your mother. To my husband, Jeff, who makes me laugh like no other, believes in me completely, and makes me a better person: Thank you for being a stellar dad and for making me happy. My love for you is forever.

—ASHA YOUMANS

Our collective appreciation for the following people is overwhelming and overflowing. We have learned more about writing and publishing in half the time from our fast-talking, tenacious, and hilarious agent, Liza Fleissig. Along with Ginger Harris, at Liza Royce Agency, we could not have landed in more capable hands. Our trust in both of you is complete. Tegan Tegani, from the get-go you were as committed to Aunt Viv, Josie, and Etta, as we were. Thank you for holding the story we wanted to tell so closely to your heart and convincing us we could do it by helping us get there. Tara Singh Carlson, thank you for being brave and acting quickly! We knew we needed to land at a publishing house that would not only care about our book but also care about us. The dedication you and Helen O'Hare gave to us during the editing process and the attention to detail provided was above and beyond what we expected. You both made sure our story would sing on the page. From our first meeting at G. P. Putnam's Sons, we knew our book had found its home.

Sally Kim, Ivan Held, Christine Ball, Alexis Welby, Ashley McClay, Lauren Monaco, Jordan Aaronson, Nishtha Patel, Meredith Dros, Maija Baldauf, Andrea St. Aubin, Kristin del Rosario, Anthony Ramondo, Monica Cordova, and Sandra Chiu, each of you touched the Bordelon family along its path to bookshelves across America, THANK YOU. You are dream makers and we hope to make you proud.

—ALLI AND ASHA

TINY IMPERFECTIONS

Alli Frank AND Asha Youmans

A Conversation with
Alli Frank and Asha Youmans

Discussion Questions

BOOK
ENDS

PUTNAM
— EST. 1838 —

A CONVERSATION WITH
ALLI FRANK AND ASHA YOUMANS

How did you two meet? Why did you decide to write a book together?

As the PreK teacher and assistant head of school, we got to know each other working on the admissions team for a private school in Seattle, Washington. We spent many admissions sessions evaluating incoming PreK and kindergarten students for their "school readiness." Swapping hilarious stories of our time with kids and their parents in and out of the classroom, we discovered we had similar senses of humor. Our conversations would often start with, "When I write a book someday . . . this gem is *definitely* going in there!"

We left our school a year apart to pursue other professional interests but kept in touch. In December 2017 on a typical dark, wet Seattle day, we meet for coffee to explore an idea for a novel based on what we knew—education. Both of us have been casual writers throughout our lives, but we wanted to integrate our two perspectives to create well-rounded characters set in the unpredictable, crazy world called school. From the get-go, we were equally on board and fully committed to the dream of writing this book. For both of us it felt like a now-or-never moment, so we chose now!

What inspired this novel?

Between the two of us we have over forty years of experience working in schools, and our love of children runs deep. Though both of us had left working in schools full time, it was difficult to get the children and their families who embraced us out of our systems. There is a lot of warmth and love in a school community, and writing about that world was a way for us to stay connected. To be able to continue to think about the growth and development of children, real or imagined, and write about it was the MOST. FUN. EVER.

With our combined professional experiences, we had a common message we wanted to bring to a broad audience of parents. We wanted to share with parents that as beautiful as their deep love, nurturing, and concern is for their babies, they also need to lighten up and enjoy the fun and hilarity of raising a child! Our experience with parents has been that too many treat parenting like a skill to master, with their child being the perfect result of their hard work and drive. If a child is not a prodigy, gifted academically, or a star athlete, the pressure can force parents to view themselves and their child as a failure. The exceptional attributes of a tiny percentage of the population has become the expectation of a typical American child. We want to see parents take a step back and enjoy their children for exactly who they are presently and embrace a wider possibility of who they are meant to become. Watching a child grow and blossom from the sidelines and not always leading from the front, clearing an uneven path, is the best place to observe the beauty of childhood.

Tell us a bit about how you work together. What is your writing process like? Has it changed over time?

Personal connection is the most important aspect to our writing process. At the beginning of every work session, we spend time shooting the breeze. We share stories about our children and spouses, or where we found a deal on facial masks, commiserating over the health issues of loved ones, or discussing our holiday plans. This time spent connecting not only deepens our relationship as friends and collaborators but also sparks the laughter and good feelings that inspires the content of our writing. Like any great pair, we complement each other's strengths and shore up each other's weaknesses. Through it all we laugh hilariously at big and small things, hoping the coffee shop we're working in doesn't kick us out for being disruptive.

When it's time to put our ideas on paper we sometimes sit side by side working on sections together, or across one of our dining room tables reading aloud to each other to work on our sentence structure and authentic dialogue. Often, we trade chapters back and forth like a game of leapfrog or assign threads of concepts from the book like the characters' relationships or the timeline of the story's school year calendar. As time went on and the book neared completion, we'd trade larger sections of the book and critique what we wrote. There were a lot of e-mails, texts, and phone calls as ideas came to us or when we needed advice on just the right word to convey an idea. Above all we checked in during all the ups and downs and inbetweens of our individual family lives to make sure we were both happy with our writing, our working relationship, and, most important, still laughing.

You have both worked as teachers in public and private schools. How much of the novel is based on your own experiences? Are there any stories that didn't make it into the novel that you wish had?

Over two decades working in public and private schools some version of most of these stories that involves a child and a parent happened to a colleague or happened to one of us. *Tiny Imperfections* is a compilation of the great joy, unpredictability, and challenge of working in schools and being responsible for the success of other people's children. The beauty of every character's story in this book is a fundamental life truth: It doesn't matter who you are—race, religion, sexual orientation—when raising a child, parents share a common goal: for their offspring to find success and happiness. And that quest can drive a parent crazy (and possibly certifiable when mixed with way too much disposable cash)! This is a beautiful fact of life that bonds all parents.

We have only touched the tip of the iceberg of our collective school stories. We believe Aunt Viv and Josie have more to share about the parents, faculty, staff, and students at Fairchild Country Day School. Stay tuned. . . .

Tiny Imperfections **is full of wonderfully laugh-out-loud moments. Did you always know you wanted this story to be funny? Was it different to write humor than to use it in the classroom? Did anything about writing humor surprise you?**

YES! We always wanted this book to be funny. Funny and honest. Kids are a natural source of material for entertainment. Their humor is unencumbered by social mores, political correctness, or fear of offense. Kids simply observe the world and call it like they experience it. This desire to explore, connect, and enjoy similarities and differences is a childhood language that is sadly, often lost in translation on the journey into adulthood.

Writing this book was our opportunity to say the things we could *never* say in school, but trust us, we were thinking. In our professional and personal lives, we both like to approach human interactions assuming best intentions. That if someone is trying to do right (even if they mess up) we are open to them. Humor is one of the few avenues of communication where people continue to be open and inviting even if the content is off color. Our hope is that with *Tiny Imperfections* our readers can relax a little bit and laugh about the best and worst in ourselves.

Even when reading the book for the twentieth time, we still cracked ourselves up! We anticipated and looked forward to some of the funnier lines of our favorite parts of the book (which differ between the two of us). We want everyone who reads this book to have a few really deep, full, laugh-out-loud moments. And then to take it one step further, if some of our readers are in a book club, have members share their favorite parts of the book and everyone can have a second big, heartwarming laugh. Collective laughter is so good for the soul!

How did you come up with Josie's character? How did you develop her voice on the page? Did anything surprise you while writing her?

We were solid on who Josie was as a character from the start, so not much surprised us while writing about her. Many of Josie's traits are a compilation of who we are as women. Like Josie, we both love beautiful clothing, we have witty tongues, and we love our children fiercely while running a tight ship and holding them to high expectations. The foundation of those traits stems, in large part, from the fact that we both come from tight-knit, loving families, like the Bordelons. What did surprise us was how difficult it was to get into Josie's head when it came to romance and the dating life she pushed aside for many years. The two of us are married women, and reaching back into the emotions of our single hearts was tough to recall. Lucky enough to have found our true loves, we knew the qualities Josie was seeking in a partner: integrity, sharp humor, self-assuredness, and of course, handsome . . . we can't forget handsome.

In the end, the love story line was one of our most collaborative, as we leaned on each other to pull at the faded memories of our past dating lives—the lust and the heartbreak.

Why was it important to you both to write this novel together? How does race play a role in *Tiny Imperfections*? What do you hope readers will understand about your partnership?

We could not have written this book alone. We needed each other's views and personal and professional experiences in parenting, education, and friendship to make this story authentic. At the outset, we wanted to express our voices, and within that framework exists race, gender, class, religion, and so many factors that often seem to separate people in the United States. We wanted to use these aspects as an important part of the backdrop but not necessarily what drives the story of the Bordelon family. Parent-child love is the essence of this story and one that transcends so many other factors that are often used to divide us. We want people to know that as individuals, we operate from a place of goodwill and humor that allows us to speak honestly about parenting and how it differs along racial and cultural lines without it being difficult or personal; it can be real and honest. The entire process led to a level of trusted intimacy between us that brought with it a lot of laughter and love between the pages of this book.

At its heart, *Tiny Imperfections* is a mother-daughter story. Why did you want to write about this relationship? Are any of the characters based on your own mothers and daughters? Do you see yourselves in Josie?

When we set out to write this book, we did not know it would become a mother-daughter story. As we collaborated, told stories, and got more words onto the page, the mother-daughter story grew. Like many mothers and daughters, our relationships with our own mothers was not one we could appreciate until we were older and could stand back to look at it from the distance of adulthood. As writers, this central theme didn't present itself until we stood back from the book as readers to see how much "mother-daughter love" shaped the story. It kind of snuck up on us. Because Josie and Aunt Viv are both single moms, we gave them the strength to be mom and dad, and we both had phenomenal role models on that front. Josie and Aunt Viv are a compilation of the best traits of parenting; the best gifts we each received from our parents.

What do you hope readers will take away from *Tiny Imperfections*?

What we want people to take away from this book is to seek connection using an open smile as a way to reach out to people who are different from you. Sometimes we tip-toe around one another straining with curiosity to learn about our differences but not knowing how to approach others for the lessons we want or need. We encourage folks to become "cultural teachers" by thinking the best of one another from the outset, being curious, and responding to curiosity with kindness. And we need to graciously forgive one another when mistakes are made surrounding culture and difference. In short, we want people to become and stay connected.

Without giving anything away, did you always know how the novel would end?

We 100 percent knew how the novel was going to end, but it was how we were going to get to our ending that was the unknown. It was beyond fun figuring out how the heck we were going to get to where we wanted to go and if we could agree on the path! The stories we swapped, the laughing so hard we're crying, and the agonizing over every word, every sentence, every piece of dialogue was truly enjoyable because we did it together. Having finished *Tiny Imperfections*, it's difficult to imagine ever writing a book on our own. Seems so lonely for a couple of social, curious women like ourselves!

What's next for each of you?

We believe that the end of *Tiny Imperfections* is just the beginning of the Bordelon family story. Our fingers are crossed that readers will want to hear more from Josie, Etta, and Aunt Viv (if you do, please send us a message in the contact section of our website, alliandasha .com) because we have so much more of their story to share with readers!

Additionally, we are working on another book idea wholly unrelated to the Bordelon family but still humorous commercial fiction—that seems to be our sweet spot. As well, we cannot stay away from kids, we both love them too much. We continue to be a part of the independent school landscape in Washington, from cofounding the International Friends School in Bellevue, to speaking in classrooms about Seattle civil rights history, to catering for graduations and board of trustee retreats. And it goes without saying, we continue trying our best, with humor and grace, to be decent mothers, wives, daughters, and friends.

DISCUSSION QUESTIONS

1. At the beginning of *Tiny Imperfections*, Josie doesn't believe she needs to date. Why? Do you think she's lonely? Do you think Josie is happy with her life?

2. Why doesn't Josie want Etta to go to Julliard? Why does Aunt Viv encourage Etta to go? Do you agree with one woman more than the other? What do you think Josie is afraid of?

3. Josie jokes about the fact that she's not forty—yet. Why are women afraid to turn forty? What does forty represent for Josie?

4. How is race explored in the novel? Were you surprised to learn that the novel was written by a black-and-white author duo?

5. Josie got her start at Fairchild Country Day School when she attended as a student, where she remembers being part of the "dog and pony show" to attract donors (p. 14). How does Josie feel about the private school world? How has it shaped her life?

6. Why do you think our society is so focused on going to the "right" school? Do you agree with the parents desperate to get their children into Fairchild?

7. Discuss how *Tiny Imperfections* portrays motherhood. What does Josie think of the overbearing parents that apply to Fairchild? How does Josie's job as admissions director influence her own parenting? Do you think it's possible to stay realistic when you're surrounded by extreme wealth and privilege? Why or why not?

8. On p. 6, Josie thinks: "The more Bay Area parents feign 'it's all good, everything will work out,' my stats show what a higher pain in the ass quotient they are." Do you think parents and parenting differ across the country?

9. Lola is the best friend that keeps Josie sane—Josie thinks "Every woman needs a girlfriend who speaks the truth" (p. 44). How does Lola help Josie throughout *Tiny Imperfections*? Do you have a best friend who keeps you in line?

10. At the end of the novel, Golden Boy tells Josie a secret that changes everything. Were you surprised by what he tells her? Have you ever misinterpreted someone's motives in your own life? Or have you pretended to be something you're not in order to achieve a goal? Do you agree with his decisions?

11. Were you surprised by how the novel ended? Why or why not?